Native Patriot

multi-award-winning author

PEGG THOMAS

SPINNER OF YARNS PUBLISHING, LLC

Sault Ste. Marie, Michigan

https://peggthomas.com/
Published in the United States of America
ISBN: 979-8-9929079-6-4
Library of Congress Control Number: 2026910363
Cover Design by Pegg Thomas *(Elements of this cover were created using AI technology)*

More Books by Pegg Thomas

Native Patriot

Salem Village

The Ragpicker~ prequel novella

The Carpenter

The Midwife

The Brewer (September 2026)

Path to Freedom

Freedom's Price

Freedom's Pride

Freedom's Promise

A More Perfect Union

Emerald Fields

Cobalt Skies

Silver Prairies

Forts of Refuge

Sarah's Choice

Maggie's Strength

Abigail's Peace

Henri's Regret ~ A Prequel Novella

Individual Novellas

Worth Fighting For

Anna's Tower

Her Redcoat

In Sheep's Clothing

Embattled Hearts

Join Pegg's Newsletter

writing updates – sneak peeks – fiber arts updates – personal content

https://www.subscribepage.com/PeggThomas

This book is dedicated to all those far-sighted Patriots who gave everything to create a nation that would become the standard-bearer for freedom and liberty around the world.

ACKNOWLEDGEMENTS

I wrote this book for our nation's Semiquincentennial in 2026. My family goes back to several Revolutionary War soldiers, without whom I would not be here.

Thomas Delano – 7th great-grandfather DAR Ancestor #A031484

Major Thomas Delano, Jr. – 6th great-grandfather, fought in both the Revolutionary War and the War of 1812 DAR Ancestor #A031485

Joel Strong – 10th great-uncle DAR Ancestor #A204479

Jeremiah Gifford, Jr. – 5th great-grandfather DAR Ancestor #A201800

Ezra M. Covell – 6th great-grandfather DAR Ancestor #A026745

James Philip Covell – 7th great-uncle DAR Ancestor #A026754

Jonathan Covell – 7th great-uncle DAR Ancestor #A204921

Aside from these Patriots, my ancestors include many pacifist Quakers, as well as Tories who remained loyal to England. It wouldn't be fair not to acknowledge them as well.

Author's Forenote

Our language has shifted since America's founding, in some ways drastically and others more subtly. In writing this novel, I polled my newsletter subscribers concerning the use of the word ***bastard***. Historically, this was a not a vulgar slur nor a curse word. It was a ***legal term***. Being illegitimate carried legal limitations, including the inability to inherit and even denial of the right to use a last name in some areas of the colonies. The limited use of the term in this novel is not to shock or offend, but to be historically accurate and bring the emotional impact that would have been felt by the characters themselves. While not vulgar, the legal term carried the impact of ***what was perceived at that time*** as a shameful heritage. My newsletter subscribers urged me to explain this up front—which was an excellent suggestion.

It is always my goal to share authentic historical fiction, portraying history with its triumphs and failures, warts and all. That is my brand of writing and reflects my passion for history to be remembered as it was and not as we wish it had been.

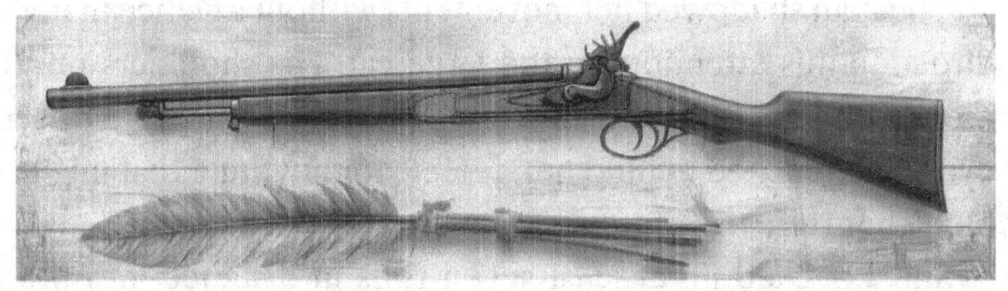

Chapter 1

September 9, 1777—Near Chadds' Ford, Pennsylvania

With hair as black as midnight, the man flowed into the tiny forest clearing in front of Grace as if materialized by her scream. Long and lanky despite the breadth of his shoulders, his crouch matched that of the panther, perched on a rocky outcropping before them. Both man and cat were illuminated by the lingering glow after the sunset. Grasping a musket at his side, the man did not point it at the panther.

The cat's long tail twitched as its yellow eyes narrowed to near slits.

"Walk backward." His voice was soothing and low, cultured, with not a tremor of unease or uncertainty.

Grace's foot obeyed his directions even as her mind clogged with fear.

"Do not turn and run, only walk backward."

Grace forced her other foot to move, then the first again.

The man shadowed her movements without a glance in her direction, his attention on the large cat. His shoulders now blocked her view of the animal's yellowed teeth and amber eyes. She reached behind her, feeling for anything that might block her retreat.

She'd backed up at least seven rods in distance into the trees, leaving the panther behind. A branch caught her linen cap and tore it from her head, dislodging the pins that secured her hair. She snatched the cloth before it hit the ground, taking another step back. Silently, she gripped her hair that fell around her face. She'd made no sound, but the man turned and faced her.

He stood straight, his back to where they'd left the cat, as if confident they were beyond its danger. Eyes barely a shade lighter than his hair met hers in the shadowed depths of the forest. The strong planes of his face were free of wrinkles, his wide mouth a straight line across his tanned skin. A dark mark divided his brow left from right, perhaps a scar. Shoulder-length hair free of a tie framed him against the deep green shadows. If not for his common hunter's clothing—a white linen shirt under a buckskin hunting jacket and buff breeches—he might have been an Indian.

"Are thee hurt?" The cultured flow of his words belied his wild countenance.

Grace smoothed the front of her apron with trembling hands while she found her voice. "I think not."

He cocked his head. "I do not believe we have met."

"Nay. I have only just arrived. With the army." Washington's army had marched in earlier that day. She should have stayed with the rest of the camp followers, who'd set up along a tributary of Brandywine Creek. She'd been a fool to stray so far into the forest, but it kept her out of reach of—

"'Tis best to stay close to a fire in the evening."

His words were warming, reassuring, not the least threatening, but still she tensed. How often had she turned away invitations to share a man's fire... and more?

"Forest predators like the panther respect fire and avoid it."

This man might speak of panthers, but they weren't the only predators. Despite the sultry air, she wrapped her arms around her ribs.

He took a step closer. "Pray accept my pardon. 'Twas not my intention to frighten thee." His brows drew together along the dark line, his eyes impossible to read.

A frog croaked in the distance, and crickets took up their evening chorus. A shiver worked the length of her back. Where was the camp? How had she allowed herself to be caught out alone with a strange man? The cultured voice meant nothing. Hadn't her mother warned her of that? Hadn't John Perkins' relentless pursuit proved it? Her throat threatened to close off again.

He retreated a step. "I would be honored to escort thee to the army's camp, should thee wish it."

Did she wish it? Nay, but what choice was left to her? Her own foolishness had caught her out.

"I would be most grateful." Had he noticed how thready her voice was? Would he pounce on her weakness as surely as the panther? Had she exchanged one dangerous beast for another?

Yet he spoke with the Quaker *thee*. Mother had installed her with Major General Greene's camp followers because of that man's Quaker beliefs. Quakers didn't walk the backstreets of Philadelphia, at least, not the backstreets where she'd grown up. That must mean something.

"Where were thee heading, miss...?" He paused, a slight tilt to his head, strands of straight black hair feathering in the breeze.

"Miss Grace. Everyone calls me Miss Grace." Because that was all the name she owned, but he didn't need to know that.

Her dress, while modest and plain, was not that of a Quaker, so Mark had expected her to supply a surname. While unconventional among those not Quaker, the use of her Christian name made things easier for him. Adding the "miss" was not something a Quaker should do, however. He'd been taught to shun any form of titles when addressing people.

"Very well, then. Call me Mark." She didn't need to know his full name. While the Quakers of Birmingham were tolerant of him, many even friendly, Mark Running Bear wasn't seen as a blacksmith or a Quaker outside of the village. He was seen as an Indian.

Did this slip of a woman see him that way too? Her eyes, the gray of a pigeon's wing, were filled with fear, her knuckles almost as white as the apron she clutched. Was it fear of the panther still—or of him? He shifted another step away, and her breathing settled into a more regular pattern.

"Where were thee heading, Grace?"

She paused, perhaps taken aback by his more intimate use of her name. "Major General Greene's division of the Continental Army. I work in the followers' encampment."

That didn't explain why she was there, in the forest. Not that it should matter to Mark.

While most Quakers didn't concern themselves with military matters, some of those coming to the blacksmith shop where he worked were free with their opinions and often argued about the state of the war. Mark had known that Washington's troops were between Philadelphia and Head of Elk to the southwest, but not that they'd veered this far north. He'd been gone since noon, it being Tuesday and his normal half day at the smithy.

"Where are they encamped?"

She pressed her fingers to her lips, uncertainty written on her face even in the diminishing light. Her eyes never left his, but she backed another step away. Why did she fear him so? Might she suspect him of being a spy for the British?

"I am a Quaker, Grace. I have no loyalty to either side of the war. I would know thy destination only to see thee safely there, not to carry the news to anyone else."

Her chin dipped, and he could no longer see her eyes. "We set up along a stream they said emptied into the Brandywine."

Harvey Run was no more than a quarter mile to the north. That was the closest stream, yet that was quite a distance for her to travel on her own with darkness closing in.

"Come, I will lead thee to the stream." He took a few steps, paused, and looked back. She was following but staying beyond his arm's reach. This one was wary, which, in light of the war, was probably a good thing. But what had driven her from the safety of the camp? It made no sense.

Neither did his strong urge to protect her.

Following Mark was like stalking a shadow—or a ghost. As silently as he'd first appeared before the panther, he slipped through the forest with only the meager light from stars in the cloudless sky. Grace closed the distance between them, her fear of getting lost in the wilderness outweighing her fear of him.

He'd made no move to accost her, even though there was no one around to stop him. His height, his build, his youth all proved she'd be no match for him if he did. *Better the devil you know than the devil you don't.* Mother's saying, one Grace had heard too many times to count.

She didn't know Mark. He'd not even offered a proper last name, perhaps because she hadn't either. And he'd called her by her first name alone, not including *miss*, as if they were intimates.

Her next thought caused her to stumble. What if he were like her? She caught herself on a low-hanging branch.

He whirled in a half-crouch, and she gasped.

He straightened. "Are thee well?"

"'Twas merely a root." And the notion they might be alike. Not that it made him any safer to be around. There were plenty of young men born to the backstreets of Philadelphia. She'd spent as much of her growing-up years avoiding them as any other men.

He continued forward, and she fell in step behind him. The night sounds surrounded them, sounds foreign to her, but nothing that caused Mark to slow or pause. He was as one with the forest, with the night. Grace's city upbringing had not prepared her for this dark wilderness. She'd been a fool to leave camp. She'd been warned, but when that soldier had come up to her, bold as brass in broad daylight, and suggested they—

"Do thee hear the water?"

Grace jumped, heart fluttering behind her stays, hands crushing the linen of her apron. "Pardon?"

He stopped. "Listen."

The burble of water over rocks came to her. A soothing sound, quiet enough that she'd have missed it if he hadn't told her to listen.

"I hear it."

"While thee are here, stay within hearing distance of the stream. 'Twill lead thee back."

Of course. Why hadn't she thought of that? Because she'd been raised in the city. Because she hadn't thought darkness would come so fast. And because fear had driven her from camp as soon as that soldier had left her. Left her and assumed she'd be there waiting for him to return. Waiting for her to... to be like her mother.

Her face was a study of conflicts, and Mark couldn't stop staring at her. In an opening in the forest, lit by starlight, she looked too frail to be in their rugged surroundings. Was she a *Wemategunis*? She wasn't much taller than the Lenni Lenape forest spirits Betsy and Sarah spoke of. The two old Lenape women enjoyed telling him stories of the *Wemategunis*. He always listened with respect, although their beliefs clashed with the Quakers' teachings. But now, seeing Grace in the starlight, he could almost believe those stories of mystical beings.

"Is something wrong?" Her voice was a reedy whisper, and her hands tortured her apron.

"Nay." He hauled in a deep breath and turned toward Harvey Run. "Follow me. We are almost there."

They reached the stream's edge, where the trees hung low over the rippling water. Mark stopped and listened. Grace halted several steps behind him, her breathing loud in the stillness. A faint whiff of woodsmoke reached him from upstream. That made sense. The land had been cleared along the stream there, and Arnold Bishop's flax crop had been harvested several weeks ago. Mark had forged a new shaft for the flyer on Arnold's wife's spinning wheel about that same time. And everyone in the area knew the farmer was sympathetic to the Patriot cause.

"The camp is that way." He pointed.

"Is it?" Grace looked around. "I am not certain. Everything looks so different."

She'd come this way in the daylight, no doubt. From the noise she'd made scrabbling through the trees behind him, she'd not spent much time in a forest.

"'Tis not much farther." He led the way, and she crashed through the brush in his wake.

Soon, voices rode on the evening breeze. Flickering light from a blazing central campfire filtered through the trees. Most people in town were abed at this hour, but the camp seemed a living, breathing thing so busy were its parts. He stopped behind the last large tree before the clearing. Grace stepped up behind him and peered around his shoulder, the first time she'd come within reach since they'd left the panther behind.

"Is this where thee belong?"

He'd have given anything to be able to interpret the expressions that flitted across her face in the light of the rising moon. She said nothing, neither did she move. He waited beside her while her breathing slowed to normal.

"Grace?"

She jumped at his voice, and he took a step back. The last thing he wanted was to frighten her any more than she already was. But she could have run past him into the camp, and she hadn't. In fact, she seemed almost reluctant to leave him now. The uneven thump of his heart had nothing to do with their swift travel through the forest. Nothing at all.

She turned hesitant eyes toward him and bobbed a short curtsey. To him. Quakers didn't hold with bowing or curtsying. They showed no deference to another human, believing that all men—and women—were created equal. Yet Mark fought the urge to bow to her in return.

"I am so grateful for what you did, getting me away from the panther and for leading me back."

"'Twas my honor to serve thee."

"Good evening, then." She bobbed another curtsey, scanned the area of the camp closest to them, and then scurried into the jumble of tents and wagons.

Even after she'd blended into the mass of humanity, lost from his sight, Mark remained. The camp itself brought back long-held memories of another time, another camp, another people. But mostly, it was the woman who held him in place with a power he'd never experienced before.

Perhaps she was a *Wemategunis*.

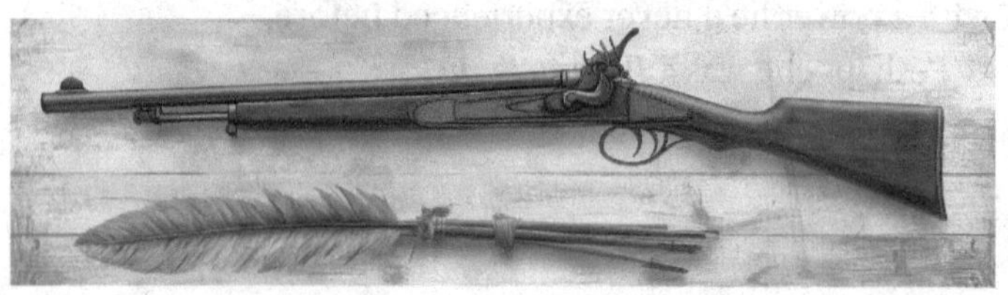

CHAPTER 2

SEPTEMBER 10, 1777

GRACE STIRRED A KETTLE filled with water and milled oats over a campfire near the center of the makeshift encampment they'd set up that afternoon. She brushed at the wrinkles of her apron with one hand and worked the ladle with the other, leaving nothing to smother the yawn that cracked her jaw.

"If you were not out at all hours doin' God knows what, you would be fit to work come the mornin'." Mistress Crenshaw stepped close to Grace, her height and bony frame covered in a black dress and deep bonnet, giving her the appearance of a specter from beyond the grave. "And think not that I have failed to notice how the soldiers sniff around you. Put one foot out of place, and I will not hesitate to see you booted from camp. I have no tolerance for the likes of you, that I do not."

"Aye, mistress." Grace couldn't move away from the woman without stopping her stirring, and to do so would risk a burnt breakfast for all of them, so she kept her eyes lowered and tried not to cringe. It wasn't as if she hadn't heard it all before. Less than three weeks in camp, and too many people had figured out where she'd come from, even though Grace had done her best to say nothing to anyone.

"Mistress Crenshaw?"

"What is it, Mistress Geyer?" Impatience leaked from Mistress Crenshaw's voice, and Grace took a small measure of comfort in knowing she wasn't the only camp follower not in the woman's good graces.

"I vonder if I might borrow Miss Grace for a special duty. The mayoor yeneral vishes a local meetinghouse to be readied for a field hospital." The Swedish lilt drew Grace's attention from the kettle. Short and gently rounded in a grandmotherly way—at least how Grace had always assumed a grandmother would be. Mistress Geyer's smile crinkled the corners of her eyes.

"The major general, you mean, and aye, if it be for him, you may take the girl." Mistress Crenshaw waved another young woman over and gestured for her to take the ladle from Grace. "But see that she is back in time to help with the supper."

"Oh, aye, unless the mayoor yeneral instructs me othcrvisc." Mistress Geyer inclined her head.

Mistress Crenshaw glared at Grace, who handed over the ladle and hurried around the fire to fall into step beside the Swedish woman.

"Poor lamb, she does not much like you." Mistress Geyer patted Grace's forearm without slowing a step.

"Nay, mistress."

"As you heard from Mistress Crenshaw, I am Mistress Geyer."

"You already know I am Miss Grace."

The older woman nodded. "I vas looking for you this afternoon after ve set up the tents ." Mistress Geyer shot her a raised-brow glance. "You vere not to be found."

"Nay, mistress. I took a walk and... I had some trouble finding my way back."

The older woman stopped and faced Grace. "Tell me plain, did a man drive you avay? Or did you sneak off to meet the one who brought you back?"

"You saw him?" Who else might have seen? Someone who would report it to Mistress Crenshaw? If so, Grace had best pack her meager belongings and ready herself for the long walk back to Philadelphia. That woman hadn't jested about booting Grace from camp. She ruled under the authority of Major General Greene himself.

"Aye, so I did, yoost as I was heading for my own bed. A tall, handsome man, I should say, with dark hair and wearing hunter's clothing."

"I did not sneak away to meet him. I vow I did not." Maybe if she could get the Swedish woman on her side... "There was a panther in the forest. He protected me and then led me back because I had lost my way. He never touched me, never asked to either. He is a Quaker."

Mistress Geyer nodded before continuing across the camp and toward the town. "See that you stay in camp and close to me. The soldiers vill not bother you if you do. I shall make certain of that."

Grace scurried after her. "Truly?" That this woman, so unlike the women Grace had known all her life, would offer her this... This what? Protection? "You would do this for me?" Dare she hope for a friendship?

"I vould. Have I not seen the vay the men look at you?" She shook her head, the frilly sides of her linen cap ruffling in the breeze. "If I had a daughter, I vould vant someone to look out for her yoost as I vill for you."

Grace's throat clogged with something she couldn't exactly identify, but before she could ponder it, they broke through a hedgerow of trees and the countryside opened before them. It was crawling with soldiers, an image that always put her on edge. So many men.

"Ve vill be vorking until dark, I fear. There is much to do to prepare. You vill be tired long before you find your bed tonight." Mistress Geyer offered another of her eye-crinkling smiles. "There vill be no returning to Mistress Crenshaw before supper. After the battle, I vill tell the mayoor yeneral that I have need of you to vork beside me. My husband and son serve under his command. He vill allow me this, I think."

That raised a smile inside of Grace, even if it didn't touch her lips.

The tongs slipped, and with a yelp, Mark jumped out of the way as the glowing metal bar crashed to the dirt floor of the smithy.

"What ails thee, boy?" Charlie Brewer, the blacksmith Mark worked for, stopped his own hammer mid-swing and scowled. "That makes three mishaps and 'tis not even noontide yet."

Mark scrambled to secure the hot iron with the tongs and thrust it back into the forge. "My mind is wandering."

Charlie brought his hammer down with a resounding clang against the iron on his anvil. Sparks jumped and arched. "'Tis all this upheaval with soldiers appearing around every corner. How are good people supposed to get on with their day? Go. Have a look. See what is happening and satisfy thy curiosity."

Mark stripped off his leather apron before his employer could change his mind. He was two steps out of the door of the smithy when Charlie bellowed after him, "Mind thee get the details straight so thee can relate them reliably upon thy return."

He wouldn't expect an answer, so Mark kept going. Charlie might think it was the armies that had taken Mark's mind off work this morning, but that was only part of it. The smaller part of it. It was the woman in the woods, the one who had robbed him of most of a night's sleep, who still held the greater part of his attention. Thoughts of her made his heart pound more than the possibility—the certainty—of a battle nearby.

How many times had Mark watched a stag in the fall with its lip curled and tongue out, tracking a doe by scent, besotted with finding a mate? For the first time in his twenty years, he understood the feeling. It wasn't a comfortable thought, but it was enticing, and it wasn't something he could shake. The need to find the young woman again hurried him on.

The smithy sat off the main street, but even there, horseback soldiers in an assortment of uniforms pointed and shouted orders to the masses of men on foot. Mark headed in the direction of the Birmingham Meetinghouse, where the local Quakers met on Sundays. There was a crowd of people flowing around it, moving in and out of the building.

Men in all manner of dress, most not any discernible type of uniform, worked to fit pieces of field artillery behind newly dug earthworks. Language uncommon among the Quaker community salted the air. The blacksmith in Mark wanted to linger and examine how the weapons were made, while the Quaker in him wanted to hurry by and not think about what the weapons would do. The Lenape in him put him on edge.

Funny how, after all these years, he still thought of them as "Quakers" and not "Friends," as those born into the Society of Friends preferred. Friend, *winkalit*, meant something different to the Lenape, a thing that incorporated brotherhood and service, not a religious connection. His mother had called them Quakers, and that had stuck with him.

He'd been just six years old when the Iroquois had attacked their band of Lenape who were pushing west, moving out of their homelands taken over by the white men. At the Iroquois warriors' first screams, Mother had grabbed him and pulled him back into the cover of the forest. If he closed his eyes and concentrated, he could almost smell the fear again, hear the shrieks of the wounded. If he turned his head, he'd see the Iroquois's spear pierce his father's chest.

Mark wiped the back of his hand across his eyes to clear those long-ago memories, striding toward the meetinghouse. People scurried in and out of the doors like ants on a kicked-over anthill. Most were dressed in plain Quaker garb, but a knot of women working near a corner of the cut-stone building were not. One seated under the window, framed by the white shutters, caught his eye.

She was small, dainty even. Her black hair roped into a thick braid reminded him of the young women of his tribe, though in her case it hung from beneath a linen cap, its end swaying near her hips on the plank bench as she worked on whatever was in her hands. Even from behind, he recognized her. She wore the same clothing and cap as she had the night before. If she'd turn, he'd see those eyes the color of a dove's wing. But would she recognize him in his Quaker clothing?

Would she want to?

Like a stag in the forest, Mark headed toward her in a straight line.

"Mark, thee are a welcome sight." Joseph Townsend came from around the building and clapped him on the shoulder. "I have been tasked with moving our benches from the floor to the balcony. Thy strength will make the chore that much faster, and then we can leave here."

Mark tore his eyes away from Grace. "Why are they to be moved?"

"Have thee not heard?" Joseph's voice rose along with his eyebrows. "Washington has commandeered our humble meetinghouse for a field hospital."

"Can he do that?"

"He has an army at his disposal. He can do whatever he pleases." Joseph leaned closer and lowered his voice. "For now. But once we have moved the benches, I am heading north. 'Tis rumored that the British might come from that direction. Howe's army will change Washington's plans."

Mark shot a glance at the women. "Are thee choosing sides in this coming battle?"

The other man shrugged. "'Tis all but certain the British will triumph. They always do. I would like to watch them march in." Joseph was year younger than Mark and well-known for getting into harmless mischief. No doubt he planned to watch more than just the marching-in. "But first we must move the benches lest they be forever stained with blood." He clouted Mark on the shoulder again and led the way into the building.

Grace had shifted, her profile now in view. She didn't look up from whatever she was folding, but her hands paused when he passed by on the way into the meetinghouse.

It wasn't much, but it gave Mark a bit of hope that she had recognized him.

It was him. The man from the woods. Grace had to steal a second and then a third glance to be sure. Deeply tanned, he might have passed for an Indian, but not as he was dressed that morning. His hair was tidied into a queue, and he wore the typical plain clothing of the Quakers. The cadence of his speech matched that of the other Quaker man. They didn't appear to have noticed her.

Mistress Geyer leaned close from the other end of the bench as they folded the bandages on the bench between them. "Is something the matter?"

"Nay, nothing." Grace picked up another length of fabric to roll into a bandage.

"Hmm." The older woman looked from Grace to the two men still conversing a few yards away. "The dark-haired one looks familiar. Is he the one—?" She broke off her sentence as the men approached.

Grace all but buried her face in her work, fingers fumbling with the strip of cloth. The men passed right beside her on their way into the building. Her fingers froze until their boot heels clomped onto the wooden floor of the meetinghouse. She raised her eyes to meet Mistress Geyer's.

"I thought so. Even more handsome in his Quaker clothing, I must say." Mistress Geyer sat straighter and stretched her back. "And by the vay he looked at you, he recognized you too."

He'd looked at her? He'd recognized her? Of course. Why wouldn't he. She was dressed the same, but she hadn't even troubled herself to put up her hair. It hung down her back like a schoolgirl's. She certainly wasn't that, not at seventeen. Her mother had been married at her age and widowed ten months after. But that had been years before Grace was born.

"'Tis best if he did not," Grace said. "We will be moving on after the battle, surely."

Mistress Geyer sighed and rested her hands on her lap. "Not all of us."

"Why not all?" Grace fidgeted with the strip of cloth. Would Mistress Crenshaw send her back after all? Why? Because Mark noticed her? She couldn't help it if someone noticed her, could she? She hadn't returned his look. That was a lesson she'd learned long ago. Never make eye contact with a man. She'd forgotten it last night with her fear over the panther, but she wouldn't forget again.

The older woman stared at something in the distance, over the heads of the other women working diligently on the bandages. "Some vill die here, if not today, then tomorrow or the next day." Sadness weighed her heavily accented words.

Ah. She was referring to the soldiers, not the women.

Grace shivered despite the warm September morning. Of course. A battle meant men would be wounded—which was why they were preparing bandages. Some wouldn't survive. Maybe even Mistress Geyer's husband or son. And here Grace had been worrying about herself. She dropped her chin to her chest and rolled her strips. She might have the least to lose of anyone here. For that, she should be thankful.

Part of her wished she had a man in her life to worry over like Mistress Geyer did, but that would mean letting someone get close enough to be special. And Grace knew enough about men to know that what they wanted from women like her wouldn't lead to anything other than heartbreak and hardships.

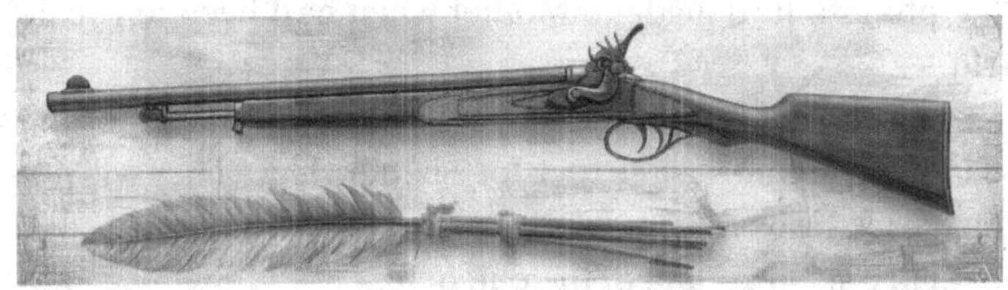

Chapter 3

September 10, 1777

Mark followed Joseph out the back door of the meetinghouse as soon as the benches were all stored in the balcony. He'd rather have left by the main door to see if Grace remained there, but Joseph had insisted they climb Osborne Hill and take in the view from there. Once on the rise, he agreed with his friend that the view was something to behold. Washington's men were gathered along the eastern bank of Brandywine Creek. Lines of soldiers guarded Brinton's Ford and Jones' Ford. Nathanael Greene's unit would be near Chadd's Ford if they'd remained where they'd been last night. If the rumors at the smithy were true, there were six divisions here with Washington.

An impressive show of force.

The sight that stirred something deep within him, something the Quakers had never been able to snuff out. Nor had the promise he'd made to Mother when he'd been ten years old.

A bit shorter than Mark, who was tall for a Lenape, Joseph had stepped onto a large rock for a better view. "They will not beat back Howe."

"Thee seem certain of the outcome."

"Of course. Howe leads the world's finest army." Joseph swung his arm in an arch toward the soldiers below. "This riff-raff cannot even clothe itself properly."

It was true that most of Washington's soldiers lacked proper uniforms. Except for the officers, most dressed in a mixture of styles that might include some part of a uniform or not. While the residents at Birmingham were largely Quaker and therefore neutral in the war, there were some firebrands, non-Quakers with Patriot leanings. If the soldiers below matched their burning desire for freedom from England, then Howe might be in for a surprise.

"Clothing does not make a fighter." The Iroquois warrior had worn only a breechclout and moccasins the day he'd struck Father down.

"Nay. Discipline does. But the uniform is part of the discipline, I say. Part of putting off self and conforming to the whole."

Mark's Lenape ancestors had worn no uniforms, but they'd painted themselves for war. It was the same concept, although the markings carried deeper meanings. "When did thee get so knowledgeable about soldiers and armies?"

Joseph waved Mark's words away. "I have ears, do I not?"

"Have thee chosen a side then?"

"Nay, of course not. 'Tis not the Quaker way." He hopped off the rock and brushed the front of his coat. "But neither will I be mistaken for a Patriot when the British march into our town."

"Thee are certain the British are close?"

Joseph laughed and pointed to the scene before them. "Washington is."

Indeed, the general must have been nearby to have amassed such a show of force. "Thee thinks Howe will come from the north? Not from the west across the Brandywine?"

"From both I should think," said Joseph. "Daniel McGee rode into town yesterday from the west. He claims he spoke with some British soldiers camped there."

"Daniel McGee is best known for a loose and thirsty tongue."

"He may tip a pint more often than he should, but he says he heard talk about marching north in the morning."

Mark studied Washington's preparations for another few minutes. McGee wasn't a reliable source, but the northern fords were narrower, easier to cross. Not that it was any of Mark's business either way. Or it shouldn't have been. Yet it was hard not to admire the ragtag group willing to face the much larger force of trained soldiers to protect what they considered their land.

"I must return to the smithy."

"Will thee join me here tomorrow to watch the fighting?"

Mark shook his head. "I plan on working tomorrow."

"Nobody will be working tomorrow. The battle will wind up in the village, in our very midst. Heed my words." Joseph rolled his eyes. "Even Father agrees." His father being one of the town elders, as much a stickler for the Quaker ways as his son was wont to flaunt them, his agreement added a sense of urgency.

Mark hurried down the hill toward the village. He couldn't say Joseph was wrong, but he hoped he was. Lucy—the woman who'd raised Mark after Mother's death—lived on the southwest outskirts of Birmingham, but a battle might erupt anywhere. He'd report back to Charlie and finish his work at the smithy, and then he should get Lucy out of harm's way.

If only he could be sure which way that was.

An elderly Quaker lady had brought by a basket of yeasty rolls around noon, but that had been hours ago. Now, evening was upon them, and the women had just finished their work at the Quaker meetinghouse. After rolling the bandages, they'd assembled the operating tables and equipment the army surgeons had brought in by the wagonload, then washed everything down according to Mistress Geyer's instructions—not the surgeons'. The older woman knew what she was doing. She'd obviously been in a situation like this before.

Grace's stomach growled as she followed the Swedish woman back to their camp.

"I have some dried beef in my tent. 'Tis not much, but 'tvill fill our bellies." The older woman stopped short.

Grace almost smacked into her. "What is it?"

"There is Mr. Geyer." She pointed to a group of men walking the banks of the Brandywine. "Over there, the man vith the blond beard and blue hat."

"I see him." He was slender and tall, a full head above the men working around him.

Moisture gathered at the corners of Mistress Geyer's eyes, but she smiled. "He makes me proud, he and our boy."

Grace could say nothing to that. She'd never felt that way about anyone, and she was pretty sure nobody had ever felt that way about her. The emotion on Mistress Geyer's face made Grace's empty middle seem even emptier.

"Come, ve must not distract the men vhile they vork." Without a second glance, the lady strode off again toward camp.

Grace looked back. The man with the blond beard had stopped and stared after them. The distance was too great to make out his features, but somehow she knew there was pride in his eyes as well. That brought a lump to her throat.

They entered camp and the lingering scent of beans and salt pork produced another growl from her middle. A woman stood by the huge kettle near the center of the camp, stirring the contents. "We are not too late for supper," Grace said.

"Aye. It smells better than the dried beef for sure."

"And easier to chew."

Mistress Geyer flashed her a wide grin. "'Tis the truth. I have an extra plate in my tent, vhich is closer than yours." She ducked inside the square canvas shelter and reemerged with two plates and two spoons, handing one to Grace. "Let us eat."

The woman stirring the pot ladled a helping onto their plates. Grace sat on one of the crates that circled the cooking fire and shoveled in a mouthful of the thick bean soup. It had more onions than salt pork for flavoring, but she didn't mind. It was warm and filling. Heaven knew, she'd eaten worse.

"'Tvill be your first battle, Miss Grace." Mistress Geyer settled beside her and rested her plate on her lap. "There are things you should know."

Grace swallowed, then set her plate on her lap as well, even though she wanted to keep eating.

"It might start tomorrow, or it might start in a few days, but 'tvill happen. And 'tvill be hard vorking in the field hospital." She grasped Grace's forearm and squeezed. "The first time I saw a soldier brought in, all covered in blood and screaming such horrible vords." She shook her head. "I yoost about lost my breakfast."

"Are you saying that we shall help in the field hospital when the fighting starts?" The beans in Grace's stomach formed an uncomfortable weight.

"Aye. Unless you vish to go back to Mistress Crenshaw. She is a bit... vell. She has a hard job to do. She must keep everyone in line in a camp made up of very different types of vomen."

Grace set her plate on the bench and pressed her hands to her middle. "Women like me, you mean?"

"Vomen who ran farms, vomen who raised children, vomen who managed stores, all used to doing things their own vay. This is vhat I mean."

"I never did any of those things." Her voice was no stronger than a spider's web. If Mistress Geyer was to be Grace's friend, she should know the truth. "My mother brought me to the camp. She did not want me to become... That is... She is a..." She slouched over, unable to look Mistress Geyer in the eye.

"Miss Grace, I saw you arrive in camp. Your mother, she vanted something better for you. There is no shame in that."

"But she earned her money by—"

"Did you earn money that vay?" Mistress Geyer interrupted.

Grace sat bolt upright on the bench. "Nay, mistress. Never. Not once."

The grandmotherly woman patted her arm. "I thought not. I have been vatching you these past three veeks. You vork hard and stay out of the men's vay, even vhen some persist. I said to myself, that girl needs a friend. I yoost needed an excuse to give Mistress Crenshaw for stealing you avay. Today gave me that excuse." The smile that wrinkled her eyes was back.

The lump in Grace's throat threatened to choke her, but she managed to say, "Thank you."

"But if you stay vith me, you vill see some horrible things once the battle starts. I vould not blame you if you vished to return to Mistress Crenshaw."

"Nay. I wish to stay with you." Partly because Mistress Crenshaw was looking for a reason to run her off, and but more because Grace hadn't ever had a woman friend who was anything like Mistress Geyer.

"Then finish your beans. You vill need all the strength you can store for vhat vill come. Afterward, ve vill move your tent next to mine."

Grace lifted her plate and scooped another spoonful of beans into her mouth. Tomorrow might be awful, but for tonight, she had enough to eat and a friend to share it with.

"'Twould be safer for thee away from the village." Mark sat across from Lucy that evening, the woman who was the last thing close to family that he had. She'd been a grandmother to him, shepherding him into the Quaker fold. Her husband, Oliver Sharp, had died years ago, and Lucy was getting on in age. Mark's and Lucy's roles were changing, with him doing more to care for her.

Or trying to.

"This is my home." Lucy's spotted and wrinkled hands rested on her lap. "What the strangers do outside of it is their business."

"They are not just strangers. They are soldiers."

"I fear no man, soldier or otherwise." Lucy's smile was serene and sincere. "The Lord will watch over me and thee, as He did when I returned thy mother to her people all those years ago."

Mark suppressed a groan. Lucy had found his mother, then a young girl, lost in the forest. She'd taken the frightened child back to her village, even though it put her in a precarious position. From that act of kindness, a friendship had formed between Lucy and his mother. But the chance Lucy had taken back then couldn't compare to the battle brewing on the outskirts of Birmingham.

While he'd accepted the Quaker teachings—for the most part—he'd seen a battle up close. He'd been too young to remember much besides his father's death, but many of his family's tribe had died that day. Mark rubbed the scar on his forehead with the pad of his thumb. Killing. That was what happened in battle.

"These soldiers have more than guns, they have cannons. One cannon ball and thy whole house could be destroyed with thee inside."

"One arrow could have pierced me—or a knife. A club could have brought me down." She covered his hand with hers. Her knuckles were gnarled, her skin spotted and thin, but the firmness in her fingers matched the resolution in her faded blue eyes. "Worry not for me. If the Lord decides to take me home, I am prepared to go. I am an old woman, Mark. I hold no fear of leaving this life behind."

It wouldn't be the Lord taking her, though. It'd be Washington's or Howe's army. The house stood far too close to Chadd's Ford for Mark's peace of mind. He blew out a long breath. "Is there nothing I can say to persuade thee?"

She chuckled. "I cannot imagine what. Even if I should desire to flee, where would I go? How would I get there?"

He enveloped her hand between both of his. "I would find a way, rent a buggy, take thee to—"

"Nay, my dear boy, nay." She shook her head, the edges of her plain cap rustling against her grooved cheeks. "I am too old to be tossed about in a buggy on some hurly-burly dash to who knows where. I am better off here, in my home."

"I will stay with thee—"

"No such thing. Thee have work to do. Charlie Brewer will have need of thee tomorrow."

Not if the battle broke loose, as it likely would with Washington's army taking its defensive position in the land south the village. But Joseph was right, Washington had been beaten back more than once. Howe's army had more cannons and more men. If the British came from the north, with Washington to the south, then Birmingham sat squarely in the middle.

Lucy patted his hand again, then stood, her knees crackling with the effort. "'Tis time for me to retire."

"So early?" He stood, ready to assist her if she needed him.

"Aye, my bones ache tonight."

She was paler than normal, the brown spots on her face more pronounced. He held his arm out for her to grasp. That she did so was a bit alarming. She usually batted him away and told him she could make it on her own. He walked her down the short hallway to her bedroom, her cane thumping on the wooden floor.

He opened the door for her. "Good night, Lucy."

"Good night, my boy. May the Lord bless thee and the Light of Christ shine upon thee." She patted his arm before entering and closing the door with a soft click.

Mark walked out onto the porch of the two-story house he'd called home for the past ten years. Would it still be standing this time tomorrow? He glanced toward the south.

Was Grace worrying about what tomorrow would bring? Would she be out of harm's way? He closed his eyes and pictured her as he'd first seen her in the last rays of evening light, fear of the panther stark on her face. Then the fear had changed to wariness.

Of him.

He was used to people being wary of him. He was, after all, a Lenni Lenape. Even clothed in plain Quaker dress and speaking as they did, people never truly forgot his beginnings. The scar on his forehead didn't help. But that wasn't what had disturbed Grace. At least, he didn't think so. Nor did he think her pausing when he walked past her at the meetinghouse had been a coincidence. Her wariness the prior evening had been more that of a woman reacting to a man... not an Indian.

That thought had robbed him of sleep last night.

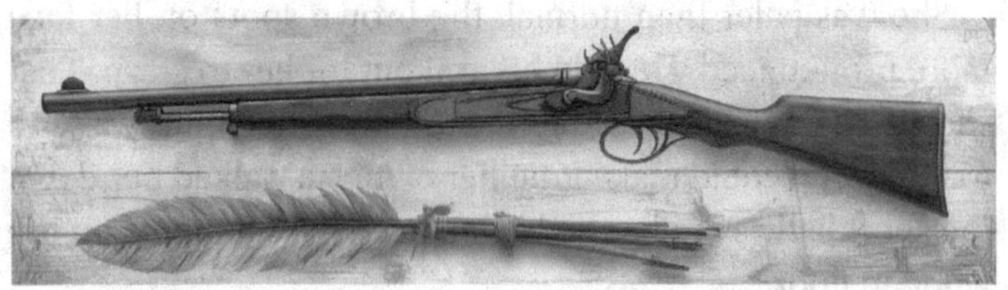

Chapter 4

GENTLE SCRATCHING AT HER tent flap pulled Grace from a fitful slumber. The light from the camp's central fire flickered around the flap's loose edges. She groaned and rubbed her gritty eyes.

"Miss Grace." Mistress Geyer's voice pulled the last fog of sleep away.

"Aye, mistress. I am rising now." She hiked herself up on one elbow to put truth to her words.

"Hurry, girl. We have much to do this day." The shuffle of feet on the packed dirt outside Grace's tent announced the woman's departure.

Grace groaned again and flopped onto her back to stare at the dark canvas above her. Not even a glimmer of sun to lighten it. Would she ever grow accustomed to rising before dawn? At times, she almost missed the backstreets of Philadelphia.

No one rose much before noon there, but avoiding the reason why was what had landed Grace in camp.

She sat and stretched, working the kinks out of her back. Her pallet consisted of a scratchy blanket and a ground tarp with not enough dried grass and cedar boughs underneath to cushion her. What there was had conspired throughout the night to poke her in uncomfortable places. Her narrow rope bed with its straw tick in her mother's rented room had been a palace bedchamber in comparison.

Grace knelt and wiggled into her stays. She pulled her same wrinkled petticoat and short gown over her equally wrinkled shift, tucking a fichu in the neckline, and then tied on her dirty apron. Mistress Geyer had warned her there would be no time to launder clothing until after the battle. She scrunched her nose as she finger-combed her hair and plaited it into a fresh braid. After tying the end with a scrap of ribbon, she secured her cap and left the tent.

Men jogged to and fro, some carrying parcels, others with the intent expressions of those on a mission, some who helped the camp followers as well as the women's husbands, fathers, brothers, and sons who stopped by to speak a word of comfort or encouragement. Women manned the main fire, ladling porridge and pouring coffee—for the Continental Army frowned upon the use of British tea—to men who gulped it down and dashed off again.

"Come vith me, Miss Grace," Mistress Geyer called from the far side of the fire.

Grace skirted the circle of standing men who ate their hasty meal. As she hurried past, one of them grabbed her arm. The force pulled her around to face a soldier's leering grin.

"Slow down, gal." His southern drawl raked across her nerves. "Where you in such an all-fired hurry to be?"

"Release me." She wrenched her arm away from him.

Several other soldiers laughed, and one slapped the man's back.

Her accoster's face reddened in the firelight, eyes shifting to his comrades and then back to her.

She took a couple of steps away.

He matched her steps, separating from the group. "We shall meet again later." His voice was low, barely loud enough for her to hear.

"Miss Grace, do make haste," Mistress Geyer called again.

He frowned at the older woman and backed up, but not before Grace read the word "later" on his lips. Fear and revulsion added speed to her feet as she raced to her friend's side.

"Thank you," she whispered.

The Swedish woman took her hand and squeezed. "'Tis a sorry thing, but ve have no time to vaste this morning, or I vould give that Dan Browne the tongue lashing he deserves. He has no reason to be in our camp, except to shirk his own duties."

"I did nothing to encourage him. I did not even know his name."

"His type has no need of encouragement. And there are too many others like him. You stay close to me. Come." She hurried Grace along, a hand at her back. "Already there are skirmishes across the Brandyvine. Someplace called Velshe's Tavern."

She'd never heard of the tavern and promptly forgot its name. But Dan Browne—that was a name she'd remember, another man to avoid. Her list was growing since she'd arrived at the camp. She did her best not to look at or speak to any man, but some would not be ignored. Especially the dark-haired one who had saved her from her foolishness in the forest, but remembering Mark didn't fill her with dread. She shook her head to rid her thoughts of him before trotting after Mistress Geyer, who was already disappearing into the mist.

Although Grace hadn't developed a taste for coffee yet, and doubted she ever would, she already regretted not being up earlier to break her fast before the day began. She glanced over her shoulder at the bustle surrounding the cooking fire, but when Dan Browne's eyes met hers, she snapped around.

There were worse things than being hungry.

The September fog hung thick until almost noon, the heat of the day made worse by it. Its cloying dampness intensified the astringent odor of burning coal until it coated the back of Mark's throat. He coughed, setting his hammer on the anvil, then took a long drink from the dipper in the bucket of drinking water they kept on the table. Removing his hat, he wiped the sweat from his forehead. A cooling fog would be a welcome relief, but that wasn't the case today.

Charlie's voice reached into the smithy, but Mark couldn't make out the words. People had been stopping by all morning, yet none to pick up an item or leave anything to be repaired. They came by to share gossip and hear it.

Rumors abounded even among the Quakers, about a minor morning battle at Welch's Tavern. A full four miles on the west side of the Brandywine, six from Birmingham, it wasn't to the north where Joseph had insisted the British would be. Although with the fog so intense, it was hard to imagine either army knew where the other was.

Charlie strode through the smithy's open door. "Nothing but rumors. 'Tisn't likely we shall know what happens till it rains down on our doorstep. Not that we should concern ourselves one way or the other."

"Thee are right," Mark said. "We Quakers should not." Of course, their steady flow of visitors at the smithy—many of them Quakers—proved they did.

"And yet we do, my lad. We do." The blacksmith blew out a breath laden with frustration and something else. A twinge of worry?

Mark hung the dipper on the side of the bucket. "It brings us no work, that much is certain."

"Bah! That will come after the battle when every wagon and gate and whatever else the army upends will need repairing." Charlie rubbed his blackened hands together. "Perhaps 'twould be the better side of wisdom for us to remove the valuables to the cellar."

Mark straightened. "Are the armies that close, then?"

"Nobody seems to know. What one man swears to as gospel, the next contradicts."

A boom sounded, far away but unmistakable. Silence followed for the space of a dozen heartbeats, then another boom.

"Well, my boy, there is our answer." Charlie nodded to the west. "And so it begins. The British must have reached the Brandywine." Another volley of booms followed. "'Twill be Greene's men at Chadd's Ford holding them off."

"Nathanael Greene?" Grace was attached to his division. Not that the camp followers were near the fighting, but if the fighters had to pull back—

"Bah!" Charlie smacked his open palm on the wooden table. "Let us move the valuables to the cellar. Mind you hide all the spare iron as well as the finished pieces and the tools. All the tools. I shall not choose a side, but I shall safeguard my belongings from both."

Pushing thoughts of Grace aside, Mark lowered himself through the trap door in the wooden floor of an addition at the back of the smithy. The cellar's ceiling was too low for him to stand upright as he worked open a hidden panel in the north wall that hid a secret room. Built decades before, the cramped space beyond was just large enough to conceal Charlie's wife and children from Indian raids—yet Mark knew of it. The irony wasn't lost on him. Charlie handed down crates of tools and iron, and Mark stacked them behind the false wall. Once everything was in place, he wedged the hidden door in again, then smeared handfuls of dirt from the floor of the cellar against the wooden walls to further conceal it.

He jumped into the opening, catching the sides and hoisting himself into the smithy.

"Well done." Charlie looked around the bare walls and work surfaces. Another volley of booms reached them, and he grimaced. "There will be no more work this day. Off with thee. But mind thee stay away from the goings on out there." He waved his hand toward the door.

"I shall." Mark stripped off his leather apron and hung it by the open door before he stepped outside. He scanned the area to the south. The dissipating fog still cloaked much of the landscape. Grace was down there somewhere. Why did she linger so heavy on his thoughts? They'd met only briefly, not more than a passing acquaintance, and yet he could still see the fear in her eyes. The urge to protect her—to be with her—pulled at him.

Like a stag in the forest.

"Mark!" Joseph jogged toward him. "Are thee free?"

"I am."

"Come with me." A barely suppressed gleefulness filled his friend's face. "The fog is lifting, so we should have a splendid view of the fighting. They say the guns are firing across Chadd's Ford."

"I ought to check on Lucy and then look in at the meetinghouse."

"Thee risk being put to work." Joseph frowned at him. "Thee could miss the whole battle."

Scenes of the battle that had killed Father flashed behind his eyes. If he missed the like again, that was fine by him. Or it should be. Yet his heart thumped a bit stronger, and he wiped his damp palms on the back of his breeches. Much as he didn't want to admit it—even to himself—Joseph wasn't the only one affected by the prospect of a battle here in Birmingham.

Then again, maybe it was the prospect of seeing Grace at the meetinghouse—if she were there—that had him restless and unsettled.

"After I have seen to Lucy, and if they do not put me to work at the meetinghouse, I shall attempt to find thee."

Joseph clapped Mark on the shoulder. "Look for me on the high ground near wherever the guns are." Then he jogged off in the direction of Chadd's Ford.

Mark turned toward home. Maybe the booming cannons would persuade Lucy to at least accompany him to the meetinghouse. The stout stone building would be a safer place for her. And much safer for Grace than an encampment of tents along Harvey Run.

The first cannon boom caught Grace unprepared. She jumped, dropping the tray in her hands.

"Easy, girl." Mistress Geyer stooped and helped Grace gather the spilled supplies. "'Tvas a long vay off, a couple of miles at least."

"Forgive me. I did not expect—"

"Of course not. 'Tis your first battle." Mistress Geyer stood and looked around the meetinghouse, then nodded. "Ve are as ready as ve can be. 'Tvill not be long now. Set that tray over there." She pointed to one of three operating tables, its wood stained by the blood spilled in previous battles.

Grace suppressed a shudder as another boom sounded, but she kept the tray steady as she set it in place. Other women, camp followers and those dressed in the plain garb of Quakers, stood in groups around the large open room or gathered near windows and the doorway. Quakers would not fight, but they would assist with the wounded—of both sides, Grace had been told.

The army's surgeon in charge at the meetinghouse, a scruffy-looking man in a tattered coat that at least appeared somewhat clean, paced in front of the makeshift tables, muttering to himself. A pair of junior surgeons and a half-dozen surgeon's mates appeared busy at keeping out of that gentleman's way. There was even a dour-looking Quaker doctor who'd volunteered his services. The atmosphere of grim anticipation was palpable throughout the large building.

"What shall we do now?" Grace asked Mistress Geyer.

"Vait." The older woman clenched her apron with white-knuckled fists. "And pray."

A volley of booms, close enough together to be almost one sound, rolled over the landscape and filled the stuffy meetinghouse. If Grace had known how to pray, she would have done it then. Nobody inside moved for several heartbeats.

"Drink now." The surgeon gestured toward several buckets of freshly-drawn spring water. "Drink often. I cannot afford to lose willing hands to this infernal heat. If you can keep food down under pressure, eat something. 'Tis well past the noon hour, and the Lord only knows when we shall have time to eat again."

The surgeon's mates hustled to obey, and the women followed their example.

"He is very smart, our surgeon," Mistress Geyer said. "Ve do not need our vorkers succumbing to heat vhen ve need them most. Drink deeply."

Grace took the dipper when it was her turn and took a tentative sip. Swallowing wasn't a problem, but fear of bringing it back up was. She didn't even look at the plate of bread and cheese someone had uncovered. The cannon blasts mixed with her uncertainty about working in the hospital had unsettled her stomach. Still, under the surgeon's bushy-browed stare, she took several large gulps of water before passing the dipper to the next woman in line.

"Here they come!" a surgeon's mate yelled from the doorway. The drumming of horses' hooves and rumble of wagon wheels reached them a moment later. More yelling, little of which Grace could understand, and then the first man was brought into the makeshift hospital. Blood covered half his face. His clothing was tattered and blackened. Those carrying him deposited him on the nearest table and raced back out the door.

The man's head rolled to the side. The brown eyes above a beardless face looked at Grace without blinking. She took a step back.

"Out of the way."

She was jostled from behind as another man was carried in and shoved onto the next table. The man groaned, his left hand wrapped around his right arm. Blood soaked the sleeve, but no hand protruded from its cuff. The surgeon and a junior surgeon bent over the second man.

Mistress Geyer stepped beside the first man and brushed her fingers over his eyes, closing them.

Grace pressed her hands to her middle.

"You, girl." The surgeon pointed at Grace. "More bandages."

She stared at the blood-smeared finger pointed her way.

The surgeon's heavy brows dropped into an ominous line. "Now!"

Grace scurried to the side of the room where they'd stored all the prepared supplies. She grabbed a tray of prepared bandages and hurried back to the surgeon. The stench of blood, sweat, and vomit rose from the man on the table. His dull blue eyes met hers.

He blinked.

She straightened, stepped back, swallowed hard to keep the water she'd drank in place, and waited for the surgeon's next order. She turned to the side as the junior surgeon cut off the man's sleeve. When the man screamed, Grace's knees wobbled. She reached out, and Mistress Geyer grabbed her arm.

"I vill assist here. You help the vomen outside."

Grace stumbled through the door and sucked in the humid air. Another male scream sent her scurrying to where women filled large laundry kettles and stoked the fires beneath them. Washing bandages and blankets in the heat and humidity was far better than being in the hospital.

Anything was better than that.

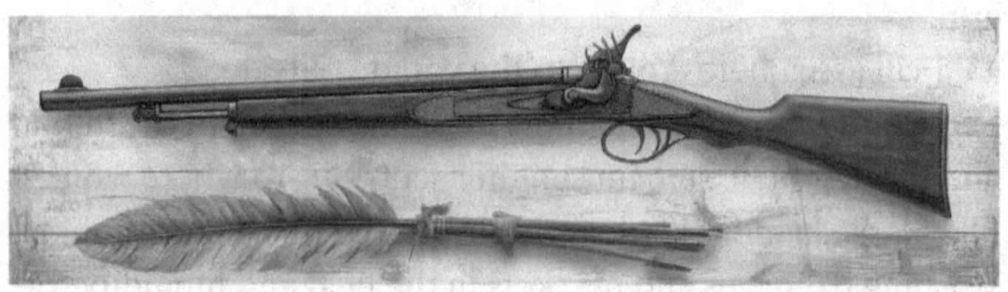

CHAPTER 5

"LUCY?" MARK CALLED AS he entered the house. He paused at the threshold, but there was no answer, so he strode into the hall, looked in the parlor and the dining room, then stopped in the kitchen. Everything was just as he'd left it that morning. Everything. He retraced his steps and peered into the dining room again. No morning teapot—because Lucy refused to change to coffee or chocolate—sat on the sideboard.

The short hallway beside the kitchen led to her bedroom. It was well past noon, though. She shouldn't still be abed. He rapped lightly on her door. "Lucy? Are thee ill?"

No answer. No rustling. Had she gone out? Another round of cannon fire shook the earth and the floorboards beneath him.

She wouldn't have gone anywhere.

Perhaps she'd stuffed her ears with cotton to muffle the sound. He rapped again, banging his knuckles on the wood. A slight sound reached him, one he'd not have heard had the cannons not paused again.

Indecision held him still for a moment. He'd never entered her bedroom uninvited. He'd only entered it on a handful of occasions in the past, and always at her beckoning. Taking a deep breath, he eased the door open.

"Lucy?"

A raspy breath was her only answer.

Mark rushed to her bedside, where her tiny frame made barely a wrinkle under the blanket. Her face was whiter than the pillow slip behind her. Her eyes were closed, her chest rose, then fell. He held his breath until it rose again.

She needed the doctor, but where would he find the man today? The meetinghouse. William Brentnall, Birmingham's Quaker physician, was likely there to help out.

"I will take thee to the doctor, Lucy." Whether she heard him or not, he couldn't say. He grabbed her dressing gown off its peg on the wall by the bed, but how was he to get her into it? He couldn't. He started to toss it aside, but hung it neatly instead. She'd want it that way. Then he tucked her blanket around her and slipped his arms underneath. He lifted, and her head lolled against his shoulder. She weighed almost nothing.

He maneuvered through the house, taking care in the doorways not to bump her. Outside, he took long, steady strides so as not to jostle her more than necessary. Her face, usually crinkled with love and kindness, remained still and slack against him.

A tightness took hold of his throat.

Lucy wasn't blood, but though they looked nothing alike, she was his only family. He favored his mother, whose dark eyes had flashed with laughter or deepened in sorrow. Her bronze skin, so like his own, had been lighter than many of their tribe. Her thick black braid, lying over her shoulder, hung almost to her waist in the manner of the Lenape. After Father's death, she had settled in the Ohio territory with the fragment of their tribe that had survived the horrible Iroquois attack. Life had been hard there, hunger always a companion. Fear and hunger had been the driving forces that had brought Mother and Maxkok—which Lucy and Oliver had pronounced as Mark—to make the long trek back to eastern Pennsylvania. Ten years ago, Mark had held Mother's head in his lap as she breathed her last, too ill from the journey, lack of food, and a white man's fever.

This moment felt the same to him.

He owed Lucy everything. She'd stepped in and raised him as a grandmother would have, kindness as much a part of her as breathing. Before he died, Oliver had made the arrangement for Mark to be apprenticed to Charles Brewer, a gruff but fair man who'd taught Mark the skill of blacksmithing. Oliver had been a farmer in his younger years, but he'd seen enough changes to know that metalworks were the thing of the future. He'd wanted Mark to succeed as a Quaker. Lucy wished that as well.

Right now, Mark didn't know what he wanted, other than to see Lucy restored to health.

He arrived at the meetinghouse and wove his way through the women working outside, ignoring their voices, until one met his eyes. Grace. He stopped short of the door.

"Lucy Sharp is ill," he said. "She requires a physician."

Three of the local Quaker women scurried past the others to reach him.

"Take her inside," one said.

"After all, 'tis our meetinghouse, and she is welcome here," said another.

The third made a shooing motion as if he were a chicken wandered into her garden, but he obeyed and entered the room in which he'd spent many hours of his life in.

The smell struck him first, then the cries, the moans, and curses never before uttered between those stone walls. Several men, including William Brentnall, bent over tables bearing the wounded soldiers. One surgeon broke away and approached him.

"What do you have?"

"Lucy Sharp. She is ill."

The man waved at the barely organized chaos around them. "Find a place to lay her down. A surgeon will see to her as soon as one is free."

"But..."

The surgeon had already turned his back, returning to a table where a patient was swearing loudly enough to loosen the cedar shakes from the rooftop.

A gentle touch, then a woman wearing an apron stained with blood pointed to an empty table. "Bring her here and I vill look after her." She grabbed a blanket from a stack nearby and spread it over the table. He lowered Lucy, still wrapped in her blankets.

Before he could say a word, the trio of Quaker ladies had swarmed around the table. They were Lucy's friends. They'd see her properly cared for. Still, he was reluctant to leave.

Another gentle touch, but this time when he looked down, it was into Grace's eyes. She nodded toward the door, and he followed her outside.

"Was she injured by the cannons?" Her voice was just as he'd remembered it from the forest.

"Nay." Mark stretched his back. Although Lucy weighed hardly enough to notice, he'd carried her clear across the village. "I found her like that in her bed."

What were the emotions that zipped across Grace's face? They disappeared before he could label them. What remained was sympathy. And for maybe the first time in his life, he let himself absorb it. He welcomed it, even, from this woman who had captured his attention despite their unorthodox meeting.

He hadn't called the old woman "mother," but Grace didn't doubt the love she'd witnessed in his eyes, nor the tenderness when he'd laid the ill woman down.

"I am sure the physician will do all he can," she said.

Mark glanced through the doorway. "'Twill not be enough, I fear."

"Oh." How did one respond to that? With his head turned, she studied his profile. The clean-shaven lines of his face were stoic, but when he turned to her again, pain lingered in the dark depths of his eyes, accentuated by the mark on his brow.

"She would not allow me to take her away from her house yesterday." He looked into the meetinghouse again. "'Twas as if she knew her time was near."

Grace had seen that same thing too many times over the years. The women of Philadelphia's backstreets didn't live to be nearly as old as the woman Mark had carried in. Even so, when their time approached, there was a knowing way about them. They died from a myriad of different causes—mostly diseases connected to their way of life or the strong drink that sustained them to do it—but they all seemed to know when their time had come. She shivered despite the oppressive heat of the afternoon.

"Pardon me. I will not distress thee further." Mark stepped to the opposite end of the meetinghouse's stone wall and leaned back against it.

Had Grace's shiver been so obvious? Surely not. But as in the forest two nights past, he seemed in tune with everything around him. Even her. Had he not turned when she'd lost her bonnet? Backed away each time she'd begun to fear him that night?

What type of man was he?

A Quaker.

But what did that mean?

They spoke differently, saying *thee* instead of *you*. They dressed differently, with no garish colors, frilly trims, or shiny buckles. And they were very religious—that was common knowledge. Even more importantly, they did not frequent the backstreets of Philadelphia. At least, if they did, it was not while dressed as Quakers. Any man could change his clothing and alter his speech, but were he truly religious, he'd not go where Grace had grown up. Ever.

She couldn't picture Mark there.

"Grace, we need your assistance." Anna Bream, a camp follower about Grace's age, stood by the laundry kettle with one hand on her hip and an annoyed crease across her brow.

Grace scurried back to her chores but positioned herself where she could watch Mark. He didn't move anything other than his eyes. Several times, she felt the weight of his attention settle on her before moving on. Always watching. Always alert. For what?

One of the Quaker women appeared in the doorway and called to Mark. In that lithe way he'd moved through the forest, he slipped inside.

"Best close your mouth and keep your mind on your work," Anna said without malice in her tone. "He be a handsome one for sure, but if Mistress Crenshaw gets word you been mooning over a man when you should be working, 'twill not go well for you."

Grace gave the boiling bandages another vigorous stir, sloshing water into the fire. "I know."

"Not that I would be telling her." Anna winked. "But the woman has a way of knowing things. She has spies in the camp. Do not forget that."

Spies? Surely not.

A few minutes later, Mark strode out the meetinghouse door and walked away without a glance in Grace's direction.

He didn't hurry, didn't pause, and that chiseled profile hadn't changed, but he was leaving. Alone.

The old woman must have died.

Mark left the meetinghouse with no thought of where he'd go. His spirit was heavy and raw.

Lucy had whispered three words to him before she died, "I love thee."

Ten years ago, Mother had whispered the same thing in the Lenape tongue. *Ktaholel*, she'd said as she slipped from the physical into the spiritual world. The Lenape and Quakers shared a belief in a creator and in life after death. It had made it easy for Mother to accept the Christian faith. Perhaps the two women were reunited again. That would please them both. Maybe later, after the pain had lessened, it would please Mark as well.

Charlie and one of his regular customers sat on the bench outside the smithy. They both nodded as Mark entered the building. Everything looked different than it had that morning, just a few hours ago. The walls were bare, barely an ember smoldered in the forge. It was empty, and so was he. Like the walls around him, something had been stripped away. It left him... exposed.

Boots thumped on the packed earth behind him. "Thee did not stay away long." The statement from Charlie held a question, even if he hadn't asked it.

Mark turned to face his boss. "Lucy Sharp is dead."

"God rest her soul." Charlie pressed a hand to his chest. "When? How?"

"A short time ago, at the meetinghouse. I found her very ill in her bed and carried her there."

Understanding written across his face, Charlie said, "That was good thinking, what with the surgeons and William set up there."

"They could do nothing for her."

The blacksmith's meaty hand gripped Mark's shoulder. "'Twas her time, I expect. She'd led a long life and contributed much to our community." The blacksmith's voice was almost a whisper. "She will be missed."

She would, indeed.

The silence they slipped into was broken by pounding hooves.

Charlie went to the doorway. "'Tis Thomas Cheyney. No doubt he carries news of the battle."

No doubt. Throughout the countryside, Cheyney was well known for his Patriot leanings.

"Thomas, what brings thee in such haste?" Charlie asked in his usual blacksmith's bellow.

"The British. They have crossed the Brandywine to the north, I reckon at Trimble's Ford. They are marching this way."

Charlie pointed toward Chadd's Ford as another cannon boomed. "But to the west—"

"They have divided their army. 'Tis only a shadow force across the Brandywine there. I have seen the large body aimed this way from the north."

"Thee have seen it?" Mark asked. Joseph had been correct. Or rather, Daniel McGee had been correct.

"Aye, and I ride to report it to Washington's troops. Do you know where their headquarters are?"

Charlie rubbed his ear, shot Mark a glance, and then said, "Thee know we Friends do not involve ourselves in wars."

"Hang it, man! That army is approaching the village. You shall be involved whether you wish it or not." Cheyney's nostrils flared almost as wide as those of his lathered horse.

Charlie looked to the north, and then to the southwest, even though buildings blocked his view of the approaching armies. He crossed his arms and nodded toward the road that led to Brinton's Ford. "'Twas said in my hearing that Sullivan's division is guarding the northern edge of Washington's troops near Brinton's Ford. Beyond that, I know nothing more to tell thee."

"That is enough." Cheyney whirled his horse and dug his heels into the beast's sides. The animal sprinted forward, spraying loose gravel as it charged ahead.

"That is done, then." Charlie dusted off his hands. "I shall go home and see to getting my wife away."

The Brewers lived in a new house on the northern edge of Birmingham. If the British were on the march in that direction—

"Do thee need me for anything?"

"Nay. 'Tis just the wife and me at home now. I shall hitch the wagon and take a drive east. She has family that way. We are long overdue for a visit." His brows drew into a bushy line. "And thee must attend to Lucy."

"The ladies at the meetinghouse said they would prepare her for burial." He swallowed against the knot at the back of his throat.

"Of course." Charlie nodded. "I am sorry we shall miss her burial. Such a humble soul."

A vigorous volley of cannon fire blasted through the midday heat.

"Thee best hurry," Mark said.

"Thee stay out of trouble till I return." Charlie clapped a hand on Mark's shoulder and squeezed before heading up the street.

Mark was alone, a situation he'd better get used to.

CHAPTER 6

"MISS GRACE? MISS GRACE!" Mistress Geyer yelled as she ran from the meetinghouse.

Grace mopped her dripping face on her soiled apron and stepped away from the laundry kettle. "I am here."

"Ve must help the surgeons pack up everything ve can carry. Now. Come vith me." The older woman spun and all but dragged Grace behind her.

"What has happened?"

"'Tis the British. They arrived from the north and vill soon be upon us. A dispatch rider yoost came through. Ve must make haste."

Grace had thought Mistress Geyer unflappable, but her jerky motions as she swept medical supplies into a clean but still damp sheet proved otherwise. Grace followed her example. There were eight women from the camp, and everyone but Anna soon held a bundled sheet loaded with supplies.

"Anna, you vill run ahead and see vhere our army is. They vill be on the move. Then return and direct us vhere ve should go. Ve vill follow you, but slower."

"Yes, Mistress Geyer." Anna lifted her skirts a bit more than decorum allowed—unless an army was at the door—and bolted south down the road toward where their camp had been that morning.

Grace's stomach rumbled. She'd had nothing to eat, and it was well past the middle of the day, but who could worry about hunger while an army marched their way? She hefted the laden sheet across her back and walked out with the rest of the ladies from Major General Greene's encampment. The army's wagons passed them, loaded with the tables and kettles too heavy to carry and the wounded who could be moved.

What about those who were too severely wounded? What would happen to them? Grace glanced back. The Quaker doctor who had come to assist stood in the doorway. Hopefully, the British would leave the injured in his care. That was probably the best anyone could hope for.

Dust raised by the wagons and horses created a dirty cloud around the walking women. Grace coughed and then wiped her forehead, doubtless smearing the dust into mud.

Mistress Geyer fell into step beside her. "'Tvill not go vell for our army, I fear."

"Why do you say so?"

"Our soldiers are in the wrong places. Instead of the armies being divided by a river, they vill be facing each other in a village." She cast a hurried look over her shoulder. "The old voman, she may not be the only civilian who dies this day."

Mark had disappeared just down the hill from the meetinghouse. Did he know that an army was about to descend upon the village? Was he even now in harm's way? Of course he must know. How could he not, with the sounds all around them?

As with the wounded left behind, there was nothing Grace could do. Regarding Mark, she shouldn't even care. Perhaps he had been nice to her, but he was just another man, no different from the men she'd spent her life avoiding. No different from the man who had fathered her... whoever he was.

Grace held no illusions about men.

When Mark climbed the slope of Osborne Hill, Joseph was standing on the same rock where they'd been the day before. Had it only been yesterday? Mark's predictable, orderly, Quaker life had been turned upside down and had its pockets shaken out. He hadn't known what to do with himself since leaving the smithy, really, since leaving the meetinghouse turned hospital, and so he'd come here.

"I have been watching for thee. I feared thee would not make it in time." Joseph jumped from the rock and grabbed Mark's sleeve. "Look over here."

Mark allowed himself to be hauled along in his friend's wake. They reached a grove of trees, and Joseph led them down a narrow path. He put his finger to his lips, although neither had spoken since his greeting, then he crouched and worked his way toward where afternoon sunlight parted the branches.

Mark crept forward, placing each foot silently as he'd been taught since childhood, and peeked between the branches. Before them spread a carpet of red and white.

British soldiers.

They covered the ground, most lying prone, perhaps even napping in the heat of the day. A tent had been erected toward the back, and by the armed soldiers around it, a commander of some sort was there. Horses were picketed beyond. More armed soldiers walked the perimeter. One glanced toward where Mark and Joseph hid. Mark drew farther back into the trees, and Joseph followed.

"I have no idea why they are camped there," Joseph whispered when they'd stopped a good distance from the soldiers. "They are giving Washington time to redirect and rally his troops."

The sun blazed west of its zenith. It must have been around three o'clock. If the British had crossed at Trimble's Ford, they'd been marching—and marching hard—for hours to be here now. "They know better than to fight with exhausted soldiers."

"Of course. Why did I not think of that." Joseph grinned and tipped his chin toward where they'd met. "Let us go and secure our spot to watch the battle." He took off at a run.

Mark followed, but without his friend's enthusiasm.

Stopping at the large rock, Joseph leaned over, hands to knees as he caught his breath. He cocked his head and looked at Mark. "Thee are quiet. Are thee not excited to witness the battle?"

"Should I be? Should *thee* be?"

Joseph straightened and waved his hand dismissively. "'Tis a once-in-a-lifetime chance. Think of it, we shall see history made here this day."

Mark shrugged, studying their village of Birmingham from this vantage point. He wouldn't admit to Joseph that the sight of all those British soldiers had stirred something in him. He didn't understand it himself. The battle was no business of his.

He needed to return and see to Lucy. He sighed.

"If thee intend to be a croaker, then by all means, do not let me keep thee." Joseph's tone was more than a little frustrated. But then, he didn't know.

"Lucy Sharp died this morning."

His friend's mouth opened and then shut, the annoyance fading from his expression. "'Tis a sad bit of news. What will thee do now?"

What indeed?

He'd not only lost Lucy but likely the roof over his head as well. Though recognized as one of the Quakers of Birmingham Meetinghouse, he was still Lenape. His skin was lighter than most of his kinsmen, and he'd learned the Quaker ways, even believed in the Quaker God, but he was still an Indian. As such, he was ineligible to own land. It wasn't a law, exactly, but established practice said that only white men could own property in Huntington County.

Perhaps Charlie Brewer would speak on Mark's behalf, but the Quakers were slow to change their ways. Ever since William Penn's son had dealt unfairly with the Lenape regarding the Walking Purchase—when Mark's people were tricked and their land stripped away—relations between the two societies had been strained.

Betsy and Sarah remembered that time. They were the last of the Lenape in this part of Pennsylvania. They didn't own the land they squatted on, living in their traditional bark hut, but they'd refused to leave, and the Quakers had left them alone. Probably because neither had a husband or children, no one with whom to leave their humble hut. At least, not that Mark knew of.

Would that be his future if he stayed? To be a lonely old man living in a hut in the woods, tolerated but not accepted by his neighbors?

Or could there be something else? Could he carve a place for himself somewhere? Maybe even raise a family.

Grace's face filled his mind's eye, and he sucked in a breath.

"I cannot stay," Mark said. "There are things to which I must attend."

"I understand. I will be at the funeral, of course." Joseph swiveled atop the rock for a better view of their surroundings.

No British were in sight within the village yet, but those napping on the other side of the hill wouldn't be idle for long. Mark must see to Lucy's burial, but that wasn't all that was pulling him back.

Grace was at the meetinghouse, and the meetinghouse was directly in the path of that swath of red and white behind him.

Loosely organized chaos described the once orderly encampment when Grace and the others arrived. Mistress Crenshaw stood at the center, shouting orders and chastising those who failed to respond promptly enough. As much as Grace disliked the woman—feared her—she couldn't help but admire the way she directed the evacuation. Tents were collapsing, trunks and bags were filling wagons and handcarts, and the horses were harnessed and waiting. Fear was visible in the movements of those carrying out the work, but they weren't giving in to it. Mistress Crenshaw wouldn't stand for that.

Mistress Geyer directed the women with her to pack their bundles into one of the wagons, then Grace followed her as she strode to Mistress Crenshaw's side. "Vhat vould you have us to do?"

"Stow your tents in a wagon or cart." Mistress Crenshaw looked the shorter woman up and down. "The men are needed to move the artillery, what we can save of it. Can you drive a team?"

"I can."

"Take that one." She pointed to a team of matching brown horses hitched to a large wagon parked near their tents. "As soon as you are packed, follow the lead wagons out."

The Swedish woman hurried to obey and Grace trotted at her side. If Mistress Crenshaw noticed her, she might assign her a duty somewhere else. Staying beside Mistress Geyer was the only comfort Grace had.

Within minutes, both tents were down and the canvas secured in the wagon Mistress Geyer would drive. The wagon was packed front to back, side to side, and some things even hung over the edges. As the older woman climbed onto the high seat, Grace stood beside of one of the horses hitched to it. It stamped its foot and she jumped back.

"'Tis yoost the flies bothering him." Mistress Geyer untied the reins and then patted the seat beside her. "Climb up."

Grace did, dropping onto the hard wood when the horses lurched forward.

"Easy now." Mistress Geyer took a firmer grip on the reins.

"Are you sure you can handle them?" Horses were beautiful creatures, but Grace had little experience with them. They'd always made her a bit fearful.

"'Tis the excitement making them nervous. They vill settle down once ve get moving."

As if to put action to her words, the wagon in front of them started rolling down the makeshift lane that led to the road.

"Do you know where we are going?" Grace asked.

Mistress Geyer pointed ahead with one finger while keeping the rest tangled in the reins. "Vherever that vagon leads us." Musket fire—from the north, not the west—reached them. "And yoost as fast as ve can get there."

Grace gripped the edges of the wagon seat, its rough wood digging into her fingers. The British wouldn't fire on wagons filled with women.

Would they?

She'd not spent much time thinking about the war back in Philadelphia. It didn't matter who ruled the country, not to Mother or the other women from the backstreets. Such things didn't change their way of life. Joining Washington's army, however, had thrust Grace right into the thick of it.

Would Mother have insisted Grace come here if she'd known the danger? Perhaps she had known and considered this the lesser evil.

Grace cringed as more musket fire sounded to their left. Perhaps Mother had been wrong.

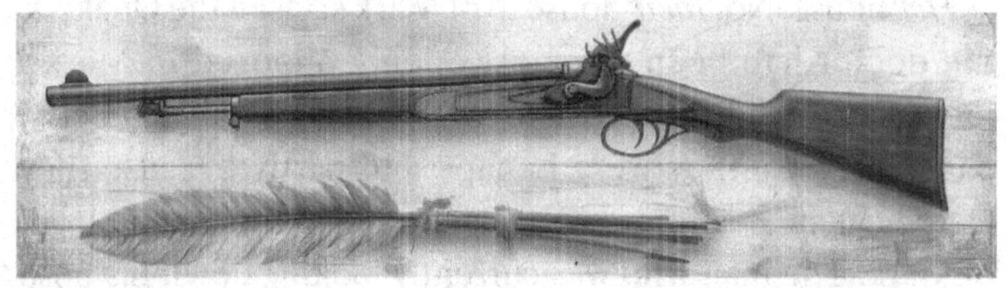

Chapter 7

THE YARD OUTSIDE THE meetinghouse was empty. Not even a laundry kettle remained. Mark walked into the building as William Brentnall knelt and drew a sheet over the face of man on the floor. The tables had been removed, the benches still stored above. Three other men on blankets were stretched out on the floor. One of them groaned.

Lucy's body was gone.

So was Grace.

"Mark? Where have thee been?"

"To see the British army. 'Tis just over Osborne Hill."

"So we heard." William gestured to the bare room. "Washington's people fled, leaving only those too wounded to move."

"What of Lucy?"

William rose and faced him, arms folded across his chest. "She was taken back to her house."

Her house. Not *their* house. Not Mark's. Of all the Quakers, the doctor had been the most openly opposed to Mark's presence. He didn't approve of Mark visiting Sarah and Betsy, partly because they were Lenape and partly because they were healers, heathen healers according to the man in front of Mark. The man who was currently looking down his nose at him.

"She will be well cared for, then." Better than Mark could have done on his own.

"Indeed. 'Tis the women's work to prepare her for tomorrow's burial, as is our custom."

Musket fire erupted outside, not too close to the meetinghouse and from the direction of Osborne Hill, where Joseph waited on his rock. Charlie would be on the road by now, heading east with his wife. Lucy was in the hands of the women who'd loved her on earth and would see her readied for burial. William would stay by the wounded men until the British arrived.

Mark had nowhere to go and nothing to do.

He could go to Sarah and Betsy. He needed to let them know of Lucy's death. The old women would welcome him, but he couldn't stay with them. Their bark hut was barely large enough for the two of them.

With heavy steps, he left the meetinghouse and headed southeast to cut around Washington's forces and work his way back near the Brandywine. He wouldn't mind seeing Grace again, but it would be better if he stayed away from the fighting. The Quakers would never grant him Lucy's house if they thought he'd been mixed up in it. Best to circle wide and avoid both seeing the battle and being seen.

He would stop at home first—Lucy's house—to change into his hunting clothes and pack a haversack with the things he might need until he returned.

If he returned.

At the house, the rustle of petticoats and murmuring of women's voices drew Mark into the dining room. The long table had been cleared and Lucy placed upon it, dressed in her Sunday best, hands folded at her waist, hair tucked within her linen cap, eyes closed. She might have been asleep, if not for the unnatural pallor of her face, its skin flattened against the bones beneath.

A round of gasps came in the wake of a boom of cannon fire, and the floor shook under Mark's boots.

"Oh, Mark." Lucy's best friend came to his side and led him to the table. "I am so sorry for thy loss. We all grieve with thee in her passing." With tears in her eyes, she patted Lucy's hands. "We have her ready for burial. My husband will be here shortly with several other men who are digging the grave even now."

"There is no time for our normal customs," another said over the rattle of muskets in the distance—but not as distant as before. "Indeed, I do hope the men will hasten back."

Mark had no words. He reached into his pocket and withdrew a carved wooden cross Mother had given to him when she'd decided to follow the way of the white man's Jesus God. He tucked it under Lucy's hands. It had been a gift from her to Mother long before he'd been born.

Several of the women dabbed their eyes.

"Is she ready?" A male voice demanded as boot heels beat against the floor.

"Indeed." Lucy's best friend rushed to meet her husband while another blast of cannon fire shook the house.

"Good, no time to waste, the British are almost upon us." Her husband pointed to the east. "Everyone should flee with all haste and not return until the battle is over."

"But we must see Lucy given a decent burial and—"

"Go, wife. The wagon is in front of our house. Grab what thee will need for several days and get on it. I shall be there as soon as I can."

Mark turned to Lucy, and after wrapping the tablecloth around her, lifted her into his arms. "Tell me where thee have dug, and I will see her buried while thee all seek safety." While Lucy deserved to have her friends around her at the burial, she wouldn't want any of them to risk their lives for it.

"My boy..." Lucy's friend started to object, but her husband shook his head and took hold of her arm.

"Mark is right," her husband said. "We must go." The house shook again. "Now."

They hurried from the room, most giving Lucy one last touch on the way out.

The husband told Mark where they'd dug the grave behind the meetinghouse. "I left my shovel there. God bless thee, boy." And then he followed the others.

Mark laid Lucy on the table again and sprinted up the stairs. He packed his haversack with his hunting clothes, a spare shirt, and other items he'd need. At the last, he crammed in both pairs of his moccasins. He slung the haversack over his shoulder and pushed it onto his back. Behind the door hung his musket, powder horn, shot bag, and tin canteen. He strapped them on before tucking his hunting knife into his boot. Then he went into the kitchen and filled a sack with all the foodstuff he could find, at the last minute adding a pewter plate, cup, and spoon. Tying the sack to his belt, he paused when he spied Lucy's money crock, where she kept her small stash of coins. They'd come from Mark's salary at the smithy, and she'd approve of him taking them, so he poured them into his palm and pocketed them.

The house shook again with a cannon blast that nearly deafened him. The British were far too close now.

He sprinted to the parlor and cradled Lucy in his arms, tucking the tablecloth around her. She looked so peaceful. Was she with Jesus even now? Was she with Mother?

Mark wanted to believe that. He wanted to believe everything the Quakers had taught him, but there was a part of him that held back. Lucy had known of his doubts. She'd prayed for him every day. Every single day. The loss hit him anew as another cannon blast dislodged plaster from the ceiling. Mark hunched over the woman who'd guarded him, protecting her from the pieces that fell. When the shaking stopped, he bolted out the door.

The hole was where he'd been told, a shovel stuck in the mound beside it, the scent of freshly turned earth strong in the air. The maple tree nearest the hole was beginning to turn already, leaves etched in a vibrant red and dancing on the breeze. Lucy would have enjoyed seeing them.

There was no coffin and no time to find one. With tender care—to match the loving care she'd always extended to him—Mark laid her in the hole and arranged the tablecloth to cover her face, dress, and petticoats. Lucy couldn't abide a dirty dress.

Musket fire rattled and the cannons continued to boom, but Mark ignored the battle sounds as he filled the hole, averting his gaze from the wrapped body until the dirt covered her. Once the grave was filled, he knelt beside it on one knee. "Jesus, watch over Lucy. She deserves that and more."

Blinking back dampness, he rose and entered the forest. He was working his way around the village toward Lucy's house when a cannon roared from nearby. A crash and a shower of debris followed. Men were shouting, cursing, and screaming.

Heart sinking, Mark waited for the dust to clear and rushed forward.

Lucy's house lay in a pile of rubble. Another loss to add to the day. When would the British stop?

A cannon bellowed from close by, probably one of Washington's replying.

Mark pivoted, loping away from the village, keeping to the cover of trees. Even if the Quakers had been willing to let him stay in Lucy's house, it was gone now. From here on out, he'd be on his own.

But there were two people he needed to see first.

The hut hadn't changed in all the years Mark had known of it. The dome top was covered with bark, held fast by twisted willow strips attached to its frame. Tucked into the forest at the edge of a tiny clearing, it had been a sanctuary for him in his younger years. Lucy had understood Mark's need to visit the two old women who lived inside. She'd encouraged him to do it. She might even be smiling down on him from heaven.

That thought lifted his spirits as he approached the uncovered door opening.

"Betsy? Sarah?"

A tiny woman stepped out of the hut, wrapped in a blanket, her head covered with a scrap of red cloth. The second woman joined her, taller, leaner if possible, wearing a wide grin devoid of teeth.

"Maxkok!"

How long had it been since anyone had called him by his Lenape name? Since his last visit to the aging sisters. Far too long. Even though the sisters insisted on using English names for themselves, they always referred to Mark in their native tongue.

Betsy, the shorter and more somber of the two, came to him and grasped his arm. "The guns, they tell us bad things are happening."

Mark laid a hand over the top of hers. "The British fight against Americans inside the town."

"Then you are right to come to us." Betsy guided him into the hut, Sarah following them. Betsy set a water-filled pot, one Mark had forged for them years ago, near the central fire, then settled herself next to Sarah, both of them facing him. "Tell us."

It was easy to fall into the familiar role of squatting by the fire and telling a story. Had his ancestors not always done the same? He explained about the battle happening just far enough away to mute all but the worst of the cannons.

When he fell silent, Sarah asked, "What are you not telling us, Maxkok?"

He raised his face to theirs. "Lucy Sharp died this morning. I have buried her behind the meetinghouse."

They raised their voices in the Lenape mourning song, the haunting cadence and sorrowful tone filling the hut. With a stab of renewed grief, Mark allowed the words to wash over him until the last note died away.

"Her house was destroyed by a cannonball." Mark spoke into the silence that had ended their song. "I have no home to return to."

"And you cannot fight against those who did it." Betsy stared through the open doorway at something beyond, but not something anyone else could see. It was how she looked when she was deep in thought. "You promised your mother, our friend, Peaceful One, to never take up weapons against the white man. It was her dying wish, and a promise you must keep."

How did one keep such a promise when cannonballs and musket shot filled the air?

The Quakers would keep it. Most of them, anyway. Joseph might not. He was enthralled by uniforms and muskets and men marching in straight lines to the beating of drums. None of that mattered to Mark. But seeing Lucy's house in a pile of rubble had sparked deep emotions within him. One in particular that he hadn't felt in a long time.

Rage.

It had gripped him hard at a young age while witnessing the Iroquois's spear pierce through his father. That wasn't the sort of thing a boy forgot. Mother's decision to bring him to the Quakers years later had been partly due to the rage that had continued to simmer, he was sure, although she'd never said as much. And he'd learned from them how to suppress the rage as much to honor her memory as to please them and conform to their ways.

Mother was gone, and now so was Lucy. Mark had no home among the Quakers, although there were some who would offer him a roof, including Charlie's and Joseph's families. But was that where he wanted to be?

A flash of dark hair beneath a white linen cap and wide eyes the color of a dove's wing filled him with a strong protective urge again. Before he left the area or did anything else, he needed to be sure Grace had gotten to safety. He pushed the rage down and got to his feet.

"Before you go, I have something for you." Sarah rose and rummaged through a basket near the wall, then she drew out a necklace made of thin strips of leather, some of them bleached almost white, others dark, and joined with knots. A small wooden cross dangled from the middle, not unlike the cross he'd tucked under Lucy's hands. "Your mother set great store by the cross. It was what brought her back here with you. I made the necklace long ago and have waited until the right time to give it to you." She lifted her cloudy eyes to his. "We may not see each other again in this life, Maxkok. Wear this to remember your heritage and your mother. Be worthy of them both."

Mark bent at the waist to allow Sarah to slip the necklace over his head. It clashed with his Quaker clothing, but he didn't care. It was a gift he would treasure. In return, Mark left half of the food he'd brought from Lucy's house, then he bid the old women goodbye.

He headed east toward where Nathanael Greene's encampment had been, but before he reached the area, he stopped and changed into his hunting clothes, exchanging his boots for moccasins. He let the front of his linen shirt hang open to mid-chest and expose the leather necklace. In further tribute to his heritage, he shook his hair from its queue and let it flow around his shoulders, as it had the night he'd met Grace in the forest. He folded and placed his Quaker garb in the bottom of his haversack before continuing on.

In the less restrictive clothing and without boot heels, he moved silently through the forest, guided by the noise as he drew closer.

The camp was in an uproar. In the distance, cannons still boomed and muskets rattled their fire, the smoke from both visibly creeping beneath the trees and spreading into camp. In what was left of the camp, people yelled, horses and mules whinnied, and dust rose as the earth was trampled by humans and animals alike. Only a few dozen people hurried about their tasks, both men and women, where before there had been at least a hundred.

Grace was not among them, but the trail of those who had left was easy to follow. Mark shadowed the trail, keeping to the cover of the forest. He wasn't afraid of being seen. He needed the comfort of God's creation around him, at least until he located Grace.

CHAPTER 8

THEY'D BEEN MOVING FOR close to an hour when the wagon's front wheel dropped into a hole. Grace grabbed onto the bench with a cry, fighting to hold her seat.

Mistress Geyer hollered and sawed on the reins as one of their horses reared to its full height, its hooves thrashing the air, the other horse squealing in fear.

Grace gasped when someone raced from the tree line and grabbed the rearing horse's bridle.

"Whoa, boy. Whoa." The horse's hooves thudded to the ground. The man turned to Mistress Geyer. "Release the reins, I have him."

Mark.

Relief didn't just flow over Grace—it gushed. Mark wore the hunting clothes he'd worn when he'd saved her from the panther.

"'Tvas the rut that set him off." Mistress Geyer was the color of chalk.

Mark adjusted the harness and spoke softly to each animal before nodding to Mistress Geyer. "Take up the reins again and hold them steady."

The older woman did as he bid, the color seeping back to her face.

When his eyes met Grace's, she couldn't look away. If the color had left her face, the burning in her cheeks attested to its return.

Someone in the wagon behind them yelled.

Mark waved to whoever it was, then examined the wheel.

"'Tisn't broken. I will give it a shove as the horses move forward. Keep them moving and hold on. The rear wheel will have to go through the same hole."

"Of course." Mistress Geyer sat straighter on the tilted seat and cracked the reins. "Pull, you two!"

The horses lunged into their harnesses while Mark heaved on the wheel.

Grace breathed a sigh of relief when he jumped out of the way, and then she held tight to the seat as the second wheel plunged into the hole and climbed back out again.

Mistress Geyer kept the horses moving but called over her shoulder, "Ve are in your debt, young man."

Mark caught up with thc wagon and jumped onto the back of it, finding a place for his feet among all the things packed inside. "'Twas no bother. Where are thee headed?"

"Ve are following that vagon in front of us. That is all ve know. Perhaps you know better?"

"Howe's army approaches from the north as well as the west. If thee keep heading east and south, thee should remain clear of the fighting."

Fear wedged itself back into Grace's throat. How could he speak of enemy armies so calmly? And yet, the lines beside his dark brown eyes deepened, and his brow creased along that vertical scar. Perhaps he wasn't so calm after all. Or maybe his grief...

"I am sorry for your loss." She blurted the words out before she could think about it. It had been obvious that he'd been very attached to the old woman he'd brought to the makeshift hospital.

"As am I," Mistress Geyer said. "She vas a gentle soul. Anyone could see that."

"Indeed." He stared toward the north, toward the rumble of cannons. "She was."

A man on horseback raced toward them from behind, his open coat flailing in the wind. "Make haste! Make haste!"

"What news?" Mark yelled.

The man drew his horse to a sliding stop, the animal blowing and tossing its head. He held the lathered animal to a walk beside the wagon. "Them Redcoats are attacking the town. They punched through the Patriots' line of defense." He gasped in a few breaths. "From the north as well as the west." The man eyed Mark up and down. "Why are you not with the men on the lines?"

"I am a Quaker."

The man stood in his stirrups, bringing himself almost nose to nose with Mark on the wagon. "'Tis not a time to cling to religion, man. Is not our General Greene also a Quaker? If a man such as General Greene can fight for our independence"—he poked a gloved finger at Mark—"so can the likes of you." He spat on the ground and then spurred his horse forward and took up his yell once again. "Make haste! Make haste!"

The wagon shifted as Mark dropped off the back. What would he do? Grace wanted to ask, but it was none of her concern. At least, it shouldn't have been.

"Young man," Mistress Geyer said, "do nothing in haste nor in grief. Today is not the day to make a life-changing decision."

"Thee are wise, mistress, but sometimes we have not the luxury of time on our side."

"Be careful." Grace's throat was still tight with fear, her words breathy. "Be safe."

His mouth tipped to one side in what might have been a smile if not for the clouded look in his eyes. Grief? Or was it something more? He stopped walking, and the wagon rolled on.

Grace twisted on the seat as Mark melted into the woods behind them, as if he were a part of nature, so like the first time she'd seen him. Gooseflesh pebbled her arms.

"Our army could use men like him," Mistress Geyer said. "But part of me hopes he stays clear of the battles. 'Tis no small thing to turn one's back on one's beliefs."

No, it wasn't a small thing. Something about Mark was starting to challenge Grace's beliefs—about men. Or at least about one of them.

Which way to go? Mark stood within the cover of the darkening forest. Twilight would be upon them soon, and with it some relief from the day's heat. Wagons rumbled away in one direction while muskets barked in the other. Hanging over all of that was the promise he'd made as a ten-year-old boy to his dying mother.

"Do not take up weapons against the white man, Maxkok. This you must promise me."

"But our people are warriors."

"They have been, I know, but the land is changing under the white man's feet. They have the Jesus God. He says it is better to be meek, to forgive, to turn the cheek when struck."

"Father was a warrior."

"And now he is dead. I would have you live, my son. Learn from the Quakers. They are good people who do not hate the Indians. Trust them."

She'd coughed then, a deep, wracking sound that had seemed to force the air from Mark's chest as well. But she had opened her eyes, and the pleading in them had caused his chest to constrict even more. She'd left her people—their people—to bring him where he could learn from the Quakers she trusted. She'd given up everything for him. Even at that young age, he knew he could deny her nothing.

"I promise."

"Ktaholel." I love you.

Mother had smiled, closed her eyes, and breathed her last.

A cannon boomed in the distance, followed by an explosion that shook him out of his past. How much of the village would survive? Was Joseph even now watching from the top of Osborne Hill? Had the rest of the Quakers made it safely out of harm's way? Should he search for them?

Or should he find Nathanael Greene and help stop the British who were demolishing everything in their path? After all, he'd be fighting *for* the whites as much as fighting *against* them. He'd be fighting for the Quakers whom Mother had loved, those who would not fight for themselves.

Washington's army hadn't wrecked Lucy's home—the British had.

The Quakers had done nothing to deserve what was happening.

The rage he'd suppressed earlier flamed back to life. He loosened the sling holding the musket to his back and gripped the gun in one hand. If he was going toward the battle, he was going armed. If he had to fire the weapon to protect himself...

He would.

He loved his mother. He loved Lucy. He respected the Quakers. But deep inside, he was a warrior, not meant to stand aside and watch the battle if he could help protect those who had for years protected him.

If the decision didn't feel quite right, at least it didn't feel completely wrong.

The wagons followed little more than a deer trail in the gathering darkness. Three times, Grace and Mistress Geyer had waited in the line of wagons while men cleared a path, chopping down saplings to create enough room for the wagons to push through. The waiting allowed a chance to stand and stretch, as she did at the moment, a welcome exercise after bouncing around on the hard seat. Grace's backside would be bruised come morning.

The horses were lathered and tired, no longer fighting Mistress Geyer. They'd left the loud noises far behind, and that helped. It helped Grace, too, but nothing distracted her from the gnawing in her middle. When was the last time she'd eaten? Not since the prior day's supper, and she'd eaten precious little then.

A shout came from the front of the wagon line, followed by several more.

"'Tis a jubilant sound, is it not?" Mistress Geyer's voice was as weary as Grace, but with an edge of hope.

Grace raised onto her toes and squinted into the gloom, but she couldn't see anything. "It might be."

The woman driving the wagon in front of them twisted on the seat and called back, "We have arrived!"

Grace hugged Mistress Geyer, then pulled back, aghast that she'd done something so... familiar. But she barely drew in a breath before Mistress Geyer wrapped an arm around her and pulled her close once again while keeping hold of the reins. "'I can tell you, I have been vorried ve vould not see camp before full dark. I have never driven a team so far, and for sure, never in the dark." She let go of Grace. "Tell the others behind us." The older woman climbed back aboard the wagon.

After shouting the news, Grace climbed up beside her and waited for the wagon in front of them to continue on. Mistress Geyer slapped the reins on the broad rumps of their team. No longer lunging, the horses leaned into their harnesses, and the wagon started forward. In a short time, the glow of many fires lit the forest around them. A man directed Mistress Geyer where to stop the wagon, and then, much to Grace's relief, more men appeared to take charge of the animals. A giant of a man leaning on a walking stick helped Mistress Geyer down first, and then Grace.

For so long, Grace had avoided the touch of any man, but her legs wobbled, and she accepted his assistance, murmuring her thanks and disengaging her arm as soon as her feet touched the ground.

"You gals look done in." The man addressed Mistress Geyer.

"That, sir, vould be an understatement." She sighed. "But ve must soldier on, must ve not?"

He combed his ragged beard with his fingers. "Would you be Peter Geyer's wife?"

Mistress Geyer straightened and faced the man. "You know my husband?"

"Your husband and son both, mistress. Fine men." He pointed to his leg. "If I had not taken a musket round to the leg, I would be with them even now. Name is Francisco, Private Francisco, at your service."

"You should be resting, private, and not helping us. You vould not vish to risk infection in your leg."

"This little thing?" He brushed at the bandage circling his leg below his breeches. "'Twill be healed good enough by morning." He looked at the pile of things in the bed of the wagon. "Which bundles are yours? I will carry them for you."

Mistress Geyer protested until it seemed Private Francisco would carry the entire load if they didn't point out their bundles.

Grace carried her haversack and the roll of canvas for her tent as he hefted the parcels Mistress Geyer pointed out. All of six feet tall, for sure, he'd have to duck through any doorway and turn to the side to get his shoulders through. Maybe she was too tired and too hungry, or maybe she was numb from everything that had happened that day. For whatever reason, any fear of the large man fell away, and Grace followed him.

It took her fumbling fingers longer than normal to get her tent set up. In that time, Private Francisco carried several more loads to where he'd deposited Grace and Mistress Geyer near fire. He'd risen from setting down the last one, still gripping his walking stick with one hand, when Grace's belly let out an embarrassingly loud rumble.

He chuckled and reached into a pouch tied to his belt, then handed her a piece of jerked meat, a staple she'd learned to eat since she'd joined the camp followers. "Here, 'tain't much, but 'twill stop the noises until you can cook a decent meal."

Grace bobbed a curtsey as she took the offering and refrained from stuffing it in her mouth until she'd thanked him properly. The smoky saltiness of the meat on her tongue made her thirsty, but she didn't care. She ripped off a bite with her teeth, mimicking what she'd seen the soldiers do, and chewed the leathery mouthful.

Mistress Geyer accepted a piece as well, tilting her head to address thc big man. "Do you know vhere my husband and son are now?"

"Major General Greene's men, all three divisions, were still holding ground off Chadd's Ferry." He thumbed his leg. "That is where I got this." Blood had seeped through the bandage.

Grace pointed to it. "You are bleeding."

He scoffed. "'Tis nothing. I tell you, I will be back in the fight come the morning." With that, he touched two fingers to his hat brim and left them.

"Vhat an extraordinary man," Mistress Geyer said.

Grace ripped off another bite of the jerky, chewed, and then swallowed. "What should we do now?"

"We should find Mistress Crenshaw and see vhat she needs." Mistress Geyer yawned, pressed a hand over her mouth, then shook her head. "But I am done in. I say ve crawl into our tents and sleep vhile ve can. Someone vill find us soon enough and put us back to vork, I bet."

With the last bite of jerky in her mouth, Grace nodded. She would have loved more to eat, but even that bit had settled her middle, and her eyelids seemed to have a mind of their own, refusing to work as they ought.

Still, once she'd crawl into her tent and draped her blanket over her to protect against insect bites, she remained awake, thoughts of the day plaguing her. Had it only been that morning that she'd arrived at the meetinghouse turned hospital? It seemed more like a fortnight. Seeing Mark bring the old woman in, the wounded screaming, the cannons, their mad rush to leave ahead of the British, Mark coming to the rescue once again with the horses... It all blurred against the back of her eyelids.

Where was Mark? Had he made it to safety? Would she ever know the answer to her questions?

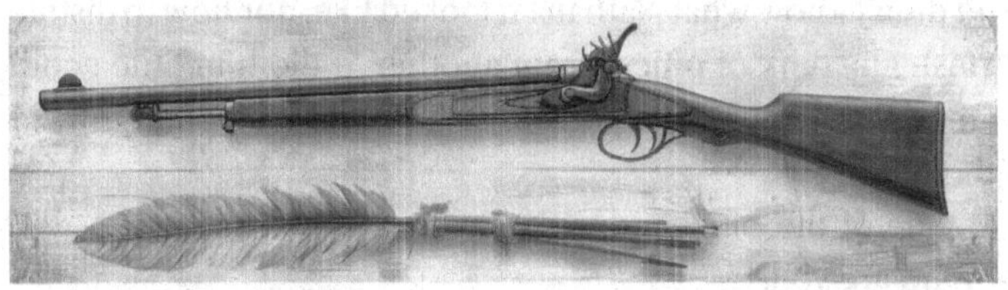

CHAPTER 9

IT WAS FULLY DARK by the time Mark found Major General Greene's fighting forces. He'd asked several retreating soldiers where to locate the man's brigade. Everyone being in a rush and many seeming to know little about what was going on, the process had taken far longer than Mark had imagined. But the fellow he'd just encountered had assured him that this was the unit he'd been searching for.

It didn't escape his notice that the only brigade not leaving in retreat from the British was the one being led by a Quaker.

Gunsmoke lingered beneath the trees, creating ghostly images of the soldiers, its acrid smell adding to the gloomy feel of the forest. The men moved with slumped shoulders, heavy footfalls, many with their chins near their chests. A weary army. A defeated army.

In the midst of the marching soldiers rode the officers on horseback. Mark scanned the faces and uniforms, but since he didn't know what Nathanael looked like, nor how to distinguish any rank of officer from another, it did him little good. Once the horses drew abreast of him, Mark stepped toward them.

One of the officers drew a sword and pointed it at Mark. "Who are you?"

"My name is Mark. I am searching for Nathanael Greene." Mark kept his musket at his side.

The man didn't lower his weapon. "Why?"

The other officers didn't stop or even acknowledge the exchange.

Mark gestured to their retreating backs. "Would thee tell me which one of them is Nathanael Greene?"

"He is Major General Greene to—did you say *thee*?" The man's brows drew together over a pair of blue eyes.

"I did."

"Are you a Quaker then?"

"I am."

The man slid his sword into its scabbard. Obviously, he felt no fear from a Quaker, even knowing Nathanael Greene. "But you do not know the major general?"

"I do not. I would, however, like to make his acquaintance."

"You carry a musket. Were you involved in the fighting this day?"

"I was not." Mark pointed toward the village, or whatever was left of it. "I live here, or at least I did."

The man scratched the blond stubble on his chin, so fair it was hard to see. "Follow me. I will introduce you to the major general when we stop to camp. Who knows? Maybe another Quaker in our midst will bring us luck." He urged his horse after the others.

Mark followed, keeping back a short distance. There were more soldiers behind him, crashing through the bracken, snapping off twigs, and the occasional muttered curse when one stubbed a toe or barked a shin in the dark. They continued on for a couple of hours until they arrived at a large river.

The place was familiar. Mark had fished in that river with Joseph and one of his brothers several years back, probably further upstream, but he knew of no other river with such a broad expanse. In the glow of the half-moon hanging above them, there were tents set up surrounding the smoldering embers of many fires. They'd arrived at the new camp—both the army camp and, judging by the number of wagons, its followers.

Women worked at fires to the far side of the encampment, their tents a hodgepodge of mismatched canvas and other cloth. Grace should be in that area.

The blond man turned to Mark. "You can pitch your bedroll, or whatever you have, under a wagon if you like. The major general is tired. Tomorrow is soon enough to see if he wishes to speak with you. Come find me then." He didn't wait for a response, just reined the horse around and rode off.

Mark spied a large wagon that looked like the one Grace had been riding on. Of course, most of the wagons were built in a similar style, but hoping he'd picked the right one, he crawled beneath it. He rummaged in the sack of provisions he'd brought from Lucy's house. Even after giving half to the old sisters, he had enough to last for a week if he was careful. He pulled out a small round loaf of bread and bit into it. Closing his eyes, he could picture Lucy at the table, sleeves rolled up, hands and forearms dusted with flour as she kneaded the dough.

His throat closed. He took a sip from his canteen, which allowed him to swallow. He wasn't hungry anymore, but only because of his grief. He still needed to eat. So bite by bite, memory by memory, he finished the loaf. He curled onto his side with the haversack under his head. He'd lost everything that day. Sorrow hung heavily on his chest, but at the same time, there was another sensation he wanted to explore. Something like... like a bird must feel the first time it opened its wings and soared.

Sleep beckoned him, demanding he close his eyes. Pondering that other sensation would have to wait for the morrow.

Light filtered through the canvas of Grace's tent. Birdsong twittered from somewhere overhead. The steady murmur of voices, the rattle of cookware, and the bark of a dog in the distance finally pulled her from sleep. Eyes gritty and mouth as dry as a week-old crust of bread, she sat and pushed the hair that had escaped her braid out of her eyes. It must be well into the morning. Why hadn't Mistress Geyer awakened her?

After finger-combing her hair into submission and braiding it again, Grace settled her cap and came out of her tent. She shook the worst of the wrinkles from her petticoats, sniffed, and frowned. What she wouldn't give for a bath. When was the last time she'd had more than a bucket of water to wash in? Not since she'd left Philadelphia. If she'd known what day it was, she could figure out how long that had been, but what was the point? It wouldn't change anything. She still smelled like the drunkards who'd populated the alleys late at night. Not that she'd ever encountered them, of course, but their smell had reached into Mother's third-floor room in the hot summers when they slept with the only window open, it overlooking the alley.

"Miss Grace." Mistress Geyer approached, drying her hands on her apron. "Did you sleep vell?"

"I did, and for too long, or so it looks. You should have awakened me."

"Nay. You need your sleep." She handed Grace a pewter cup of water. "Yesterday vas taxing for you."

"For you as well." Grace sipped the water, savoring every drop.

"I have been vith this army for more than a year." She dipped more water from the bucket and filled Grace's cup. "My husband and son yoined with Mayoor Yeneral Greene in August of 1776 at Long Island. I am used to this life now."

Grace looked around the camp. "Will we move on today?"

"Ve have yet to receive vord, but 'tis being said that the British have stayed put along the Brandywine. Our men with Mayoor Yeneral Greene held them there vhile the rest of Vashington's troops made it out safely."

"Have you heard from your husband and son?"

Mistress Geyer shook her head. "I have had no vord, good or bad. I hope they vill find me yet this morning bringing only good news."

What must it be like to have a loved one here? The constant worry must be difficult. Not that Grace had any idea what it was like to have a husband, brother, or even a father.

"Vell, look who *has* found us." Mistress Geyer gestured toward the edge of the forest.

Grace raised her cup to drain the last of the water and turned, expecting to see Mr. Geyer. Instead, Mark walked toward them, a large turkey dangling from one hand. She almost choked on the water. How had he found them again? His hair was loose, as when she'd first seen him, his skin bronzed by the sun and set off by the whiteness of his linen hunting shirt and the inky blackness of his hair. Around his neck was a tangle of leather strips that would have made him look like an Indian, if not for the wooden cross attached to them.

Why did her heart skip a beat? Because she hadn't expected to see him again, of course. It was good to know that he'd escaped injury, that he was well. That must be the reason.

He stopped beside Mistress Geyer. "Good morning." He held up the turkey. "I found this fellow in a tree at daybreak. Would thee like fresh meat for thy fire?"

"Goodness, aye." The Swedish woman set down her bucket and took the bird. "'Tvill be a feast for our supper, vill it not, Miss Grace?"

"Aye." But her empty belly twisted into a knot when Mark's dark eyes met hers.

She wanted to look away, as was her habit when a man noticed her, but there was something—

"There is porridge in the pot at the fire. You vill eat vith us, please." Mistress Geyer ushered Mark to the fire.

Grace fell in step behind them. No doubt she'd be put to work plucking that turkey after they ate, a job she hated, but the thought of fresh meat for supper had her mouth watering and her belly rumbling. If only the army would stay long enough for the bird to fully roast.

And if Mark would stay to enjoy it with them.

"You." The officer who had spoken to Mark the night before appeared as Mark finished a bowl of porridge sweetened with molasses. "Come with me." He pivoted and marched off.

"If thee will excuse me," he said to Grace and Mistress Geyer, then rose and followed the officer.

They approached a circle of tents around another fire, this one larger, as were the tents. Horses were tethered to the rear, and armed guards surrounded all of it. Mark's escort stopped in front of a guard standing before a tent. "I have brought the Quaker to speak to the major general."

The guard slipped inside and reappeared a moment later, nodding to Mark's escort.

"Come." The officer held the tent flap open.

Mark entered. He'd never seen anything quite like it. Inside, a thick rug covered the ground. On one side was a wooden cot with rope supports holding a stuffed canvas ticking, a woolen blanket folded at the end. A wooden table and two spindle-backed chairs took up the other side of the tent. *It must take most of one wagon's bed to move this tent and its furnishings alone.*

On one chair sat a man who might have blended in with any company. He was large, in his middle thirties, clean-shaven with a long, straight nose, and unpowdered hair receding at the front. His regal bearing, even seated, might have been due to the cut of his uniform and its ornamentations, befitting an officer, no doubt. There was absolutely nothing about the man that said he was a Quaker.

Mark's escort removed his hat and addressed the officer. "This man is—" He looked at Mark.

"Mark."

The escort frowned at him. "He says he is a Quaker. Says he lives near where we fought along the Brandywine."

"Mark." Nathanael's voice was deep and unruffled. "Thee are part of the Birmingham Meeting?"

"Indeed." Mark kept his answer short, unsure of what would happen in the next few minutes.

"I am sorry for the destruction of the property there. I hope thee were not unduly affected."

"The house I lived in was destroyed."

The big man rubbed his jaw and eyed Mark up and down. "Thee say thee are of the Society of Friends?"

"I was raised by Lucy Sharp after my mother died. The Friends accepted me there."

"Ah." Nathanael dropped his elbow to the table. "Have thee Indian blood?"

Few people asked that of Mark, but wearing his hunting clothing, he wasn't totally surprised by the question. "I am of the Lenni Lenape tribe."

"William Penn was a friend to the Lenni Lenape."

"His sons were not." The words left Mark before he'd thought them through.

Nathanael glanced down, but he nodded. "'Tis a shame, that." Then he raised his eyes to Mark's. "What are thee going to do now?"

"I know not." But something struck him then. "Perhaps thee need a scout. I know much of this area."

"'Tis doubtful we will be staying here. Would thee pick up a musket against the enemy? The British?"

Mark didn't flinch or hesitate. "Not if I can avoid it." He could keep that much of his promise to his mother, at least. "However, if my life were threatened, I would defend myself." Which would honor his warrior father.

"A scout." Nathanael drummed his fingertips on the table.

Mark nodded.

"Thee can move quietly, unseen through the forest?"

Mark stood a little straighter. "As my father and uncles taught me."

"I believe I could use thee." He rubbed his jaw again. "But not, I think, as an enrolled soldier. Nay, not that. As willing as thee might be now, 'twould test thy Quaker resolve, I think. I like the idea of an independent scout. However"—he held up one finger—"I have no idea if I will be able to pay thee anything for thy service. Indeed, I can barely guarantee pay for those who have signed papers of commitment. Our new Continental Congress is tight with its purse strings."

"I understand. If it pleases thee, I can find side work as a blacksmith, should the need arise."

"Thee are a smith?" Nathanael's brows rose along with his voice. "'Twas my occupation before the war as well." He stood and came around the desk with a noticeable limp and thrust out a hand. "Smithing is an occupation I am authorized to spend Congress's money on."

Mark shook the offered hand, his own nearly swallowed by Nathanael's. The man might not work the forge anymore, but his grip was that of one who'd spent hours swinging a hammer against iron.

"Welcome to the Continental Army as a special scout assigned personally to me. Thee will need no uniform. What thee are wearing will do nicely. And when we need an extra smith, I will contract the work to thee."

"Thank thee for the opportunity."

"Thank me not, Mark. Thee will earn thy way here or find another place."

"Major General Greene." The guard who'd stayed outside opened the tent flap again. "General Washington approaches."

"Thee will excuse me?" Nathanael dismissed him that quickly, and the escort all but shoved Mark from the tent.

Once outside, they waited for General Washington to pass. It was easy to see why he inspired men to follow him, given his size and regal bearing. When he glanced at Mark, there was a kindness amidst the weariness of his face. He murmured something to the guard and then entered the tent.

Mark turned to his escort. "Where shall I stay until Nathanael has need of me?"

"'Tis Major General Greene," the officer growled. "Give the man the respect he is due. I am Brigadier General Nash, and you may address me as such. I assume Major General Greene will assign me to keep an eye on you." And he didn't sound best pleased by that.

Using titles would take some getting used to. Quakers considered all humans, even a Lenni Lenape orphan, to be equal in the sight of God. But Nathanael—nay, Major General Greene—hadn't flinched when the guard had called him by that title. And it was obvious that Brigadier General Nash would accept nothing less.

If Mark were to fit in with the army, even as a scout and smith, he'd have to adapt.

Chapter 10

"Here is a bit of sacking for the bird." Mistress Geyer handed it to Grace. "Bundle it vell."

She took the fabric and secured the plucked turkey within it. They'd gotten word moments before that their camp was to move out again. Any thought of a bath in the river had been squashed. Instead, they must hurry and pack and get their wagon in line.

A disturbing word had reached them as well. Not only had the Continental Army been driven out by the British forces, but they had lost almost all their field cannons. When the British had arrived, they'd shot and killed the artillery horses first thing, making it impossible to move the heavy guns mounted on their carriages.

The loss was a bitter blow to the Patriots.

The turkey and their cookware again on the wagon, Grace began dismantling her tent. She pulled the back support pole free. When the canvas dropped to the ground and unmasked her view, there was Mark, coming toward her. She was struck with a sense of relief. Was it from seeing that he'd not been in trouble with the soldier who'd come for him? Or was it knowing he was close in case they needed him again? Either way, the sight of him lightened her heart.

"We are to move again." Of course he could see that for himself, but she didn't know what else to say.

"Indeed. If 'tis agreeable with thee and Mistress Geyer, I will travel with thee."

That made her heart skip a beat. "You are coming with the army?"

He glanced around and lowered his voice. "Not the regular army, not as a soldier. I will scout for Major General Greene."

"Should you not travel with him, then?"

Mark shook his head. "Brigadier General Nash, the officer who came for me this morning, said I should find a place to travel within the followers' camp. As I know no one else"—he shrugged—"I hope thee do not mind if I join thee when not scouting."

Know her? He didn't know her at all. If he did, he would likely keep his distance, him being a proper Quaker and all. And yet, he didn't look like a Quaker now, nor had he when they'd first met. He looked rugged and wild and... and handsome. Flustered, Grace dropped the canvas she'd picked up to fold.

"Allow me." Mark took the weighty material and folded it neatly. "That one is thy wagon, is it not?" He pointed to the correct one.

"'Tis."

"Mark, how good of you to come and help." Mistress Geyer spoke from behind Grace. "Could you fold my tent as well? I have emptied it already." Mistress Crenshaw called her name, and Mistress Geyer bustled off again.

Mark made short work of dismantling the other tent, folding it and storing it in the wagon along with all of its poles. He glanced at Grace. "Where are thy horses? I can hitch them for thee."

Where? How would she know anything about the horses? "With all the other horses, I suppose."

"Which pair pulled thy wagon?"

Grace shook her head. "They all look alike to me." They were big and scary and covered with flies in September's heat.

Something like a grin tugged at one side of his mouth. "I shall inquire of the hostlers." And then he was gone.

"Girl!" Mistress Crenshaw's voice broke over Grace like a bucket of cold water. "Do not just stand there, move. Help the laundresses."

Grace scurried to do the woman's bidding but managed to keep an eye on Mark at the same time. While she pulled damp clothing off the bushes and stuffed them into the empty kettles, Mark spoke with a man near the horses and returned with a pair of the brown beasts already harnessed.

"Is that not the Quaker man you were making eyes at back at the field hospital?" Anna's elbow caught Grace in the ribs. "He looks like an Indian in those clothes. Handsome enough though." She lowered her voice. "Do not let Mistress Crenshaw see you slacking off or ogling him."

"I do not ogle." Grace grabbed an armful of the bats used to stir the big laundry kettles and lift the scalding cloth from them. "You think he looks like an Indian?" His skin was deeply tanned, but so were many of the men she'd met since leaving Philadelphia. Men on the frontier spent their days outside, and it left them weathered. But an Indian? Her own skin was duskier than most and had grown more tanned since she'd arrived at camp, and she certainly wasn't an Indian.

Anna giggled. "As if an Indian would speak like a Quaker, all *thee* and *thy*."

Of course not. Grace had never heard an Indian speak, but everyone knew their language was guttural and harsh, not cultured as Mark's was. She loaded the bats, relieved to have worked that out, then she hurried back to the laundry fire, now reduced to a few glowing ashes, and searched for anything left to load.

"So this is where you have been hiding."

The male voice coming from behind Grace crawled up her spine like a spider. She whirled.

Leering brown eyes scoured her from toes to linen cap.

She suddenly wished she were dirtier, smellier, and even more repulsive. But his black curls were sweat-plastered to his head and his uniform coated with grime, so maybe no amount of dirt would repel Dan Browne.

"I have a pile of laundry needing to be done." He took a step closer, the smell of him threatening to overwhelm her. "When we set up camp this evening, I shall search you out." He took another step closer and raised a hand as if to touch her.

"Grace?"

She wanted to run to Mark and hide behind him, but Dan Browne's face contorted into an angry mask that kept her rooted in place.

"Mistress Geyer sent me to fetch thee." Mark's voice remained even and measured. "She wishes thee to join her at the wagon." He stepped beside the other man and shot a glance his way. "Now."

That released her feet, and Grace scurried away. She didn't stop running until she reached the wagon, but there was no sign of Mistress Geyer. Grace crouched behind the vehicle, keeping it between her and the men still speaking near the remains of the laundry fire.

Had Mark lied to allow her escape?

One of the horses hitched to the wagon snorted and stomped a hoof. Startled, Grace ducked. When she'd caught her breath and peeked over the wagon again, both men were out of sight.

She slid to the ground and rested her back against the large wheel. Mark had come to her rescue—again—and then just strode off as if it were nothing. What manner of man was he? And why was he showing her so much attention without asking for anything more? She drew in a deep breath and grimaced. Perhaps the smell of her put him off.

Once they were stopped for the night, she would find a way to wash off the sweat and grime and don her fresh dress and petticoat. Dan Browne hadn't been put off by her smell, but Mark had walked away. Instead of feeling relief, it bothered her. And it bothered her that it bothered her.

Leaving the broad river behind, the army's wagons rolled north. General Howe and his British troops remained to the west, while Philadelphia—which housed the Continental Congress—lay east of them. With women driving the wagons and Mark having nothing else to do, he'd decided to practice his scouting skills.

What he'd wanted to do was take down the curly-haired man who'd made unwanted advances on Grace. The pallor of her face and the fear in her eyes had made plain—as well as the way she'd raced away when Mark had given her the opportunity—that she didn't welcome the man's attention. Mark's reaction had been swift and strong, the desire to pummel the man to the ground. Instead, he'd lied. He'd done it to give Grace a reason to escape.

But he'd still lied.

The Lenni Lenape strongly disapproved of lying, but to the Quakers, it was a sin. They were quite firm on that point. Justifying the sin by thinking it was helping another did not mitigate the sinful act. Lucy would have advised him to repent during his personal prayers and ask for forgiveness.

Except Mark didn't want forgiveness—yet. He wanted to smash a fist into that filthy soldier's face.

Over the years, he'd honed his ability to be dispassionate in the face of all manner of insults and innuendos. Not everyone in the Quaker community had welcomed him with open arms. Lucy had explained that several had lost loved ones to Indian attacks. When he'd bristled, she'd asked him if he harbored ill will toward the Iroquois warrior who had killed Father. Of course he had—he still did. In her own gentle way, she'd explained that those who were not happy to have him in their midst saw in him the reminder of what they'd lost. So he'd learned to ignore the subtle, and often not-so-subtle, insults sent his way.

All of that training had vanished with one look at Grace's stricken face.

Mark needed to regain his calm, and moving through the forest, far enough from the wagons to lose their noise, allowed him to become one with the wilderness around him. The day was gray and dreary, the scent of rain in the air, but it felt good to be in the forest. Having already bagged a turkey that morning, he ignored the rabbit that tore down the deer path ahead of him, as well as a pair of squirrels chasing each other from tree to tree.

Once his anger dissipated, curiosity got the better of him. He angled farther to the west, in the direction of Birmingham. He wouldn't enter the village that had been his home for half of his twenty years, but maybe he'd learn something useful to Nathanael—Major General Greene. He'd best learn to think of the man by his title lest he slip and refer to him in the Quakers' familiar way.

He ran along the forest paths he'd known since childhood. The lingering taint of gunpowder in the air kept him from sinking into memories of those times. Every sense alert as he drew closer, he moved off the path and into the trees. He hadn't gone more than a few rods when a voice reached him. He crouched and waited until it came again from the path he'd just left. The words were foreign. At the smithy, he'd overheard talk of Hessian soldiers with Howe's forces, so the language was probably German. For sure it wasn't anyone from a Native tribe, who spoke with a cadence very different from that of the European languages.

Not that Mark would have shown himself to any Native warriors either. Most tribes had sided with the British—including the Iroquois. His banked anger threatened to surface again. Over the years, Lucy had warned him that he needed to forgive those who had killed Father, but he hadn't been able to. Not completely. Not like the Quakers would have. It may have been the sticking point that kept him from fully accepting their way of life, even though he believed in their God.

More unintelligible words followed in different voices, a larger group than he'd first thought. Mark kept as still as a tree root grown up from the ground, glad he'd donned his hunting coat even in the heat, as it hid the white of his linen shirt. He closed his eyes and concentrated on the tramp of feet. How many were there? At least a dozen, likely more. Where were they heading? He traced the path in his mind's eye. It twisted and turned, as most wildlife trails did, but if they stayed on it, they'd come to the wide river.

Where they'd discover Washington's forces had already left.

Mark waited patiently, a light drizzle sifting through the leaves above and dampening his hair and clothing. When he estimated a half hour had passed, he rose and continued toward Birmingham. The smell of gunpowder grew stronger, even with the rain. How long would it take for its stink to wash away?

Once he arrived at a small rise just east of the village, the drizzle turned into rain as he worked his way to the top, keeping to the cover of trees and brush, scanning his surroundings. When he reached the final summit, he dropped to his belly and crawled forward until he could see the village.

Broken trees were scattered around, no doubt felled by cannonballs. The remains of Lucy's house weren't visible from where he was, but the smithy was still in one piece, as was the meetinghouse. No one moved along the streets, perhaps due to the army encamped around them or because of the rain, which was now soaking him. He'd left his hair loose again, and because he'd never favored wearing a hat, water matted it and dripped off its ends.

He turned his attention to the encamped army, which showed no inclination to move. In contrast to the rush and bustle of Washington's forces, Howe's gave all the appearance of being half asleep.

Movement in red caught Mark's eye. Not far from him, a pair of soldiers approached, each with a musket at his side, bayonets fixed.

Mark burrowed into the tangle of brambles he'd hidden behind, ignoring the prick of more than one thorn in the process.

"Did you hear that?" One of the soldiers lifted his musket and looked toward Mark's hiding place.

A small bird, disturbed by Mark's presence, flushed from the brambles and soared away.

"Just a bird," the other soldier said. "The colonials are long gone, run with their tails between their legs like the whipped dogs they are." The boast and bravado might have been earned, but he'd missed the meaning of the bird.

His uncle had taught Mark to watch the birds. They often signaled where danger lurked by fleeing from it. And even the

British should know that a bird would prefer to stay on its perch than fly in the rain. Had he been a panther, the soldiers in front of him might be the ones on the run. It was not likely that their muskets would fire. Rain made the gunpowder in their pans inoperable—which explained the bayonets.

If he'd been a soldier, Mark could have slain both men before they'd reacted. Few could match him in throwing a knife, a skill he'd perfected while learning to forge knives at the smithy. The one nestled in his moccasin was perfectly balanced to throw, and the smaller knife at his belt was nearly as good, as he'd proven that morning when he'd used it kill the turkey.

But he wasn't a soldier, so he waited and listened.

The soldiers complained about the weather as they passed by Mark's hiding spot. They were out of his hearing when someone approached them. Mark had to shift to get a better view.

Joseph.

Mark's friend joined the soldiers without pause, and from his gestures, appeared to be answering their questions. Not unfriendly questions, or Joseph wouldn't be smiling and pointing toward the village.

His friend was giving them information.

Joseph had chosen a side after all, but who was Mark to pass judgment? Hadn't he done the same? Yet he couldn't help feeling betrayed as Joseph turned and walked away with the two soldiers. The British soldiers who had brought the fighting right into Birmingham—their home.

Washington had stayed on the banks of the Brandywine until pushed by those Redcoats.

When the three were out of sight, Mark wiggled out of his hiding place and crept back into the forest. There was nothing left for him in Birmingham. He'd made his choice. As much as he appreciated everything the Quakers had done for him, his future was now with the fighting Quaker, Nathanael Greene, and a gray-eyed young woman Mark hoped to know better.

Chapter 11

"THERE IS PLENTY OF turkey to feed the laundresses and us," Mistress Geyer said to Mistress Crenshaw, "but I need Miss Grace to tend to the cooking. Ve cannot afford to vaste food, especially fresh meat."

Grace turned the makeshift spit over the fire with the trussed turkey on it, keeping her face lowered, eyes on her work. She held her breath, waiting for the woman sergeant—for that's what people had taken to calling Mistress Crenshaw behind her back—to agree. There was a loud sigh, and apparently a silent agreement, before the woman stomped off.

Mistress Geyer came to her side. "Ve need a strong person to lead the camp followers, but that voman takes it to the extreme, I think."

"Thank you for keeping me here." Grace looked up then. "I fear she dislikes me too much, that she would find fault in whatever task she gave me, if only to have a reason to send me away." And where would Grace go? How would she return to Philadelphia? She didn't even know where they were.

"I vill speak up for you, should that happen."

A warmth she'd rarely felt settled over Grace. Mother had always sheltered her, of course. Taught her to behave like a lady in spite of things and taught her to read and write as few women did, certainly not the women where Grace had grown up. Mother had learned those things as a girl and young woman, before she'd run off and married against her parents' wishes. When her husband had died, she'd been left to fend for herself, because her family had cut her off. There were so few choices for a woman on her own. Mother had tried taking in washing and mending, but it hadn't paid the rent, much less covered the cost of food and clothing. She'd been open with Grace about what had happened, and very clear that she wanted something better for her daughter.

Grace had never imagined that would mean being left with the camp followers of General Washington's army.

Which wouldn't have happened at all if not for John Perkins, the son of a prominent family in Philadelphia. He was a regular at the house where Mother worked, and he'd followed her to their rented room one night, where he'd seen Grace. He'd taken to watching for her, following her if she went to the market, and approaching her with his inappropriate remarks. As if Grace were...

Like her mother.

Grace had struggled with shame at her mother's occupation for much of her seventeen years. Not that Mother was like most of the backstreet women. With her education and manners, Mother didn't fit in with the majority of them, the strumpets, as they were often called. Grace had understood what that term meant by the age of five or six. Mother had left her in the company of Granny Avery, a Christian woman who had reached out to Mother many times, offering her a way out of the life she lived. Why Mother never accepted the offers she never explained to Grace. How different their lives might have been if she had.

Grace swiped a damp tendril of hair from her face. She might not like to be hunched over a fire, turning a turkey on a spit while hoping the British Army didn't descend upon them. But she'd long ago learned that bemoaning her position did nothing to improve it.

"That nice young man has returned." Mistress Geyer's voice pulled Grace back to the present, and then the woman was called away by someone with a question.

Mark came to the fire, leaned over the turkey and sniffed. "I have thought of this bird for the past hour. It smells even better than I imagined." He flashed Grace a grin. With his hair loose and slicked to his head thanks to the rain that had, thankfully, stopped, he looked even more like an Indian.

"'Tis a young bird, and should be tasty." She didn't know what else to say. She certainly didn't want to comment on the aroma, not when she was so conscious of her own unwashed state.

"I must speak with the major general, then I will return and sample thy cooking talents." He left, working his way through the maze of cooking fires. A camp of their size was divided into groups for meals. Mistress Geyer—and now Grace—cooked for the laundresses, who spent enough time stirring pots over a fire. They didn't have time to cook meals as well.

Pots!

Grace used a stick to lift the lid on the one nestled in the embers of the fire. With a rough spoon that had been hastily carved, she stirred the simmering dried peas, then she checked a second pot of heating water. At the right time, she'd stir in a batch of greens some of the women had foraged while they walked. When everything came together, their evening meal would be something of a feast.

Mistress Geyer returned, and Grace worked up the nerve to ask, "Would you watch the meal for a few minutes while I wash up?" Heat filled her face, but it wasn't from the fire.

"Of course." The older woman took the spoon from Grace. "And vhen you are done, I shall do the same. Ve vill both feel better to eat our dinner, I should think."

Grace scurried to her tent, grabbed a small bucket the laundresses weren't using, and headed for the creek they'd camped near to fetch clean water. It would be cold, but on such a hot and humid day, that didn't seem like a bad thing. Her longing to be washed free of sweat and wearing clean clothing had nothing do to with Mark, to be sure. But for whatever reason, she looked forward to seeing him when she didn't smell like something that had crawled onto a hot rock and died.

"Hessians?" Brigadier General Nash practically barked the word at Mark. "How do you know they were Hessians?"

"I assume they were, as I could not understand their language. Also, while working at the smithy, news came of Hessians fighting with Howe's forces."

"How do you know they were not Indians? Several tribes are reported to be fighting with the Brits as well."

"I know what Indian languages sound like."

"Ah, I had forgotten." The officer sized Mark up and down. "You are an Indian under that Quaker demeanor."

Mark stood straighter, not liking the inflection in the other man's voice. "I am Lenni Lenape. I am also a member of the Birmingham Meeting of the Society of Friends. The Quakers do not value any human over another. They teach that all are equal in the Lord's sight."

"Do you believe that?" The words were thrown down as a challenge.

Mark had already lied once that morning, something he still needed to deal with, so he wasn't going to add to his sin. "I try to."

The brigadier general snorted, but not in a disrespectful manner. "For the record, I think those Quakers should fight to hold what belongs to them—to us—but I can respect a man who holds to his beliefs." He turned and headed for the circle of leaders' tents. "Come with me."

The tents were set up as they had been near the river, with the horses on a picket line behind and soldiers standing guard. Nash—Mark didn't know his first name even to think of him by it—told the guard at the largest tent's door that they needed to speak to the major general about important information, and they were allowed to enter.

If Mark hadn't known the camp had moved, he would have sworn this was the same place he'd been in before. Every piece of furniture was arranged in the exact same position, and even the rug appeared in the same spot within the tent, squared to the outside walls. He'd heard of military precision, but it hadn't occurred to him that it was detailed down to every last item. Obviously, it was. Or at least it was with Major General Greene.

"What news?" the major general asked without looking up from what he was writing at the table.

"Hessians, sir," Nash replied.

That brought the ranking officer's head up, dark blue eyes snapping to Nash. "Where?"

"If your new scout is correct, between us and the main body of Howe's army."

Those blue eyes focused on Mark. "Tell me what thee saw."

"I saw nothing, but I heard them speaking a language I knew not. From the footsteps, I would say more than twelve of them, but fewer than twenty."

Nathanael—Major General Greene—leaned back on the spindle chair, making it creak under his weight. "There were plenty of Hessians on the battlefield yesterday. Alexander's division faced off with them. Stephen's division on the high ground held them off as long as they could." He let out a snort. "Sullivan fared no better. Those Hessians are fierce fighters."

"Who are they, exactly?" Mark asked.

That drew an annoyed frown from Nash, but Nathanael answered. "They are hired soldiers from the German states. Their German rulers run well-disciplined armies and make a lot of money leasing them to the British to fight their wars. If only our Continental Congress had the money to hire them." He turned his attention to Nash. "With so few men, they were likely scouts. Nevertheless, double the patrols, alert the guards, and pass the word to all commanders."

"Very well, sir." Nash jerked his head at Mark, indicating they were leaving.

Outside, he turned to Mark. "You may prove useful yet." Then he strode toward another tent and entered.

Mark made his way back to the wagons and a turkey dinner he was looking forward to, not only for the meal, but for the company of a certain young woman. First, however, he would wash away the day's grime.

Lucy had been strict about cleanliness at the table. The pang of her loss stole his breath for a few heartbeats. Mistress Geyer, although she neither looked nor sounded like Lucy, seemed to be a woman cut from the same cloth. She had obviously taken Grace under her protection, much as Lucy had taken in Mark. For Mistress Geyer, he would make himself presentable.

And if Grace noticed—that was fine with him too.

Grace glanced around for the tenth time in the past two minutes. Why was she so nervous?

Mistress Geyer leaned close. “Are you vatching for Mark? He vill be here, vorry not.”

Worry not? She wasn’t worried, she was nervous. There was a difference, wasn’t there?

And then, there he was, wearing the Quaker clothing she’d seen him in back at the field hospital, his hair in a queue. But he still wore the moccasins.

Grace dropped her eyes back to the work at hand and finished deboning the turkey onto a platter. The peas were cooked and the greens simmered to perfection. It had surprised Grace how quickly she’d adapted to cooking outdoors for large amounts of people instead of small amounts for herself and Mother cooked over a brass brazier. Even Mistress Crenshaw had remarked on how tasty one of her meals had been—perhaps because she hadn’t realized Grace had made it.

“Are ve ready?” Mistress Geyer asked. At Grace’s nod, she called to the women who shared their fire.

They lined up with their plates and cups, and Grace served them as they came by, led by Mistress Crenshaw. Mistress Geyer manned the coffeepot—the largest Grace had ever seen—pouring the dark brew into the waiting cups. Grace scooped portions of turkey, peas, and greens onto each plate.

“This smells wonderful,” Mistress Crenshaw said before moving off to sit on one of the nearby crates they used for chairs.

“You are doing vell, and this she notices,” Mistress Geyer whispered. “She may be gruff, but she is fair.”

At the end of the line of women, there was Mark. Gone was the wild Indian, replaced by the cultured Quaker. His eyes met hers, and she had to force herself to look away. What was wrong with her? She filled his plate a little more full than she had for the women. After all, he'd provided the turkey, and men had bigger appetites, or so she'd been told.

"'Tis a feast for sure." He smiled at her, teeth white against the weathered bronze of his skin.

Her stomach flipped in response, but not in a bad way. Not out of fear. Not in a way she'd ever felt before. It stole her voice, so she simply nodded. Once he moved off to sit on a fallen tree trunk a short distance from where the laundresses enjoyed their meal, she dished up portions for herself and Mistress Geyer.

"Come, ve vill sit with Mark." Mistress Geyer left no room to argue, not that Grace wished to.

A distant rumble of thunder reached them. The one thing they didn't need was more rain. The ground was still soggy from that morning's shower, which made Grace thankful for the tree trunk to sit upon. Mark had waited for them before eating, his plate full, head bowed. When they settled on the trunk, Mistress Geyer in the middle, he raised his head.

"'Tis the Quaker way to pray silently over our meals." He searched their faces. "I know not how thee practice prayers."

Praying? That wasn't something Grace had done until coming to the Continental Army. It was said that General Washington himself had commanded his troops to pray before their meals. Usually, one of the laundresses would speak a few words. It made Grace terribly uncomfortable. She knew nothing about the God they prayed to, and she was pretty sure God wanted nothing to do with her.

"I vill say a simple prayer out loud, if you do not mind." At his nod, Mistress Geyer bowed her head and gave a soft prayer of thanks.

Grace bowed hers as well and did her best not to fidget. After the amen, she lifted her face. A tall blond man was striding toward them. She nudged Mistress Geyer and pointed.

"Peter!" Passing her plate to Grace, the woman rose and hurried to him.

"Who is Peter?" Mark asked.

"Her husband."

"Ah. I am happy for her that he survived yesterday's fighting."

"As am I. I hope her son did as well." By the grin on Mr. Geyer's face, he must have good news.

Mark shifted on the tree trunk, and Grace realized they were alone, although within full sight of the rest of the camp. She set the extra plate down and made a show of straightening her petticoat, which allowed her to inch farther away from him. Had he noticed her clean clothes? Or that she no longer smelled like an alley drunk? Would a Quaker even know what an alley drunk smelled like?

Hungry as she was, it was difficult to eat with such conflicting emotions battering at her. Yet among all her emotions and questions there was one thing missing entirely. Fear.

Why did she not fear this man?

Another rumble of thunder was her only answer.

Perhaps her lack of fear was what she should fear the most.

Chapter 12

The downpour had started shortly after supper the evening before, and continued through the night. Stretched out on his side beneath the wagon, Mark listened to the wind drive raindrops into the oiled canvas Mistress Geyer had loaned him. Without it, he'd be drenched.

He pulled a corner back and studied the camp. Dawn had broken, but few people were up and about. The laundresses had rigged canvas on poles over their work fire, another canvas on the side blocking the wind, and two of them huddled there even though the fire had gone out below the large washing kettle. What sense was there in washing clothes they couldn't dry? Perhaps the women would have a day of rest. Sunday wasn't until tomorrow, but Mark had a feeling that Sundays would mean little to an army. How many people there even knew what day it was? Would Mark be able to keep track of the days after weeks or months with the army? Probably not.

That brought a wave of sadness. While he came up short of accepting everything the Quakers had taught him, he believed in the Lord's prescribed day of rest and worship. Even when the meetinghouse had remained silent, on the Sundays when nobody seemed to have a direct word from the Lord to share, Mark had always been able to feel His presence among them. He could question the Quaker practices, but not the God they followed. The God Mark followed too.

Mother had been convinced it was the same God the Lenni Lenape believed in, *Kishelemukonk*, the one who created everything. Over the years, he'd come to agree. It just felt—right. One God. One Creator. And the Savior? Mark understood those Quaker teachings and embraced them as well. The Jesus God was God in a way he didn't understand but felt to his bones. That was enough for him.

The idea of not gathering to worship on Sundays... it would take getting used to, along with everything else about living with the army.

As he gazed out from his makeshift shelter, Peter Geyer emerged from his wife's tent carrying a crate. Mistress Geyer followed and hurried to the central cooking fire, which was also sheltered beneath a length of canvas suspended with poles. She grabbed a long stick and poked where the canvas sagged, letting loose a torrent of water, while Peter knelt and coaxed last evening's embers back to life.

If not for the weight of the British Army just a few miles away, it might have been a normal domestic scene.

A rivulet of water defied Mark's canvas covering and pattered on his shoulder, signaling it was time to rise.

Three steps out into the rain, his moccasins were heavy with mud. He glanced back at the wagon, its wheels settling into the soggy earth. They wouldn't need to worry about the British Army that day or the next. No one would be moving anything heavy until the rain tapered off and the ground firmed up. It wouldn't be a good day for hunting, either. And scouting? Even at his most careful, he'd leave a trail any child could follow back to the camp. So how would he spend the day?

He ducked under the canvas covering the cooking fire.

"Good morning, Mark." Mistress Geyer pulled porridge makings from the crate. "Did you stay dry last night?"

"Indeed. Thank thee, again, for the use of the canvas."

She waved a dismissive hand. "'Tis little enough thanks for that turkey last evening."

"I have not eaten so vell in months." Peter patted his lean middle. "Any chance you can find another one?" His blond brows rose with his question.

Mark pointed out into the rain. "Not in this. The birds will be huddled under cover wherever they can find it, as will the rest of the animals."

"Only humans are daft enough to be out in this veather," Peter said.

"Oh, hush." Mistress Geyer wagged a finger at her husband. "Have ve not rigged our own shelters to stay dry? That makes us smarter than the animals." Despite the scolding words, her voice was tender, and Peter's eyes sparkled with humor.

"Oh!" A female voice cut through the rain drumming on the canvas overhead.

Mark turned in time to see Grace grab onto the supporting pole of her tent to keep from sliding in the mud. He sprinted into the storm, his moccasins better in the mud than Grace's buttoned boots, and reached her side. "Take hold of my arm." Once she had a firm grip, he brought her to the fire, ducking underneath the canvas once more.

"That was quick thinking, lad." Peter looked at Mark's feet. "'Tis an interesting choice of footwear."

Mark still wore his Quaker clothing but had kept his moccasins on because... well... he just preferred them. He hadn't had much trouble learning to wear Quaker clothing, although he'd missed the freedom of running in just a breechclout and moccasins, but that had been too scandalous for Lucy.

"They are easier for... hunting." He'd almost said scouting, but he wasn't sure if he was supposed to tell people what he was doing or not. He'd already told Grace, but maybe he should refrain from telling anyone else.

"I imagine they are." The older man straightened, moving to look past Mark. "He found us."

"My boy!" Mistress Geyer pressed the spoon she'd been using into Grace's hands and waited for the tall young man to duck under the canvas with them. While he had Peter's height and colorings, his features bore an unmistakable likeness to Mistress Geyer. She threw her arms around him, and he gathered her close, pressing his face against her linen cap.

Much as Mark had once pressed his face against his mother's braided hair and Lucy's linen cap. A lump in his throat had him turning away, where he met Grace's glance. In the depths of her eyes, he saw the same kind of loss the scene had brought to him. Was she, like him, alone in the world? Why else would she be with Washington's army? Unless...

Was Grace a camp follower because someone she loved served in the army? Of course, she was. Wasn't that why the women worked so hard for the cause? They supported the men who fought—men they loved. It could be her father or a brother. She wasn't married, or she wouldn't have introduced herself as *Miss Grace*, but what if it were another man whom she loved?

Mark didn't like that idea.

Mistress Geyer made introductions, beaming at her son, John. Grace murmured a greeting but kept her eyes lowered to the kettle and the porridge she stirred. Mark shook the man's hand. They were similar in age. "I was sent to find you, Mark." His English lacked the heavy accent of his parents. "The major general wants to see you after you eat. He was particular, that you should eat first." He leaned a little closer. "Which means he is going to put you to work." A chuckle went around the company.

Reassured by John's humor and relaxed manner, Mark took the bowl of porridge passed to him. They all ate while standing, including the laundresses who crowded in under the shelter, while rain continued to slap against the canvas. When he was finished, he handed his bowl to Grace.

"If the rain stops, and if the major general needs me not, I will try to bring some meat back for supper."

"How will you keep your powder dry in this?" John asked, having easily overheard in the cramped space.

Mark patted the knife at his side. "I have my knife." He ignored the man's skeptical expression and ducked under the canvas into the rain.

But more than the water cascading over his head and down his back, it was the thought of Grace serving the army to support another man that jabbed at him. He had no right to feel that way, no right at all.

And yet, he did.

Would she ever be fully dry again? Grace huddled inside her tent. There wasn't enough dry wood to keep both the cooking and laundry fires going, so Mistress Crenshaw had let the laundresses take the afternoon to rest. Until they needed another field hospital, Grace and Mistress Geyer were back to working with and cooking for the laundresses. Mr. Geyer and John had headed back to their own fire with their unit. The fighting men were broken into smaller groups who shared a fire and combined their rations for cooking meals.

The meal for Grace and the other laundresses that evening would be turkey broth and whatever they could combine to go with it. The turkey carcass was stewing over the embers while Grace and the others relaxed. Every so often, the wind would bring a whiff of it to her tent. She pulled in a deep breath. Even though the meat had been devoured the night before, the broth smelled heavenly after the monotonous diet of salt pork.

Someone scratched on the canvas of her tent. Mistress Geyer would call out, as she always did. Could Mark have returned? Her stomach did that thing it did whenever she thought of him. She rose to her knees, untied the tent flap and opened it.

Dan Browne's leering face greeted her. "I heard you gals wasn't busy today, so I thought maybe we could get to know each other better." He started to push his way into her tent.

"Stop!" The word came out as a shout, but Grace didn't care. She raised her voice even more. "Go away! Leave me alone!"

"Grace?" Mistress Geyer's voice came from her tent, set up only an arm's length from Grace's.

"What are you doing?" Dan's face turned from a leer to a glare, his low voice grating against her ears. "Shut up." He made no move to leave.

"If you do not leave right now, I shall scream loud enough to bring Mistress Crenshaw as well as Mistress Geyer." Grace did her best to stand her ground, considering she was kneeling in a tent.

"You little—"

"Mr. Browne." Mistress Geyer's voice came from behind the man. "Vhat do you think you are doing?"

He moved, unblocking Grace's view. Mistress Geyer stood behind him, an iron fire poker in her hand.

"This woman lured me here—"

"A lie. I know better. You had best stay avay from her, Mr. Browne, or my husband, he vill have a vord vith your commanding officer." The older woman, her accent thick in her ire, gave a sharp jerk of her head. "Now you go, and do not show your face around our fire again." For emphasis, she smacked the palm of her hand with the fire poker.

Under his breath, he said to Grace, "This ain't over between us." Then he was gone.

Grace collapsed onto her bedding, which was growing wet from the open door flap.

"Come into my tent." Mistress Geyer gestured to her. "He vill not be back today, but ve vill stay together."

On legs that trembled, Grace followed her friend into the larger tent. Would it never stop? What must she do to avoid men like Dan Browne? Mistress Geyer was protected by a husband and son and—

The thought hit her like a bolt of lightning.

If she were married, Grace would be protected as well. Marriage wasn't a thing to be considered where she'd grown up. It was something that happened to other women. Respectable women. Even Mother had never mentioned such a thing to Grace, instead, having spoken at length of her finding a position in a large house, perhaps even as a governess.

Who would marry the bastard daughter of a backstreet Philadelphia strumpet? Not even a man like Dan Browne. He didn't want a wife, he wanted... he wanted someone like Mother. The shame Grace struggled most of her life to hold at bay threatened to overtake her as she settled on a small crate in Mistress Geyer's tent.

She lifted her eyes to her friend's. "What am I to do?"

"To start, you are going to move in vith me in this tent." Mistress Geyer pointed at the ground beneath the oiled canvas she used as a rug. "And ve vill tell Mistress Crenshaw"—raising a hand, she silenced Grace's protest—"so she knows that man had been bothering you. She vill see that you are the innocent one in this situation. I vill make sure of that."

"But what about when Mr. Geyer is here?"

The older woman paused, then her faced creased in a gentle smile. "Perhaps on those nights, you can stay vith one of the other laundresses."

Grace slumped forward, her elbows resting on her knees. "I wish he had never seen me. The same with the others I have told to leave me be."

"You cannot help being a lovely young voman, and they cannot help but notice you. However"—Mistress Geyer gave a firm nod—"noticing and menacing are two different things. That man, he is not velcome here anymore. I vill make sure Mistress Crenshaw knows this too."

Having someone to champion her meant more than Grace could say, but it wouldn't solve her problem in the long run. The same as hiding away with the army hadn't. She'd only swapped being harassed by a Philadelphia dandy for a grime-encrusted soldier. Of the two, she'd have preferred—

No. She had no preference for either of them.

Mark, on the other hand, had shown himself to be a man of... of what? Principles? Integrity? Things Grace hadn't had much exposure to, for sure. But things Mother had taught her to value, had insisted Grace live by. Things Mother had assured her existed somewhere beyond the backstreets of Philadelphia. Had Grace managed to find them in a Quaker man who, when dressed in his hunting clothes, looked as wild as an Indian?

If so, the laugh was on her. For no self-respecting Quaker would ever look at the likes of Grace.

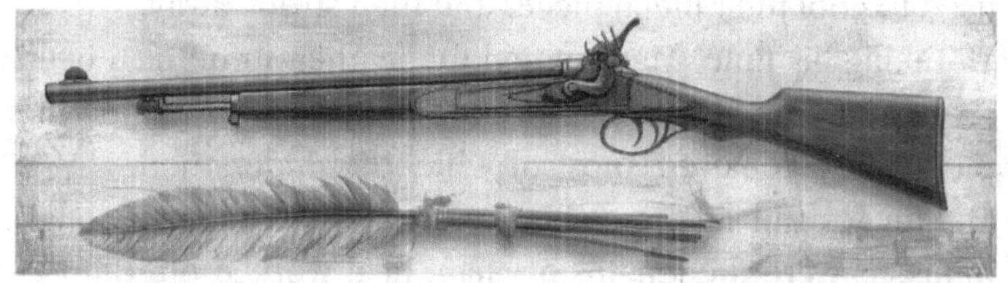

Chapter 13

Mark flexed his shoulders to ease the tightness in them. Sweat plastered his shirt to his back and soaked the waistband of his breeches. The front of his hair had long ago escaped its queue and hung in damp strands on either side of his face. He smelled of smoke and hot iron. For the first time since the shooting started, two days past, he felt almost normal.

"You did all right." Lemuel Trigg, the company blacksmith Mark had been assigned to for the day, gave the praise grudgingly. He'd eyed Mark up and down when he'd arrived with Nash, looking none too happy to have another blacksmith at his canvas-sheltered forge. The man was intimidating in size alone, towering half a head above Mark and easily half a foot broader in the shoulders. His inky black hair was threaded with gray, and his dark brown eyes carried all the warmth of a wolf standing over its kill. "Come earlier tomorrow. We have much to do." He tossed his tongs into the iron bucket they used to cool their metal pieces and then strode away.

Taking his time, Mark untied the leather apron he'd been given and draped it over a stack of crates. He examined the pieces he'd repaired, most of which he understood. Hasps and hinges and singletree brackets were all common enough items, as were the lengths of chain he'd worked on. But the other things? They were part of the war apparatus. Parts of the cannon carriage they were building were all new to him. One soldier, a giant of a man had carried one of the smaller cannons out of the battlefield on his back. Due to his heroic effort, they had not lost that cannon, but needed to build a new carriage to haul it on. Preferably before the next battle. With Howe's forces so close, that could be whenever the rain let up.

Neither army was moving through inches-deep mud.

Mark ducked outside the temporary smithy, and within minutes, he went from sweat-soaked to rain-soaked. Even so, he longed for a bath. He headed for the creek. It wasn't large, coming only to his waist in the middle, but he flopped back and let it wash over him, Quaker clothing and all. He pulled the tie from what remained of his queue and shook his hair out in the clear water, feeling the grime from the forge lift away. He hadn't thought to grab soap on his way out of Lucy's house, but at least he could rinse off the worst of the dirt and smell.

He climbed out of the creek and was headed for his dry clothing under Mistress Geyer's wagon when he remembered his promise to bring something back for supper. The sun tilted far to the west, and the women no doubt already had supper cooking, but he took the long way around camp, scanning tree limbs for any roosting turkeys or grouse. All he got for his effort was an earful of cuss words from a guard for walking in his way.

Arriving in camp, he searched for Grace, who stirred whatever was cooking in the pot. He'd talked himself out of his irrational disgruntlement at realizing she likely had a man somewhere in Washington's forces. Any man must be a father or brother. No woman would follow a man she wasn't married to or related to into a war. At least, he didn't think so.

She looked up as he approached.

"I am sorry to say, I have brought nothing back to eat."

"We have enough." A wrinkle appeared on her brow. "You should get out of those wet clothes before you catch a chill. Evening will be upon us soon."

Not that it was all that chilly in the evenings yet, but she had a point. "I will do as thee say."

That brought a ghost of smile to her lips.

He crawled under the wagon and dug through his belongings. Sheltered from the camp by canvas, he managed to change his clothing, pulling on his dry pair of moccasins last and leaving his hair free to finish drying. By the time he emerged, the clouds had begun to break up overhead, and the rain had ceased.

Grace was ladling out bowls of soup when he returned to the fire. She filled a bowl and handed it to him along with a spoon.

"Thank thee." The other laundresses were already seated and eating, having set up crates outside since the rain had stopped. Mark looked around for somewhere to sit.

"You can join Mistress Geyer and me over by the tent." Grace pointed to where the other woman already sat with a bowl resting on her lap.

"I would like that." He waited for her to fill her bowl, then walked with her. There were only the two crates set out, but he overturned a bucket and sat on that. He bowed his head and said his prayer in silence. When he raised it again, both women watched him. "'Tis my custom to pray before all meals."

"I am sure," said Mistress Geyer, "but 'tis different to do so vithout vords. I already said my prayers." She spooned up a mouthful of soup and nodded to Grace. "'Tis very good."

Grace flushed under the other woman's praise, as if she weren't used to receiving such a thing. But how could she not be when she was such a fine cook? Mark took a spoonful of the soup. It was thick with greens, something the women would have foraged locally, but there were also dumplings, little knots of wheat dough. Lucy had made something similar, and he loved them.

"I am glad I cleaned up for such a fine supper." Mark spooned up more.

"Vhat did the mayoor yeneral need you for today?" Mistress Geyer asked.

Mark swallowed his soup. "Blacksmithing."

"You are a blacksmith?" Surprise filled the older woman's voice.

"Indeed." He shrugged. "'Tis a good occupation. It came in useful today. There were many things to be repaired after the battle." Too many things with too little iron with which to repair them, but there was no sense worrying the women about that. "Besides making this excellent soup, what did you ladies do today?"

The women exchanged glances, Grace giving the barest shake of her head. Mistress Geyer pressed her lips together in a firm line, then turned to Mark. "I had to varn that Dan Browne to stay avay from our Grace."

Grace seemed to melt in on herself, eyes on her bowl, from which she'd eaten nothing yet.

Anger churned in Mark's middle, not mixing well with his soup. "Dan Browne?"

"Aye, and he has done it before. Vile man, that he is." Mistress Geyer nodded toward Grace. "She vill be in my tent from now on, you can be sure of that."

They finished their meal in silence, Grace barely eating anything, and Mark tasting nothing but his anger.

Someone approached, footsteps muffled by the soft earth, but loud enough to awaken Mark. The inky darkness of a cloudy night sky didn't allow him to see anything. He slid his knife from his haversack and waited, the sound coming closer to the wagon under which he had taken residence these past three days.

"Mark?" Nash's voice was low and hoarse. "Are you there?"

Mark slipped out from under the wagon, knife still in his hand. "I am."

The whites of Nash's eyes flashed in the darkness. "No need for the knife. Not yet." He came closer. "The major general wants you to scout to the east. One of the pickets reported seeing movement, but he couldn't be sure if it was human or animal, and he had orders not to leave his post."

"What does the major general expect me to find?" Mark had slept in his hunting clothes, except for his coat. He tucked his knife into his moccasin before pulling his coat out from under the wagon.

"He does not believe the bulk of Howe's forces would move in the night, but the Hessians? They might. See what you can learn and report back with all haste to the major general." Nash left him, making just as much noise as when he'd arrived. Moving quietly in a white man's heeled boot was a problem.

Mark slung his shot bag and powder horn over his head and shoulder, letting them rest across his chest, then picked up his musket. He didn't want to use it, but he might need it to protect his life. How far he'd come in the five days since the battle along the Brandywine. Since Lucy's death. How much farther would he go? Not just on the land, but in his faith?

Those would be things to ponder at another time.

He was getting good at putting off such thoughts.

He crept away from the tents of the laundresses, past two smoldering fires near soldiers' tents, and finally deep into the forest. The rain had been intermittent for the past three days, turning mud into a quagmire around camp. In the forest, everything was wet, making it easy to see that it hadn't been churned by boots and horse hooves. Mark was able to move silently through the damp grasses, ferns, and leaves. It wouldn't be long before a fresh carpet of colored leaves littered the ground. Then it would be more difficult to move without noise.

With the sky hidden by clouds, it was impossible to guess the time. His body, while fully awake, held to a sluggishness that let him know he hadn't slept nearly long enough. It couldn't be too far past midnight.

Every dozen rods or so, Mark stopped and crouched to listen. The night animals were out. Bat wings slipped through the air. In the distance, a lone owl hooted. Small things scurried in the underbrush. Insects clicked and frogs sang. The music of the forest was beautiful, something he'd always enjoyed.

And then a whiff of something reached him.

He waited, sniffing, trying to catch it again. So faint he might have missed it, it was there. The scent of wet wool. It took a lot to get wool soaked, but they'd had more than enough rain to achieve it, and wet wool not only had a very distinctive odor, but it could take days to fully dry.

He must have been close to have caught the scent, so Mark felt his way to where he thought it came from. Hands on the ground, toes of his moccasins finding purchase without making a sound, he moved. A stray beam of moonlight escaped the clouds and filtered through the canopy of leaves and needles overhead. Not very much, and not lasting very long, it allowed a glimmer of light to strike against metal.

Mark flattened to the ground. The soldiers were at rest, but not sleeping. Not unless they could sleep sitting up with their backs to the trees. He waited for another break in the clouds, but they kept their stubborn hold on the sky. With infinite patience, Mark crept closer. Each hand, each foot, placed with care, each breath pulled in softly and released the same way. He'd moved maybe half a rod when someone coughed. Mark froze. The sound had come from his left—not from the soldiers ahead of him.

Fear raced up from his fingertips, down his shoulders, and ended at his toes. Every nerve was tingling in response when someone called out in a growled whisper of words Mark couldn't understand.

He'd found the Hessians.

Not only to his left, but to his right, men rose from the forest in answer to the words.

Mark wasn't surrounded, as none were behind him, but he'd nearly crept into the center of them. He silently chided himself for his carelessness as he backed away, still low to the earth, still feeling out each step.

More of the foreign words were issued as the men assembled in lines. It was apparent by the outlines that they wore uniforms. The clouds hid the color other than thin slashes of red, but they weren't British army. Nor were they the ragtag men of Washington's army. These were disciplined soldiers, bristling with weaponry, and ready for war.

Mark stopped when he deemed he'd gone a safe distance and listened to the men move out. As far as he could tell with no stars to guide him, they would miss Nathanael's camp by a few degrees to the north. But not by many. He needed to alert the major general as soon as possible.

Word came before first light that they were to pack the wagons and be ready to move when the command came from on high. Grace and Mistress Geyer put out leftover flatbread that they'd baked over the fire the day before, and the laundresses ate while working. There was so much to pack. All the laundry equipment, their tents and poles and oiled canvases. Not to mention crating up the foodstuffs, cooking supplies, bedding, and personal belongings. It was a daunting task to complete in a morning, much less in the hour they'd been given.

And where was Mark? Grace didn't want to worry about him, but how could she not? He'd been gone when they'd been awakened long before sunrise. He must have been called away first, but why?

"Miss Grace"—Mistress Geyer shoved the last of her bedding into a crate—"pack up Mark's belongings. Ve cannot leave them here." She pointed to an empty crate. "Use that one."

"Since we share a tent now, you could call me Grace."

Mistress Geyer tilted her head. "Very vell. Run along, Grace, and get Mark's things packed."

The pleasure brought on by the familiar address from the woman who was protecting her fell away as Grace reached Mark's sleeping area beneath the wagon. It felt wrong to touch his personal items, but the other choice was to leave them behind, and Mistress Geyer surely knew what was best. Grace put his bedding in the crate first. Not a trace of warmth remained in it. He'd been gone for a while. His belongings were few, a haversack and a pair of moccasins he'd left out to dry. Where were his musket, powder and shot? She felt around in case she'd missed anything in the darkness beneath the wagon, but there was nothing more. She covered everything with the oiled canvas, as they did for all the crates to keep the contents dry, then she crawled out, dragging the crate behind her.

"Thank thee for doing that."

Grace nearly slapped a hand to her heart to stop its wild flight at Mark's voice. Some due to surprise, and some because he had that strange effect on her.

"I did not mean to startle thee."

"And yet, you did." Her voice was sharper than she'd intended, but it only earned her a slow grin.

"I believe that is the first time I have ever heard thee snap at someone."

"'Tisn't a thing to be admired." She stood and brushed the damp grass from her petticoat. "I should have thought before I spoke."

"'Tis good to know thee can—and will—speak up for thyself." His brow creased along the odd line on his forehead. "Especially with men like Dan Browne in the camp."

Dan Browne. The name sent a shiver through Grace. He hadn't returned since Mistress Geyer had ordered him to leave, but his parting words, *this is not over between us*, still rang in her ears. He wasn't the type of man to give up on what he wanted. She'd been down this path before with the Philadelphia dandy who had pursued her for months. A woman alone had so few options.

If only she were worthy of something more. If only she were worthy of a man like Mark.

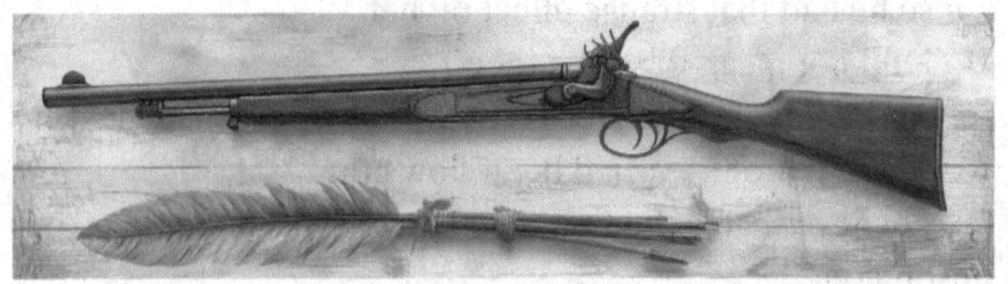

Chapter 14

After making his report to Nathanael, whom Mark remembered to address as Major General Greene, two soldiers had arrived with news that the Hessians—Mark had been right about who they were—had set a course to arrive at White Horse Tavern, a well-known stopping place on the way to Philadelphia from the west. In the morning light, they had also spotted the rest of Howe's forces following in the distance.

"I must speak with General Washington." Nathanael had pushed his way through his crowded tent and left.

Nash had given the orders to pack up, assigning Mark to help Lemuel Trigg after seeing to his own belongings. Since Grace had done that chore for him, he went to help the blacksmith.

When Mark appeared, Lemuel turned on him with a growl, pointing a hammer at his chest. "Who are you?" He demanded.

"'Tis I, Mark."

"Then why are you dressed like a dirty Indian?"

"The major general sent me on a scouting mission." Mark glanced at his hunting clothes and back at the big man. "'Tis better to dress in hunting clothes for that." He'd always worn his Quaker garb for working the forge, not wishing to burn a hole in his leather hunting clothes.

Lemuel didn't lower the hammer, and it shook as if he were restraining himself from throwing it at Mark.

"That hair, that skin." Pure hatred poured out with each carefully spaced word. "You are an Indian."

Mark squared his shoulders. "I am Lenni Lenape. I am also a Quaker and a blacksmith."

"Liar." The word was a snarl and the big man launched himself at Mark.

They hit the ground together, slapping into the mud. Mark concentrated on keeping the hammer away from his head, not an easy task when it was held by the well-muscled arm of a larger man. A cry of "Fight! Fight!" arose from around them, and men flocked to watch. With a twist and shove, Mark disengaged from Trigg. Younger and leaner, he regained his footing first and backed up, crouching with his arms spread wide. He didn't pull the knife from his boot, even though Lemuel continued to brandish the hammer.

Lemuel charged, looking for all the world like a raging black bear if not for the hammer in his paw. Mark waited until he was almost within reach, then lowered his shoulder and ducked, coming under the deadly swing of the hammer to drive his shoulder into the larger man's stomach. But it cost him. The hammer's handle came down on the lower part of Mark's back. It took an act of will to twist away again and keep on his feet.

"What the devil is going on here?" Nash's voice cut through the crowd of men who now ringed the fighters, most egging them on. "Trigg, drop that hammer." A groan of disappointment rose from the onlookers. "The rest of you, back to work. We move within the half hour. Whatever you have not packed you will leave behind." Anger lashed from Nash's voice, and the men scattered.

Nash pointed a finger at Lemuel while keeping out of his reach. "I said, put that hammer down."

"He is a dirty Indian." Lemuel spat, a trickle of blood staining his lip. He pointed the hammer at Mark again. "I will not work with the likes of him."

"You will do what the major general orders you to do, soldier, and what I order you to do." Nash pointed to the ground. "Now drop that hammer before you wind up shackled to the back of a wagon for the march."

The bear-like growl from Lemuel had Mark balancing on his toes, ready to dodge the flying hammer, but the big man released it and let it fall to the ground. "I will not work with a killin', thievin' Indian."

"If he wanted to kill you, he would have pulled that knife in his boot." Nash gestured toward Mark's moccasin, where the hilt of the blade was visible.

Lemuel eyed it, then he glared at Mark. Hatred, as stark as Mark had ever seen, burned there. "All Indians are killers, liars, and thieves."

Where the words came from, Mark didn't know, but he uttered them anyway. "Who did thee love who was killed by an Indian?"

Lemuel turned his back and stomped away letting loose a string of vile words, cursing Mark and every Indian ever born.

"His wife and daughter," Nash said. "Butchered in their cabin while Trigg was out hunting." He sighed and turned to Mark. "You showed good judgment, not pulling your weapon."

"I am a Quaker." He met Nash's look. "But I did not become one until after my father was killed by an Iroquois. I understand his anger and hatred. Without the Quakers, I would be like him."

"Those Quakers took away your anger?" Nash sounded disbelieving.

"Nay. But with the help of their God..." Mark shrugged. "Some days, I still need to turn it over to Him afresh."

Nash shook his head. "Well, I am just glad not to have a dead body here this morning. Best you keep your distance from Trigg in the future."

"But the forge work?"

"He shall have to do it on his own. I can afford to lose neither a good scout nor a half-crazed blacksmith. You are both too important to the cause." With that, Nash left.

Mark circled wide of the forge and made his way back to the wagon. Where else could he go? He wasn't part of the army, not a soldier, and by the faces of those who had egged Trigg on, Mark would remain an outsider. An Indian. While they hadn't seen him that way before, they all would now.

Including Grace.

Carrying the last crate to the wagon, Grace met Mark approaching with the team of horses. What would they have done without him? Mistress Geyer had proven she could drive the team, but hitch them? As he got closer, something in Mark's expression, along with the mud coating his clothing, stopped her in her tracks.

"What happened?" she asked.

He held the reins of the big beasts in one hand and brushed at the wet mud with the other. "'Twas nothing."

"Nothing does not cover you in mud." She shoved the last crate into place and dusted off her hands.

Mark hadn't moved, and his expression hadn't lifted. He looked... defeated.

She stepped closer, almost within touching distance of the horses. "What happened, Mark?"

His sigh was deep and heartfelt. "The blacksmith learned that I am Lenni Lenape." He raised his eyes to hers, deep and dark and searching.

The eyes of an Indian.

Fear rooted her to the spot, her mouth dry as she formed the words, "An Indian?"

With another weary sigh, Mark turned the horses and hitched them to the wagon. Then he left without a word. Without a backward glance.

Mark was an Indian.

"Vhy are you standing there, Grace?" Mistress Geyer called. "Come and help the girls with the laundry equipment." The older woman waved her over. "Ve have no time for vool gathering today."

"I know, I just...I just..." Grace stuttered.

"You can *yoost* later. Now, ve must work."

The next half hour kept Grace too occupied to think about Mark's revelation, but once they were on the wagon and it was moving in the line, she turned to Mistress Geyer. "Mark said he is an Indian."

"Aye, vell, I suspected as much." Mistress Geyer slapped the reins on the broad rumps of the team to keep them moving.

"You did?" Grace's question came out in a squeak, and the older woman glanced at her.

"He has the look, I think, but not the manners. He vas raised by the voman he brought to the field hospital that day. A sorrowful thing it vas to see him vith her vhen she died."

"But he is an *Indian*."

"Vhat difference does that make?" There was an underlying note of censure in Mistress Geyer's voice. "Does he not help us vhenever he can? Bring us meat for our supper? Hitch the horses and carry vater and the like?"

"Aye, he does, but—"

"Listen to me, Grace. Ve live in a good country, soon to be a free country, if the Lord vills it so. The Indians, they lived here first. Ve are the ones who pushed our vay in."

"But the massacres against the settlers?" Grace couldn't let it go. "What about all those people who were killed?"

"Look around you." Mistress Geyer's nod took in the line of wagons and those who walked alongside them. "Many people vill be killed in this var. 'Tis vhat happens in var. The Europeans came and took over the Indian land, an act of var. You cannot expect they vould not fight back, can you?"

"I suppose... I suppose not." Grace fell silent, partly because she didn't know what to say, and partly because Mistress Geyer sounded more than a little vexed with her. But mostly because she felt betrayed. She'd trusted Mark. For the first time in her life, she'd trusted a *man*. She'd even—she squirmed on the hard wooden seat—imagined herself longing to marry him.

And he'd lied to her.

The horror on Grace's face would live with Mark for a long time.

He'd never tried to hide who he was, but neither had he expressed it. Not all of it, anyway. He was quick enough to admit to being Quaker and a blacksmith, but slower to own his Lenni Lenape heritage. If he'd been as dark as his father instead of inheriting his mother's lighter skin, people would have known at a glance. Some still did, as Lemuel had proved, if he dressed the part. It was his Quaker clothing and speech that made people overlook what would otherwise be obvious.

After all, what Indian could act so *civilized*?

He'd heard that comment and others in those early days when he'd gone to live with Lucy and Oliver. Even Quakers weren't above prejudice—not all of them, anyway. Lucy had helped him to understand their fear, not of him personally, but of what he stood for. He'd mended his ways, worn their clothing, spoke only their language until he could scarcely remember his own, adopted their mannerisms. Even accepted their God for his own.

Yet in the end, some still looked at him as if he were a monster.

Like Grace had.

He was too old to have hurt feelings. That was a childish thing. But he walked away from the wagon and lost himself in the forest. Away from the noise of the army, he curled up under a huge red pine and let his mind go blank, as he had when he was a child. Back pressed against the rough bark, breathing the musty scent of the earth, listening to nature going on about its business, he felt grounded. He felt closer to his people, the Lenni Lenape, but farther from the Quakers and Lucy.

Grief welled in him again.

Maybe grief was the reason he'd been so drawn to Grace. The simple need to connect with another human being after Lucy's death. No, that couldn't be it. He'd been drawn to Grace at their first meeting in the forest, when that panther had frightened her. Lucy had died the next day. Meaning his attraction to Grace had been that of a man to a woman. It was as simple—and as complicated—as that.

He must release any idea of Grace in his life, and it felt like a blow to the chest, as if Lemuel's hammer had found its mark.

What was he to do now? He had no home. No people. Nothing except a fragile bond with the fighting Quaker,

Nathanael Greene. Major General Nathanael Greene, who wanted him to scout. Scouting gave him a purpose and a chance to use his skills. If he stayed with the army, he could keep an eye on Grace, at least, even if they never spoke again.

Because men like Dan Browne were still there.

The going was difficult. Their horses labored to pull the wagon through inches of mud churned up by the many foot soldiers, horses, and wagons ahead of theirs. Grace felt sorry for the beasts, their coats soaked with sweat, white lather gathering wherever the harnesses rubbed their bodies, nostrils flared as they sucked in great lungsful of the cool air.

Grace pulled her shawl tighter around her shoulders. They'd been either hot or wet ever since she'd joined the camp followers. The cool morning breeze was a refreshing change, for as long as it would last. A quick glance at the gathering clouds on the horizon said more rain was coming.

Hills rose on both sides of the valley they traveled, with fall's color showing in soft yellows and blazing oranges. A soldier who'd ridden by and spoken to Mistress Geyer had named them the North and South Valley Hills. Not very original, but descriptive.

Not interesting enough to take her mind of off Mark, however.

Where had he gone? Maybe more to the point, why did she care? If he hadn't outright lied to her, at least he'd misled her, which was close to the same thing.

A little voice in the back of her head reminded her that she hadn't been honest with him, either. She'd shared nothing of her past nor owned up to the fact that she had no last name because her father hadn't married her mother to give her one—assuming the man ever even knew she'd existed.

Mother wouldn't speak of him. Grace had learned early on not to ask. Questions about her father had been the only thing that had caused Mother to lash out at Grace.

A shout from an outrider coming down the line of wagons distracted her.

"Keep in line. Follow the wagon in front of you. Camp will be set up over the hill. Keep in line..." He repeated his message, never stopping the horse who splashed mud with every step.

"Where are we?" Grace asked.

"Novhere I have ever been before," Mistress Geyer said, "but still vest of Philadelphia, for sure. Yeneral Vashington vants us to keep Howe's army avay from the city. Mr. Geyer said our men in Congress need time to evacuate."

Grace twisted on the seat to face her friend. "General Washington thinks the British will take Philadelphia?"

"Aye. Ve have not enough men nor ammunition to stop them. Ve can only slow them down. They vill likely spend the vinter there."

Would Mother be safe in the city with Howe's forces there? Of course she would be. She and the backstreet women would be in demand with a city full of soldiers who had little to do until the snow stopped and the mud dried off the roads.

"Vashington must find someplace for our army to take shelter before the snow flies. Ve need time to build cabins and forage for food. 'Tis a lot of vork to feed an army through the vinter. There vill be hardship." She shot a glance at Grace. "If you are thinking of returning to Philadelphia, I vould not blame you."

Return to the city with John Perkins and his insistent pursuit of her? A city now filled with the enemy.

When had Grace started thinking of the British as the enemy? She wasn't a Patriot. At least, she hadn't been. But she'd found a fragile sense of belonging here, due in large part to the Swedish woman holding the reins. Sure, there were men to avoid here as well, but there was also Mark.

Mark, the man who'd protected her, helped her, even befriended her—and lied to her. The Indian.

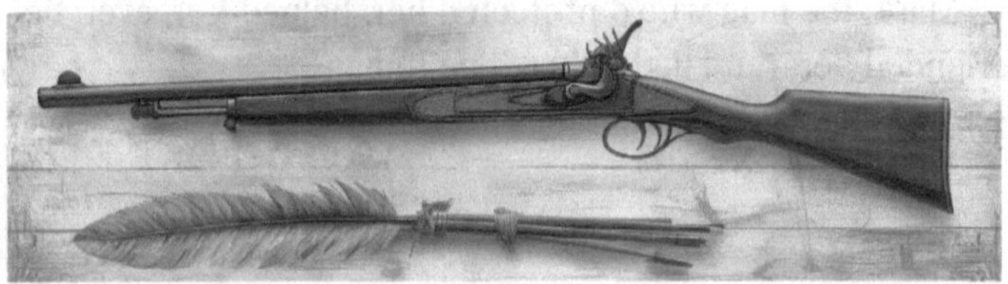

CHAPTER 15

MARK WORKED HIS WAY along a forested hill, passing the wagons, which now lagged far behind the foot soldiers. In the openings between trees, he caught a glimpse of the officers out in front. Mounted on horses, they were easy to identify. Nathanael would be with that lot. Mark loped along, running easily on the drier high ground along a well-traveled path marked with the hooves of deer and elk, even occasionally the pawprints of wolves.

Nature had its own warriors, but unlike men who fought over land, wolves killed to survive.

The path angled toward the summit of South Valley Hill, and Mark followed it, losing sight of the army below. He slowed as the trees thinned out, moving silently, keeping to the cover that was there. On the other side was a crossroads with a tall building flanked by several smaller structures. An inn, no doubt, where travelers could get a meal or spend a night. It must be White Horse Tavern, the one the soldiers had mentioned. Such inns sprouted along the newly expanding network of roads that had followed the white man west.

The white man. How long had it been since Mark had thought in that term?

Since Grace had learned he was an Indian.

Movement to the west distracted him. With so much rain, there was no dust, but as he waited, the movement became men, and the men became an army. The British army, heading right for the inn at the crossroads. If the soldiers had been correct, the Hessians were already there, and what was approaching was the bulk of Howe's men.

Mark needed to let Nathanael know. He moved away from the hilltop and worked down the other side, running where he had good cover. He slipped past two soldiers who were keeping watch—for British soldiers, not for an Indian—and not in the right spot to see what Mark had. It didn't take him long to pass the bulk of Washington's forces and locate the officers again. Mark made his way to Nash's side.

"Howe's army is approaching the inn just over the hill."

"Are you sure?"

"I saw them myself. They are a long way off yet, but by the uniforms, they look like regulars. The Hessians are likely already there."

"The major general assumed they would be." Nash rubbed his jaw with a gloved hand. "You are the first to report. I shall let him know."

"What would thee have me do now?" Mark asked.

Nash looked him up and down. "Until we know for sure if you will fight, Quaker, 'tis best if you stay with the wagons until the shooting is over."

He heeled his horse and rode forward toward Nathanael.

Back to the wagons—and Grace. With a sinking stomach, he worked his way down the column of men, staying in the trees and out of the mud as much as possible. He came to the end of the soldiers and their limited number of cannon carriages and pack mules loaded with ammunition, but there were no wagons of the camp followers in sight.

Mark broke into a lope again, his long strides covering the ground. Around a shallow bend in the valley, he found them. The wagons had left the road and were snaking up the side of North Valley Hill using a path hacked out by a half-dozen men with axes. Whoever was leading them must know the territory, because although there wasn't a real road, they were climbing a manageable slope with only brush to remove, not trees. It would lead them to the top of the hill farthest away from the tavern.

It didn't take long to spot Mistress Geyer's wagon in the line. The wagon was stopped, the tired horses with their heads hanging to their knees. Mistress Geyer kept hold of the reins, but Grace was not beside her.

When he worked his way closer, voices reached him, the jingle of harnesses, the stomp of hooves. The wind shifted, bringing the scent of sweaty horses. He emerged from a stand of young pines and searched for Grace. Not that she'd be glad to see him, but he wanted to know she was safe. A group of women walked along the waiting wagons, kettles hanging from some hands, others carrying crates, and some with poles slung over their shoulders.

Grace was easy to pick out. Her hair, nearly as dark as his, was braided and hung down the center of her back, swaying at her hips with each step. Her arms were wrapped around a crate. Even from the distance, it was easy to see she lived up to her name, moving with grace and ease.

Mark caught up to them ahead of those working to clear brush and before the women reached the summit.

Anna, the laundress most often working alongside Grace, noticed him and called out, "So you found us, Mark."

At his name, Grace looked around, her expression blank.

"Thee look as if thee could use some help." Anna carried the largest kettle, so Mark eased it from her grip.

"Bless you," she said. "I do not mind giving that up." She shook her hand and flexed her fingers.

Grace said nothing, but neither did she look away.

"Where are thee going with all this," he asked.

"We have been dispatched to start the fire and prepare soup, enough to feed the workers and wounded. 'Tis said there will be fighting yet this day." Anna wrinkled her nose. "And rain, to be sure."

The clouds had drawn closer, but so far, the wind had yet to rise.

"Thee will need water." Mark searched the area. To his right was a thick stand of cedar trees. Since they usually grew in wet ground and the hill was no place for a swamp, there was likely a spring nearby. He nodded in that direction. "Let me see what I can find."

One of the other women spoke as he turned away. "Handsome enough, he is."

"Have you not heard? He is an Indian. There was quite the fight in camp this morning."

The comment stirred the anger in Mark.

The woman continued. "The blacksmith nearly crushed his head with a hammer. My man told me all about it."

Finding the spring didn't lighten Mark's spirits much, if at all. As when he'd first joined the Quakers, he was back to being just an Indian. Could he prove to be more than that with time? Should he have to?

Did he want to?

Grace bit the inside of her lip to stop herself from defending Mark. What would the other laundresses say if she did? Anna had suspected that Grace was drawn to him ever since she'd caught Grace staring at him in the Quaker village's field hospital.

Until that morning, she would have been correct. Until that morning, Grace had been thinking far too much about the man who'd rescued her from the panther. Until that morning, she'd even, for just a moment, allowed herself to dream of something more.

Then she'd learned the truth.

But when he'd approached them, walking up the hill in that loose stride she'd come to recognize as his, her heart had done that stuttering thing it did when he was near.

While everything she'd been taught, everything she'd heard over the years, said she should fear him, maybe even hate him, Grace had wanted to defend him as he'd walked away. He'd gone to find water so they wouldn't have to find it themselves and then lug the kettle back.

Mark had always been thoughtful, respectful, helpful, and... and kind.

"He is also a Quaker."

The other women turned to Grace as Mark disappeared into a grove a trees.

She looked around the circle of faces staring at her, some with curiosity and others with something close to hostility. Anna wore a knowing smirk.

"Mark has been nothing but helpful and kind to Mistress Geyer and me," Grace continued, "and to all of you when he brought us that turkey for our supper." No one spoke, so she plunged on. "Our enemy is not fetching us a kettle filled with water." She pointed to the general direction she thought the soldiers were. "Our enemy wears a red coat and will attack those we care about soon. We must do as Mistress Crenshaw told us and ready a fire and food for the wounded."

Anna stepped to Grace's side and put an arm around her shoulders, facing the others. "She is right. If Mark almost got beaten by the blacksmith, 'twas likely because—being a Quaker—he would not fight back. 'Tis probably why he is helping us now and not with the army. Let us not speak of him unkindly. Let us be about our work."

As the other women moved off, Grace whispered to Anna, "Thank you."

Anna shrugged. "He might be an Indian, but he seems far more Quaker to me. And so far, I have never had to beat a Quaker off with a stick—unlike a few other men in this army."

Grace giggled—giggled! It was a sound she barely recognized, but it felt good. Anna was right, Mark was still the Quaker he'd been when he'd brought the old woman to the field hospital, and left without her, shoulders hunched in grief. The same man who had backed her away from the panther, and given her an excuse to flee from Dan Browne.

Shame burned deep in her chest.

All her life, she'd avoided people she didn't know, not just men, but women too, because of their unkind assumptions of her. She was Grace without a last name, the daughter of a backstreet Philadelphia strumpet. A nobody with manners too haughty to fit in with the backstreet women—Mother had seen to that—and yet too lowly to fit in with... with anyone else.

Until Mistress Geyer and Mark.

Had Grace let her own prejudice ruin her one chance at something more?

The spring was larger than Mark had expected. It meandered for a short distance from where it bubbled out of the hill, then pooled near a rocky outcrop. The pool was large enough to plunge the kettle in to fill it. The water must go underground from there, for he could see no other runoff from it. He pulled the dripping and now very heavy kettle from the clean water and headed in the direction the women had gone. He'd leave the water for them and then swing back to see what was happening with the army. The idea of staying near the laundresses and their fire—near Grace—no longer appealed to him.

By the time he found them just over the hill, the women already had their poles set and were slinging the canvas covering over them. Grace waited nearby with a small pile of bark and brush at her feet. The metal container in her hand would hold the remnants of last evening's fire, a smoldering ember she'd coax back into a flame. She half turned toward him and offered a timid smile.

Mark nodded, set the kettle down, and headed back for the army.

"Mark?" Footsteps rustled the damp grass behind him.

He should ignore her and keep moving, maybe even break into a run. But his steps slowed to a halt. He didn't turn, just waited for her to catch up.

She stopped beside him, both of them gazing toward the wagons struggling to make their way up the muddy hill as the wind rose and the first spattering of rain dampened his face.

"I must apologize for my reaction to what you said this morning." The words were low but not grudgingly given. They sounded sincere, if a little painful to say. Yet he sensed the pain came from her own embarrassment, and not his heritage.

"Worry not about that. 'Tisn't the first time, nor will it be the last."

"But if anyone should have reacted better, 'tis me." Her voice was barely audible at that point, and he turned to see her eyes laden with sadness.

"Why, Grace?"

She wiped the dampness from her cheeks, whether from rain or tears, he wasn't sure. "My heritage is nothing to be proud of, I assure you."

He stiffened, and though he tried not to display any emotion, she shook her head. "Not that you cannot be proud of yours. Oh. I am saying this all wrong."

"What did thee wish to say?" He kept his voice even, not yet sure if he should be offended or not.

"I am trying to say that I do not even know who my father was."

That explained the misery pooling on her bottom eyelids. Among the whites, being born outside of marriage was considered a sin. Churches were harsh with children born in such situations, unlike the Quakers. And when he'd been given so much grace, how could he not extend that same grace to... to Grace? Her name took on a whole new meaning for him.

Mark put his hand to her elbow. "Thee need not tell me this."

"If you knew the whole truth, you might think differently."

"I doubt it." He explained about the Quaker's beliefs and what that meant for him. "If the Lord accepts us as we are, should we not also accept each other in the same way?"

She opened her mouth, but a cannon blast from the opposite hill reached them.

"I should get the fire started." She lifted the metal container she still held, now spotted with raindrops. "Wounded will be coming."

"Go." He gestured to where the canvas was up and secured to its poles. "I will see where I can be helpful."

After she left, Mark started down the line of wagons coming toward him. Another cannon blast rumbled across the valley dividing the two hills. He stopped by Mistress Geyer's wagon. "Do thee need me to help with anything?"

"Not unless you can make this rain stop."

"Only the Lord can do that." He wiped his face with his sleeve.

"Then I supposed ve vill yoost have to carry on." The old woman chuckled and slapped the reins on the tired team. "Not much farther. On vith you."

Mark jogged back down the hill, keeping his footing thanks to his moccasins. Boots would have been too slippery. He followed the mud-churned path to where the wagons had branched off, then the army's trail along South Valley Hill. He picked up where the soldiers had started up the hillside, following where the grass was beaten down by boot prints. No wagons had been pulled up here. It was too steep for them. Even without the easy signs to follow, he could have located the army by the sporadic musket fire.

Soldiers spread out in a line roughly three miles in length along the south-facing slope. Mark had overheard their number as nearly ten thousand. Seeing that line, he could believe it. As always, the officers were easy to locate, knotted together under a stand of trees and circled by their subordinates. It was Nathanael Greene's group, so Mark headed for them.

Nash noticed him first and strode toward him. "Did I not send you to help with the wagons?"

"They are nearing the top of the north hill now and did not require my help."

The heavens opened then, the torrent drenching both of them before they could retreat to the merger shelter of the trees. They stood under the dripping branches, visibility no more than three rods ahead of them. The next rumble that shook the hill wasn't cannon fire—it was thunder. How could an army fight a battle amid a storm such as this?

The dismal conditions matched the hollowness of his chest. It was easier to stand there in the pouring rain than try to figure out his next move.

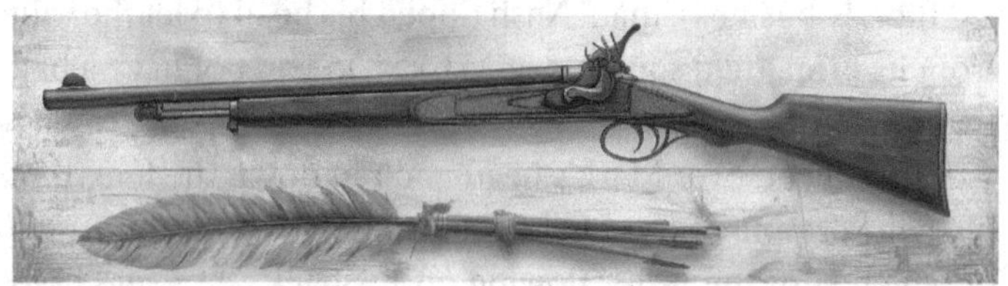

Chapter 16

MARK LEANED CLOSER TO Nash to be heard above the rain. "Do thee know how many men Howe has with him?"

"Our cavalry estimated their forces at just under twenty thousand."

Nearly double that of Washington, but Washington had the high ground. If only they could see the enemy through the downpour. Thunder growled across the landscape, the ground once again trembling under Mark's feet.

"We cannot fire the cannons if we cannot see our targets." One of the officers shouted in frustration.

"'Twouldn't matter if we could," Nash said to Mark. "They will not fire with wet gunpowder, and neither will the muskets. Washington is going to have to make a choice, bayonets or withdrawal."

"Bayonets?" That stirred the memory of his father being speared.

"Bloody business, that." Nash tipped his head to let the rain from its brim, then squinted at Mark. "Do you not have a hat, man?"

Rain sluiced over Mark's head and ran down the length of his hair, dripping onto his leather hunting jacket, the fringe of which kept the water flowing off his back. "I never cared for them." Perhaps because he'd not learned to wear one as a young boy.

Nash shook his head, then looked away when a mounted soldier brought his mount up beside Nathanael Greene's and spoke to the major general. Several others crowded around, but Nash stayed by Mark under the shelter the trees offered. "We shall know what that is about soon enough."

"Where are the followers?" Nathanael's bark broke through after another rumble of thunder.

Nash strode forward, and Mark followed.

"The scout says they are just over the North Valley Hill, already setting up camp."

Nathanael's gaze swept over Mark. "Washington wants us to move to the northeast. Return to the camp followers and have them repack everything and load the wagons. I shall send someone to lead them to us shortly." He turned to the next man with another order.

"Go on." Nash nudged him. "Make haste."

Mark left, and within a dozen strides, he couldn't see the men behind him. Heavy rains didn't usually last very long, but the clouds overhead were so thick and dark, it looked like evening while it was barely midmorning. Already soaked to the skin, he ignored the rain as best he could while concentrating on keeping his footing. Even in his moccasins, it was not an easy task. The return to South Valley Hill took longer than his journey from it.

When he arrived, the wagons were all atop the hill, and poles covered in oiled canvas had been erected, sheltering people from the rain. The news he brought wasn't going to make him friends with any of them. Since Mistress Crenshaw was the woman in charge, he searched her out first. She wasn't hard to find, as people tended to give her plenty of space. She was under a shelter with just two other women.

"Mistress Crenshaw." Mark slipped under the cover of the canvas but didn't crowd close to her. "The major general wishes thee to repack the wagons and await his word to move out. He shall send someone to lead thee to the northeast in due time."

Hands planted on her hips, she snapped at Mark. "And does the major general expect us to sit in the pouring rain until such time as his courier arrives?" Her voice gained volume with each word.

"I believe he does."

"Then he shall surely be disappointed." Her hands left her hips to cross her arms over her breast. "I shall not expose the women to such conditions only to watch the lot of them fall ill within a few days. I will not."

What was he supposed to say to that?

Muttering a word that sounded like "men," Mistress Crenshaw turned her back to him.

Now what? Over the formidable woman's shoulder, he caught a glimpse of a dark braid hanging from a linen cap under another canvas shelter. Ducking out into the rain again, he headed that way.

Mistress Geyer saw him first. "Mark, come out of the rain." She motioned him over. "You should get into some dry clothing." She clucked over him not unlike Lucy would have, and it brought his grief to the fore again.

"'Twould do me little good," He wrung out his hair, which he hadn't bothered to queue that morning. "The major general wants the wagons repacked and ready to move."

Worry creased the woman's brow, and Grace moved to her side.

"However, Mistress Crenshaw would have none of that. She said too many people would fall ill."

"I share her concern," Mistress Geyer said before someone on the other side of the shelter called her away.

"How bad was it over there?" Grace nodded toward the other hill. "Are there many wounded?"

"Not that I saw, but then, the rain made seeing anything difficult."

"At least the shooting has stopped." Grace hugged her middle.

"It had to. The gunpowder got wet."

"I had not considered that." She eyed him up and down. "You should stand by the fire and let it dry you before you catch a cold."

Not a bad suggestion. Mark followed her to the middle of the large laundresses' shelter where the fire threw out its heat. While not a cold day nor a cold rain, neither was it exactly warm. Within minutes, steam rose from Mark's buckskin coat. Several of the women edged away from him, and he couldn't blame them. Wet leather wasn't the most pleasant odor to be found.

Grace handed him a cup of something smelling much better. He took a sip, enjoying the herbal concoction.

"'Twill warm your insides." She gave him a shy smile.

They were on better footing now, the touchy subject of his lineage—and hers—having been crossed. Where did that leave them? Mark was committed to scout for Nathanael Greene, and he was happy to hunt for the laundresses in return for his meals. Working with the blacksmith was no longer an option, but he shouldn't need coin as long as he could hunt and barter.

Mark still didn't know why Grace was there, huddled under a canvas in the middle of nowhere waiting out the storm. She wasn't here because of a father, she'd made that known. He'd seen no other man come to her. Had she followed another man here? If that were the case, he hadn't watched over her as Peter did with his wife, so whoever he was wasn't worthy of Grace.

Maybe that meant Mark had a chance.

Or maybe it meant the other man was among the dead. Perhaps he'd been killed in a previous battle.

Mark might stand up to a rival, but how did one stand up to a martyr?

Before Grace could interpret the thoughts lurking behind Mark's eyes, the odd mark on his forehead drew together into a thin line, and a courier arrived.

"Why are you not packing the wagons?" The man stood in his stirrups and shouted, gesturing toward the wagons with one arm, the other hand controlling his snorting horse as well as the extra horse he led by its reins.

"Are you here to guide us on?" Mistress Crenshaw gave an answering shout, sounding none too pleased by the man's arrival. But then, when had she ever sounded pleased?

"As if I could while you are *unpacked*."

"Nonsense. Only the shelters were unpacked, not the tents or the supplies." Mistress Crenshaw clapped her hands as she turned to address the rest of the camp followers. "Pack up. Make haste. We are to move out in five minutes."

The courier snorted louder than his horse, but then, he probably hadn't seen Mistress Crenshaw in action before.

Everyone else had.

With at least a half a minute to spare, the wagons were packed and the teams hitched. Mark had taken care of the horses for Mistress Geyer's wagon before moving off to help others. Grace had helped dismantle the laundresses' shelter, roll the canvas around the poles, and load them back into the wagon. She was on the wet seat next to Mistress Geyer before the lead wagon rolled out.

The horses, washed clean of sweat by the downpour, had enjoyed at least a short break. They leaned into their harnesses and, because the journey was downhill this time, stepped out with their ears perked, which Grace had learned meant they were in a good frame of mind.

The thunder had moved off, taming the wind a bit, but rain still sheeted down from the heavens. Upon Mistress Geyer's instructions, Grace had kept back a smaller oiled canvas. She had her arm around the older woman, whose hands were busy on the reins, and held the canvas in place as best she could around the both of them.

Where had Mark gone?

She peered through the dark rain until, finally, she spied him ahead of them, mounted on the spare horse the courier had brought. Mark rode along the line of wagons coming toward them, seeming to speak with each driver in turn. When he reached their wagon, his eyes met hers for a moment before he concentrated on Mistress Geyer.

"The courier is leading the wagons down the hill. Keep a full rod between thy wagon and the one in front of thee. Should the wagon become mired, wait on the seat for someone to help thee. Should the wagon begin to slide, keep the horses moving forward and in line with the wagon in front." He glanced at Grace, then back to Mistress Geyer. "If the wagon is ever in danger of going off the path, abandon it with all haste."

"Vhat you are saying is that ve vill be in a dangerous spot soon, am I correct?" Mistress Geyer asked.

"Indeed. The path will narrow ahead with a steep cliff on thy right side."

Grace's stomach dropped.

"Worry not." He met her eyes. "This team is well-trained and able." It was with an effort that he focused his attention on Mistress Geyer again. "Keep them slow and steady and thee shall be fine."

Easy for him to say. He looked as if he'd been born on the back of that horse. But the beasts scared Grace, and she wasn't sure she wanted to depend on them for her safety. On the other hand, she couldn't abandon Mistress Geyer to the elements. Grace had a job to do, keeping them both as dry as possible.

If she believed in the God of heaven, she would have started praying.

The hills weren't normally dangerous, but water had saturated the ground for days, turning it into a quagmire beneath the feet of men and horses alike. Mark nudged his horse forward, a gift from Nash after someone had found it running loose. The saddle, blanket, and bridle said the animal had been ridden by a British officer. The man may have been killed by cannon fire, or the horse may simply have spooked in the nearly continuous rumble of thunder that had shaken the hills when the battle began. Either way, Mark was happy to have it.

A shout erupted ahead, and he urged the mare faster but let her pick her own way through the wagon ruts and muck. They arrived at the place where the cliff dropped off at one side. A wagon had slid, its right back wheel off the path and hanging in the air over the cliff. It was the wagon with most of the cooking supplies on it. A wagon they could not afford to lose.

The women had climbed down and waited ahead of the team. Those men who hadn't been fit to fight that day, some with arms in slings, some leaning on crutches, several with bloody wrappings around their heads, had control of the frightened animals and were doing their best to coax them forward. Even as he approached, the back wheel slipped farther to the right.

Mark stood in his stirrups. "Stop the team." He brought the mare beside a man with a crutch near the back of the wagon. "Have thee a stout rope?"

"There should be one on each wagon." The man waved to the wagon behind them.

Mark wheeled his mount around, and by the time he got to the wagon, the woman seated beside the one driving handed him the rope. "Take this." There was fear in her eyes and her voice. As well there might be, since they would need to traverse the span next.

With the rope, Mark returned and handed it to the man. "Make a bowline knot and secure the rope to the axle. I shall use the horse to steady the wagon as it finishes the crossing."

"Just make sure you let it go if that wagon shifts over, or it will pull you and that horse both to your deaths." With that less-than-cheery thought, the man did as Mark had bid him, then handed the other end back.

Mark shifted in the saddle, bringing the rope underneath him. It would take more than his hands to steady that wagon. He'd need his full weight to hold on. If this didn't work, they'd have to unhitch a team and try to secure the wagon that way, but it could get tricky if the two teams didn't work together. Mark breathed in and bowed his head, asking the Lord for help. When he looked up, he nodded to the man with the bandaged head who held the reins of the team. "Take them forward."

He did, and the rope tightened. Mark gripped it with both hands, using his knees and lower legs to control the mare. She responded, proving she'd been well-trained by someone. The tension increased as the team struggled to move the wagon, which was determined to continue its path over the edge. Mark heaved with all his strength, tempered by years at the forge, his muscles straining the wet leather of his coat sleeves.

Inch by inch, the wagon moved forward. Step by step, Mark kept the mare moving with it, the drag of the wagon's back end threatening to pull his arms out of their sockets, but he didn't let go. The mare slipped once, going down on one knee, but even as the onlookers gasped, Mark hung on. The span with the drop off wasn't more than three wagon lengths long, but it felt like forever before the team's hooves got better purchase on firmer ground and hauled the wagon up the incline at the end of the span. Several people cheered.

Mark let go of the rope and rubbed the mare's dark brown neck beneath the wet black mane. "Thee are as brave as three horses. I shall call thee Naxa." It was the Lenni Lenape word for *three*. He rode her up to the men who had handled the team. "We must unhitch two other teams and bring the remaining wagons across with four horses, alternating the two extra teams to let them rest between passes."

One man, his head swathed in a bandage that leaked reddish rainwater down the side of his face and stained his coat, stepped forward. "We will see to that, if you will pony the teams back across." At Mark's nod, he gave the orders, and a matched team of heavy black horses was led to him. Naxa laid her ears back as if to tell the team who would be in charge, but she turned when Mark asked her to and led them across the treacherous stretch of ground.

By his count, over half had made it to safety, but not yet Grace and Mistress Geyer. And the crossing would only grow more tricky with each passing.

CHAPTER 17

THE SHIVER THAT SHOOK Grace to her core had nothing to do with being wet and tired and hungry. It had everything to do with Mark on the dark horse behind the wagon crossing the dangerous stretch of path ahead. He held a rope tied to the wagon's rear axle, and kept it from sliding toward the expanse of gray sky to their right. If anything went wrong, he might be pulled off the ledge with the wagon to disappear over the side. Her heart skipped a couple of beats until the wagon in front of them made it to the other side.

Their wagon was next.

Mistress Geyer had tied the reins off on the brake handle, but it probably didn't matter to the horses. The tired animals stood with their noses almost to the ground, dozing in the gentle mist that surrounded them—all that remained of the storm.

"I vill not lie." Mistress Geyer turned to Grace. "I vish ve did not have to cross that."

"Mark will see us safely to the other side." Grace wanted to believe it and had no reason not to, having had a good view of him shepherding the wagons in front of them. Their wagon was near the end of the line, just six more after them, and they'd been waiting in line for well over two hours. Hitching and unhitching the horses, making the crossing, bringing the extra teams back, it all took time.

It also took its toll. Not only was Mark's face showing the strain, but his horse's hide was lathered, the mist not saturating enough to wash it away. How much more could man and horse take before they were too weary?

At least the rain had abated and the ground wouldn't be taking in more water. Plus, Grace had been able to lower the oiled canvas and rest her weary arms. Keeping that heavy thing over their heads had been more taxing than she'd expected. She rubbed her arms with the opposite hands.

"Are you cold?" Mistress Geyer asked.

"Nay, just sore."

Mark was coming toward them with a fresh pair of horses in tow.

"Are thee sure thee wish to stay on the wagon?" His brow furrowed with the question. Several other women had decided to walk across, allowing one of the injured men to drive their teams.

"For sure." Mistress Geyer untied the reins and took them in hands that weren't quite steady. "Ve vould only lose our boots if ve tried to valk through that mess."

Grace had been ready to get down and let a man take over, but out of deference to her friend, she said, "We shall be fine." She attempted a confident smile, but his furrow didn't budge.

Two men on the ground got the new team hitched in front of their horses, handing the extra reins to Mistress Geyer. Another man secured Mark's rope on the rear axle.

"Whatever thee do, keep the wheels turning." Mark paused and looked straight at Mistress Geyer. "Do not let the horses stop. Keep moving no matter what."

Again, Grace had the illogical urge to pray. Instead, she called to Mark, "Would you pray for us before we cross?"

His eyes rounded, but his slow smile caused that wonderfully disturbing sensation in her middle. "I already have." Then he nodded to Mistress Geyer. "When thee are ready."

"Dear Lord, see us through to the other side, if it be Your vill. And please, Lord, let it be Your vill." The older woman cut a glance toward Grace and then urged the horses forward.

When they reached the drop-off, the wagon felt different, as if it slid more than rolled in the deep muck left by all the wagons having churned through it. When it slipped sideways, she gasped and hung on with all her strength.

Naxa's feet slid and she scrambled for footing. He kept the rope taut while sending a silent prayer that the horse could prevent the heavy wagon's back wheels from sliding off the cliff. With each passing wagon, the crossing became more dangerous. The thick mud covered a slab of rock that would hold the weight of the wagons with no problem. The danger was in sliding sideways toward the steep drop-off.

Naxa was getting tired. The mare was a fighter, but her sides were heaving between Mark's knees, and her neck dripped white flecks onto the dark mud. She needed a rest.

The wagon slid a little more, and Mark hauled back on the rope, his own muscles quivering. He should have sent someone else to bring this wagon across, but he'd wanted to be there for Grace. He'd wanted her to see him as something other than just an Indian.

Would his wounded pride—his need to impress—lead them all into disaster? Where had the years of Quaker teaching about humility and meekness gone?

There wasn't time to ponder that as Naxa slid again, snorting and tossing her head.

"Easy, girl. We can make this last crossing." Mark squeezed his knees tighter to the mare's sides, willing her to steady. She responded, arching her neck, muscles rippling under the skin. "Good girl. 'Twill be our last today." He had to let his voice and legs do the work, because he couldn't let go of the rope. The strain against his arms and shoulders nearly robbed him of breath.

The wagon slipped again, and Grace's gasp pulled his gaze upward. He forced it back down. He couldn't let himself be distracted. They were halfway across, where the ground angled up. The most dangerous span was just ahead. The wheels were turning, Mistress Geyer keeping the horses moving.

But one of the lead team went to its knees.

Men shouted from the other side, several sprinting forward to grab the horses' bridles, but the damage was done.

The wagon had stopped.

Getting it moving again as the mud coagulated around the wheels would take a herculean effort, and Mark didn't have it. Neither did Naxa. The mare dropped her head, sucking in lungsful of air. She kept her position, which allowed Mark to keep tension on the rope.

But if the wagon started to slide now, all their effort wouldn't be enough. One man and one horse couldn't save it.

Or the women on it.

"What should we do?" Grace's voice came out too loud and too high-pitched, but with the cliff so close, and Mark's warning still in her ears, she couldn't fight back the rising panic.

"Ve vill vait for the men." Mistress Geyer nodded toward those helping the fallen horse as it struggled to rise.

One soldier yelled for another team to be brought and hitched, but then...

The back of the wagon shifted.

"Mark!" Grace twisted on the seat. "Help us!"

"I am doing all I can," he called back in a low voice. "Try not to shout. The horses need to be calm now."

"He is right." Mistress Geyer followed his example, her voice barely above a whisper. "Best to stay quiet."

Stay quiet? While their wagon slid off the cliff?

Oh, why had Mother brought her here? What Grace wouldn't give to be back in their room above the alley, safe and warm in the city. Maybe she should have stayed, maybe even considered what John Perkins had offered her. Could being kept by a rich and influential man be worse than this?

Mark's gloved hands on the rope held them steady, his blacksmith's muscles pressing against the sleeves of his coat, his legs controlling the horse. The furrow on his brow was deeper than she'd ever seen it. Sweat glistened on his face, his hair wet, his expression grim. But he wasn't giving up. He wasn't letting go.

Would a man like John Perkins have risked his life for Grace?

The wagon shifted again, the back inching closer to the edge causing Grace's stomach to drop as well. The top of a tree—the very top branches—were level with the wagon, its trunk planted far down the hillside. If they were to slide over the edge...

"See the branches there?" she whispered to Mistress Geyer. "If we start to go over, grab onto one of them. 'Tis the only chance we have not to be crushed on the rocks and trees below."

"Good thinking." The older woman's face was set but pale. "Very good thinking. But I am still praying that the men get us out of this wagon and all, with the Lord's help."

Praying.

That urge came over Grace again, unmistakable and undeniable and unignorable. For the first time in her life, she squeezed her eyes shut and cried out silently to the Lord. *I do not know if You are truly there, or if You even care about someone like me, but Mistress Geyer is a good woman. Please save us for her sake, if not for mine. Amen.* That was what people were supposed to say at the end of a prayer, wasn't it? Faint memories of the old woman who had watched her as a toddler came back. The woman had been a Christian and had prayed over Grace many times. How had Grace forgotten that? Why did it seem so clear now, while death hung less than an arm's length away?

The men in front of them had the horse back on its feet and a third team hitched by the time she opened her eyes. The new lead team was past the drop off, but only just, allowing a man to stand to the outside of the right-hand lead horse. Another man stood beside the left-hand horse. That one said to Mistress Geyer, "Just keep the reins steady and let us guide the horses now."

The older woman pulled in a trembling breath and nodded. "I have no other choice," she said in a low voice to Grace. "There are no reins long enough to feed back to me from that lead team."

"Are you ready, Mark?" The same man called back.

"I am, but my horse is weary. I know not how much more she can take."

"Even if you lose the right rear wheel, these horses should be able to pull the rest through." He sounded confident, but panic returned to Grace. She didn't want even one wheel hanging over the edge of the cliff.

"Here we go." He urged the horse next to him, while the man across urged his horse to lean into its harness.

Leather creaked, chains groaned, horses snorted, and Grace clung to the wagon's seat. But the wagon didn't move.

"Mistress," the one giving directions called back again. "Hand the middle teams' reins to the girl, and use the wheel horses' reins to get them moving. They are the key to unsticking the wagon."

"I cannot drive horses!" Grace kept her voice low, but her panic bled through.

"Nor vill you. The men are controlling those up front." Mistress Geyer sorted the leather straps in her hands and handed two to Grace, who stared at them as if they were vipers.

"Thee can do this, Grace." Mark's voice reached her, full of calm and confidence. "Take the reins so that Mistress Geyer can drive the others. 'Twill be fine, thee will see. Just keep the reins up off the horses' backs."

Grace swallowed the fear that climbed her throat and took the leather straps. They were thick and foreign in her grasp.

"Here we go," the one giving directions said. "Slap those wheel horses now, mistress."

Mistress Geyer did, and the wagon shuddered as the animals responded. The men up front yelled encouragement, whether to Mistress Geyer or the horses, Grace wasn't sure. But the wagon moved forward.

And sideways.

"Come on, Naxa." Mark's voice from behind was tense, but Grace couldn't turn to look, fearful that she'd drop the leather in her hands. She didn't know what might happen, but it wouldn't be good, or Mark wouldn't have told her to keep the reins up.

The wagon crept forward and sideways. Men shouted from behind, but Grace didn't understand what they were saying, or maybe she didn't want to, because the tree top beside her drew closer.

"Keep them moving." The leader urged everyone forward. "They are almost to firm ground."

He must mean the lead team, which was a long way ahead of the wagon. The tree continued to grow closer.

"I cannot hold it." Desperation filled Mark's voice and squeezed Grace's heart.

"It should be fine," someone yelled back. "We are close enough, thank God. We are going to make it."

Hope surged in Grace, and she practically strangled the reins in her hands, determined not to let them fall against the beasts working so hard to save the wagon—and their lives.

Then the wagon slipped again—and tilted.

"Hang on!" Mistress Geyer yelled, all attempts to calm her voice gone.

"The back wheel is off!" shouted the fellow on the right side of the lead team.

"Mark?" Grace added her voice to the mix. "Are you all right?"

There was no answer.

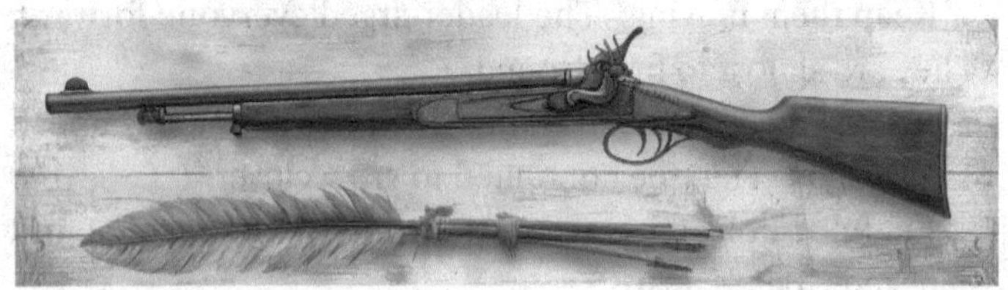

Chapter 18

NAXA'S HOOVES FLAILED IN the mud. The gallant mare was too weary. She slipped, and her hindquarters went out from under her. Mark launched himself from the saddle, keeping both hands on the rope. His feet hit the mud, but even his moccasins couldn't find purchase. He landed on his hip, still clutching the rope. Skidding forward, he was unable to stop the wagon's motion toward the cliff.

Grace's cry of his name pierced the air, but he was too focused on the remaining back wheel sliding ever closer to the drop off to answer.

Lord, provide a way of escape!

The prayer was a shout in his thoughts, nearly drowning out the voices of the men who were on firm ground now with the lead team of horses. *If I could just stop that wheel.* But there was nothing for him to grab onto.

Then a dark muzzle came into view, and Naxa was beside him. "Good girl." Mark looped the rope around his right wrist, and then grabbed onto the saddle's stirrup with his left. "Whoa, Naxa, whoa."

The mare stopped, and so did Mark's sliding, but the strain of holding the rope and the stirrup was more than he'd be able to stand for long.

"Get those horses moving!" he yelled to the men up ahead as the saddle leather groaned under the strain.

Answering yells didn't make much sense, but the wagon lurched forward, the middle team of horses must have reached good footing. Mark let the rope slide through his hand, keeping enough tension on it to prevent the wagon's rear wheel from slipping off the path, if not by more than a hand's span.

When the wagon's right rear wheel was firmly back on the path, Mark released the rope and collapsed back into the mud, staring up at Naxa. "Thee are an amazing animal." She blinked at him, then blew a breath that made her nostrils quiver. Had the Lord sent the mare to rescue Mark and the wagon? Was she the answer to his prayer?

"Mark!" Grace's cry reached him. He sat and raised a hand to let her know he was all right, but he remained seated there in the mud, catching his breath and marveling at how one of Lucy's favorite Bible verses could explain what had just happened. *Also we know that all things work together for the best unto them that love God, even to them that are called of His purpose.* If he'd never fully understood that before, he did now. If Nash hadn't sent him the mare, if the mare hadn't run from its previous owner... But the Lord was over all of it.

Mark climbed to his feet, weighted down with new layers of mud, and led Naxa off the cliff to where the wagon had been stopped farther up the trail. There were more wagons to bring across.

"You are done in." The man who had taken charge of the lead team came to meet Mark.

"Thee are right." Mark looked down at himself. "And desperately in need of a bath."

The other man chuckled. "Well, we are going to unload the remaining wagons and pack the contents across before trying to bring them up. That last one was probably the heaviest wagon left and the most likely to slide, but we can't take the chance." The man strode away, issuing orders.

Unpacking the wagons and bringing everything over on horseback would take the rest of the day, leaving Mark time to find a stream or a spring or somewhere he could wash off before the mud dried and fully encased him.

Naxa's ears perked beside him, and he glanced up.

Grace approached, each step hesitant as if she feared his reaction. Or feared him? Surely not. He'd given her no cause to, and she'd seemed to have made peace with his Indian blood.

"Grace, 'tis good to see thee made it over without harm."

"Thanks to you." Her voice was soft and full and... captivating.

Mark rubbed a hand down Naxa's sweaty neck. "'Tis Naxa thee should be thankful to. I could not have stopped the wagon from going over the cliff, but she did."

"You did it together." She summoned a small smile but kept her distance from the horse.

"Come." He motioned her closer. "She will not hurt thee. Come and touch her, show her thy gratitude."

"Touch her?" Grace took a step back, but he doubted she even realized it. It was a movement born of fear. Why was she afraid of the horse? Well, at least it was the horse and not him.

Emboldened, he reached for her hand. "Come on. 'Tis time thee were introduced." She slipped her fingers into his grimy ones, and he brought her closer to the mare. "Grace, this is Naxa. 'Tis a Lenape word for the number three, for she has the courage of three horses, as she has shown us today." He turned to the horse. "Naxa, this is Grace. Her name means favor or blessing."

"It does?" Instead of looking at the horse, she searched his face. "How do you know that?"

"'Tis how the word is used in the Bible."

"Oh, of course." Her words lacked conviction. Did she not understand the meaning, or did she not think it applied to her?

"Thee can run thy hand down her face. She enjoys that." Mark demonstrated and then waited for Grace to copy the movement.

It took her a few breaths, but she finally lifted her hand and touched the mare's face, running her fingers down the broad forehead to the velvety nose, where they lingered. "Her nose is so soft. I never imagined."

She'd never touched a horse before? Mark had learned to work with and ride horses in the Quaker village, where they relied heavily on the animals for all means of transportation as well as working the land. His Lenape tribe had not used them except for a couple of the warriors. The women had used dogs to pull the sleds with their belongings.

Grace raised her eyes to him. "What you and Naxa did, it saved our lives. How can we ever thank you?"

A slightly disturbing sensation started in Mark's chest. If it was pride, it wasn't the boastful kind, but the kind that lingered after a job well done. Surely that couldn't be a sin, could it? He rubbed his chest and cleared his throat. "'Tis enough to have thy friendship, thee and Mistress Geyer." He added the last part as an afterthought, so as not to sound too... too what?

It wasn't as if he were declaring himself a suitor. Even if Grace could, in time, come to accept his Lenape heritage, a man didn't declare himself while wearing more mud than buckskin.

The way she looked at him before returning to the wagon and Mistress Geyer, however, had a whole different sensation warming inside him.

Mistress Geyer and Grace, along with the laundresses, were instructed to set up camp not far ahead of the drop-off. It would take hours to bring the remaining wagons over. The rain had finally stopped, even the mist clearing off as evening approached. Grace stirred their largest pot filled with salt pork, along with wild onions some of the women had spotted growing along the way. Salt pork had never been Grace's favorite meal, but the army seemed to have little else on which to feed itself. And that only supplied by local Patriots, according to Mistress Geyer. Without it, the soldiers would have to forage for their supper, as the camp followers did much of the time.

Perhaps Mark would bring them another turkey soon. Where had he gone? He'd disappeared after their talk, when he'd coaxed her into petting the horse.

She rubbed her palm against her apron, still surprised that she'd done it. Although Naxa wasn't nearly the size of the team that pulled the wagon, she still seemed very large when Grace stood next to her. And brave. Grace would never forget the horse going to Mark the way she had, and then standing still, taking the weight of the wagon's rope, leaning back and holding her ground.

And Mark. He'd been in danger of being pulled in half, one arm holding the rope and the other holding onto the saddle. He was so brave. The image of him standing between her and the panther would forever be engraved behind her eyelids. How could she have thought badly of him because of his parentage, especially since she'd no idea who had fathered her? Surely, Mark had saved their lives that day.

And yet, the prayer she'd thought came back to her. Had it been just Mark and the horse? Or had God intervened?

"Let not that soup scorch, girl." Mistress Crenshaw's voice raked across Grace's ears, and she resumed her stirring.

"Aye, mistress."

To Grace's shock and disbelief, the woman's face softened. "You have had a fright today, but 'tis over and time to move on. We have a camp to feed and precious little to feed them." The words were almost... almost kind.

Mistress Geyer joined Grace by the fire, and they watched the other woman walk away. "She is a good voman. You must remember that. She carries the responsibility for the camp followers on her shoulders. Mayoor Vashington himself appointed her to the position."

"I understand."

Mistress Crenshaw couldn't allow things to become unruly, or what would happen to them? She'd seen Grace as a threat to the orderliness of the camp. Could it be that Grace had finally passed muster? If so, the harrowing experience by the cliff might have been worth it.

"Ah, here comes Mark." There was an extra layer of fondness in Mistress Geyer's voice as she looked beyond Grace.

Dressed in his Quaker clothing, Mark joined them at the fire. His raven-black hair was wet, but every speck of mud had been removed. In one hand, he carried his wet hunting clothes, also cleaned of mud. In the other, he held a brace of rabbits and a squirrel. "'Tis too late for supper, but 'twill make a pot of something for tomorrow."

"Vonderful." Mistress Geyer took the game. "Any chance to cook something besides salt pork is a blessing, is it not, Grace?"

A blessing—like her name. Heat fired along her cheeks. When had anyone, other than Mother, ever thought of her as a blessing? Men had always eyed her as if she were something to be devoured, but when Mark had looked at her earlier beside the horse, it had been different—as if he saw someone nobody else had ever seen.

What a fanciful notion. She gave the pot another vigorous stir. "I look forward to cooking tomorrow's supper."

Mark moved off, no doubt to find bushes to drape his clothing over to dry.

As the last emptied wagon reached safety and the exhausted men and women joined the camp, Grace was kept busy ladling soup and handing out the biscuits Anna baked over the fire. Grace filled bowl after bowl held over the pot, barely glancing up until one man left his there, even after the bowl was filled. Grace looked up and into the eyes of Dan Browne. His head was swathed in a bandage, dried blood marring the right side, but even injured, he leered at her.

"With this bump on my head, I can stay close for the next few days." He raked her up and down with his eyes. "I look forward to seeing more of you."

Grace's belly knotted, and the scent of salt pork mixed with the odor of his unwashed body. She had to fight the urge to gag.

"Move on," the man behind him said. "We are all hungry."

Dan leaned closer and whispered, "I am hungry for more than this slop." Then he left.

The next man stepped up, leaning on a crutch. He glanced at Dan and then back to her. "Watch out for him, missy. He be bad news."

As if she didn't already know that. But Grace gave him a wan smile and filled his bowl.

What would she do if Dan Browne came back? She was sleeping in Mistress Geyer's tent, so the man wouldn't accost her there, but could she avoid him while going about her duties in camp? What if he followed her when she fetched water? Or lurked in the bushes when she hung laundry to dry?

Fear rippled through her as another bowl was held over the pot.

"Grace? What is wrong?"

Mark's voice edged the fear aside. How had he known she was afraid? She'd learned early on to mask her emotions, a skill Mother had insisted on, saying there would come a day when she would need it. But Mark seemed able to read her very thoughts at times. She looked into his dark eyes and found only compassion there.

"Dan Browne was just here."

Mark scanned the area, but the other man had melted into the crowd. He faced Grace again. "I will stay close." Then he took a seat on a nearby barrel to eat his soup.

Just his nearness allowed Grace to relax again, smile, and continue to serve the rest of those waiting in line. When she was done, she swung the pot away from the heat and helped herself to a bowl. Mark remained on the barrel he had chosen, and Grace sat on the one next to it. Such a bold move almost shocked her, because she'd never sought out the company of a man before. But Mark was more than just a man. He'd become her protector. Not in the way John Perkins had offered her "protection," but in a way in the same way Mistress Geyer had. Well, almost.

Mistress Geyer's presence never made Grace's insides warm and her cheeks flush.

Grace ate her soup in silence, content to be near the first man she'd ever begun to trust, the man who had saved her life—more than once.

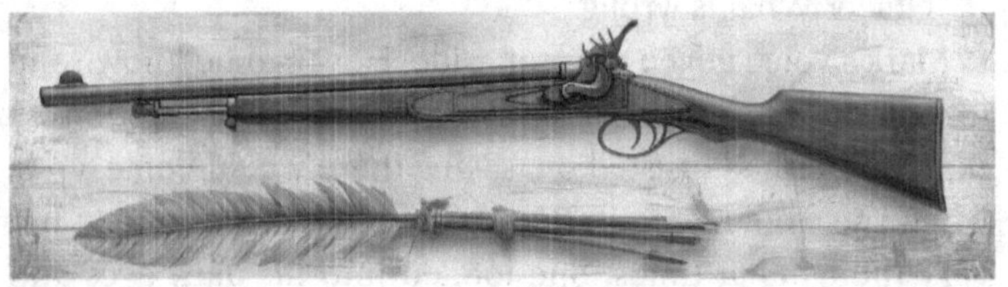

CHAPTER 19

THE ARMY HAD BEEN on the move for six days of painfully slow progress on the saturated ground. Mark relaxed in the saddle and watched the camp followers prepare for a day spent in one place. Word had come down the line that they would be staying put for perhaps several days. That might account for the smiles on travel-weary faces and the happy chatter that reached him from his vantage point on the hill.

Grace worked beside the cooking fire, no doubt preparing a kettle of porridge, a filling meal to start the day. He never had a problem finding her among the crowd. Not that she was so different, neither her manner of dress nor the way she wore her hair, but that she was... she was Grace.

The countryside all around was new to Mark. He'd never been so far east or north. It was populated by farms on rolling hills separated by woodlots, some marshes, and creeks that probably emptied into the Schuylkill River, which they had yet to cross. Rumor had it that Philadelphia was to their southeast more than a day's hard ride, and that following the Schuylkill would lead a person right there.

In the distance, a lone rider on a chestnut horse approached the army's main camp at a full gallop. No dust was raised, the ground not yet dry enough, and the blue of his coat was evident. A courier for Washington's army.

After one last check to be sure Grace was safe in the company of Mistress Geyer, for Dan Browne still convalesced in the followers' camp, Mark turned Naxa toward the main army's camp, over a mile away. He urged the mare into a canter, her hoofbeats adding to the urgency the courier's presence had kindled.

Arriving in the camp, he sought out Nash.

"Mark!" the man bellowed. "Where the devil have you been?"

Mark brought Naxa to a halt beside Nash's mount. "With the camp followers. Was that not where thee expected me to be?"

"Yes, yes, of course it was." Frustration came off the man in waves. "I should have sent for you." He pounded his fist into his thigh, startling his mount. "Maybe if you had been with the scouts—but maybes do nobody any good."

Apprehension tingled along Mark's spine. "What has happened?"

Nash waved a hand toward the courier's lathered chestnut, standing with its sides heaving next to the major general's tent. "A massacre has happened. Brigadier General Anthony Wayne's division at Paoli, cut down by those murderous Redcoats. With bayonets." The last two words came out with a mixture of venom and disgust.

Bayonets, a method of killing not unlike the Iroquois's spear that had taken his father's life. Anger churned inside Mark, an anger he would need to repent of and give over to the

Lord. Again. He brushed his thumb over the old scar on his forehead. A remembrance.

"They attacked last night, after dark, without adequate warning from the guards. The men were asleep. Too many were lost." Nash's voice dropped. "Men we could ill afford to lose."

"What can I do?" He kept his voice low and even, despite the turbulence raging inside of him.

"What can any of us do?" Nash shook his head, then speared Mark with a narrow-eyed look. "The wounded will be here shortly. We have scant provisions. Washington had hoped Wayne's division would capture some from the British. Hunt for whatever meat you can find and take it to the camp followers. The wounded will be taken there."

Mark wasn't sure what he thought he'd be asked to do, but hunting? For sure not that. He was angry enough to fight, wanted to fight, wanted to engage those who had torn up his town, leveled Lucy's house, and now slaughtered good men as they slept. He wanted revenge.

Avenge not yourselves, but give place unto wrath: for it is written, vengeance is mine: I will repay, saith the Lord.

The Bible verse came to Mark like a slap on the face. How many times had Lucy and Oliver quoted that to him when he'd first arrived in their home? He'd been full of equal measures of anger and grief and had lashed out more than once at those who had not accepted him among the Quakers. He'd even lashed out at Lucy and Oliver a few times, to his everlasting regret. But their gentle patience, their understanding and compassion had won him over. Never once had they retaliated for what he'd said or done. They had shown him another way, a better path to follow.

Could he stay on that path during wartime? If Lucy had survived, he'd be back in Birmingham, taking care of her. What did he have now to hold onto?

A pair of dove-gray eyes came to mind.

Eager for a day to wash her own clothing and not just the uniforms of the officers who demanded their clothing be spotless, Grace lugged water from the nearby stream, thankful it was in full view of everyone. Mark had disappeared first thing, and Dan Browne had once again made her uncomfortable while collecting his ration of porridge. The man looked fit enough to be back with his division. He was playing up his injury more than necessary. Yet who was she to question it? That was the surgeon's job.

A shout arose as a lone horseman approached.

Mistress Crenshaw hurried across the camp to intercept him, and several of the wounded men grabbed their muskets. But the rider wore a blue coat—not red—and appeared to be in no hurry. When he reached Mistress Crenshaw, he didn't dismount, simply spoke to her, turned the horse around, and headed back to the army's main camp.

Grace poured her two buckets of water from the creek into the largest washing kettle, then wiped her wrist across her damp forehead. "I wonder what that was all about?"

Anna paused in shredding the hard lye soap into the kettle. "I suppose we shall know soon enough. I just hope he did not leave new orders for us to move again."

"Anything but that," said another of the laundresses.

Mistress Geyer bustled over to Grace. "Leave that and come to assist me. Ve vill be getting vounded men here shortly."

"Was the army attacked?" Anna, the tallest woman in the group, stretched onto tiptoe and scanned the camp, which was visible, if too distant to discern anything.

"Not Mayoor Yeneral Greene's camp, but another vas. A terrible business." The older woman wagged her head. "Come,

Grace. You remember how to lay out bandages and all from the stone field hospital, do you not?"

Grace nodded, but her stomach pinched. The thought of packing up and moving again now sounded much better than what was to come. The broken men, the smell of blood and vomit, the screams that had rent the air—she never wanted to see or smell or hear anything like that again. But she lived with an army, so what she wanted didn't matter.

Mistress Geyer issued orders for Anna to build a new fire closer to where the surgeon would be working and to bring the kettles and get the water boiling. She took Grace by the arm and propelled her along to the far side of the camp where larger tents were already being erected.

"Why must the men be brought here?" Grace asked.

"The Mayoor Yeneral knows he must keep the vounded avay from the healthy soldiers. 'Tis too disheartening for the men to see vhat happens to their fellow soldiers. 'Tis our Christian duty to assist as best ve are able."

If Grace fainted and lost her breakfast, how was that going to help anyone?

"Once ve have everything ready, you can stay outside and keep the bandages and cloths clean." She gave Grace a pointed look. "That Dan Browne vill not bother you there. He should be back with the other men anyvay." She snorted. "Yoost keep the bandages and cloths clean. Even if they have no time to dry, vet and clean is better than bloody and dirty. The Bible says to cleanse all filthiness of the flesh and spirit. Ve cannot help the poor men vith their spirits, but ve can see their flesh cleaned, at least."

They arrived at the first large tent and set about doing as they had in the meetinghouse turned hospital. The same young men were assisting the same surgeon. Grace and Mistress Geyer worked side by side until the noise from outside heralded the first wagonload of wounded.

Grace ducked out and hurried to the fire Anna had roaring under the kettle. It wasn't long before the rumors of what had happened filtered toward them. A massacre in the night, men run through with bayonets, some hacked to pieces, many taken as prisoners of war. Despite the warmth of the day and the heat from the fire, a chill settled over Grace. Would the British soldiers follow the wagons of wounded to their camp? Would they attack in the night and stab them all to death? Surely not the camp followers, the injured men and the women who followed after and supported their husbands, fathers, and brothers.

They wouldn't, would they?

She wished Mark were near.

At a likely watering spot near a stream, far away from both armies, Mark crouched in the cover of brambles and waited. He'd left Naxa tied to a tree just inside the woodlot, where she could graze. A turkey or rabbits wouldn't be enough to feed the wounded—assuming they were many—along with the camp followers. He needed to bring in a deer. The path he'd followed since leaving the horse was riddled with the distinctive hoofprints. The air was still and wouldn't carry his scent, and he was back in his hunting clothing, making it easy to blend into the background. How many times had he done this same thing to provide meat for Lucy? And before that, he'd gone out with his uncle and the other hunters of their Lenni Lenape village.

If he had a bow and arrow, could he still shoot as straight as he once had? Or was he too accustomed to a musket in his hands? Maybe, if he had time, he could fashion a bow for himself and the arrows to go with it, but they'd need to stay in one place for a while for him to locate the right type of wood and flint, and he'd need another turkey to provide the feathers for fletching.

Lost in his thoughts, Mark didn't see the young buck until it was almost to the stream. It had two points on one antler and three on the other. Old enough to be meaty, young enough to be tasty. The animal approached the water with its head up, ears swiveling, alert for any danger. There were panthers and wolves in the area. Even a hungry bear might try to bring the buck down. But not today. Today, the men back at camp needed the meat to recuperate from their injuries. In the manner Mark had been taught as a young child, he muttered a blessing on the animal he was about to take, thanking it for sustaining his people. The urge to fight had left Mark again. The need to kill to survive was a different thing. He eased the musket into position and waited for the best shot. Then, he squeezed the trigger.

The musket rammed into his shoulder, and gunpowder billowed before its muzzle. Mark rose and stepped beyond the gray cloud. The buck was no longer in sight, but he tracked it to where it had fallen some three rods from the stream. It took him little time to dress it out and drag it from the woodlot.

Naxa, a seasoned warhorse, didn't flinch as Mark hauled the gutted carcass across her saddle. The scent of blood was strong, but she'd doubtless smelled it plenty of times in battle, even though, judging by her teeth, she was fairly young.

He mounted behind the carcass and headed back to camp at a slow trot to keep the buck from banging against Naxa's shoulders. The angle of the sun said it was well past noon. His stomach grumbled. He'd missed breakfast and eaten only a handful of late-season blackberries he'd found in the woodlot.

He kept Naxa close to the trees, although he was well north of where the armies should be. Something colorful caught his eye, and he moved the horse closer to inspect it. It was a persimmon tree, several of them, in fact. Mark dismounted and plucked the fruit from the branches, filling the haversack that had come on Naxa's saddle. Most of the fruit was still unripe, and he put those in the bottom. The riper fruit he put on top to avoid it getting squashed. And the very ripest he ate, smiling when Naxa helped herself to one. He moved her farther away from the tree.

"'Twould be best if thee did not eat such things. Horses are made to eat grass, not fruit."

The mare snorted and shook her mane, the buck moving with her motions. Mark could have eaten another dozen of the soft, sweet fruits, but that wouldn't get the meat to camp. He grabbed just two more, mounted again, and set off.

They arrived in camp about an hour later, and he stopped Naxa near the cooking fire. Grace wasn't there. Another laundress told Mark that she was helping outside of the hospital tents across the camp.

"The meat is for the wounded," Mark said. "Should I take it there?"

"Nay." The girl wiped her forehead with the back of her wrist. "Leave it here. They have their hands full with other things there, and glad I am not to witness it." She pointed at a trestle table nearby. "Leave the deer there, and I shall skin it."

"I would like the hide, if thee do not mind." One of the things he'd learned from Betsy and Sarah was how to tan a hide. In the tribe, that had been a woman's task, and no man would have done it. But among the Quakers, the line between male and female work was blurred, and while Betsy and Sarah had been scandalized at the notion of teaching him, Lucy had encouraged it. Once the old women had grown used to the idea, they'd even taught him to make his own moccasins. The two pair he had would wear out eventually, so the hide would come in handy.

"I shall set it aside for you."

"Thank thee. I also have persimmons, a few of them ripe, and the rest should ripen soon."

That brought a smile to her face. She set her spoon aside, took the haversack, and emptied it into a large wooden bowl. Her grin widened at the bounty. "'Twill make a few tarts, I should say. A more than welcome treat."

Mark took back the empty haversack, then laid the buck's carcass on the table. He cared for Naxa, tying her to the picket line next to the wagon teams before heading to the hospital tents.

It wasn't difficult to spot Grace near the kettle over the fire, but finding her in the company of Dan Browne resurrected Mark's urge to fight.

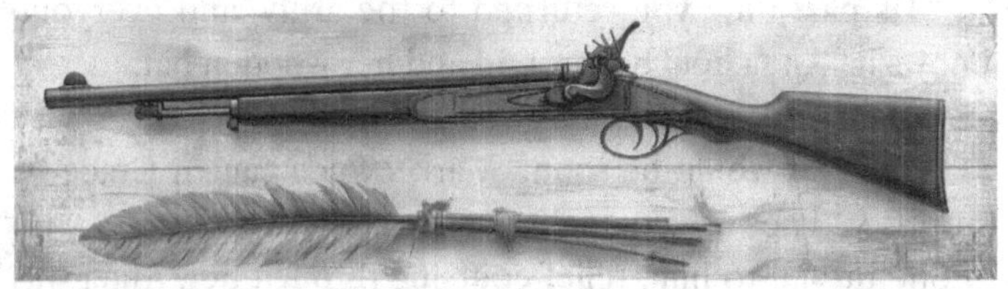

CHAPTER 20

"I TOLD YOU TO leave me alone." Grace dumped another heap of disgustingly bloody bandages into the already dirty water. She needed to haul in clean water again, but how? If she went to the stream, Dan would follow her. Everyone was so busy caring for the injured, who would notice?

Anna returned from delivering an armload of washed linens to the tent. Seeing Dan, she picked up one of the heavy wooden bats they used to stir the wash and scowled at him. She was a couple of inches taller than Dan and appeared more menacing than him at the moment. "You have no business here, Dan Browne. Be off with you."

"My business is my own," he shot back, but he also retreated a step.

"Then take it elsewhere." She shook the bat at him. "We have work to do and men with honest injuries to attend to."

Dan's scowl deepened, but he backed another step. "My injury was honest. I near to got my head bashed in."

"'Tis past time you returned to the army, and everyone knows it." Anna held her ground and her wooden bat.

"I shall return when I am good and ready."

"Pray that would be soon." Mark's voice caught Grace by surprise. "Thee are no doubt needed there."

She turned to him, relief coursing through her. Anna was doing a good job of fending Dan off, but with Mark close by, she felt safer. Then she noticed the blood on the front of his coat and top of his breeches. "You are hurt!"

"Nay." He brushed at the drying blood. "'Tis from a buck I brought in." He tipped his head toward the hospital tent. "I was sent to hunt for the men so they would have meat to hasten their recovery."

Footsteps retreated behind Grace, and she turned as Dan disappeared around a tent. "I wish he would leave me be."

"Between my bat and him"—Anna poked her thumb at Mark—"we can keep Dan Browne away."

"You were doing a good job of it, even by yourself." Grace smiled at her tall and fearsome friend.

"'Tis because the last time the dog came sniffing around, I let it be known who my father is." Anna grinned. "He would not wish to upset the daughter of Sergeant Bream, the man he must report back to, now would he?" She winked.

"Indeed, thee seemed to have things well in hand before I arrived." Mark nodded to Anna, but there was a thread of tension in his voice. It wasn't obvious, but Grace heard it.

"Is everything all right?" she asked.

"'Twill be." Mark watched where Dan had gone. "When that man is back in the regular camp."

"Ugh." Anna had come closer to the fire. With her bat, she lifted the bandages and rags Grace had added to the kettle, and red water streamed off them. "Twill not do. We must make another trip to the stream for fresh water."

"Allow me to do that for thee." Mark walked to where several buckets were stacked and took two.

Grace followed and took two more. "'Twill take both of us, and Anna can empty the dirty water." She pointed toward the stream. "'Tis right over there."

"I worry about thee with Dan Browne lurking about." The tension was still in Mark's tone. "Perhaps I should put a burr in someone's ear concerning his return to the regular camp—the sooner, the better."

Nothing would make Grace happier, but... "Can you do that without causing trouble for yourself?"

A wry smile pulled at his lips. "I think so, but what can the man do to *me*? 'Tis thee I am concerned for."

A scream from the hospital tent reached them, even though they'd moved a distance away. Grace cringed. There'd been too many cries throughout the day. Men in such unbearable pain, men having hands, arms, or even legs sawn away. Her stomach rebelled at the thought.

As if he'd read her mind, Mark lowered his voice and said, "'Tis a bad business, war."

"I am glad you are a Quaker and will stay away from the fighting." The words came out in a rush, but Grace didn't wish them back. She meant them. The thought of Mark being hurt—maybe killed—was too awful to contemplate. But why had her words caused him to grimace? Had she overstepped the boundaries of their friendship?

Of course she had. Others may look at Mark as an Indian, but everyone—even Mark—knew her to be something just as bad. Or worse. As hard as Mother had tried to raise her like a lady, everyone knew that Grace was nothing but a bastard. How she'd hated that word growing up. She'd been born of sin and was destined to live a life stained with it. Hauling water and helping in the camp was going to be her life until the end of the war.

She had no idea what would become of her afterward.

"Is something bothering thee?" Mark carried the two larger buckets, leaving Grace the smaller two. They were almost back to the fire, and she had not said a word since telling him she was glad he didn't fight.

She looked up at him. "Do you think the British will come? Here, I mean, to our camp? Might they follow the wagons of the wounded?"

"'Tis doubtful. They know Washington would not be here, and 'tis him they must find and stop." He set his buckets near the kettle. "Surely they are headed for Philadelphia now, to take possession of the city." Instead of reassuring her, that seemed to distress her all the more.

"What is it, Grace?" He kept his voice low, although Anna had stepped away.

"My mother is in Philadelphia."

"The British are not known for being a danger to ordinary citizens. As I understand it, and I have only what I overheard at the smithy to go by, the people in the city may have to take in soldiers, quarter them during their stay, but they should come to no harm."

"As if having a Redcoat living in one's house were not bad enough." Anna joined them. "They must feed them, do their laundry, clean up after them." The tall woman snorted. "'Tisn't right, I tell you. They treat us colonists as if we were dirt beneath their feet, all looking down their long noses at us."

Similar comments had found their way into the smithy for the past few years. The British had alienated the colonists with their restrictive ordinances and unfair taxation. Mark didn't know what had struck the final blow that had sparked the revolution, but those fighting were fighting for their homes, their families, their way of life, and even more compelling... their very freedom. Mark had benefitted from that freedom with the Quakers.

When he'd lived with the tribe, there had always been the threat of raids by other tribes, and of course, clashes with the white men who ventured that far west. Not that there hadn't been peaceful, happy times. Running through the forest in his breechclout and moccasins, the wind in his hair, racing with his friends. Stories told around the warm fires at night in the longhouse where he and Mother had lived surrounded by other families, relatives of his mother. Journeys with his uncle, who had taught him to hunt and to fight and the ways of a warrior, as much as a young boy could learn.

Ways he'd put aside to fit in with the Quakers.

"Mother lives in a rented room. I do not think she would be able to house a soldier." Grace's brow wrinkled as if that didn't erase her fears.

She'd said she didn't know who her father was. Her mother must have raised her alone. As awful as it'd been watching his father killed, at least Mark had known him for his first six years, been loved by him, and loved him in return.

"Dump in the water." Anna finished shaving soap into the kettle before stepping out of the way.

Mark lifted the buckets and poured the water. Even with four, the kettle wasn't full. "I shall fetch more to fill it up, and leave the buckets filled for thee."

Grace nodded and stirred the kettle, but whatever was bothering her still creased her brow.

Was it Dan Browne? Mark took a firmer grip on the buckets' rope handles. He'd ride to the main camp later and see if Nash could have the man recalled to duty. Even as he thought it, guilt pricked him again, as it had when Grace had declared she was relieved that Mark didn't fight. Could he, in good conscience, demand another man fight because he was fit—when Mark himself refused to do so?

He was an Indian and a Quaker, but he wasn't a hypocrite. He'd have to keep close to Grace himself to ensure her safety.

A prospect that was in no way unpleasant.

In their shared tent many hours later, Grace and Mistress Geyer readied themselves for sleep.

Grace pulled her blanket over herself against the chill of the mid-September night. "How many men were brought in?"

"I lost count, but one of the nurses said fifty." The older woman pulled a shawl around her shoulders before sinking onto her narrow cot. "It seemed like more. So many vere badly torn up. 'Tvas nothing short of butchery, if you ask me." She clicked her tongue. "Savagery. There is no other vord for it, to be sure."

From all the blood they'd laundered out of the bandages and rags and the soldiers' clothing, Grace had no doubt Mistress Geyer was telling the truth. It'd taken Grace a long time to get every last trace of it washed from her hands and from under her fingernails. The coppery scent of it still clung to her skin, even after all the scrubbing with lye soap.

"I hope ve vill have a rest now, give the men time to heal." Mistress Geyer rolled to her side and faced Grace. The light from the fire outside shone through the canvas of the tent enough that they could see each other. "The deer Mark brought in vill last us a couple of days, but I hope he vill hunt again soon. Ve have very few provisions left, not enough to feed the camp, much less all the vounded."

"When I see him, I will say as much." Grace shifted to get more comfortable on her layer of pine boughs under an oiled canvas that served as her bed. "He told me today that the British will march to Philadelphia and occupy the city."

"I have heard the same."

"My mother is there."

"I had forgotten that. You must vorry for her."

"Of course I do." But Mother made her living off men, and it didn't really matter what color coat they wore. Nothing much would change for her or the other women of the backstreets. Yet she couldn't shake her worry.

Despite the hard work in the camp, the scant food, and the ever-present problem of men who wanted her attention, Grace was glad to be there. Any urge she'd had to flee to the city was gone. And it wasn't hard to understand why. She squirmed further under her blanket and closed her eyes. The image of Mark's face, his hair loose, his eyes locked on hers, stayed with her. In spite of everything, she was content to remain with the camp because of him. Not just him, of course. There was Mistress Geyer too. What would have happened to Grace if the kind woman hadn't befriended her and taken her into her own tent?

Dan Browne's ugly image pushed Mark's aside.

If Grace returned to Philadelphia, all her mother's attempts to raise her as a lady would be for nothing. Mother had known it. Grace had seen the truth in her eyes. If she returned, Grace would become just like her mother. There was nothing else for her in Philadelphia. Nobody would hire her as a governess in that city, even though she could read, write, and do math.

Grace was stained by her beginnings.

What was it Mark had said? She tried to remember his exact words from that day on the hilltop in the rain, after he'd explained about the Quaker beliefs. *If the Lord accepts us as we are, should we not also accept each other that way?* She'd told him that she didn't have a father and he'd not backed away from her. He'd not acted at all displeased nor said anything unkind. He didn't know about Mother, however. Could he learn even that and still look at her as if... as if she might be worthy of his... ? She struggled with the notion that had first come to her days ago.

Worthy of his love?

Could he marry someone who wasn't a Quaker—or an Indian?

Could she marry someone who was both? What little she knew of weddings was that they took place in the bride's parents' home. The idea of standing in her mother's rented room with Mark was unthinkable, but she was not yet twenty-one and would need Mother's consent to marry.

No minister would perform the ceremony, of course, so they'd have to find a justice of the peace.

The gentle snoring of Mistress Geyer interrupted Grace's fanciful thoughts, which was just as well. Such thoughts could lead to nothing. Nothing but heartache.

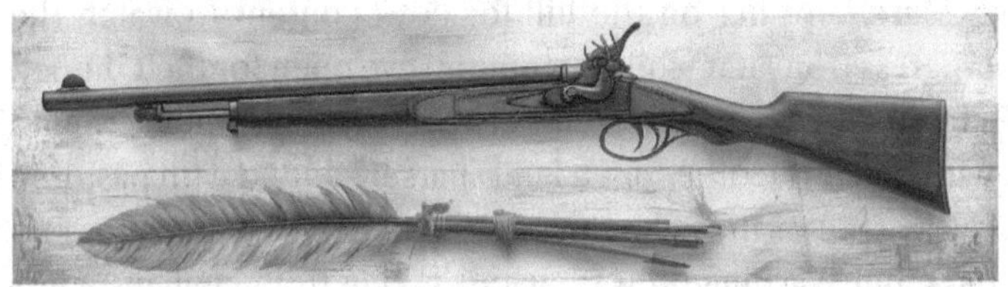

CHAPTER 21

IT'D BEEN A WEEK and a half since the wounded from the Paoli Massacre had arrived at the followers' camp. Mark tugged his neckcloth higher to combat the chilly morning breeze. The almanac he'd seen earlier on Nathanael's desk had been crossed off up to the first Friday in October.

Many of the wounded men were back on their feet and had returned to their units, including Dan Browne. Only the grievously wounded would be left behind in sympathetic Patriot households. As for the rest of the army, they were on the move again.

Naxa stamped her foot and shook her mane. She'd proven herself a good companion while hunting these past days, bringing in meat to feed the wounded and the camp followers, but this was what she'd been trained for. A war horse, she sensed that they should be moving out with the masses below them.

Mark kept her on the hill for now, content to watch the progress from afar while keeping an eye open for their dinner. The line of wagons snaked between two hills, one carpeted with pines, the other open land sparsely dotted with pastured cattle. One of those bovines would feed both camps for two days, but Washington was against taking from civilians without compensation. And the army had nothing to compensate them with, according to Nash.

Stealing was stealing, whether it was meant to feed an army or not, and stealing was a sin. Washington wasn't a Quaker, but from everything Mark had heard since coming to the camp, he was a Christian man on firm moral footings. That caused more than one of the lesser officers, including Nash, to grumble. Mark, on the other hand, admired the general for his stance.

It was one thing to keep your moral compass during good times. It was something else again to keep it during stressful or dire times. Mistress Geyer had cautioned him about that. It was something Mark still struggled with when he thought of Lucy and her house blown to ruins, but the struggle was lessening.

Killing deer and turkeys, and even a black bear to feed the army was nothing like turning his musket—and now the bow and arrows he'd had time to fashion—on another human being. He'd been angry enough, grieved enough, right after the battle at Birmingham to take up the gun and use it. Three weeks had passed, and he'd had a lot of time to think and settle into his new routine. His rage was once again under control, and his grief hit him less hard if no less frequently.

The mare shifted beneath him, giving a loud snort that blew twin plumes of white into the air.

"All right, girl. I am woolgathering this morning." Mark scanned the countryside before and after the line of wagons.

Seeing nothing to alarm him, he turned the horse toward the trees and touched her sides with his heels.

Hours later, he brought a turkey, a raccoon, and a partridge to where the wagons had stopped to rest the horses and eat a quick meal at midday. He'd taken all three with his bow and arrows, saving his lead shot and powder, the army having none of either to spare.

"Vhat a blessing you are." Mistress Geyer came to Naxa's side and took the carcasses from Mark. "Ve vill make wilderness stew for supper. Now rest your poor horse and have a bit of bread and cheese." She pointed to where Grace was slicing both on a makeshift table consisting of a plank put over two barrels.

Mark tied Naxa and got in line. When it was his turn, he got not only a slice of bread and cheese, but a brilliant smile. Had Grace any idea how appealing she was? Once again, that feeling of being a stag in the forest came over him, and he had to force himself to look away. He settled on the ground not far from Grace and ate his meal. He'd filled his canteen at the stream where he'd watered Naxa not even an hour prior. The water was still cool and refreshing.

When Grace approached, he rose and looked around for something for her to sit on.

"Do not bother yourself." She came to stand beside him. "I have sat all morning on that hard wagon seat. Being on my feet is a good thing."

He couldn't help but notice, not for the first time, that she didn't pray before she ate. When Mistress Geyer prayed, Grace always bowed her head, but if they ate separately, she never did. He wanted to ask about that, but she wasn't a Quaker, and he didn't know how other churches did such things. Perhaps they only prayed when more than one was present. While that seemed odd to Mark, his Quaker ways undoubtedly seemed odd to others.

When Grace finished eating, she turned her face to his. "Have you heard where we are going?"

"Nay. The major general told me to stay with the followers and to hunt. But I did overhear that the orders came from Washington himself."

"Mistress Geyer is hoping we are heading somewhere to set up camp for the winter. She said we shall need to build shelters and forage for food to feed ourselves through the cold months."

He hadn't thought about that, but it made sense. "I wonder where they stayed last winter."

"She said a place called Morristown, in New Jersey, a long way from here."

"'Tisn't likely the army would go back to the same place. The British have probably destroyed it, and would certainly know about it."

"Indeed. She said they built a log-house city there, and that we shall have to start from scratch in a new place."

With maybe six weeks before the snows came? That wasn't enough time to build shelters and store away food. Mark had grown up knowing lean times. The Lenni Lenape were growers and gatherers as well as hunters. The women were skilled at growing corn, beans, and squash as well as harvesting berries, roots, and nuts in their seasons. The warriors hunted for meat and fished. But even so, when the snow lay thick around the longhouses and the howling winds shook the bark coverings, there was hunger inside. Dark days with never enough to eat. It had been that deprivation, along with Mother's long friendship with Lucy Sharp, that had driven her to travel alone across the Ohio territory and most of Pennsylvania to bring Mark to Birmingham.

Mistress Crenshaw's voice cut into Mark's musings. "Back on the wagons! Time to move on!"

"What will you do this afternoon?" Grace asked.

"More hunting." Mark picked up his musket and bow, slinging them both across his back. "If what Mistress Geyer says is true, the camp will need the meat."

Grace wrapped her shawl around her shoulders. "And 'tis cool enough to keep it for a few days, should you bring extra." She glanced around the camp, now bustling in preparation to depart. "Unless we get more wounded."

They were heading almost straight east, while Philadelphia was to the southeast, but that didn't mean they wouldn't encounter more Redcoats before they were done. The British outnumbered Washington's forces by a wide margin. Howe could afford to divide his army, something Washington had done at the Battle of Long Island the previous year, which had nearly ended the war before it'd fully begun. Word of that devasting defeat had even reached the smithy in Birmingham and had kept tongues wagging for weeks.

Mark untied Naxa and mounted, then rode a wide loop around the line of wagons and those who walked beside them, scanning and scouting, looking for any sign of the enemy.

It still shook him sometimes, thinking of other people as enemies. He'd grown up with that mindset, mostly toward the Iroquois, but the Quakers had instilled in him a different way of looking at things—that all of mankind had been made in the image of God and was precious to Him.

Even the Iroquois.

Even the British.

His scouting complete and no danger sighted, he turned Naxa toward the main army, traveling south of them by several miles. On the roundabout way he traveled, he took shot at another turkey, his arrow flying true. He bent from the saddle and grasped the end of the arrow, pulling it and the turkey off the ground in one fluid motion. His uncle would have been proud of that shot. Proud that Mark had remembered how to balance the shaft of his arrows with fletching that allowed them to soar with such accuracy. It was a skill every Lenni Lenape boy learned.

It took Mark a while to locate the army. They were ahead of the followers' camp and not exposed in open country. They were traveling a road through dense forest when he arrived. Nash was easy to spot with his pale blond hair. Mark rode up beside him.

Nash leaned over and eyed the bird. "Please say that turkey is for me."

"If thee wish." Mark had already removed his arrow, so he passed the carcass over. "The followers' camp has theirs already."

"Anything besides salt pork is priceless." Nash secured the bird's feet to his saddle with a leather strap. "How go things in the other camp?"

"Most of the women were walking when I left, the wagons driven by the wounded who can handle the reins. They are gathering what they can forage for food as they walk."

"We should do the same, but 'twould slow us down."

Mark glanced at Nash. "Are thee in haste to get somewhere?"

"Washington's courier was here no more than an hour ago. Howe has taken Philadelphia and moved his men to winter in Germantown. We are to march—all night if need be—to engage the British there."

"Germantown?"

"Just north of Philadelphia." Nash frowned at him. "Have you been nowhere, man?"

"Ohio Territory and western Pennsylvania, even north once to the big water when I was very young. Not this far east, however."

"That will change tonight. Ride forward with me."

Mark urged Naxa to follow Nash, and they came up to Nathanael and his more senior officers.

"Major General Greene," Nash said. "Mark is here. Where would you have him direct the followers' camp?"

Nathanael turned in his saddle and spied the turkey tied to Nash's horse. His eyebrows rose. "I assume thee brought that, Mark."

"Indeed."

The sigh that escaped Nash probably signified his resignation to sharing the bounty, if they were able to cook it after the march and before the impending battle.

"Good man. I hear thee are keeping the wounded well supplied. In the future, we may need thee to spread thy hunting efforts to include the army here."

Mark warmed at the praise. "As it pleases thee."

"The followers' camp, sir?" Nash prompted.

"Keep them at least ten miles northwest of us. The fighting will no doubt be intense, and we shall need them for the wounded." Nathanael shook his head. "I like not the idea of arriving travel-weary to the fight, but those are our orders." His eyes met Mark's. "Do not cross the Schuylkill River." With that, he faced forward and urged his horse on.

Mark reined Naxa to the side of the column, following Nash.

"Our scouts say the British are all south of us," Nash said, "so your followers should be safe, but keep your eyes open. Should you spy even the thread of a red coat, ride to me in all haste." He glanced over Naxa. "I have heard your mare can handle the strain. Word of her bravery moving the wagons reached even the major general. He was impressed."

Mark stroked the horse's neck. "She is a good mount."

Nash cleared his throat. "I hope to see you again after the battle." The words were spoken softly by a man who understood what was to come.

"I hope to see thee as well." Mark stopped Naxa and held her back as Nash galloped to catch up to the other mounted officers. Would he see any of them again? As the foot soldiers passed by, one glared at Mark.

Dan Browne.

The man's hatred ran deeper than just having his attempts with Grace foiled. Mark could feel it to his bones. It was his Lenape blood that riled Browne. Mark had dealt with enough prejudice in his life to recognize it. He could practically smell it.

That a woman looked with favor on him—an Indian—while rebuffing Browne had to be the greatest insult the man could imagine. He would always see himself as superior to Mark because of the color of his skin, no matter how much it stank. Nothing Mark could do would change that. Only God could heal such hatred.

Mark reined the mare around and into the forest. He had his orders.

"Hello, ladies." Mark walked his mare up to the two women. Both were young and attractive, but Grace was the one who made him feel as if he'd come home. "Thee should catch up to the wagons and stay close. We may be traveling well into the evening."

"Has something happened?" Anna glanced around.

Grace's gray eyes remained on Mark, so he addressed her. "The army marches to meet Howe's forces. We are to keep our distance but be close enough to attend to the wounded."

"Again." The word slipped from Grace on a breath.

"Do you know where?" Anna asked.

"A place called Germantown."

"'Tis near Philadelphia," Grace said. "I was there once as a child, holding Mother's hand, walking through the snow. I remember light from candles in the windows reflecting on the snow." From her winsome smile, it must have been a fond memory.

No fond memories would be created by what was to happen there when the armies clashed. "Catch a ride on the wagons if thee can. It may be a long night, and the day to follow even longer." He urged Naxa ahead of the women.

"Where are you going?" Grace called after him.

He turned in the saddle. She was beautiful standing there, eyes meeting his, mouth slightly open as if she couldn't wait for his answer. What would it be like to have a home somewhere and a woman like her to greet him at the door after a day of work at the forge? Not just any woman—Grace. He cleared his throat to gather his thoughts before he could answer. "To scout a place to set up camp before it grows too dark."

He clicked to the mare, and she cantered off, but he looked back twice to be sure the women were hurrying to catch up to the wagons. And maybe just to see Grace again. Assured they had obeyed, he thumped the horse with his heels and let her gallop the length of the line of wagons. He nodded to Mistress Crenshaw as he passed the lead wagon upon which she rode. He'd already filled her in on the orders from Nathanael.

Once ahead of the wagons, he slowed Naxa to a trot she could maintain for miles. The land was flattening out, the higher hills behind and to the north. As the sun crept toward the horizon, Mark angled to the southeast. He topped a low rise. In the distance, sunlight gleamed off water. That must be the Schuylkill.

A shallow valley with a creek flowing through it flanked a curve in the river. No cattle were in sight, and no homesteads nearby. So close to the river, the creek probably flooded in the spring. This time of year, however, it would make a good camp, offering fresh water and plenty of grazing for the horses. It would also keep them on this side of the river, as ordered. Nathanael hadn't made a fuss about that order, but there had been a reason for it, Mark was sure.

He headed back to the wagons. They would need to speed things up. No doubt Mistress Crenshaw would give him an earful, but orders were orders, whether he was officially in the army or not. Getting the women settled before full dark was his main concern.

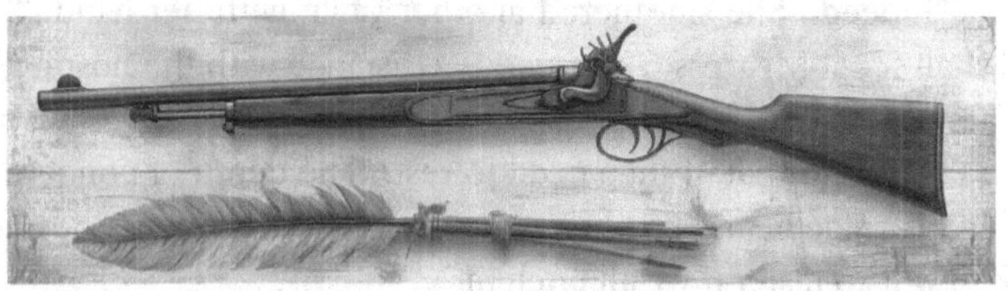

CHAPTER 22

GRACE ROSE FROM POUNDING the last tent post into place with a rock and stifled a yawn.

Mark had pushed them hard to reach this place. They'd been delayed when two of the wagons got mired in a creek they crossed. It must be near midnight, the stars above so clear and bright, but with a line of clouds banked to the west. The clouds would make for a warmer night, but they didn't need rain again. Grace had just gotten used to being fully dry.

It was past time to sleep, but Mistress Geyer remained at the hospital tents. As much as Grace's blankets were calling her name, she headed in that direction instead.

"Are thee all set up?" Mark's voice came out of the darkness beside her.

Grace startled but was not afraid. How odd it seemed, after all the years of avoiding men, that his presence was more calming than any she'd ever known, perhaps including Mother's.

"Indeed." She smothered another yawn with her hand. "I shall see if Mistress Geyer needs assistance with the hospital tents."

"I can do that, if thee need to rest." The depth of concern in his voice nearly had her agreeing, but she shook her head. "'Twill go faster if we all pitch in."

"Then I shall join thee." He fell into step with her, the darkness curling around them except for the brilliant points of light above and the scattered fires throughout the camp.

The hospital tents were on the opposite edge of the camp from the laundresses. Mark sprinted forward and helped two of the surgeon's mates steady the main pole of the largest tent while others secured the outside poles. Grace sought out Mistress Geyer.

"You have everything ready for sleeping already?" the older woman asked.

"I have gotten much faster at it." Grace had known nothing about tents or camps or much of anything before joining the followers. Her education had been swift and sometimes blunt when her faults and ignorance were pointed out. But she had survived those first weeks, had earned a grudging acceptance from Mistress Crenshaw, and had even been praised for her work preparing tasty meals. Mother would be shocked to learn her daughter was cooking for all the laundresses in camp and doing a good job of it.

Grace worked on the surgeon's trays with Mistress Geyer, getting everything ready for whatever might come in the morning. It was honest work, even if it didn't pay. She was learning skills she'd be able to use after the war. Cooking could transfer to a domestic situation, perhaps working in a big house in some city. Not Philadelphia, of course, lest any man in the house had visited her mother. She'd have to move somewhere like New York or Boston and start a new life.

Alone.

She peeked at Mark through the darkness, his black hair loose and blending into the shadows, but the white of his hunting shirt visible beneath his open coat. Could Mark ever look at her and see past her less-than-respectful beginnings? Not in the way Dan Browne or others of his ilk looked at her, but like Mark sometimes did. Those times that made her uncomfortable, but not in a frightful or repugnant way. In a way she wished to explore, in a way that hinted at something more, something better than she'd ever imagined.

"Ve are as ready as ve can be tonight." Mistress Geyer put a hand to her lower back and twisted, her spine popping with the motion.

Time to put aside a silly girl's daydreams and get back to reality. "Then we should seek our beds. Mark said tomorrow could be a very long day."

"I expect he is right, since he heard from the mayoor yeneral himself."

Casting one last glance at Mark across the camp, and looking away when their eyes met, Grace left with Mistress Geyer. Tomorrow would bring more wounded, more dying, more work, and little time to fret about what would happen after the war. But tonight she could sink into her blankets and—just for a few minutes—let her mind indulge in her daydreams again.

Reality and the war would return with the sun.

Fog so thick he couldn't see two strides ahead of him greeted Mark as he crawled from under the wagon before daybreak. The laundresses' fire had burned to embers, making a tiny orange smudge through the fog. He knelt and coaxed them back to life, adding scraps of wood someone had left next to the fire the evening before. In the kindled flames, the fog seemed denser.

Would Washington's plans proceed in such weather? How could anyone fight against those they could not see?

The women who shared the fire emerged from their tents as the camp stirred to life. They were used to rising before the dawn, being ready to move at a moment's notice. Or, as with this morning, preparing for their part in the battle. No army could survive without the brave women who followed after and did so much of the difficult work. The clean-up work. When they weren't patching up wounded, they were patching the clothing and tents, knitting socks, even mending shoes and boots as best they could.

Grace slipped from her tent, almost spectral in the fog. She disappeared into the brush that grew near the camp, no doubt to attend to her personal needs.

Mark turned his back and waited, hands held to catch the warmth of the fire until a scream broke the stillness.

Grace.

Her scream echoed in the fog as she stepped back.

A man was lying on his back with his head nearest to her, hair matted with dried blood, his outline murky in the fog. He looked up at Grace with dull eyes and blinked.

"Grace!" Mark's voice cut through the fog.

"Here. I am here." She couldn't take her eyes from the wounded man. His coat was green with bright red trimming and large brass buttons, his breeches, which had once been bleached nearly white, but were now a mass of dirt and stains. He wore leather boots that pulled up above his knees.

Mark rushed to her side, a knife in his hand. "Are thee all right?"

"Aye." She pointed to the soldier. "I found him there. I nearly stepped on him."

"A soldier." Mark walked around the man, who followed him with his eyes. "What is thy name?"

The soldier shook his head, then grimaced.

Two more men from the camp crashed through the brush, both with muskets in hand. The first one stopped and pointed his weapon at the man on the ground. "He be a dirty Hessian!"

Mark stepped between the two men, right in front of the musket.

Grace gasped.

Mark raised a hand toward the man from camp. "The man is injured. He is no threat."

"He has killed plenty of our boys." The musket didn't waver.

"He will kill no one today. Neither shall we. The man is defenseless."

"Check him for a knife." The musket-wielding man nodded toward the one in Mark's hand.

Mark turned his back on the musket and knelt beside the wounded Hessian. "Do thee have a knife?"

The Hessian shook his head, but it was clear that he didn't understand the question.

"I do not think he speaks English," Grace said.

"Most likely not." The second wounded soldier who had come with the one holding the musket pulled a long knife from his belt and showed it to the man on the ground. "Got one of these?" He tapped the blade and pointed at the Hessian.

Very slowly, keeping eye contact with Mark, the Hessian tapped the side of his coat.

Mark reached in and withdrew the blade, then he patted down the rest of this clothing. He turned his face back to the one still pointing the musket. "He is disarmed. Help me get him to the hospital tent. He needs the surgeon."

"We should just shoot him."

"Nay!" Grace stepped in front of him, pushing the muzzle of his gun aside. "'Twould be murder."

"He be a Hessian!" the man roared in her face.

Strong hands moved her out of the way, and Mark faced the armed man. "He is a human being, created in the image of God, the same as thee and I. He is disarmed and in need of the surgeon. Help me get him there, or go back to camp."

"I will not help a Hessian nor take orders from a lousy Indian." He tried to raise the musket again, but the other soldier from the camp seized his arm.

"Go back, Harold." Something passed between them, the moment stretching in silence blanketed in fog, and then Harold stomped off.

The remaining soldier gestured to the Hessian. "You take his feet." He slipped his arms behind the man's shoulders. Between them, they carried the Hessian.

Grace followed, heart still beating wildly against her ribs.

The laundresses were in a huddle near the fire, but Anna and Mistress Geyer rushed forward when they emerged from the fog and brush.

"Are you all right?" Mistress Geyer eyed Grace up and down.

"Fine. 'Twas just the fright of almost stepping on him in the fog. He needs the surgeon."

"I vill see to it." The older woman hustled off after Mark and the other man carrying the Hessian.

"I wanted to run in after you," Anna said, "but those two men who followed Mark told us to stay. And then the one returned with his musket and looked fit to kill someone."

"He was. He would have shot that soldier where he lay, had not Mark stopped him." Grace would never forget the way Mark had stepped right in front of the musket's barrel, fearless, and faced Harold down. For that matter, so had she. Her knees grew a little weak.

"'Twas enough excitement already, but we are sure to have more. Come on, the porridge is almost done. We had best eat while we can."

That Hessian was only the first of who knew how many wounded they'd see before the day was over. Without a chance to get over the shock and fright, Grace plowed ahead in preparing the simple morning porridge. Yet in the back of her mind was Mark standing up to Harold, protecting the wounded man on the ground just as he'd once protected her from the panther.

The Hessian had passed out before they'd arrived at the hospital tent. Mark and the other man had laid him on a table at Mistress Geyer's instructions, and then left him in her care until the surgeon arrived.

Mark walked out of the tent with the one who'd helped carry him. "Thank thee for thy assistance."

"'Tis nothing." He lifted a bandaged hand. "If not for this, I would be back in the line. Surgeon's not sure if I will ever be able to shoot a gun again, but I can lift and tote and do my part." He stopped and faced Mark. "Pay Harold no mind about the Indian talk. Those of us who been here to get healed, we know where our dinners have come from. I thank you for it."

"As thee can lift and tote, I can hunt. We all do our part." But it helped, in an odd way, knowing that others who could no longer fight were still serving in other capacities. Mark felt a little less alone in that way. "I suspect we shall both be busy once the battle starts—if it can in this fog."

The distant *boom* of a cannon answered that question.

Mark strode back to the laundresses' fire, his belly growling. He waited his turn, then took a bowl of porridge from Grace.

"Did the surgeon see to the Hessian?" Grace asked.

"I left him in Mistress Geyer's care."

Grace nodded. "She will see to things, then."

Mark took his bowl and sat on a crate nearby, ignoring the distant cannons. He needed to eat. He'd just about finished it when Grace joined him.

"Thank you for looking after that man. I should not have screamed, but 'twas the last thing I thought to see in the fog."

"I imagine so." He couldn't help the grin that tugged at his lips. "Thee likely frightened him more than he frightened thee."

She chuckled. "I am not so terrifying as the panther, though." She turned her dove-gray eyes to him. "Am I?"

Grace was a lot of things—she caused conflicting emotions to course through him—but she was never terrifying. He shook his head.

"Thank you for not allowing Harold to shoot him. Even if he is the enemy, he is harmless now. 'Twould have been wrong to kill him."

"Indeed." *Even if he is the enemy.* Would Mark have felt the same way if the man had been an Iroquois? That thought hit a little too close to something he wasn't willing to dissect. He stood and carried his bowl to the wash tub, Grace following him. "I must saddle Naxa and ride toward the battle." Another *boom* reached them, followed quickly by three more.

"Why? You will not fight, will you?"

"Someone must lead the wounded back here, and nobody with the army knows exactly where we are."

"You will be careful?" Her eyes pleaded with him.

"Of course." As careful as anyone could be riding into a fog that covered friend and foe alike. "If thee will pray for me."

"Of course I will." But a frown smudged the smoothness of her brow. He wanted to wipe it away with the pad of this thumb, but such a gesture was too intimate for... for whatever was between them. *Lousy Indian.* What right had he to touch her at all? He could promise her nothing.

Not even to survive the day.

Lord, keep him safe. He is a good man. He believes in You, so You should watch over him.

The prayer went through her thoughts as if put there by someone else. It was just... there. Could it truly be that easy to talk to God? Might He listen to the likes of her?

"Grace?" Anna appeared at her shoulder. "He will return, but we have work to do." Another cannon boomed, sounding even more eerie with the fog. "Help me set up the washing fire near the hospital tents."

Grace nodded, but didn't move.

"Make haste, girl, before Mistress Crenshaw catches you mooning over him."

Mooning? That jerked Grace out of her thoughts and into action.

While they were setting the kettles in place, Mistress Geyer joined them. "The Hessian is settled. You did not find him any too soon, Grace. The surgeon said he was close to death from lack of vater and food."

"Could anyone speak to him?" Grace asked.

"One of the vounded from Paoli, he spoke to the man in German. Said his name is Franz. Now"—Mistress Geyer pointed at Anna—"you must help me vatch over our Grace. No more stumbling over the enemy for her."

Our Grace. Even under the circumstance, that phrase made her feel like... like she belonged.

Anna nodded solemnly, if with a humorous twist to her lips. "I shall do my best."

"Good girl." Mistress Geyer eyed them both up and down, then nodded. "Two good girls." Then she hurried back into the hospital tent.

Grace worked alongside of her friend, and even after the fright she'd had that morning, she felt strangely at ease. People were looking out for her, Mistress Geyer, Anna, and Mark. The sense of belonging that Mistress Geyer calling her *our Grace* had started settled back over her. Amid the fog, the chill, and with the impending arrival of wounded men, suddenly, she couldn't think of anyplace else she'd rather be.

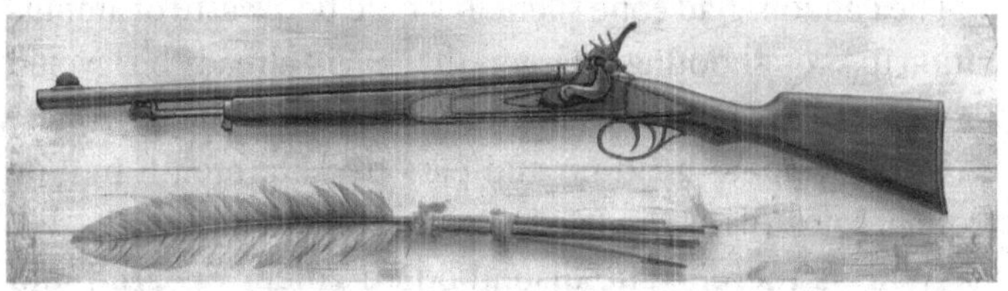

Chapter 23

As foggy as it'd been in the follower's camp, it was even worse as Mark rode closer to the battle. He was forced to keep Naxa at a walk, following the boom of the cannons. Washington must have had his forces in place before the fog had settled, and the cannons trained on their targets. There was no way the men manning the artillery could see what they were firing at now.

Riding closer, the rattle of muskets joined in. Of course, sound carried differently through fog than it did on a clear day, so he wasn't sure exactly how close he was. He located a ford, and Naxa entered the river without hesitation. Even in the fog, the place was obviously well traveled. Likely the same ford the army had used the evening before. He pulled his feet out of the stirrups when the water threatened to reach them, but then Naxa found firmer footing and soon they were on the other bank. He gave the mare a chance to shake off the excess water, and then pointed her toward the sound of the muskets.

The cannons had gone silent. It would be a waste of ammunition to keep shooting at targets that might already be leveled or moved elsewhere. Washington's army had none to waste.

Naxa stopped, head up and ears perked, breath puffing from her nostrils as she tried to scent something ahead.

"Who is there?" The disembodied voice was gruff and straight ahead.

Mark sat in silence, unsure how to answer. What if the man asking the question was a British soldier?

The barrel of a musket came out of the fog, followed by a soldier in a blue coat. "I said, who are you?"

"A scout for Major General Nathanael Greene."

"Greene?" The man didn't lower his weapon, but he glanced around. "Where the devil is that man? He was supposed to be covering our flank."

"Which direction is the flank?"

The man used his musket to point to his right. "I thought it over there." Confusion colored his tone.

Musket fire erupted from nearby, and Mark ducked.

"If you find Greene, tell him to cover the blasted flank," the man yelled as he disappeared back into the fog.

Naxa snorted and tried to follow, but Mark stopped her.

What should he do? If he kept going forward, he'd likely stumble into someone, but would it be Washington's Army or Howe's? Or would he walk into the musket fire? How best could he serve Nathanael at this point? The camp was set up and ready. There was nothing for him to do there. In the back of Mark's mind, he could almost hear Lucy's voice. *Have thee prayed about it?*

Shame had him bowing his head, right there amid the musket fire and fog and uncertainty. *Lord, I should have come to Thee first, not tried to figure this out on my own. Show me the way to go. Show me what Thee would have me do. Give me guidance, and I will follow it.*

When the answer came, it was stark and clear in a way Mark had never experienced before. *The ford.* The words accompanied an urge so strong he couldn't ignore it.

Lifting his head, Mark reined the horse around. "Come on, girl." They reached the ford on the river and didn't need to wait long.

The rumble of the wagons reached him before he could see them, even though the fog was beginning to thin. There were two of them, one right behind the other, both pulled by four-horse hitches driven by blue-coated men and traveling fast. Mark recognized the heavily bearded man driving the first wagon. He'd been one of those among the injured from Paoli.

Mark raised his hand and called out, "Over here."

Once both wagons were on solid ground, the bearded man said, "Ain't you the one who hunts for the followers camp?"

"I am."

The man jerked his thumb toward the back of his wagon. "We got a mess more wounded for you."

"Follow me." Mark wheeled Naxa around and urged her into a trot. The wagon horses could keep that pace, and the sooner they got the wounded to the surgeon, the better. He angled back and trotted Naxa beside the first wagon. "What happened back there?"

"Who knows? We could see nothing after the fog rolled in. Washington divided our forces." He shook his head, which was still sporting a thick bandage from the last battle. "I am not even sure everyone got into position before the fighting began."

"I can guarantee you they did not," said a man from the wagon, who held one arm to his side with the other hand, but was able to sit upright. "We pushed them Redcoats back at first, and should have been able to run them clean into

Philadelphia, but no one came from the other side of the line. I think the forces there were in retreat."

"We do not know that for sure," the bearded man said. "It was too hard to see anything."

"What the fog did not hide, the smoke from the cannons did," the wounded man said. "It hung in the fog, making everything murky as a bog."

The farther they traveled from the river, the more the fog thinned. Mark pointed toward where the camp was hidden in its shallow valley. "Keep going straight and over that hill in the distance, the one with the three pines on top, one leaning to the right."

"I see it," the bearded driver said.

"I shall return and guide any more to this point." Just as the Lord had directed him.

"There will be more." The wounded man stood. "We shall be lucky if half our men make it out of that mess."

The driver sent the man a glare. "Sit down and close your mouth." Then he cracked the reins across the backs of the teams and the horse jolted forward, sending the wounded man sprawling into the wagon's bed. By the grunts and curses that followed, more than just the driver were annoyed at him.

Mark waved the second wagon on and then returned to the river's ford. As he neared it, voices reached him, including the moaning of wounded. He followed the sounds. Two more wagons climbed onto the bank of the river, the first one driven by a man with a bloody rag tied around his leg.

"Are thee looking for the followers' camp of Nathanael Greene?"

"That we are." The wounded driver swayed on the bench seat.

"Are thee fit enough to drive?"

"Guess I have to be." He swayed again and pointed to the wagon's bed. "Those back there are in worse shape than me."

Mark glanced at the next wagon and froze. The blond hair was matted with blood, and the blue eyes dull, but it was Nash. The man listed to one side, staring at Mark but not appearing to see him.

"Nash." Mark dismounted and tied Naxa to the wagon, then climbed onto the seat. "Nash? Can thee hear me?" There was blood trickling from Nash's ear, down his neck, disappearing under the collar of his coat. The glazed blue eyes met Mark's, and he nodded.

"Move over and let me drive." Mark took the reins, and Nash slumped back against the seat, eyes closed. But he was still breathing. There was nothing Mark could do except get the wagons to the hospital tent, so he gave the reins a slap and hurried the horses on, passing the other wagon. "Follow me to the surgeon's tent."

Someone in the wagon's bed said, "Thank God, you found us," and a weak chorus of "amens" followed.

Nash rousted enough to add, "Leave it to the Lord to send us a Quaker. Nobody in his right mind would be in that place without being ordered." Then he fell silent, eyes closing.

Never again would Mark strike out on his own without praying for guidance first. Not after this. Not about anything.

Grace paced in front of the fire she'd kindled outside of the hospital tents. The largest kettle was suspended over it, filled with water already near to boiling. She'd rolled every length of bandage she could find. There was nothing else to do but wait.

And pray.

She'd prayed near the cliff, and they'd made it safely across, but they might have without her pitiful attempt at a prayer. Then the prayer for Mark's safety earlier, which had come so easily. It remained to be seen whether or not it would be answered.

What she knew about Christians and their God was that He had no use for the likes of her. Church was for people born into intact families surrounded by those who cared for them. In Grace's world, it had been only Mother and her, and Mother's way of earning a living did not fit with anything connected to a church. Even Grace knew that much. More than once she'd seen people filing out of a church, and upon seeing her and Mother, lift their noses and turn away.

But Grace's concern now was the battle raging across the Schuylkill River. The cannons had started up again after a long pause. Each time one boomed, she flinched. Was the fog lifting there too? Could they see to shoot at each other again?

Where was Mark in all that? That question was the reason for her restlessness. Did he take up his musket to fight? He'd left with it slung across his back, along with his bow. He carried them everywhere now, saying he couldn't pass up a chance to bring meat back for the camp. If seen armed that way, would he be mistaken for a soldier? Shot before he could proclaim that he wasn't?

"Wagons coming in!" One of the lookouts Mistress Crenshaw had stationed on the rise surrounding their camp shouted. "Two of them!"

"'Twill be our wounded," the surgeon bellowed from the largest hospital tent. "Everyone drink water, as much as you can." He gave the same advice he'd given each time.

Like the other times, Grace managed only a couple of swallows, so tight was her throat. This time, it wasn't just the horror coming at them, but fear for Mark that added to it. When the wagons crowned the rise, she stretched onto her toes, scanning the faces of those on the seats. Neither was Mark. But of course, he'd ridden out on his horse. He wouldn't be on a wagon.

Unless he was in the back among the wounded.

Lord, please, let him be all right. Mark is a Quaker, after all. He believes in You.

After all her struggling with the notion, the prayer flowed through her thoughts like honey, calming her spirit enough to enable her to rush forward with the others to help the soldiers to the tents. She scanned the faces she could see and let out a breath of relief that Mark wasn't among them before leading a man who could walk, but had taken off his shirt and wrapped it around his face and eyes. She steadied him, holding onto his arm and trying not to think about touching a man's bare skin. Mother had done her best to drill modesty into Grace—but war changed everything.

Handing the injured man over to one of the surgeon's mates, Grace hurried to the second wagon. Again, she searched for Mark and blew out a breath of relief when she didn't find him. Others were assisting the wounded away from the wagon, except for one man, near the front, lying on his side, the back of his blue coat facing Grace.

"Can I help you down?"

He didn't answer her, didn't move. Had he passed out?

Grace climbed into the wagon and went to his side. "Sir? Can you hear me?" She put her hand on his shoulder, and he rolled onto his back. Vacant eyes stared up at her, mouth slack, the front of his neck blown apart.

Grace gagged and reeled backward, making it to the edge of the wagon before losing her breakfast over the side.

"You all right?" asked a large bearded man with a bandage wrapped around his head.

Grace wiped the back of her hand across her mouth. "I do not know if I shall ever be all right again."

"Sure you will." He reached up to hand her down.

Even a month ago, she wouldn't have allowed him to touch her, but Mark's steady friendship was changing her. She put her hand in his and accepted his support until her feet were on the ground.

"Thank you." She pointed to the man in the wagon. "He is dead."

"The other driver sent me back to carry him to the burying spot they have marked out."

"Are you well enough to dig graves and drive a wagon?"

"Oh, this?" He touched the bandage. "'Tis only that my eyesight is a bit blurry. I can drive the wagon or dig, but I cannot see well enough to shoot yet without the risk of hitting one of our own."

"That would be terrible." Hitting one of their own soldiers instead of the enemy. What could be worse than that? He might even shoot a friend.

"'Tis a tragedy, and one I fear may be happening behind us." He lifted his chin toward the sound of another cannon boom, which seemed closer than the ones before. "Fog so thick a man cannot see his own boots. How can a man know what he is shooting at?"

"Two more wagons coming in!" shouted the lookout.

"I should return to the hospital tents." Grace moved past him. "They will need every hand."

"Bless you for being here to help us." The big man touched the brim of his bandage in an informal salute.

Grace scurried away, shaken as much by his words as the dead body behind her and the chaos in front of her. He'd blessed her—Grace without a last name—for being there and helping, sincerity in both his voice and expression. But even more shocking, there had been nothing else. No leering, no attempt at an intimate touch, no threat of... of anything.

Perhaps Mark wasn't the only man who defied her previous opinion of men. But where was he? She shuddered as the image of the man in the wagon came back to her. "Please, Lord, do not let that happen to Mark."

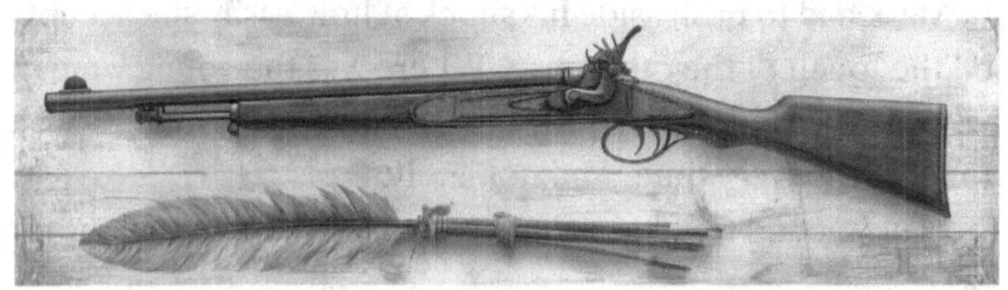

Chapter 24

MARK PARKED THE WAGON as close to the hospital tents as he could get. One of the surgeon's mates and several women rushed forward to assist. Mark set the wagon's brake and tied off the reins, then jumped down and reached back for Nash, who seemed to have been in and out of consciousness throughout the drive.

"Come on," Mark said. "Let me help thee down."

Nash moaned and half-leaned, half-fell into Mark's arms.

Bracing under the weight, for Nash was not a small man, Mark steadied them both against the wagon. With the wound to Nash's head, Mark didn't want to upend him over his shoulder and maybe increase the bleeding.

"Mark?" Grace's voice reached him. "Can I help?"

"Indeed. We must get him into a tent."

Grace came to Nash's side and pulled his arm across her shoulders.

Mark had to push aside his shock at how easily she accepted the touch of the other man. Where was the young woman who had shrunk away from his very nearness, much less a touch? Not every time. And not lately.

"The second tent has room." Grace led them in that direction.

Mistress Geyer met them at the entrance and motioned to an empty table on the side. "Over there."

It took all three of them to get Nash onto the table. He seemed to have little control over his movements, and had said nothing at all.

Mistress Geyer pushed a bundle of cloth at Grace. "Back to the fire and the vashing."

Grace whirled and left the tent.

"She has no stomach for vorking in here." Mistress Geyer's voice was free of scorn. She simply stated the fact.

"But she is a hard worker outside, and we need thee women to do both." Mark leaned over Nash, who had closed his eyes again. "I leave thee in good hands with Mistress Geyer." There was no response. He straightened and addressed the older woman. "I must return to lead more here. Please give him whatever he needs."

"Is he a friend of yours?" she asked.

That made Mark pause. Nash was a soldier, not a Quaker, not someone he'd have spent time with except for the war. But he'd accepted Mark almost from the start, despite their differences.

"He is." With that, Mark left the tent.

Grace was stirring the great kettle, smoke from the fire swirling with the lingering fog around her. As much as he would like to speak with her, they both had jobs to do. He turned in the other direction and climbed aboard the now empty wagon he'd driven in, Naxa still tied to the back.

The bearded man who'd driven the first wagon climbed aboard that one and called to Mark, "Shall we see who else we can bring out?"

"Indeed." Mark turned the team and headed up the slight incline and past the lookout there. Their path was easy to see, crushed wet grass evident in mist, all that remained of the cloaking fog of the morning. It must be nearly noon, the sun a pure white gleam through the gray above.

The other driver urged his horses up beside Mark's wagon. "Those cannons are getting closer. Washington must be in retreat and heading north. I think we should look for another ford rather than return to the one we used. If we are in retreat, that ford will be swarming with Redcoats."

The man being a soldier, Mark took his advice and turned his wagon on a direct path to the river. "I saw what might have been a place to ford here last night before full dark, but I cannot be sure."

"Lead the way." The big man let his horses stop and then followed Mark's wagon as they threaded through a tangle of willows.

Mark had seen the spot from the top of a hill that was behind them. He tried to picture it in his mind again. The lead left horse in his four-horse hitch snorted and shook its head, harness jingling, then tried to veer off. Mark started to correct the animal, but stopped. The Lord had given Mark a clear nudge to return to the ford before. Could He be using the horse to direct him now? A month ago, he might have dismissed the idea, but not today. He let the horse's rein go slack, and it angled them to the left, the other horses following his lead.

Nearly half an hour later, Mark was second-guessing his decision to trust the animal when the gurgle of rushing water reached him. They broke free of the willows, and Mark stopped the wagon. He scanned the landscape for any hint of movement. A hawk soared high overhead. Across the river, a fox disappeared into the brush.

The bearded man walked to Mark's side. "That water is moving fast, but it appears to be shallow enough."

"'Twill be a trickier crossing. We will have to keep the horses moving at a good clip. If they slow too much, the pull of the water might be too much for the wheels."

"I agree. I would not attempt it here with a two-horse hitch."

Neither would Mark. He wasn't too comfortable even with the four. "Do thee think we are too far north of the fighting? I have not heard a cannon in quite a while."

"Hard to say." The big man scratched under his beard. "I suspect we may be running short of ammunition. General Sullivan's troops had little enough to start with. Before I left the fray, word was that General Muhlenberg sent those Redcoats running with a bayonet attack. Payback for Paoli, if you ask me."

"Our job is to get the wounded out so they can fight another day." Mark tightened his grip on the reins. "I shall cross first right over the stones. None look large enough to cause a problem with the wheels."

The other man grunted and returned to his wagon.

"Okay, teams." Mark flicked the reins. "Move out and do not stop." He guided the horses to where the river appeared the shallowest, the rocks visible under the rippling water. Then he put the reins in one hand and pulled the whip from its holder beside the seat. With a flick, he cracked it in the air above the animals. They surged forward, the wagon tilting down the short slope and splashing into the river. One of the wheel horses shied at the water and tried to ram into its teammate. Thankfully, the lead pair kept on course as the skittish horse's teammate nipped it back into line. Mark had to trust that Naxa would follow on her tether.

Near the middle of the river, where the water reached to the horses' hocks, Mark cracked the whip again. The horses kept moving forward, but Mark could feel the drag of the water against the wagon's wheels. Another whip cracked behind him along with a shout, but Mark couldn't take his attention off the horses ahead of him.

They made it to the other side, where the river was deeper and the slope of the bank longer. "Get up there!" Mark added his voice to the whip's crack, and the lead horses scrambled onto the bank. He cracked the whip again when the wheel horses reached it, then held on as the wagon lurched from the water. He kept them moving, clearing space for the following wagon, before he stopped the teams on level land and looked behind. Naxa shook herself, then lowered her nose to grab a mouthful of the tall weeds at her feet.

As the other wagon topped the bank, the bearded man grinned at Mark. "I would not want to make that crossing come spring!"

With the runoff from snow and the season's rain, the ford would be impassible then.

"Which way do thee think we should go?" Mark asked. "North or south?"

"Your guess is as good as mine."

They sat in silence for a few minutes, giving the horses a rest. A distant *boom* answered Mark's question.

"It came from straight ahead, so we are in retreat." The man's expression turned weary. "I thought this time we might actually win one."

How difficult it must be to keep on fighting and see so few victories. That was what had driven Mark's tribe into the Ohio Territory, the inability to triumph over the more powerful and numerous Iroquois and the neverending advance of the white man. They'd been a beaten band of Lenni Lenape hoping to start over in the west. Mark knew nothing of their whereabouts anymore, but he hoped they'd had some victories and found a place to call home.

"Do you know the area ahead?" the other man asked.

"Nay. I have never been across the Schuylkill before."

"Let me lead then." He flicked his reins, waking up his horses.

Mark followed. It wasn't long before the rattle of distant muskets reached them. The fog had burned away, but the sun was still hiding behind a thick layer of clouds. They kept to a narrow road leading them under a canopy of trees, many of their colorful leaves carpeting the path, tall spires of pines and spruce standing among the maples, oaks, and aspens. They traveled at a walk, the bearded man's head swiveling from side to side. The muskets were closer now, and when Mark pulled in a deep breath, the sting of gunpowder hit the back of his throat.

"You there." The call came from the trees. "Wait."

"Whoa." Mark hauled back on the reins as someone moved branches aside to reveal two men, one in a blue coat leaning heavily on the other, who was coatless. Only the coatless man had a musket across his back.

"What unit are you from?" called back the bearded driver.

"Greene's," the upright man said as the leaning man in the blue coat raised his face to Mark.

Dan Browne.

"How far ahead are they?" the bearded man asked.

"Not sure. We got separated during the retreat. Dan here took a slug to the leg. Help me get him on a wagon."

Mark set the brake and tied the reins to it, then jumped down. Not that he wanted to help the man who'd threatened Grace, but neither could he drive off and leave him. Between the two of them, ignoring Dan's cursing, they got him on the wagon.

"What will thee do?" Mark asked the other fellow.

"No powder left, but my bayonet is sharp. If you would be so good as to let me ride with you, I shall rejoin my unit."

Mark hesitated only a moment, then unstrung his powder horn and handed it to the soldier. "Give me thy empty one and take this. 'Tis nearly full."

"'Twill leave you without a way to defend yourself." But he unstrung his horn and passed it over.

"I have my bow if needed."

"You any good with it?"

"Good enough. Climb aboard." Mark took his seat, and the other man joined him on the bench. Apparently, he'd no more desire for Dan's company than Mark had.

The bearded driver nodded at Mark, then led the way again. The stink of gunpowder grew stronger, the musket fire louder, even though there was less of it. Three horsemen in blue uniforms appeared from around the bend of the path in front of them.

"Halt!" The order came as muskets were raised and trained on them.

"Wait a minute." The officers from the back rode forward. "I know that man on the second wagon. You scout for Major General Greene, do you not?"

Mark recognized him as well, one of the officers who was always around Nathanael. "I do."

He rode forward, but the others still had their weapons up. "Are these wagons for the wounded?"

"They are. We will take them back to the followers' camp."

"Praise the Lord and follow us." He whirled his horse and motioned for the others to do the same.

"I must say, things were tense there for a moment." Mark's passenger on the seat looked at him. "Rotten timing, losing my coat when I did, but a Redcoat's bayonet split it right down the middle of my back. I am lucky to still be breathing."

"What about me?" Dan Browne asked from the wagon's bed. "Why are you not taking me back to the camp? Ain't I wounded enough?" The bandage around his leg was bloodied, but not enough to threaten his life.

Mark started the horses forward, following the other wagon. "Once the wagon is full, I shall head back. Or thee are welcome to get off and walk." He ignored the rest of Dan's complaints.

They'd traveled no more than a quarter of a mile when they came to a horrific scene. Men littered the ground, mostly from Washington's forces, but some in red coats as well.

Nathanael rode toward them and addressed the officers. "Thee found the wagons."

"More like they found us," said the man who'd recognized Mark.

"See that our wounded are loaded, then take the rest of the men northwest." Nathanael passed the first wagon and came to Mark's side as his passenger climbed down to help load the wounded.

"Good job, finding us. When thee arrive back at camp, tell Mistress Crenshaw to keep the wounded there. I doubt Howe has any desire to cross back over the Schuylkill, but keep thy eyes open. When Mistress Crenshaw says the wounded are ready, thee will find us to the northeast." Nathanael gave Mark a nod. "I know not exactly where, but thee can track the army and find thy way."

Mark sat a little straighter on the seat. "I will find thee."

Nathanael reined his horse away, but turned back. "'Tis not a small thing thee are doing, Mark. I need men I can trust. Thee have proven thyself one of them. Well done." He gave Mark a crisp nod, then rode away.

Mark waited until the wounded filled the back of his wagon, most of them able to sit up, which made enough room for the few who couldn't, including two wearing red coats. When both wagons could hold no more, Mark passed the reins over to a man with an injured leg who said he could drive, making room for the final wounded man in the back.

After untying Naxa, Mark mounted and led the way back to the river. Not only had he not fired a shot, but he'd given away the last of his short supply of gunpowder. Nevertheless, the kind words from a fellow Quaker—the Fighting Quaker, as the men called him—had given Mark peace. He was serving the army without being a part of the fighting. He was keeping his word to his mother, even holding to the beliefs of the Quakers by serving the wounded and helping the women.

If he could just win the full trust of a certain woman, his life would be complete.

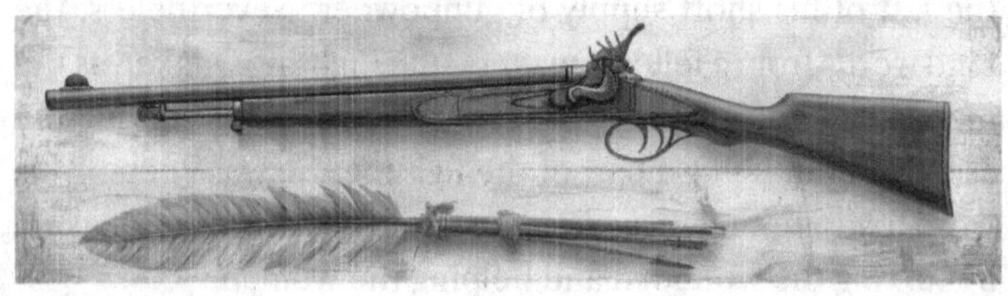

CHAPTER 25

"WHAT DO YOU THINK you are doing in my camp?" Mistress Crenshaw's voice rose above the groans and cries of the wounded in the hospital tents.

Grace finished pouring fresh water into the large kettle, and then went to investigate. Anna joined her.

A wagon filled with women had stopped in the middle of the camp.

Grace's heart leaped until she got a better look at them. Then it sank to the soles of her feet.

Even with thick wool shawls wrapped around them to keep out the chill and the plain linen bonnets they wore, the garish color of their dresses and false red painted on their cheeks showed them for who they were. Grace took a step back, but before she could turn away and flee—

Mother's eyes met hers.

She sat on the front seat of the wagon beside a burly man who was ignoring Mistress Crenshaw's demands that he remove his wagon and its occupants in all haste. Mother's faded blue eyes, the blond hair carefully enhanced with the use of saffron and chamomile to keep it from showing gray, and the tired droop to the corner of her mouth were as familiar as Grace's own reflection, although she looked nothing like her mother.

"Grace?" The name was filled with longing and uncertainty, perhaps even vulnerability.

It squeezed Grace's heart nearly in half. Instead of slinking away, she picked up her petticoats and hurried to the wagon.

"Are you all right?" That seemed safer than asking why she was there in the camp with a wagonload of backstreet women.

"I should ask you the same." Mother's mouth turned up in a hesitant smile. "If I had known how badly things would turn out, I would not have—"

"Am I to understand that you know this person?" Mistress Crenshaw towered over Grace.

For the first time since she'd met the woman, Grace held her ground. "This is my mother."

There was a gasp behind her, whether from Anna or one of the other laundresses, it was hard to say. Whoever it was, word would be all through the camp by sundown, destroying Mother's careful planning when she'd left Grace outside the first camp and told her to walk in, claiming she had nowhere else to go and would work hard to earn her keep.

It had almost worked. Mistress Crenshaw had never quite trusted her, had always thought Grace might bring trouble. That woman was now glaring at her, disgust and contempt written across her face.

Grace squared her shoulders, ready to accept whatever punishment was about to fall upon her. "Allow me to introduce you to Prudence Fisher. Mother, this is Mistress Crenshaw. She oversees the camp."

"Who have ve here?" Mistress Geyer bustled in and took a stance beside Grace, speaking to Mother. "Have you come to help vith the vounded?"

"Help them?" Mistress Crenshaw swept an arm to incorporate the entire wagonload. "These creatures? The type of work they do will not be done in my camp."

"These 'creatures,' as you say, have two hands, do they not? Ve have more vagons coming back vith more vounded. Hands ve need." Mistress Geyer turned her face up to Mother's again. "Vill you vork?"

"That is why we came." Mother looked at Mistress Crenshaw. "We bring food and clothing and shoes, as we heard many men lack these things. Even more"—Mother leaned down and dropped her voice—"we bring two barrels of gunpowder, labeled as molasses. Please, see that it goes where it is most needed."

"Food and clothing?" Mistress Crenshaw had not expected that, the consternation in her expression changing to something else, but Grace couldn't quite say what. "And gunpowder?" She faced Mother again. "Can you remain with the wounded and leave the rest of the men alone?"

"We will." Mother turned and looked at the women now standing in the wagon bed behind her, five of them. They all nodded, but a couple of them did so with smirks. Mother faced front again. "Where shall the driver unload what we have brought?"

Within minutes, Mistress Crenshaw had everyone in motion. But while the wagon was unloaded and the other woman whisked away by Mistress Geyer, Mother came to Grace's side.

"You did not have to claim me, my dear." She cupped Grace's cheek with one hand. "I would have understood had you not wished to."

Tears pressed against the back of Grace's eyes. "You *are* my mother."

"Which makes things more difficult for you, I know."

"What brought you here to the camp?"

"Oh, there are still Patriots in the city, some of whom I know." Mother didn't elaborate. She didn't have to. "They figured Howe's men wouldn't stop a wagon full of women on an outing before the weather turns cold."

"More wounded coming!" The shout came from one of the lookouts. "Two wagons loaded."

"'Twould seem we arrived just in time." Mother's smile was easy and practiced, but the love in her eyes was genuine—and it was for Grace alone.

Grace motioned for Mother to follow her to the hospital tents. "What foodstuff did you bring?"

"Oh, the usual. Flour and oats, molasses and cornmeal, dried peas, crates of potatoes and onions, salted fish and pork."

Mother named the food as if it were commonplace. "'Twill be a feast and a pleasure to cook with all of that."

"Cook?" Mother's eyebrows shot up. "Is that what you are doing here?"

"Aye. I have no stomach for tending the wounded. But even Mistress Crenshaw compliments my cooking. Mistress Geyer, the Swedish woman, she taught me. She has become a mentor to me." Grace glanced away. "A protector." Guilt crept over her for admitting it to Mother, who had done the best she could to protect her daughter.

Mother grasped Grace's hand and squeezed it. "I am glad. I hoped an older woman would look out for you."

Grace's heart warmed at her mother's words.

Up ahead, a rider led the wagons in.

Mark.

His eyes met Grace's, and they widened as they flicked to her hand, still held by Mother's. What expressions passed over his face flicked too quickly to be sort through, but he turned to the wagons and spoke to the driver of the first, directing him where to park to unload the wounded. When the colorfully dressed women came out of the tents to assist the men inside, Mark backed his horse out of the way.

A flock of strumpets must be the last thing a Quaker had expected to find upon his return, unless it was witnessing one holding Grace's hand.

Mark had never visited the type of women who lent their strength to the wounded men, ignoring more than a few ribald comments from the lesser injured among them. He wasn't ignorant. Talk of such had reached him at the smithy, along with dire warnings from Charlie Brewer to stay away from them. Not to mention the Bible passages, especially from Proverbs, that explicitly commanded men to avoid such women. Up close, it was easy to see that none of them were young, despite the red on their cheeks and their high-pitched chatter. But that wasn't what had shocked Mark.

Grace holding hands with one of them had.

Lucy had taught him to be polite toward all, even those who fell short. That was how she termed those who did not live by the Scriptures or know the Light of Christ, those who didn't believe in the Creator of the universe, whom he'd first been taught about by his mother.

Perhaps Grace had simply been being polite as well.

He didn't believe it, though.

Even across half the camp, he hadn't missed the stricken look she'd given him, as if she'd been caught out doing something wrong. She must know the woman, but how? She'd told him she came from Philadelphia, and they were close to that city, so perhaps she'd met the woman there. But why would Grace know a woman like that? Grace, with her gentle manners and meekness.

After dismounting, he shot another glance at the approaching pair. The older woman was of fairer skin with pale hair and eyes. She looked nothing like Grace's dark beauty. They headed straight toward him, not the tents.

"Mark." Grace stopped in front of him. "I would like you to meet my mother, Prudence Fisher. Mother, this is Mark. He scouts for the major general and helps here in our camp."

The woman—Prudence—glanced first at Grace, and then back at him, her look pointed and searching.

Mother? *She* was Grace's mother? Lucy's training kicked in. "A pleasure to meet thee, Prudence." Grace not knowing her father suddenly made sense. Tragic sense.

"Thee?" Prudence took a half step back, hand pressed to her chest. "A Quaker in the army?"

"Nay. I am not in the army. As Grace said, I am but a scout."

Now her eyes narrowed. "A scout with a musket and a bow?"

"I am also a hunter."

"The best we have," Grace added. "He brings in meat we need to feed the wounded."

"But the bow." Prudence cocked her head. There was no disapproval in the action or her voice when she asked, "Are you an Indian?"

"I am Lenni Lenape." He touched the bow's string that rested against his chest. "I am also a Quaker, a blacksmith, and currently a scout."

"A man of many talents." She looked between him and Grace again.

"Grace!" Anna yelled across the distance. "I need your help, now."

"I must go."

"Show me where I may be useful." Prudence started toward the hospital tents. "We shall have to leave in the morning, but you have our undivided attention until then."

As they walked off, Mark wrestled with the implications of what he'd learned. Surely Grace had not been one of those women. Everything about her was too... too what? Too innocent. Too shy. Too perfect. They needed to speak before he jumped to any conclusions. When they did, he was sure she would confirm his faith in her. But if she didn't? If she couldn't? Could he accept her background as—?

"Mark!" Mistress Geyer waved him over to the second hospital tent.

He met her at the doorway. "What is it?"

"Your friend, he asks for you."

"Nash is speaking?" Surely that was a good sign. Mark ducked beneath the tent flap. It took a moment for his eyes to adjust to the gloom, but then he spied Nash lying on a pallet on the floor, a heavy bandage wrapped around his ears, his blond hair pushed up at the top. Mark knelt beside his friend. "Nash?"

Eyelids fluttered, and Nash frowned, squinting up at Mark. "Mark? Is that you?"

"Aye. How are you feeling?"

"Like I have been run over by a wagon." He fumbled for Mark's arm, and then grasped it in a strong grip. "But I cannot see, not like I should."

"What can thee see?"

"Light and dark and movement of the two." His voice dropped to a whisper. "Nothing else."

"What has the surgeon said?"

"That I took a hard blow to my head, which I already knew, and that my vision may or may not return. 'Tis in the hands of God, he said."

"Then I shall pray and ask Him to return it."

"I was hoping you would." Nash's grip tightened. "And if you could, ask Major General Greene to pray as well. I have heard that God listens to you Quakers, and that you listen to Him."

Mark let the impact of that settle over him. "I believe God listens to anyone who believes in Him and prays to Him, as long as they pray to no other god. But understand that listening and granting are not always the same thing. We must pray that His will be done in all things."

Nash let go of Mark. "You are saying God might wish me to be blind?"

"I am saying, I will pray and if I see the major general, I will ask him to pray as well. But first and foremost, thee should seek the Lord thyself."

"I have never been much of a praying man." Nash's admission came softly, but not belligerently.

"There have been times when I was not either, but I will tell thee why I always resumed the practice." Mark settled himself more comfortably on the ground and explained how the Quakers believed that all could speak to the Lord and receive the Light of Christ in their lives. Then he explained the Lenni Lenape's belief in a single creator God, Kishelemukonk, and believed he directed other spirits to interact with the people. Not unlike the angels, perhaps. If two cultures with such differences could agree on the same principle, how could it not be the truth? "They even agree that at one time, the whole earth was covered with water."

"Thank you." Nash's words were a whisper again, his eyes closed. "You have given me much to think about."

"Rest now. I will return later." Mark rose and looked down on his friend. What would become of Nash if his sight didn't return? What life had he other than the army? That could be a discussion for another day. For now, he'd find a quiet place and ask the Lord to return Nash's sight. And for wisdom for himself concerning Grace.

Grace had only meant to bring Mark's friend a drink of water. She hadn't meant to eavesdrop. But once Mark began explaining about the Quakers' beliefs and then his Indian beliefs and how they were so similar, she hadn't been able to walk away. It was all foreign to her. Her mother wouldn't have been allowed in a church, of course, and as she'd grown, Grace had just assumed she'd not be welcome either. Certainly not if the people inside had known where she'd come from.

Mark knew her whole story now. She was the child of a strumpet. What must he think of her? The same as everyone else who knew. They all assumed she'd follow in Mother's chosen profession.

But listening to his words about the Lord, and not just the words, but the *way* he spoke them, as if they came from his very heart, had moved her. When he stood, she whirled and fled the tent, the cup of water in her hands sloshing over the brim and dampening her petticoat. She didn't stop until she reached the tent she shared with Mistress Geyer. Then she put the nearly empty cup down and sank to her knees.

Lord, I know You not, but according to Mark, You know me. According to him, You will listen to me. I hardly know what to do with that. Nobody much has ever listened to me except for Mother, and she does not lead a good life. But then, You know that. You know everything, or You could not be God. That much Grace had worked out for herself. *I want to ask You to bring sight back to Mark's friend. He seems a good man. He said nothing to me other than to thank me for bringing water the first time.* She had only approached him because Mistress Geyer had told her he was Mark's friend.

Now came the hard part. *Lord, I want to believe in You like Mark does. I want to have the peace he has. I hear it in his voice when he speaks of You. I want to live an honorable life, like he does. While Mark says I must ask it be Your will, and not my own, I do not understand exactly what that means. I am willing to learn, however, if You will teach me.* Somehow, that was the most frightening part of her prayer.

What if God didn't want to teach her? What if He rejected her, ignored her as so many people had in the past?

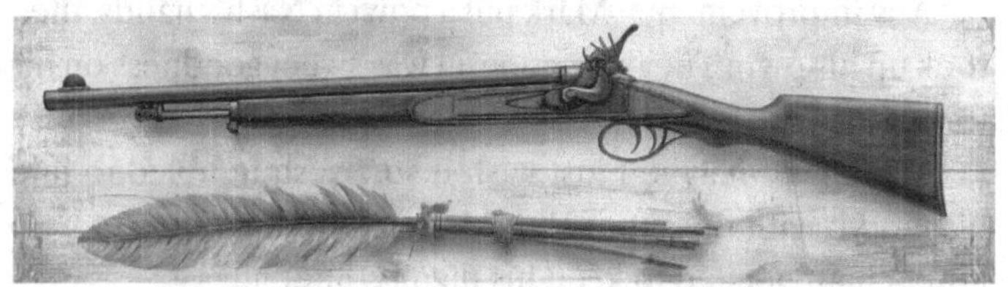

Chapter 26

Steam from the porridge added the tang of molasses to the morning air. The camp had run out of that sweetening days ago. The women from Philadelphia had brought that and more, food and other provisions—including rum, which Mistress Crenshaw had confiscated for the surgeon's use only. That and their promise of leaving this morning were probably the only reasons Mistress Crenshaw had tolerated them staying even one night. Still, they had worked with the wounded, showing themselves willing to do whatever tasks were necessary. They'd even earned a bit of praise from the crusty old surgeon.

Mark knelt beside Nash's pallet. "I have brought thee porridge." His friend struggled to sit, and Mark set the bowls down to steady him. "Easy now."

"The world wants to tilt this way and that." Nash blinked and looked around, squinting.

"Any improvement?" Mark put a bowl in Nash's hands, then took up his own. The first spoonful was sweet goodness on his tongue.

"Maybe. Or maybe I just wish it so." Nash fumbled to find his mouth with the spoon, but Mark resisted the urge to help him. A man needed to keep his dignity, after all.

They finished the porridge in silence, listening to the women delivering bowlfuls to the other men, several of them kneeling and spooning it for those unable to feed themselves. Too many were in that condition. Some were unable to eat at all. The camp wouldn't be able to move for several days, if not weeks.

Nash set his empty bowl down. "I prayed last night."

Hope surged in Mark. "And?"

"I can hardly believe it, but it felt as though someone or something was right beside me." He snorted. "I could not see it, of course, but if I had been brave enough, I think I could have reached out and touched whatever it was."

"'Tis a fine start, I would say." Mark remembered that feeling when he'd sat beside Lucy, a grieving and confused boy who'd lost his mother, and prayed to God using both the names he knew Him by.

"I misjudged you at the start." Nash brushed a hand across his eyes. "I am sorry for that."

"How do you mean?"

"I have only ever wished to be a soldier. My father was, and his father before him. When you asked to see the major general with your Quaker *thee*, I could not imagine you being useful at all. Everyone knows that, aside from the major general, Quakers will not fight. But what you are doing here, this is important." Nash squinted at him, blinking several times. "You are a patriot as much as any other. I had forgotten how much the army depends on the non-fighters. Like the women in this camp, the surgeons, their helpers. We could fight without them, but more would die. We would miss the comfort of the socks they knit and clothing they wash and mend. 'Tis not everyone's lot to be a soldier."

"I struggled with that," Mark admitted.

"What you told me last evening, about God, I hope you can tell others the same. You gave me hope."

"Nay. The Lord gives hope."

"Well, 'twas you who pointed the way."

Uncomfortable with the praise, Mark gathered the empty bowls. "I will return later today. Rest now." He left the tent and went in search of Grace.

She wasn't hard to find, cleaning up after the last of the porridge had been served. She straightened as he approached and set the bowls on her worktable.

"Nash ate every bite."

"I am glad your friend is getting better."

She was lovely. Too lovely to have ever been one of those—

"Grace?"

They both turned at her mother's call and waited for her to join them, her colorful dress wrinkled and spotted with blood and dirt after working with the wounded.

"Grace, dear. We must be away soon. Mistress Crenshaw is quite insistent about that."

"I am sorry—"

"Nay, do not be." Prudence shook her head. "'Tis nothing we have not heard before, and will again." She gazed up at Mark and crossed her arms. "I have seen how you look at my daughter. I would know your intentions before I leave. I did not raise Grace to follow in my footsteps. She has been gently reared for a better life, and she deserves more than I could give her on my own."

Mark glanced at Grace, who'd blanched nearly as pale as her apron, then back at her mother, his mind churning.

"I know not Grace's wishes. We have not spoken of such things. But for me, rest assured, I have only the highest regard for thy daughter." He wrestled with what to say next.

Prudence didn't move, and Grace made not a sound.

Sweat popped out on Mark's brow, despite the cool morning breeze. "Thee probably wish better for her than an Indian for a suitor." There. He'd said it. Now he would hold his tongue until she replied, no matter how long it took.

It took an uncomfortable length of time until Prudence turned to Grace. "Many times you have asked me about your father, and I told you nothing."

"You said never to ask again, and I did not."

"Indeed. You were a biddable girl even from the start. 'Tis why I worked so hard to keep you out of my trade." Prudence touched her daughter's cheek, all the love of a mother in that motion.

Mark was flooded with relief to know that Grace had not been one with the women who were gathering at the wagon hitched and ready to drive them back to the city. Back to a way of life his Grace had not been a part of.

Grace drew in a breath that quivered in the stillness. "Do you mean to tell me now?"

Prudence glanced at Mark again, then back to her daughter. "I believe I should. I loved your father. He was not one of the men who, well, you know. He was good man. He wanted me to marry him, in fact. But I was stupid, you see. Afraid. I had chosen poorly when I married my husband, who abandoned me for other women and died at the hands of someone he had cheated at the card table. I could not see myself dependent on anyone else ever again, not even your father. And not just for that reason, but because it would not have changed my position much."

Grace's brow crinkled with questions. "But being married, you would have had his protection and respectability."

"More to the point, I should have thought of you. You deserved a father. But you would have still been considered an outcast."

"Because you were pregnant before the wedding could have taken place?"

Prudence shook her head. "Because of who he was."

"Was?" Grace almost pounced on the word. "Is he no longer living then?"

"I heard he died in an uprising led by that Indian from the west, Pontiac."

Grace pressed a hand to her chest. "He was a soldier?"

"Not in the way you think." Prudence once again touched her daughter's cheek. "I knew him as Sammy, but his real name was Singing Turtle. His Iroquois name."

Mark felt the words like a punch to the stomach.

Grace was Iroquois—like those who had killed Father.

Her olive-toned skin and black hair, so unlike Mother's fairness.

Grace had always attributed that to her father, of course, but never—not once—had she ever suspected the truth. Philadelphia was filled with people from all over the world, from Greece and Spain and other areas where people looked like her. The sailors at the wharves were among the most colorful of the city. She'd just assumed her father had been one of them.

She was the daughter of an Indian.

"Grace, dear." Mother's words came as from a cave, hollow and distant. "I would never have told you had you stayed in the city. Had you not met this young man who follows you with his eyes but keeps his hands to himself."

"I am an Indian?" The words tasted foreign on her tongue.

"Partly, my daughter, my beloved." Mother knelt beside where Grace sat on a barrel. "Your father was half Iroquois and half French. A man who lived between two worlds, where I was too fearful to join him."

When had Grace sat down? Her ears buzzed and her heart thumped against her stays. Could it be true? It must be. Mother had never lied to her. She'd withheld the truth, but had never lied.

"Sammy. You said his name was Sammy?"

"That is the name he used. He had left the tribe and was working at the wharfs. That was how we met." Mother bowed her head, but not before Grace caught a glimpse of the blush staining her cheeks. Not a blush painted on, but one drawn with emotions.

"I am glad you told me now."

"Prudence!" One of the women in the wagon called out. "We are waiting."

Mistress Crenshaw stood beside the wagon, arms crossed, looking ready to drag Mother away if she didn't move on her own.

"I must go." Mother rose.

Grace rose with her. "Thank you for coming, for bringing the supplies, for... for telling me."

Mother's arms came around her, and Grace sank into the embrace. She didn't want to let go, but it was time. She dropped her arms, and Mother walked away without a backward glance. She stepped up into the wagon, and it drove away.

Letting out a sigh, Grace turned to Mark.

He was gone.

She scanned the camp, but there was no sign of him. Had Mother's interrogation driven him away? Surely, he wasn't put off by the revelation about her father. He was Indian himself, after all. An ache throbbed in Grace's temples. She massaged them with her fingertips.

"Are you quite all right?" Mistress Crenshaw's voice cut the morning air like a hot knife through butter as she approached. "You are white as snow, girl."

Grace shook her head. "'Tis nothing." The woman's snort said she wasn't believing that, but Grace hurried on. "Just news my mother brought."

"I cannot think it was anything good." Mistress Crenshaw cast a disapproving eye at where the wagon disappeared over the rim of the valley they camped in. "Never is with that sort."

Grace tried not to bristle under the criticism. "She is still my mother."

To her utter surprise, Mistress Crenshaw's face softened. "Of course she is. I should not have said that." She touched Grace's arm. "Pray, forgive me. It has been a long night, but 'tis no excuse."

"She wanted better for me. That is why she brought me to the camp. 'Tis why she left me outside to walk in by myself, so you would not see her and judge me harshly."

"And yet, I did." Mistress Crenshaw shook her head. "'Twas your pretty face and the way the men ogled after you. I had no idea of the other." She swept a hand toward where the wagon had disappeared.

Grace smiled. "Mother did her best to raise me for a better life."

"She did a fine job of it."

The praise for Mother tightened Grace's throat, so she nodded in response. She couldn't judge Mistress Crenshaw harshly for her thoughts about Mother's profession, for she'd had the same thoughts more than once herself. The older woman patted her shoulder awkwardly, then moved off.

Grace scanned the camp again, but there was still no sign of Mark. She plunged her hands into the washwater, the white suds contrasting with her dusky skin. A smile tugged at the corner of her lips. Where once the idea of Indian blood would have horrified her, now it offered her hope. She was more like

Mark than she'd understood. It felt as if a barrier to her dreams had been removed.

Iroquois.

Mark thumped his heels against Naxa's sides, urging the horse to greater speed. He'd grabbed his musket, the newly filled powder horn and shot bag, along with his bow and a trio of arrows. He would hunt, even though the Philadelphia women had brought food. They could save the salted meats for another time if he brought in fresh.

Hunting would give him a purpose. Something to keep his mind busy, to keep at bay the images of the Iroquois attacking his band of Lenni Lenape, his people, his family—the spear that had pierced his father. His rage and hatred of the rival tribe boiled up despite the pounding of hooves beneath him.

What if Grace's father had been part of that attack? What if the blood that flowed through her veins had come from the one who had drained the blood from Mark's father?

There was no way to know.

At a thick stand of trees, Mark slowed Naxa to a walk. He'd find no game if he charged in, crashing through the forest like a raging bull elk. Bad enough he'd acted like a stag around Grace all these weeks. He pulled a hand down his face, trying to erase his thoughts.

He needed to concentrate on the hunt, breathe the forest air, stalk the animals that would feed the wounded in camp and the women.

Grace.

Ever since he'd met her, he'd considered himself not worthy of her because he was an Indian. Now he knew the truth.

She was an Iroquois. His enemy.

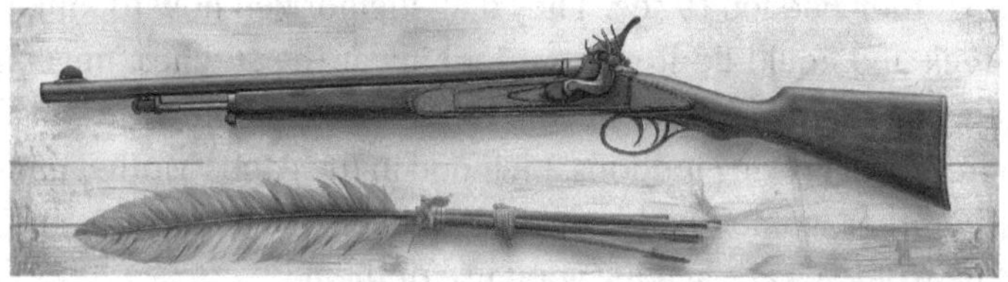

CHAPTER 27

FOUR DAYS LATER, GRACE had barely had a glimpse of Mark, and they'd exchanged nothing more than a few polite words. Everyone was busy, either tending the wounded, managing the camp, or cooking staggering amounts of food to feed everyone. While she couldn't fault Mark for being busy—he'd brought in fresh meat every day—it was easy to see that he made no attempt to approach her. That settled like a lead weight on her spirit.

Evening came, its darkness settling around the camp, and there was still no sign of Mark. Grace hung the last of the washed bandages on a rope strung under the canvas that sheltered the laundresses' fire. The air smelled of rain and no stars shone through the heavy clouds above.

In the distance, an owl hooted. Grace shivered and wrapped her thick wool shawl around her shoulders, then she picked up her knitting and joined the circle of laundresses who were already at work by the feeble light of the fire. Not that they needed to see. They'd all memorized how to knit a sock and could do it without looking at the stitches, fingers feeling their way from needle to needle, wrapping the wool around in flowing motions. Included in the goods Mother and the other women had brought had been skeins of yarn, and the women were making good use of them.

Walking through the hospital tent, she'd noticed more than one man's bare feet sticking out from beneath the blankets. With winter coming, the men were in dire need of socks. Did Mark need a pair as well? Thankful that the darkness hid her warming face, Grace bent over her knitting. With the day's chores accomplished, she couldn't help but relive the moments when Mother had asked his intentions. She'd nearly died of embarrassment, but that had turned to joy with his answer and Mother's tacit approval.

But then he'd left and kept to himself.

Was he as embarrassed as she'd been? Was that why he'd left without a word? Or was it something else? Mother had been bold enough to assure him that Grace had never lived the lifestyle he would certainly have disapproved of. But maybe... maybe just knowing that her mother was a strumpet, that she earned her living in such a socially unacceptable way, maybe it was too much for him, being a Quaker.

Pain laced through her.

As the yarn slid around her fingers, the urge to defend Mother rose within her. After all, Mother and the other *socially unacceptable* women had brought much-needed supplies. Their offerings may have come tainted with their sins, but they had come. Where were the supplies promised by the Continental Congress?

"Grace?" Mistress Geyer approached, her steps slow. "I am off to bed. Vill you be up long?"

"Nay." She tucked her knitting away and stood. "I shall join you." She wished the rest of the laundresses a good night, then followed Mistress Geyer to the tent.

Mistress Geyer picked up the stub of a candle, but set it back down again. "'Tis too bad your mother did not bring any candles vith her. Ve could have used them."

"But she brought many other things." Grace couldn't help her defensive tone as she stripped off her gown and petticoat. It was still warm enough to sleep in just her shift, and with Mistress Geyer nearby, safe enough too.

"Oh, my. I did not mean to say othervise. We are blessed by the many things those vomen brought."

Those women. How often had Grace heard her mother and the others called that? Mark must think of them in the same way. And perhaps, even with Mother's bold statements to the opposite, perhaps he now saw Grace that way too.

On the rim of the hillside overlooking camp, Mark sat on Naxa, ignoring the pattering of raindrops. He brought no fresh meat today. He'd been to see Nathanael, to learn what he could of the army's movements or lack thereof. He'd been sent back with a message for Mistress Crenshaw, but it would keep until morning.

No light shone from the tent Grace shared, yet her figure wasn't among the women leaving the fire's canvas shelter and walking to their tents.

He missed her, and it was his own fault. He had plenty to do—they all did—but that wasn't an excuse. The time he'd spent away from camp had been necessary, especially once the fifth and sixth wagonloads of wounded had arrived the day after the battle. The hospital tents overflowed, men sleeping no more than a hand's breadth away from the next man, including Nash, whose sight had not returned. The poor man was suffering through terrible headaches now, unable to sit upright without losing his balance and emptying his stomach.

Mark had spent a good deal of time in prayer over that. The Lord would answer, but whether with a yes or a no. Only time would tell.

As much as he worried for his friend, most of his prayer time had been taken up with Grace. As he'd promised himself in the middle of the battle, he would not go forward again without guidance from the Lord. The shock of learning she was an Iroquois had passed. In hindsight, the shock must have been greater for her. While she probably held nothing against the Iroquois in particular, she'd been repulsed upon first learning of his Lenni Lenape heritage.

She'd not only learned who her father was, but that he was dead. Did one mourn for those they'd never known? Mark had been raised in such a different culture. While he had no siblings, the longhouse of his people housed his mother's relatives. He'd been related to everyone born in that longhouse, the only outsiders having married into it. Had he stayed and taken a Lenni Lenape for a wife, he would have moved to her family's longhouse, and the tradition would have continued.

The Quakers had a different standard. For one thing, they married only among fellow Quakers. To marry outside of the faith was to be put out of the meeting. Who else would they marry anyway, when Puritans and Anglicans saw them as heretics? Mark had never heard of it happening in his ten years living in Birmingham and attending the meeting there.

Yet here he sat in the rain pondering the wisdom of asking Grace to allow him to court her. Prudence had all but given her consent already, and as Grace had no living father, there was no one else to approach. The only thing keeping him at a distance was the answer to his prayers. He waited. He listened with his heart as Lucy had instructed him. But so far, he'd heard nothing from the Lord.

Perhaps the timing was wrong. Perhaps it wasn't a *no* but a *not yet*. Or perhaps, in spite of his growing attachment to the young woman, the wise thing to do would be to ride away. He could slip into the forest and disappear easily enough. The army was east of them across the Schuylkill. Southwest was Birmingham, where he could work in the smithy again. Or farther west, he could find his mother's people, although that would go against her wishes.

The wind picked up and the raindrops became a slanting sheet of water, causing Naxa to shake her head.

"Thee are right. 'Tis time to join the others." He urged the mare forward. "I to crawl beneath my oiled canvas, and thee to shelter between the larger beasts who pull the wagons."

They'd no more than entered camp when a man slipped between the tents of the laundresses, crouching near the entrance to one. The dim light of the dying fire outlined his profile when he turned his head.

Mark spurred Naxa forward, bringing the mare to a foot-stomping halt inches away from Dan Browne. "What are thee doing here?" Mark took no caution to keep his voice down. It wasn't Grace's tent, but the man had no right to be near any of the women.

Dan stood, arms extended in front of him as if to keep the war horse away. "What right have you to ask my business?"

Mark leaned forward in the saddle. "The right of a man protecting women from the likes of thee."

"What makes you so high and mighty?" Dan spat the words. "You ain't nothing but a dirty Indian and everyone knows it."

Several tent flaps had opened, but it was Mistress Crenshaw's voice that cut between Mark and the man in front of him. "Dan Browne? If that is you, and you are well enough to be skulkin' around in the dark, you are well enough to rejoin the army." She thrust out an arm, pointing to the east. "Be gone with you and pray you have no need to return to my camp."

"You cannot kick me out of this camp." Dan drew himself up.

"She can." Mark allowed Naxa to take another step closer, all but pushing the man against the tent behind him. "She has full authority under Major General Greene himself. I carry a message from that man to her this very evening."

"My injury—"

"Did not stop thee from creeping about the camp." Mark lowered his voice. "'Twill not stop thee from walking from it, even if I must follow thee every step of the way." He leaned from the saddle so that only Dan could hear him. "If I see you near these women again, I shall personally make sure thee can never accost another again. The Lenni Lenape have a way to treat men like thee."

The man's eyes went to the knife hilt showing about the top of Mark's moccasin, and he took a step back.

"Be gone." Mistress Crenshaw stood in the rain, every inch the woman in charge. "Leave now and I shall not send word to Major General Greene. Fail to leave, and he will hear from me at the first opportunity."

Dan glanced around at the growing crowd, including several men who'd been drawn to the scene. "I need my things from the hospital tent."

"'Tis happy I am to see you get them." A fiery-haired man, leaning on a crutch, hobbled forward. "And to see your backside leaving camp—for good."

"Thank you, sir." Mistress Crenshaw inclined her head toward the man before turning to Mark. "And thank you for stoppin' him from his ill intentions."

"Aye," added the young laundress who'd poked her head out of the tent Dan had been crouched beside. "I want nothing to do with him, but he will not leave me be."

"He will now." The man with the crutch used it to prod Dan none too gently ahead of him.

Mistress Crenshaw pointed to the laundresses' fire. "Come. Let us be dry while you tell me what the major general said."

To Mark's surprise, another man came and took Naxa, saying he'd see her settled and fed, so Mark followed. When he passed Grace's tent, she smiled at him before withdrawing back inside. Then he ducked beneath the canvas awning and joined Mistress Crenshaw.

"You have been to see the major general?"

"I have. He wishes me to convey his deep gratitude for all thee do here."

She dipped her head, a slight if weary smile gracing her usually stern face.

"His units will be moving frequently, to keep the British guessing, but he wishes thee to remain here. I assured him we have a good spot with shelter, water, wood for fuel, and game to hunt."

"Thanks to you."

"He also wished to prepare thee for the possibility of more wounded coming."

She planted her hands on her hips. "And will he send me more tents in which to house them? Of course he will not." Her lips firmed into a flat line.

"He has requested more provisions from the Continental Congress, but as thee know, they were driven from Philadelphia by the British, and no one seems to know their present location."

That earned a snort.

"I have been saving back the deer hides from hunting," Mark said, "but I cannot both hunt and tan them. If thee could spare two or three of the women to do that chore, we could perhaps fashion two more tents."

"As if I have anyone to spare from any chore." But she sighed and nodded. "'Tis a good thought. I shall ask if any of the women are familiar with tannin' or any men among the wounded who can do the work."

"If not, I can teach them. 'Tisn't difficult, but 'tis time consuming."

That raised her eyebrows. "You are a man of many talents, Mark. I know not how we would get along without you."

"Thee would find another, I have no doubt."

"Not with your modesty and moral standards, I am sure." She cocked her head at him. "I have never had much to do with Quakers before, nor Indians. You are makin' me rethink my opinions."

What could he say to that?

Before he landed on an idea, she walked away, saying over her shoulder, "I will see who can help you with those hides tomorrow. Have a pleasant sleep tonight."

Mark removed his coat and shook the worst of the rain from it before crawling beneath his oiled canvas under the wagon. He'd hoped to use two or three of those hides to fashion his own tent and perhaps make a pair of moccasins with the leftover parts. Still, he was dry and warm enough for now. He got comfortable on the pallet of cedar boughs he'd cut and stacked and covered with another piece of canvas. They kept him off the damp ground.

Then he closed his eyes and prayed. *Lord, I know Thy timing is perfect, and Thy answer is just. I want to be true to Thee, the Lord of all creation, and I want to pursue Grace. Guide me, however, in the way Thee would have me go, as Thee did during the battle when Thee turned me back to the ford to lead the wounded out.* That had been such a clear leading. Why wasn't God giving him a clear direction now?

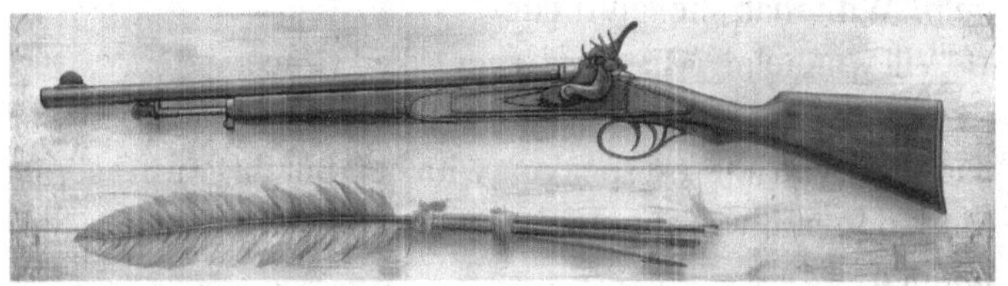

Chapter 28

THE RAIN HAD MOVED on by morning's light, but everything was wet. Wet and cold, water still dripping from the canvas that sheltered them around the laundresses' fire where Grace and the others ate their breakfast.

"I require two or three women to tan deer hides for makin' tents." Mistress Crenshaw joined them beneath the awning as Grace scraped the last of her porridge from her bowl. "The major general expects more wounded will arrive, so we need them as soon as possible. Who knows anythin' about tannin'?"

Grace looked at the other laundresses, but none spoke.

"I know a little bit," Mistress Geyer said. "As children, ve used tanned rabbit hides to make mittens in the old country. But I vould need someone to show me how to get started again, and I have never tried a hide so big as a full deer."

"Mark has agreed to instruct you," Mistress Crenshaw said, "so I will leave it to you to arrange that and pick two more to help." With that, she left them.

"Vill you help?" Mistress Geyer asked Grace.

After five days of silence, was it the right thing to do? Mark had shown no interest speaking with her. But this wasn't about Mark or her, it was about wounded men needing shelter. She nodded.

"Good." Mistress Geyer pointed at Anna. "And you? Ve vill need strong hands to do a good job of it."

"Working with smelly old deer hides." Anna looked at the other laundresses and shrugged. "If my father came in wounded, I would want him to have shelter, so how can I refuse?"

The rest of the women looked relieved not to have been volunteered and hurried off on their normal errands.

"The cold vill keep the vorst of the smell avay," said Mistress Geyer. "This I remember from my childhood."

That was a small blessing in return for Grace's stiff fingers.

Mark approached their fire, a bundle of deer hides in his arms so large he could barely see above them.

They'd have to tan all of those? The enormity of the task made Grace's stomach drop.

"'Tis a kind thing, giving your furs for the vounded." Mistress Geyer cleared a crate for Mark to pile the hides on. "And much appreciated."

"'Tis my pleasure." His eyes met Grace's for a moment, then he motioned for them to sit on the barrels and crates near the fire. He gave them each a hide, and then launched into an explanation of how to scrape every bit of the fat and membrane that clung to the underside. He emphasized the necessity to being careful not to tear the hide itself. A torn hide could still be used, but patching made it smaller and more likely to leak in the rain. From his pocket, he withdrew a handful of rocks that had been chipped to an edge. "Use these instead of a sharp knife." He laid a hide on his lap and showed them the way to hold the rocks and stretch the hide while using it. "'Twould be better to have the hides stretched on a frame, but we have no frames, nor time to make them. This will work."

The instructions were clear and precise, and never once did his eyes meet Grace's again.

While she nursed the grudge that grew within her, Anna and Mistress Geyer mimicked Mark's actions.

Anna peeled a long strip of membrane with dangling bits of fat and even a few leftover flecks of meat on it and held it up. "'Tisn't as hard as I had feared."

"In lean times"—Mark pointed to the strip—"we would cook that with the rest of the membranes for our supper."

Grace pressed the back of her hand to her mouth, but thought better of that move when the hide smell on her fingers nearly choked her.

Mark chuckled. "Thee would think differently if thee had nothing else to eat."

"Ve have you to hunt for us, so ve can eat meat and not..." Mistress Geyer held up a short piece she'd removed from the hide on her lap and dangled it in the air.

"At least for now." Mark sobered. "Come the dead of winter, what my people called 'the hunger time' when food becomes scarce, things could change."

"'Tis vhy you need to hunt now," Mistress Geyer said. "Ve can save the salted and dried meat for those times if ve have fresh meat now. Go on." She made a shooing motion at him. "Ve can finish this, and vhen you return, you can show us the next step."

Mark rose. "Thee are right. I must bring in another deer or two. We will need the brains to rub into the hides to finish them properly."

Brains? Grace's stomach rebelled, and her breakfast threatened a reappearance as Mark walked away.

"Vell, that part I did not remember." Mistress Geyer wrinkled her nose.

Anna's nose matched the older woman's. "I have heard some people eat brains."

Grace spent the rest of the morning wrestling with the membranes that didn't wish to leave the hide while keeping her breakfast down and swallowing her annoyance with Mark. That last part didn't work. Her annoyance rose and blossomed into a simmering anger she barely understood.

The buck had a proud rack, polished to a high shine on the young trees Mark had seen roughed up along the path. With patience drilled into him from childhood, Mark waited for the animal to move into a position where he could get a killing shot. The buck was equally patient, approaching the stream with caution that had served him well for years, as evidenced by the many points on his antlers. Caution had kept the beast safe from the panthers, wolves, and coyotes roaming the forest.

But caution left Mark with too much time. Time to think about Grace with her hands on the hide, doing her best to copy his movements. As with everything, she applied herself wholeheartedly to the task. He'd never seen her shirk a duty given to her. Not once. He could picture the two of them working side by side, learning and growing and building a life together.

So why wasn't God answering Mark's prayer for guidance?

Forgiveness.

It wasn't an actual word he heard, but more of a whisper in his soul.

As if the buck had heard it as well, it bolted forward.

Mark raised his bow, drawing the string tight in the same fluid motion, arrow firmly in his fingers, but the dense growth and the buck's speed didn't allow for him to get the killing shot. The white flag of the animal's tail disappeared into the swamp beyond the stream, the splash if its hooves growing faint in the distance.

Lowering the bow and easing the string, Mark slid his arrow back into its quiver.

Forgiveness for what? Was he to forgive Grace for something? Or did she need to forgive him? Neither made sense. He remained there, puzzling over the revelation, until his feet grew cold. All the puzzling in the world wouldn't bring meat back to camp, so he walked to where he'd left Naxa.

The mare lifted her head as he approached, ears pricked.

"Let us try farther up in the hills." He swung into the saddle and reined the mare around. *Forgiveness*. He needed to stop thinking about the word and concentrate on finding game. He applied his heels to Naxa's sides.

The edge of the hide tore under Grace's hands, the third rip and the hide was barely more than half done. If it'd been a hide for Mark's personal use, she would have gladly punched holes in it, but it was for the injured, the brave husbands and fathers, sons and brothers of the women who worked around her. She groaned.

"I think we could all use a break." Anna stood and set her hide on the crate she used for a seat. She lifted her arms and stretched. "Come on, you will feel better for it."

Grace followed her friend's lead. The stretch made her back pop and snap like a pan of corn over the fire. Anna swung her arms open and wrapped them around herself and repeated the motion, so Grace did too. It felt good to move after being hunched over the smelly hides for hours on end.

Fuming about Mark's lack of interest.

"You have not smiled all day." Anna bent to peer into Grace's eyes. "You do not look sick in body, so it must be in spirit. Or could it be a matter of the heart?" She arched an eyebrow at Grace.

"'Tis nothing."

"While Mistress Geyer is busy with dinner and 'tis just the two of us, tell me what happened between you and Mark." She took a step back and raised her hands at Grace's glare. "I see I have diagnosed the problem."

"There is nothing to tell."

Anna tilted her head and examined Grace as if she were a mouse who'd sneaked into the pantry.

"Truly, there is not. He no longer speaks to me, and I know not why." There. She'd said it out loud.

Mistress Crenshaw approached, and Anna scooped up her hide, plopping on her crate and working again. Grace did the same, both keeping their heads down until the woman had passed them by.

Anna's hands stopped and she leaned over her hide and whispered, "Do you think your mother's visit had something to do with it?"

Of course everyone knew the whole of Grace's story since Mother's visit. Oddly enough, the women treated her just the same, and if anything, the men with a level of respect she hadn't felt before. All except Mark, of course.

"I wish I knew." Grace ran the sharpened rock over her hide with more force than prudence, adding another small tear at the edge.

"I could ask him for you."

"Nay!" The word came out as half a shout. She lowered her voice. "If he wished to speak with me, he knows where I am."

"Oh, very well." Anna shot Grace a glance as she bent over her work. "But if you change your mind..."

"I will not." The past was the past and couldn't be changed. If Mark held her upbringing against her, nothing Anna said would make any difference. Nothing Grace said would either. She'd been a fool to ever imagine someone like her had the hope for a future other than what she was doing now—working for someone else.

Once the war was over, she'd seek a job in service as a maid or perhaps a nanny, even though she had little experience with children. But she could learn. She'd proved that here in camp. She could do whatever she set her mind to... except where men were concerned. She'd been better off when she'd refused to speak to or even make eye contact with a man. That was what she planned to do again.

The poor hide took a beating as she scrubbed every last particle of membrane from it.

The sunlight was already waning as Mark steadied his bow, string pulled back to his cheek, eyes unblinking on the doe in front of him. He'd seen a second buck and another doe earlier, but hadn't had a shot at either. If he didn't bring this one down, there'd be no fresh meat for tomorrow's meals at camp, nor another hide to tan.

Shutting out all thoughts of Grace and forgiveness and what that all meant, Mark barely breathed as the doe picked her way across a narrow opening in the forest. When she paused, he loosed the arrow. It flew straight and true, entering behind the shoulder. She sprang forward four bounds before toppling to her side.

Mark notched another arrow and scanned the area, watching for anything else that might have been tracking the doe.

When no wolf or panther came forward to claim it, he moved from the cover of the trees. Standing over the animal, he thanked the Lord for the means to keep the camp fed another day.

Naxa was dozing next to the tree where he'd left her when he dragged the deer from the woods. The doe was a big animal, too large to hold over his legs, so he hefted her across the saddle. The steady mare didn't flinch at the deer or balk at the added weight when he mounted and sat behind the saddle. He reined Naxa around and urged her forward.

A full hour and a half west of the camp, they traveled along a narrow road with little worry of running into any British. Mark let Naxa settle into a slow trot, her naturally smooth gait making it a comfortable ride even from the back of the saddle. Their shadow grew longer in front of them as the sun sank toward the horizon. Mark relaxed and let his mind empty of the worries of the day, until a trio of riders appeared around a bend in front of them, three feathers protruding from the *kastoweh* hats they wore, two pointed toward the sky, and one pointing to the side.

Iroquois.

His hatred for the Iroquois, which always burned just below his skin, heated him to the boiling point. Mark hadn't touched the precious gunpowder in his powder horn since he'd refilled it from the supply Prudence had brought, but he stopped Naxa and unslung the musket, then dribbled powder into the flash pan.

Of the three men, two swung their guns off their backs. The third man raised one hand, and they all stopped. Then the one who'd raised his hand came forward, alone, at a slow walk.

Mark shouldered his musket, looking down the barrel as the man advanced. The warrior didn't touch his musket nor alter his slow pace. Despite the hatred surging within him, Mark hesitated. Shooting anyone was against everything the Quakers had taught him. In the fading light on a narrow road facing his worst enemy, a battle raged inside Mark. The image of Father with a spear through his chest warred against the image of Lucy's gentle face. He let his finger rest on the trigger, a hair's breadth from discharging the weapon.

Forgiveness.

CHAPTER 29

MARK GAVE THE UNWANTED word a mental push to the side and glared down his musket barrel at the approaching man.

He stopped no more than a rod away, still without a weapon in his hand, and spoke in a language Mark didn't understand. When Mark didn't respond, he asked in heavily accented English, "Who are you?"

"'Tis none of thy business."

"You Quaker?" The man's eyebrows rose to the edge of his *kastoweh*. "You not Indian?"

"I am both." Mark ground the words out, his grip on the musket tightening.

The other man shook his head. "Not Quaker with musket."

Mark flinched.

"Quaker not shoot." The man pointed to one of the men behind him. "Never Miss, he shoot and you die."

"What do thee want?"

"We hungry. Want food." He gestured to the deer.

"Thee cannot have it. 'Tis food for the soldiers."

The man shifted in his saddle, his horse sidestepping. "What soldiers?"

The Iroquois sided with the British. If Mark was going to get out of there with his life, he was going to have to shoot someone. Oddly enough, even through the rage and hatred, the thought saddened him. But he wouldn't lie and add to his list of sins. "George Washington's."

The dark face in front of him broke into a smile, and he shouted something in their own language back to the others. Then he nodded to Mark. "Oneida." He thumped a hand to his chest. "Broken Rock." He pointed to the two men, who were now approaching, their guns lowered but still in hand. "Never Miss. David Crow. We look for Washington. Oneida help Washington."

Mark kept his musket raised. "The Iroquois side with the British."

"British bad." Broken Rock shook his head. "Bad for Iroquois. Oneida"—he made a slash with his hand—"break away. Find Washington."

They didn't know where Washington was, or they wouldn't be heading west. Mark knew little of the Oneida other than they were part of the Iroquois Confederacy and lived far to the north. These men must have been traveling for many days, even weeks. Their weary-looking horses attested to that.

Broken Rock thumped his chest again. "Fight at Fort Stanwix. Fight Mohawk there. Big fight. Many die."

Nash had spoken of the battle at Fort Stanwix, of Indians fighting with the British as well as with the Americans. Mark couldn't remember the details. Broken Rock's face turned grave, and his voice deepened, convincing Mark he spoke the truth. But he was Oneida, and the Oneida were part of the Iroquois.

Forgiveness.

Time slowed and the air around Mark grew thinner and clearer. The word had nothing to do with Grace or the British. It had nothing to do with the men in front of him. It had everything to do with what had happened to his father. Lucy's words, spoken years prior, came back on the clear air as if he heard them for the first time. *For if ye do forgive men their trespasses, your heavenly Father will also forgive you. But if ye do not forgive men their trespasses, no more will your Father forgive you your trespasses.* Almost of its own accord, his musket came to rest over the body of the deer.

"Thee are heading in the wrong direction." He slung the musket across his back again. "Come with me. We will eat at the camp." He looked Broken Rock in the eye. "Together."

The Oneida spoke among themselves, then Broken Rock nodded.

Mark rode past the men, ignoring the prickling between his shoulders as he presented his back to them. The *clomp* of their horses' hooves let him know they followed. He kept going, and in the silence, he opened his heart to God, the Creator of both the Lenni Lenape and the Quakers.

I forgive him, Lord, the man who killed my father. Not because I wish to, but because Thy word says I must. I wish to obey Thee because I trust Thee. Lucy tried to make me understand, but I could not. Not until Thee sent me the word. Thank Thee, Lord.

With a touch of his heels, he sent Naxa into her slow trot. He wasn't foolish enough to think that the anger—the hatred—of the Iroquois would be easy to erase, but oddly enough, something inside of him felt lighter.

Darkness fell and there was still no sign of Mark. Not that Grace needed to see him, but they needed the meat he should have brought. They'd had enough to feed the wounded their supper, but the laundresses and others had eaten a meatless meal, choosing to save the salt pork.

She scrubbed the last kettle clean, then wiped sweat from her brow. What she wouldn't give for a bath. Even with the cool temperatures of mid-October, working over the cooking fire and washing up afterward made her sweaty and—she sniffed—stinky. She wiped her hands dry and went to the tent she shared with Mistress Geyer, where she grabbed the last precious sliver of scented soap she'd been hoarding, her clean shift, dress, and petticoat, then headed for the small stream that fed into the river. With Dan Browne gone, and the men generally ignoring her now, she was emboldened enough to have a real bath for the first time in far too long.

Just please, Lord, do not let me almost step on another wounded Hessian.

The prayers were easier now, coming almost unbidden at the oddest moments. But once thought, there was a peace that settled around her heart.

At the stream, she stripped to her shift and shook her hair free of its braid. Half a moon in the cloud-free sky highlighted the sparkling water as it flowed toward the river, babbling over a patch of rocks that jutted out of the streambed. On her first step in, the cold water stole her breath away and gooseflesh pebbled her skin. She set the soap on a rock. Then, undaunted, she plopped down in the stream. The water level rose to just below Grace's shoulders. Taking a deep breath, she leaned back until the water enveloped her, but only for a moment before she sputtered to the surface. Remaining seated on the sandy bottom of the stream, she fumbled for the soap and then lathered her hair. She tried to imagine herself in her mother's small copper bath in front of the brazier they used to heat their room, but that didn't stop her teeth from chattering.

She lifted her arm to soap it and studied its length illuminated in the moonlight. How had she never suspected that her father was an Indian? Well, half Indian, but he must have been raised as one to have been named Singing Turtle. Plenty of swarthy men populated the docks in Philadelphia, dressed in gaudy colors with gold rings in their ears. No doubt Mother had entertained more than a few. Any one of them could have left her with her dusky skin, but Grace had always suspected that her father had been someone special. Mother's refusal to speak of him, for one thing, but also the way she grew sad the few times Grace had dared to mention her father.

A horse snorted nearby.

Grace ducked into the water until it covered her to her chin. She shivered and clenched her teeth to stop their chattering.

Another snort, followed by a guttural word in a language Grace didn't know. It sent another type of chill through her. It was one thing to contemplate her father being an Indian or knowing Mark was one. Meeting an Indian in the woods while nearly naked and freezing was... terrifying. She sank even lower, barely keeping her nose out of the water.

More guttural words, and then came a voice she knew all too well.

"Water thy horses here. The camp is just beyond."

Mark.

Four horses and riders stopped at the stream not three full rods away. They were upwind of her, and she could smell the horses and other odors on the breeze. If they'd stopped on the other side of her, would they have smelled her scented soap? Would it have given her away?

When the horses finished drinking, lifting their dripping muzzles and snorting droplets that sparkled in the moonlight, Mark pointed toward the camp. "That way." The others moved out, and when one looked back, Mark moved his horse to block his view of Grace. When they were past him, Mark twisted in his saddle to look straight at her.

How had he known she was there? She hadn't moved, had barely breathed.

He said nothing when their eyes met, just faced forward and clicked to his horse, following the Indians.

Had he once again found her wanting in some way? She hadn't been able to read his expression in the moonlight. Did he judge her harshly for desiring a bath? Anger brought a welcome surge of warmth. She sat up and rubbed the soap between her hands, working a lather that she scrubbed into her hair. If she wanted a bath, she'd take a bath, and mister high-and-mighty Mark the Quaker Indian could think what he liked. After dousing and rinsing her hair, she stood and soaped the rest of her beneath her shift, then sat down and rinsed, her teeth chattering fit to break before she was done. She scrambled to the bank and dried herself with her dirty dress before donning her clean clothes.

Grace marched back into camp, wet hair trailing over her shoulders and dampening her dress.

Mark and the three Indians were eating near the fire, Mistress Geyer flittered around, waiting on them. When she saw Grace, her expression turned from worried to shocked.

"Grace, dear. You vill catch your death in this cold. Come and varm yourself by the fire."

She'd rather chew rocks than spend a moment in Mark's company, but she wasn't stupid. Neither was Mistress Geyer, so she took the good woman's advice and stomped as close to the fire as she dared, letting its warmth steam away the lingering dampness from her clothing and begin to dry her hair.

The Indians ignored her, stuffing their faces with whatever was in their bowls, using their fingers. Mark let his spoon settle in his bowl, his gaze following her movements as she fluffed her hair to hurry its drying. But she didn't meet his look. She was past making eye contact with any man. What had happened at the river had been beyond her control, but from now on, she was in charge of who she looked at and who she spoke to. Including Mark.

Especially Mark.

"These men have come to assist Yeneral Vashington." There was a waver of uncertainty in Mistress Geyer's voice. "And Mark brought us another deer. Enough to feed camp tomorrow and another hide to tan."

Grace smiled at her. "That is good news. We should be able to fashion two small tents with the additional hide."

Mark set his bowl on the ground. "I had hoped—"

"If you will excuse me," Grace said to Mistress Geyer. "I believe I shall retire early tonight." Without a backward glance, she strode toward their tent with her back straight and head up. It was rude, and Mistress Geyer might berate her for it later, but Grace didn't care. Mark hadn't spoken to her for days, and she wasn't about to pretend all was well just because he'd dragged along a few Indians who said they wanted to help Washington.

Mark stared after Grace, then looked to Mistress Geyer. The woman's mouth had thinned to a firm line, but he had a feeling her disapproval wasn't about Grace's rudeness when her blue eyes focused on him.

"Mark, find a place for these men to sleep, and you can take them to the army in the morning. The major yeneral vill know vhat to do vith them." Her accent thickened, which could be from worry or displeasure.

He rose and motioned for the others to follow.

"One from stream," said Broken Rock, "she angry to you."

Mark wasn't surprised the others had noticed Grace, her face above the frigid water, hair floating around her like a living thing, beautiful in the moonlight. Thankfully, it'd been dark enough that nothing had shown from beneath the surface. Not that it would have bothered the other three, who were used to communal bathing. It was Mark's Quaker upbringing that rebelled at such an invasion of her modesty and privacy.

They arrived at the wagon. "This is where I sleep. There is room for the four of us."

One of the men spoke to Broken Rock and their conversation grew into a heated discussion among the three of them. Finally, Broken Rock faced Mark again. "They are uneasy, sleeping trapped beneath a wagon."

Mark grabbed his bedding and wadded it into an easy-to-carry bundle. "Come. We shall sleep near the horses tonight."

It would be cold without any clouds, but at least it wouldn't rain. Mark spread his bedding near Naxa, who blew out a soft snort. The other men arranged themselves in a semi-circle. A fire near their feet would have been nice, but Mark doubted the others would appreciate it. They would prefer to remain unseen and cold than warm and backlit by a fire. Distant memories invaded his thoughts as he settled for the night. Memories of his mother and father and the long journey to the Ohio Territory. Just before he fell asleep, the memory of his father's death came to him again. *Forgiveness*. Instead of growing angry, he visualized himself handing the hatred over to the Lord of all creation.

It wasn't easy. Even in his half-dream state, he wanted to snatch it back and hold it firm. But Lucy's words—words from the Bible—convinced him yet again to let go. Would the struggle get easier with time? He hoped so. Following the Lord in all ways was the best choice for him, for anyone. Of that, he had no doubt. And he had another issue to deal with.

Lord, if it be Thy will, allow me to speak with Grace soon and learn the desires of her heart in regards to me.

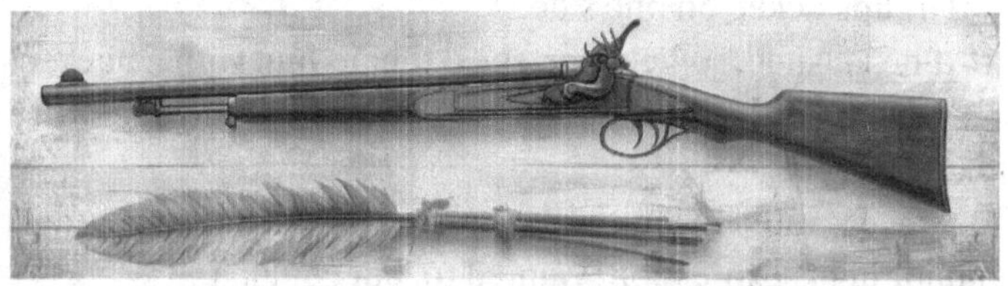

CHAPTER 30

GRACE ROSE EARLIER THAN normal and crept past Mistress Geyer. She rekindled the cooking fire and went to the stream for fresh water to make the morning porridge. When she saw the man bent over the stream scrubbing his face, she almost fled.

Mark.

Fleeing wouldn't get the porridge made, so she squared her shoulders and approached. Naturally, he was in the only spot where it was deep enough to dip and fill the buckets without getting her boots or clothing wet. And it was too cold this morning to chance that.

He looked up, then rose and reached for the buckets.

Stubbornly, she refused to turn them over. "I can do it."

"I know thee can. But 'tis my wish to assist thee."

"'Tis my wish that you leave me to get about my work if your morning ablutions are finished."

His lips ticked on one side.

If he laughed, so help her, she'd thump him with a bucket.

"I have not heard the term 'ablutions' from anyone other than Lucy."

Grace wanted to look away from the mixture of sorrow and humor in his expression. Wanted to, but couldn't.

"Come." He reached for the buckets again. "Lucy would have my hide like one of those deer should I not assist thee. Do not make me turn away from her gentle teaching."

What could she do? Remembering the old woman's creased face, Grace released the rope handles to him.

He plunged both buckets into the stream, drew out the fresh water, and then came to her side. "I would speak with thee, if thee can spare a moment."

"Perhaps later." She turned her back and took a step away.

"I will be gone soon, taking the Iroquois to Nathanael Greene, and then perhaps on to General Washington. I know not when I shall return."

That stopped her. She faced him again. "Why do you wish to speak to me now, after ignoring me ever since my mother left?" There. He could explain himself. Whether or not she wished to understand was still up to her.

"Because I have prayed for wisdom, and the Lord brought thee here this morning."

She crossed her arms. "What did you pray for?"

"Wisdom concerning thee and me."

Grace braced herself for his dismissal, letting her anger grow as the moment dragged out. Anger that he'd ignored her for so long and made her feel inferior.

"But first, the Lord had to show me the error of my ways." His eyes met hers again. "I have harbored a hatred, a very old and deep hatred that often turned to anger. I needed to forgive someone." She must have looked as confused as she felt, because he continued, "Not thee, of course. 'Twas someone from my past."

"What did this someone do?"

He looked away. Was he nervous?

Her anger eased, but she ignored the urge to go to his side.

"He killed my father."

Grace's quick intake of breath had Mark looking at her again. She hadn't known what to expect, but certainly not that. "How can you forgive someone who killed your father?"

"On my own, I could not." His lips quirked. "'Tis only through trusting in the Lord of all creation that I could take that step."

"I do not understand." Grace took a step backward. "I could never..."

"If thee come to trust in God, thee could."

"What has God ever done for me?" Her words came out in a cry, as if wrenched from her soul. "You know my background. The Lord has had nothing to do with me."

"Thee said thee prayed at the cliff."

She had. And she'd felt... something. Not to mention the other prayers, the ones that came almost naturally now. She wasn't ready to share that. Not yet. It was all too new and too uncertain. "I was afraid. I knew not what I was doing."

"We often find the Lord through trying times. 'Tis how I found Him, left as an orphan, taken in by Lucy and shown the Lord's love and caring."

Grace took another step back. "The only one who ever loved or cared for me was my mother."

"And yet, thee reached out to Him when thee were afraid. So in thy heart, thee know He is real."

"I do not—"

"Did thee reach out to anyone else?"

Grace opened her mouth, then snapped it shut. What could she say? She hadn't. Hadn't even thought of anyone else. Why? *Because there is no one else.* The thought came from somewhere, but Grace shook her head. "I must start the porridge." She whirled and lengthened her stride.

Mark kept pace with her without spilling a drop from the buckets.

"What did the Lord tell you about me?" She didn't look at him and braced herself for the worst.

"He brought thee to the stream—to me." He stopped. "Grace?"

As if his voice had thrown a rope around her and pulled it tight, she stopped.

"Why are thee running away from me?"

She had porridge to cook and hides to finish tanning and... and she didn't know why, but she blinked back tears she didn't want Mark to see and kept her back to him. "I have things to do."

He passed her, not stopping again until he'd poured both buckets into her porridge kettle. Then he set them down and faced her. "When I return, we will speak more." He strode off toward where the horses were picketed.

He would ride to the army, into possible danger. Grace's chest ached with the thought that something might happen to him. What if he never returned? What if her angry words were the last between them?

"I am heading to see the major general." Mark sank to the ground next to Nash's pallet. "Do thee wish me to take him a message?"

"Tell him I am improving and should be able to return shortly." Nash sat up, but had to brace himself, no doubt still plagued with dizziness.

"I can see that."

"I am serious." Nash looked straight at Mark with eyes that were clear and focused. "I only see one of you now. You look no prettier than you did before I got hit on the head."

"And the darkness?"

Nash shrugged. "'Tis improving, truly. Just not as fast as I wished. But tell me, why are you returning to the major general now?"

"While hunting yesterday, I came across three Iroquois—they claim to be Oneida—searching for General Washington."

"Indians?" The word all but burst from his friend.

"They say the Oneida have broken from the Iroquois Confederacy, that they wish to join forces with Washington." It would be good for Mark to think of them as Oneida—not Iroquois. It brought less temptation to let the hatred seep back.

Nash squinted toward the light at the tent's flap. "You believe them?"

Mark wouldn't have thought it possible even the morning before, but now...? He did. That alone was proof the Lord was involved. "I do. There are just the three of them, not a force to come up against an army. They show signs of having traveled a far distance." Then he cleared his throat. "And they did not kill me."

"For that, I am grateful."

"I shall take them to the major general. He can decide if they are to go any farther."

"That is wise." Nash leaned closer and dropped his voice. "If we could get some of the tribes on our side, 'twould even things out. Too many are allying themselves with the British. But 'tis hard to trust those we have so recently fought against."

He referred to Pontiac's Rebellion, of course, and before that, the French and Indian War.

"Times change, my friend." Mark stood. "Keep out of trouble until I return."

"Once the headaches and dizziness pass, you can escort me back to the troops."

Nothing would make Mark happier than to see Nash restored to full health, but only time would tell. He left the tent, passing Anna who had arrived carrying a tray with bowls full of porridge.

The Iroquois men were finished eating by the time Mark reached the cooking fire. He wolfed down a bowl of the porridge, then saddled Naxa and headed away from camp. Broken Rock rode beside him, his face impassive as he scanned their surroundings. They didn't speak much—there wasn't any need. These men wanted to find Washington, and Mark had already agreed to take them as far as Nathanael's army.

They arrived at the last place Mark had met with Nathanael, but the army had moved again. It wasn't hard to follow their trail. An army couldn't very easily cover its tracks.

By the time they reached the new camp, it was nearly nightfall. They were met by the sentries, and one of them, recognizing Mark, led them to the commander's tent which was, as always, surrounded by an armed guard.

The Oneida wisely kept their hands well away from their weapons. Instead of being invited to dismount and enter the tent, they waited as Nathanael was called outside.

He did not look best pleased to see Mark with the trio of warriors.

"What is the meaning of this?" His voice broke the uneasy silence.

"These Oneida wish to meet with and join General Washington in the fight against the British," Mark said.

"They do?" Nathanael's scowl said he was less than convinced. "Why?"

"My people," Broken Rock thumped a hand over his heart, "fight British. British bad for Oneida."

"Oneida." Nathanael snapped his fingers. "Are thee not part of the Iroquois Confederacy?" His voice rose in challenge, and several of the armed guards lifted their weapons.

Best to let Broken Rock state his own case, so Mark remained silent, even though Nathanael's glare had swung to him.

"No more." The Oneida made the same slashing motion he'd used with Mark. "Others join British. Oneida no." Then Broken Rock looked Nathanael up and down. "You Quaker?" He'd obviously heard the *thee* in Nathanael's question.

The major general drew himself to his full and impressive height. "I was."

Was? Mark shouldn't have been surprised. Nathanael's Quaker meeting must have rejected him for his stance on fighting. As Mark's would also reject him if he picked up a weapon against another human. They might even do so for the small role he was filling in the war.

Broken Rock nodded. "You change sides." He thumped his chest again. "Oneida change sides."

"Do the others speak English?" Nathanael asked.

"Only Broken Rock speak white man's words."

"Mark?" Nathanael turned to him. "Can thee speak their language?"

Mark shook his head. "'Tis too different from Lenni Lenape."

That earned Mark another scowl before Nathanael shouted for another interpreter to be found. Then he motioned Mark to dismount and follow him to the tent. Once inside, he faced Mark. "We shall get all that sorted out, but tell me, how are things in the followers' camp?"

"Nash asked me to tell thee that he is getting better and hopes to return soon."

The big man cocked his head. "Will he?"

"He is improving, but I cannot say how soon he will be fit to ride."

Nathanael went to his chair and sat, drumming his fingers on the table. "I could use that man, but not if he cannot ride."

"I wish I could do more." Mark meant it, but he also felt the restriction of his convictions more clearly than ever, the Quaker training winning out over his warrior ancestors.

"Nay." Nathanael squinted at him. "I know what thee are going through. Once, I had the same choice to make. This"—he spread his arms to take in the tent—"is where my destiny lies. 'Tis the answer to my prayers. However, the Lord may not seek the same from thee. Above all, be true to Him, Mark. 'Tis the best all of us can do."

There was such sincerity in his eyes that Mark had to swallow the lump forming in his throat. "I do wish to help, in whatever way I can."

"There are more ways to be a Patriot than by shouldering a musket." Nathanael rose and paced from his cot to his desk, his limp more noticeable than normal. "I have another job for thee, and Nash if he is up to it. Washington wants to attack Philadelphia yet this winter, but the other generals are against the idea. In the meantime, we need to secure a place for the army to spend the winter. Provisions must be amassed." He ran a hand over the top of his head, smoothing his hair back. "It must be within a day's march of Philadelphia, have a good water supply, adequate wood for fires and building shelters, and"—he whipped around and faced Mark—"it must be defendable against attack. We cannot assume that Howe's forces—or his Indian allies—will not march to find us."

"Thee wish me to scout out such a place?"

"Indeed. Report back to me within a week. Thee are dismissed."

Mark hesitated. "About the Oneida—"

"Leave them to me. Winter quarters are what is most important right now. I cannot spare even one fighting man to scout them out."

Mark turned to leave.

"When thee next reach camp, send me every man who can see straight and walk this far. I need bodies. I needed them yesterday."

"I will." Mark exited the tent. The Oneida and their guards were gone, no longer his responsibility. He took a deep breath and blew it out.

If he returned to camp, Nash would insist on going with him, even though he could barely sit upright on his pallet, much less in a saddle. A day's march from Philadelphia left a lot of territory to cover, but if it could be close to where the followers' camp already was, it would be easier to move the wounded. Their present camp would not do. Come spring, the river would flood as snow runoff to the north overflowed its banks. Mark pinched the bridge of his nose, digging through old memories of hunting with his uncle and walking in circles to locate a wounded deer. The same principle would apply.

Someone had tied Naxa to a nearby tree. He untied her and led her to the officers' cooking fire.

A grizzly man wearing a grouch glared at him from under a ratty tricorn hat. "What do you want?"

"Major General Greene is sending me on a scouting mission. I need provisions for several days."

"I have barely enough to feed the officers." The old man shook a dripping spoon at him. "If you be a scout worth your salt, hunt your own food."

That was plain enough. Despite the darkness, Mark mounted and turned Naxa to the north. He'd sleep hungry tonight and hunt in the morning. First for food, and then for the army's wintering ground. The quicker he could get that done, the sooner he'd return to Grace and they could work through their differences.

Lord, Thy timing is always perfect and good. Grace needs Thee, but she knows it not. Reveal Thyself to her that she may understand Thy lovingkindness. The silent prayer lifted his spirit as Naxa carried them into the night.

Chapter 31

Grace slapped a chunk of the salted pork, part of the shipment Mother had brought, onto her worktable. Mark had been gone for three days, and they'd cooked the last of the deer he'd brought in yesterday by boiling the bones and serving a thin if nourishing soup. Today she must dip into their reserves. Mistress Crenshaw hadn't been happy about that, but the wounded men who'd been fit enough to send out to hunt the day before had come back exhausted and empty-handed.

Where was Mark? Had he found the army and delivered the Indians? Or had they turned on him and killed him somewhere in the forest? They could have run into a British patrol and be on their way to one of those ghastly prison ships the soldiers sometimes talked about in hushed voices.

Had her cold reception of him that last day made him decide to deliver the Indians and ride on—away from her?

She pressed her hand to her stomach, which wanted to twist inside of her at that thought. She'd been unkind. He'd shared about his father's death, about his willingness to forgive the killer because God demanded it. But once he'd mentioned God, she'd bristled like a riled porcupine. If he did ride on, she could only blame herself.

Lord, if You are near, protect Mark from danger. I would rather him ride away than die at the hands of those Indians or the British, even if I never know the outcome.

There. She'd prayed. Only time would tell if it did any good. Which she doubted. And yet, she didn't. A part of her wanted to believe. Mark believed, and he was different from anyone she'd ever known, even her old nanny, who had spoken of God but lived like everyone else around her. Mark didn't. He was... he was a good man, strong and kind and...

"Vhat are you making vith the salt pork today?" Mistress Geyer's voice made Grace jump. "I did not mean to frighten you."

"I was woolgathering." Grace grabbed a knife and began hacking the meat into pieces.

"You miss Mark, no doubt." A gentle sigh followed the woman's words. "As I miss my Peter. I vish the camps vere closer, that I do."

"Do you think 'tis because of the fighting that they leave us here?"

"Aye." The older woman shielded her eyes with her hand and looked to the east, not that they could see anything beyond the forest across the river. "But they must move us soon if ve are to be ready for the vinter. I pray they do."

Grace took her bottom lip between her teeth for a moment, but then blurted out her question. "Do you believe in prayer?" The shock on Mistress Geyer's face had Grace looking at her stilled hands, clenching the knife and meat. "I was not raised going to church, you know."

"Nay, I suppose not." The flustered woman lifted a hand toward Grace, then let it drop. "I did not think... that is... I yoost assumed..."

"'Tis all right. Thee knew not my full background until recently."

Then a warm arm came around Grace's shoulders, and a gentle hand cupped her chin, bringing her face around to meet the kind, faded blue eyes of her friend. "The Lord is bigger than the church, you know. He is the head of the church, for sure, but He also lives here"—she motioned to the camp around them—"vhere ve are. Ve can pray to Him at any time no matter vhere ve are."

"And He listens?" Because she'd prayed for Mark, she desperately wanted to hear that He did.

"Alvays He listens to His children."

"But I am not. I have never believed in Him."

"Never?" Mistress Geyer cocked her head. "Do I not remember you asking Mark to pray back on the cliff?"

"Because I know *he* believes."

"You must have believed enough to ask, enough to trust God vould answer Mark's prayer, did you not?"

Had she?

"You vould not have asked him to pray to a God you did not think existed, now vould you? Vhat vould be the point in that?"

Indeed. Grace searched her friend's face. "You think I do believe?"

"I think you must." Her smile was beautiful and loving, and Grace stepped into her full embrace.

"How can I know more about the Lord?"

"Talk to Him. Talk to Him often and then vait and listen for His response."

Grace leaned back but kept her hands on the other woman's arms. "He will speak to *me*?" Her last word came out with a squeak.

"Oh, not the kind of vords you hear vith your ears, but the kind of vords you hear vith your heart."

"I do not understand."

"Nay, you vill not at first." Mistress Geyer shook a finger under Grace's nose. "But do not let that stop you. Believe and trust and the knowledge—the understanding—'tvill come in time." She smiled again, full of love and understanding. "Choose first to believe."

"What is going on here?" Mistress Crenshaw descended upon them with a scowl and planted her fists on her hips. "Why is supper not started?"

Mistress Geyer turned to her with the same expression she'd bestowed on Grace. "Grace needed a bit of encouragement. I am sure you can understand that, can you not?" She took the other woman by the arm and led her away, speaking about the need to send out gathering parties now that the laundresses were not cleaning the soldiers' clothing.

Grace returned to chopping the meat and then slid the salty globs into the pot she'd left to simmer. Together with wild onions and carrots Anna had gathered the day before, it would make a stew Grace could stir dumplings into later. But as her fingers worked, her mind churned with Mistress Geyer's words.

The Lord listened. He'd heard her prayer. And if she listened back, He might speak to her.

She wasn't sure if that reassured her—or terrified her.

Kneeling beside the dying fire, Mark blew the embers back to life. He positioned the remains of last evening's rabbit on the spit to warm. Cold rabbit wasn't a bad breakfast, but it was a chilly morning, and he relished the idea of something hot in his middle. It wouldn't be long before frost sparkled on the leaves blanketing the ground. More had fallen in the night, the wind shaking them from the trees.

Lucy had loved this time of year. She would brew a pot of tea and sit by the window to sip it, watching the leaves drift down in their colorful patterns and exclaiming over the beauty of the Lord's handiwork. Too often, Mark had only seen the work involved in raking and removing them to the small garden to cover the root crops for the winter, only to rake them again in the spring and burn them, then spreading the cooled ashes on the garden and working them into the soil.

He rose and moved Naxa, tying her where she could reach a good swath of grass and weeds. He hadn't camped near water, but they couldn't be too far from the river, so he'd fill his canteen and let Naxa drink when they reached it. He'd already found a couple of sites that the army might use for the winter, and while either would work, he wasn't satisfied with them. The water supply for one would likely freeze over, and the other might not have enough wood to see them through building, heating, and cooking until spring.

After he'd eaten and put out the fire, he saddled Naxa and moved on, once again working in circles. It was midafternoon before he came to a valley on the northern edge of the restrictions Nathanael had given him. The site was on the banks of the Schuylkill River, so water would be no problem. The fast-moving river would be easy to keep open enough to draw water, even in the coldest weeks. There was a plateau that would be defendable, and surrounding it all, including on the other side of the river, was plenty of standing timber. A stream fed into the Schuylkill that would create yet another defensible barrier to attack. It reminded Mark of a place where his tribe had once wintered long ago.

On the same side of the river as Mark were scattered a collection of farms, not unlike those on the outskirts of Birmingham. Sorrow tugged at the edges of his thoughts as he took in the sight of the neat buildings, houses and barns, surrounded by barren fields, the harvest no doubt having been gathered into those barns. A flock of sheep rested on one hillside and small groups of cattle dotted the area.

He'd found what Nathanael needed, and the camp followers wouldn't have to go far to reach it.

As much as he wanted to return to the camp, he must first report to Nathanael. He rode toward the nearest farmstead. A man waded among a pen of squealing pigs, dumping a bucket of slop into a wooden trough as Mark approached.

"Hello," Mark called.

With the pigs now grunting in their feed, the man heard him and raised a hand in greeting.

"Can thee tell me the name of this place?"

The fellow looked up at him. "I thought thee an Indian when thee rode up. 'Tis good to hear thy speech."

"'Tis a common mistake." No sense in telling the man more.

"This be the Valley Forge meeting."

"I am from the Birmingham Meeting."

"A long way from home." The farmer scratched above his ear. "What brings thee north?"

"I am on mission for a friend." Best to leave it at that. "Thy valley is beautiful. I trust the harvest was good this year."

"It was." The man snorted and shook his head. "But the British left little of it for us to sustain ourselves through the winter."

"The British were here?"

"Aye, not a month past, close to five hundred as best I could account."

Nathanael would want to know that, as would Washington. There'd be little help from the locals to feed the army.

He tipped his head toward the other side of the river. "Is the hunting good over there?"

"Good enough in the spring, summer, and fall, but much of the wildlife will push south ahead of the snows."

Hunting would have to be farther out then, more good information. At least they could spear fish in the river to supplement their meat.

"Thank thee for the information. I shall pass it on to my friend."

"If he be thinking of moving here, tell him best to wait for the spring. 'Twill be a lean winter for sure."

"I shall pass that on." He aimed Naxa back to Nathanael, pushing her into a lope once out of sight of the farmer.

It wasn't an ideal location, but it was the easiest to defend, for sure, and had all the water they'd need. Being among a settlement of Quakers would benefit the army, as they would not take up arms against them nor help the British in any way.

Or would they? Joseph might have been doing that very thing the last time Mark had seen him, walking with the British soldiers, talking and laughing.

There was no perfect place. Mark would give Nathanael the information on the three best he'd found. While he would choose Valley Forge, Washington would have the final say.

The ride back to Nathanael's camp took him most of the day. They'd moved again, farther east away from the followers' camp. He'd have to spend the night and start back in the morning.

He found the general's tent and nodded to the guards, who let him pass. They'd grown comfortable with his comings and goings. He slipped from Naxa's back, and one of the soldiers led her away. It gave him an odd feeling, being treated as if he were someone of importance. Odd in the sense of not knowing quite how to respond to it, but also odd in that it didn't seem to fit who he was, neither as a Quaker nor a Lenni Lenape.

The guard beside Nathanael's tent announced his presence, and the general called him in.

"What have thee found for me?" The big man didn't bother with pleasantries.

"Three places that will suit thee for wintering the army." Mark detailed each one, their locations near the river, along with their strengths and flaws.

Nathanael tented his fingers together, elbows on the desk, and listened, never taking his eyes off of Mark until he finished. Then he sat back in his chair, the wood creaking in protest beneath him. "Which would thee choose?"

Mark hadn't expected to be asked his opinion. "Valley Forge."

The general studied him for a moment. "Because 'tis populated with Quakers?"

"Because 'tis the easiest to defend and the farthest from Philadelphia while still being a day's march away." Mark weighed the truth of his words and added, "And maybe somewhat because of the Quakers."

"Thee think them harmless?" There was an underlying tone that Mark couldn't quite identify.

"They are pacifists. They will not fight."

"What thee say should be true, yet here I am." The general spread his arms, then let them drop to his sides as he leaned forward. "And here are thee."

"I am not fighting." Why did Mark feel the need to defend himself?

"Thee are scouting, thee are assisting the effort, even if thee never use thy weapons against another man. Think thee that the Quakers in this place..." He raised his brow.

"Valley Forge."

"Aye. Valley Forge. Think thee they would not do the same for the British?" There was a definite challenge in his tone. "The work of people like thee is essential to an army."

"I had not considered that."

"Nay." Nathanael waved a dismissive hand, as if to wipe out his words. "And why would thee? 'Tis my job. Thank thee for the information. Return in five days, and I should be able to give thee direction to where Washington will decide to move the followers' camp." He gave Mark a message for Mistress Crenshaw before dismissing him.

The guard at the entrance to the tent said, "Get yourself to the cook's fire. Someone brought in an elk this morning. For once, there be plenty for all."

Mark took his plate of roasted elk with a hard biscuit and squatted to eat near where Naxa grazed from her tether. The meat was hot and filling, the biscuit a chore to chew, but he was hungry and persevered, washing it all down with water from his canteen. Tomorrow, he'd speak with Grace again. And after that, he had a decision to make.

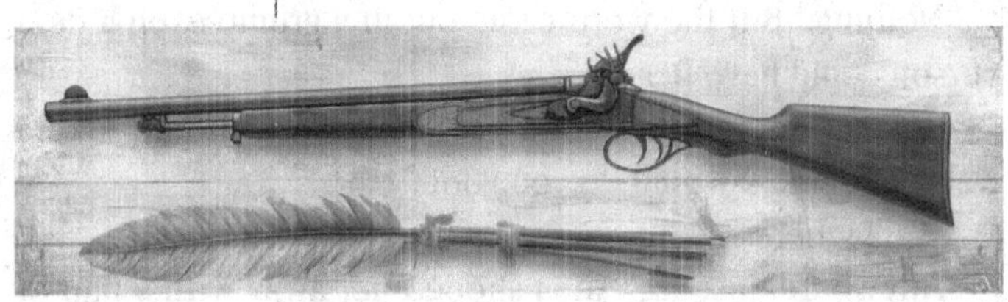

Chapter 32

The never-ending chores—rising early, cooking the porridge, cleaning up afterward, only to start the noon meal, and then the evening meal—created a monotonous existence. Packing up and moving again would at least give them something else to do. And yet, Grace had enough to eat, warm clothing, and a tent to share with Mistress Geyer. She should be grateful.

Instead, she was miserable.

God hadn't answered her prayer. At least, she didn't know if he had. It'd been five days since Mark rode away, the longest he'd ever been gone from camp. Would he return at all? Was he on his way back to the Brandywine? Or was he lying dead somewhere, unknown and unmourned?

She threw her washrag into the cleaned kettle and wiped her chapped hands on her apron.

"What has you in a mood?" Anna stoked the fire to ready it for baking the bread she'd shaped into round loaves.

"Nothing." But the word came out in a grump even a deaf person could have heard.

Anna stood and stretched her back. "You should take a walk. The break would do you good."

"Walk where?"

"Anywhere, just go." Anna shooed her away with a flap of her apron. "Get away from the fire, away from the food, and relax for a time. You work too hard."

What else was there to do? But Grace had grouched at Anna enough already, so she kept the question to herself. "Perhaps a walk along the river would be good."

"There, you see?" Anna beamed a smile at her. "Off you go."

She'd gone a few steps before turning back around. "Thank you, Anna."

"Go." Another flap of the apron sent Grace off again.

The river was smooth without a puff of breeze to ruffle its surface. The sun had climbed halfway to its zenith, reflecting in sparkles that normally would have delighted her. Grace pulled the head off a tall stalk of dried grass and shredded it in her hands. What was wrong with her? She'd not been this moody even while living above the alley in Philadelphia.

Before she'd met Mark. Before she'd known who her father was. Were all her troubles caused by Indians? Or just men?

She dusted the bits of grass off her hands, then sat on a flat rock near the water. *Why am I so unhappy, Lord?* The prayer came unexpectedly, and she looked around as if someone else had asked it. Perhaps Mistress Geyer was right. Perhaps Grace really did believe in the Lord. Gathering her courage, she folded her hands in her lap and plunged on.

Please let Mark be unhurt, wherever he is. He is a good man, too good for the likes of me, I know. She struggled to voice her deepest fears, but if she was talking to the Lord, didn't He already know them? *I know not what will happen to me after the war. I would like to get married and have a family.* But that wasn't all of it. She squeezed her hands tighter. *With Mark.*

Remembering what Mistress Geyer had said, Grace waited. She kept her eyes shut, let her head drop forward, her chin resting on her chest, and she listened.

In the distance, a crow squawked long and loud, berating whatever had disturbed it. Nearer to her, a bee buzzed, no doubt gathering the last of summer's nectar in preparation for winter. From across the river, a squirrel chittered. All normal sounds, but nothing from the Lord. Still, she waited.

"Grace?"

She nearly jumped out of her skin.

When he first saw her sitting there on the rock, Mark stopped Naxa at a distance and enjoyed the vision. She was lovely, maybe not in the fashionable way, but the Quaker in him cared nothing for fashion. If she were a Lenni Lenape woman in the summer, she would be bare to the waist. Uncomfortable with that thought—or knowing he should be—Mark shoved it out of his mind's eye.

When she didn't move after many minutes, he grew concerned and heeled Naxa forward, her hooves pressing almost silently into the damp earth.

"Grace?"

She gasped and leaped to her feet, eyes wild. "What are you doing here?" Her words tumbled out like water over the rapids.

"I was on my way back to camp and saw thee. I did not mean to startle thee."

"And yet, you did. Again." She hugged her arms around herself. "You have made a habit of that."

That was certainly true, but never intentionally. "Pray, forgive me."

"Pray?" She looked around and then back at him, her eye rounding.

What was she thinking behind those dove-gray eyes? He was shocked when she rushed to Naxa's side and rested a hand on his mare's neck. She, who was afraid of horses.

"I did, Mark." A smile lit her face. "I prayed. Truly, from my heart."

In one smooth motion, he was off of Naxa and facing Grace. He forced himself to keep his arms at his sides. "What did thee pray for?"

"That you were unhurt." The smile grew wider. "And here you are! I listened, with both my ears and my heart as Mistress Geyer told me to, but the Lord didn't answer me. Instead, He sent you here, to me."

Throwing caution to the wind, Mark opened his arms. To his delight and surprise, Grace stepped into them. Her arms came up and around his neck, her body pressing along the length of his, and her laughter filling his ears.

"The Lord is real. I know that now. Not because He brought you back, but because... because He just is. I can feel it deep inside of me. It feels like..." She paused and pulled back to look him in the eye. "It feels like joy."

Mark cleared his throat from the tightness that had formed there. "The Quakers call that the Light of Christ. When thee come to accept the Lord as thy Savior, the Light of Christ comes to thee. And Grace?" He leaned forward until their foreheads nearly touched.

"Aye?" Her voice was breathless, as it should be on finding the one true God, the Creator of all things.

"Thee will never be alone now. The Light of Christ will go with thee always."

She pressed a hand to his chest, nearly robbing him of thought. "You feel it too?"

He felt all sorts of things he shouldn't at the moment, but he nodded. "Lucy made sure I understood, but in truth, I learned of the Creator as a young child in the longhouse of my mother's family, from stories told by elders around the fire."

"Do all Indians believe in God?"

"The Lenni Lenape do."

"What of..." Indecision was painted across her face. "What of the Iroquois? Would my father have known?"

The longing in her voice pierced him to the soul. She'd never met her father, but she was concerned for his beliefs. He'd only seen the man as an Iroquois, painted and wielding a spear, perhaps the very man who had taken his father's life.

"I know not the ways of the Iroquois." He pushed the hair that had escaped his queue away from his face. "There is something I should have told thee after thee learned about thy father. 'Tis what kept me distant for a while."

She gave him a tiny nod to continue.

"My father was killed by an Iroquois, speared through the chest. I saw it happen." He rubbed his thumb along the line that marked his forehead. "'Tis where I got this scar."

"Oh, Mark." Her hand fluttered to her throat. "I am so sorry."

"Mother tried to pull me out of harm's way, but the warrior who had stabbed my father threw a knife. Mother deflected it, taking a cut on her arm. The knife flipped and hit me right before one of our warriors put an arrow into the Iroquois. I watched it with blood running down my face. I have harbored a hatred for that man and all his tribe ever since."

Grace reached up and traced his scar with a feather-light touch, her voice barely a whisper as she said, "I am part Iroquois."

For the first time in her life, Grace wished with all her heart that she didn't know who her father was. Mark's eyes, normally dark and unreadable, filled with pain. One of her father's people had killed his father, and he'd seen it happen. No wonder he hadn't wished to be near her.

"Indeed." Mark cupped the side of her face with a warm hand. "Learning that forced me to do what I should have done long ago."

"What was that?"

"Forgive the man and his people."

So that was what he'd been talking about before he left. "How can you, after what he did?"

"As thee now understand, the Light of Christ gives us more strength than we have in ourselves. And He wishes us to forgive."

"You could not have been very old. I cannot imagine what it must have been like for you."

"I pray thee never face anything like that, but if thee do, resist not the Lord's help, as I have done all these years." He let his hand drop and took a step away. "Forgiveness is a powerful thing."

She missed his warmth. "But that man, he will never know you forgave him."

"'Tisn't about him knowing, 'tis about me. The hatred and anger I carried inside hampered me from being the man I should have been. Lucy knew that and did her best to make me see it, but I resisted her as well."

"And now? Why did you do it now?"

"Because of thee." The sorrow lifted from his eyes, replaced by another emotion that brought a flush to Grace's face. He'd changed on this matter because of her. Did that mean...?

"Does thy mother know the Lord?" His question stopped her wayward thoughts.

"If she does, I am sure she would have told me." She stepped beyond his reach and bowed her head. "You know my mother is not a good woman."

"She is lost, but the lost can be found."

She dared a peek at him, and there was no condemnation in his expression. "How?"

"With the Lord, all things are possible."

"Can it be truly that simple? Does everything come down to trusting in the Lord?"

"Simple? Nay. But possible? Aye." He smiled at her. "We know not all the answers, but God does."

Grace didn't understand, but there was reassurance in his answer, and strength. Strength she sensed that she could lean upon when she needed it.

How could he make her, who was so new to knowing God, understand what had taken him years to grasp? *Lord, give me the right words.* "Since thee have accepted that the Lord is real and alive in thy life, surely thy mother can as well."

"You do not know what 'tis like for her in Philadelphia." She shook her head. "'Tis not at all like your Quaker village."

"We Quakers are not ignorant of the ways of the world." That brought her face up. "If we were, how would we know what we reject?"

"I had not thought of that."

"I was taught that we are to be *in* the world, but not *of* the world."

She scrunched her face. "Like you are *with* the army, but not *enlisted*?"

That hadn't occurred to him before. "Not exactly the same. It means, we are to live among those who know not the Lord that we might be an example and a light to show them the way."

Her eyes grew large again. "As you did with me."

That warmed his insides in a whole different way. "If I did, then I am humbled and very grateful."

"But my mother..." She looked away again.

"Shall we travel to Philadelphia and speak with her, together?"

"'Twouldn't be proper."

"Because we are not married." It wasn't a question, it was the truth. An unmarried man and woman traveling alone together wasn't socially acceptable—certainly never among the Quakers. But the largest impediment to a marriage had been removed—Grace now believed.

Naxa snorted behind him and shook her mane, which snapped Mark out of the silence that had formed around them.

"Grace?" He extended a hand.

She looked at it, and then into his eyes, but didn't move.

There were many things boiling inside of him, words and emotions he couldn't have sorted out if he'd had to, so he waited, keeping his hand steady, eyes locked with hers in what he suspected was a ritual as old as time.

Grace inched her hand toward his, their fingers barely touching at first, the slightest tremor transferring from hers to his.

He moved his other hand to cover their fingers, and she slid her hand the rest of the way into his with a sigh.

He pulled her closer, until their hands were trapped between their bodies. "Will thee have me to be thy husband?"

She searched his face. "Do you ask only so that we can travel together to speak with Mother?"

"*Ahotasu.*" The word came unbidden from his past.

"What does that mean?"

"It means beloved. That is what thee have become to me. I will marry thee if thee wish to travel to Philadelphia or not. I will spend the rest of my life with thee, no matter where we go."

Her arms encircled his neck again, but this time without laughter. This time, when their foreheads touched, it was only to pause before their lips did the same. Wonder filled Mark. Little over a month ago, he'd lost everything. Now, he held everything in his arms. But he needed to be sure. He raised his head and whispered, "Are thee sure?"

A single tear rolled onto her lashes and slid down her cheek. "I am." Then her eyes widened. "If I am to finally gain a last name, what will it be?"

He'd never told her? With the tip of his finger, he brushed away her tear. "Running Bear. 'Twas my father's name, and now my last name."

"Grace Running Bear." Her smile sent a wave of longing through him.

The next hurdle was to find someone who would marry them, a Quaker and the illegitimate daughter of a strumpet. If he had to ride around the countryside for a week, he wouldn't return until he'd succeeded.

Chapter 33

As Mark approached the pallet, his friend sat up, visibly more steady than before. The happiness the sight brought him was nothing compared to the past hour in Grace's company, but it was there all the same.

"I see thee are much improved." He dropped cross-legged on the ground beside Nash.

"Not only is there just one of you, but you do not weave like a reed in the wind anymore." Nash grinned. "Hold up some fingers."

Mark displayed three.

"Three. See? My vision has returned."

"All of it?"

Nash sobered a little. "Close up, at least. The distance is still foggy, but looking at it no longer makes my stomach want to empty."

"That is good news."

"I want to hear where you have been these many days." Nash cocked at eyebrow. "If Major General Greene sent you on a mission, you should have returned for me."

"So I could have tied thee to the saddle and ridden slowly beside thee to hold thee upright?"

"'Twasn't as bad as all that."

Mark hiked an eyebrow at his friend, who shrugged and looked away.

"I could have stayed upright, at least until I needed to empty my stomach."

"Exactly why thee needed to remain here and continue to heal."

"Enough about me. Where did you go and what did you do?"

Mark explained his mission, what he found, and the three wintering places he'd recommended while Nash hung on every word, a man starved for news of the world outside the hospital tent.

"So this Valley Forge is the best of the lot?"

"I believe so. The major general seemed taken with the report of it as well. The one problem will be finding enough food. The British took most of the harvest when they passed through."

"'Tis good we have such a hunter as yourself with us." Nash leaned back against the tent post by the head of his pallet. "I know you are a good scout and more reliable than most, that you take pride in what you do, but why the jovial disposition this afternoon? It must be more than a good report to the major general."

His friend was perceptive. Mark had done his best to dampen his emotions before entering the tent. But perhaps Nash..."

"Are there any among the army who can legally perform a marriage?"

Nash's mouth dropped open, and Mark made a shushing motion with his hands. He didn't need the whole camp advised of his plans.

Nash leaned forward, his voice low. "Who has caught thy interest?"

"Her name is Grace. She cooks for the laundresses and wounded."

"That angel with the black hair and dark eyes?"

Mark nodded, for Grace was the only black-haired woman among the laundresses, but he also pushed down a stab of unease that Nash had noticed Grace enough to consider her an angel.

"You are a lucky man. Do you know what she did for me? And not just for me but also for several of the wounded here these past few days?"

"Tell me." Mark knew Grace would do nothing improper, but he still fought down an element of unease.

"She wrote letters to our loved ones for us. I could not write because I could not see. Henry over there could not write with his broken hand. Bob and Claude never learned their letters. The doctor gave her paper and ink, and she wrote what we asked." His face reddened in the dim light of the tent. "She even helped me word the letter to my mother so as not to worry her overmuch. I would not have thought of that."

His Grace—an angel. Mark could almost preen like a ruffled grouse in mating season.

"She is kind." He grinned at Nash. "Kind enough to agree to marry me, if we can find someone who will perform the marriage."

"What is the problem?" Nash's brow wrinkled. "There are towns nearby. Some must have Quakers among them."

Mark looked out the open tent flap at the busyness of the camp beyond. People milling around doing the mundane chores that would feed, clothe, and keep the residents safe.

How to explain things to Nash, who hadn't been raised in a church?

"The Quakers only marry among themselves. They will not marry me to anyone not a Quaker."

"So Grace becomes a Quaker, and the problem is solved."

If only that were true. It would be a drawn-out process, her background would be brought to light, questions would be asked and answers demanded. The Quakers were welcoming—they'd proven that when they'd taken him in—but he'd been a child. Adults they accepted far more gradually into their ranks, after proof of their conversion was well accepted by the way they lived among the Quakers. Getting married by that route could take months. Neither Mark nor Grace had even a roof over their heads. And frankly, Mark wasn't willing to wait. He loved the Quakers and embraced most of what they taught, even their concept of forgiveness now, but there was also the issue of the war and his non-combat involvement in it.

"'Tisn't as easy as that. Best I find someone else, perhaps a justice of the peace."

"Of course." Nash smacked his palm to his forehead. "Henry, right over there." He pointed to a man sitting up, his arm in a sling and his hand wrapped in thick bandages. "He is a justice of the peace from somewhere in Massachusetts."

"Think thee he can perform a marriage here, in Pennsylvania?" Hope surged through Mark.

"During a war?" Nash raised his voice. "Whyever not?"

"Hush." Heads turned toward them, the men eager for any sort of distraction as they recuperated. "Would thee call him over and introduce us?"

"Mistress Geyer?" Grace arrived at the tent they shared and stuck her head inside, although it was unusual for either of them to be in there in the early afternoon.

The older woman turned while kneeling, a skein of yarn in her hand. "Grace? I thought Anna had run you off for the afternoon." She came out of the tent.

"She did, and... and..." Grace couldn't control the smile that burst forth. "He asked me to marry him." She barely breathed the words.

"Did he? Well, it took the man long enough." Mistress Geyer was all smiles, wrinkles nearly hiding her eyes. "And of course, you agreed."

"Aye." She looked around still keeping her voice low. "But now what?"

"Now you vait for him to make the arrangements. Mark is resourceful, I say he vill have things in order soon."

Grace looked down at her worn and stained dress. "I wish I had something—"

"Of course!" Mistress Geyer's voice raised the heads of those by the fire. "Come and look."

Grace followed her into the tent.

The older woman rifled through the trunk that held her belongings. The scents of lavender and old leather wafted through the tent before the woman sat back on her heels, a dress in her lap.

"Ve must make alterations to fit you, of course." She held up the lovely moss-green fabric with creamy lace trim. "'Tvas my vedding dress. 'Tis one of the things I could not part vith. My Peter, he laughed at me for bringing it vhen ve could pack so little. Men. They do not understand such things."

"You would let me borrow it?" Tears welled in Grace's eyes, large enough that she couldn't blink them away.

"I vill gift it to you for you to keep from now on."

"I cannot take your dress!"

"Of course you can." Mistress Geyer pressed it into her hands. "I have no daughter to pass it on to, you see. 'Tis vhat Peter teased me about. I believe the Lord had me bring it for yoost this purpose."

"I... I..." The soft fabric draped over Grace's lap like a hug. She lifted her face to her friend, who was blurry through the tears. "I can never thank you enough."

"Yoost be a good vife to that young man, and that vill be all the thanks I need."

"I will. I promise."

"Slip it on. Let me see vhere ve need to tuck and sew."

The rest of the afternoon went by in a blur of needles and thread, laughter and advice, and more than one warm hug. The sort of things Mother should have been there to do for her. A mixture of guilt and sorrow threatened to worm its way in several times, but Grace pushed it away. Mother was who she was, but that didn't mean she couldn't change, that she couldn't start a new life once she came to know the Lord.

Mark had promised to go with her and speak to Mother once they were married.

Married. Wouldn't Mother be surprised?

News spread throughout the camp, and the wedding was set for the next day, October eighteenth, a Saturday according to Mistress Crenshaw's calendar. Men he hardly knew had been clapping Mark on the shoulders and back until he was fairly bruised. Henry Colburn had willingly agreed to marry them, and much to Mark's relief, he'd declared the reading of the banns could be waved during wartime. Grace's kindness to the wounded soldiers had no doubt made his decision an easy one. Several of the men had congratulated Mark there in the hospital tent, all of them with a kind word about his wife-to-be.

Wife.

Mark rested beside Naxa, overlooking the camp from the hill to the south. He'd been hunting all day. The large doe and three fat turkeys slung across his saddle would feed the entire camp after the wedding. He searched for the tent made of fresh deerskins, the same skins Grace had helped to tan and sew. Enough of the wounded had healed and returned to the army that they didn't need another tent for them. The one newly set up on the edge of the camp would be their home—starting tomorrow.

Grace was at the fire, her braid hanging down her back from under her linen cap, the end swaying around her hips. Before Mark could get too lost in that view, the rattle of wagon wheels reached him. He guided Naxa under the cover of some shrubby trees and watched the backside of the hill. Whoever it was had taken no measures to hide their arrival.

It wasn't one wagon but two that came into view. Filling the back were a collection of colorfully dressed women. The one seated beside the driver of the wagon that led the way was Prudence, his soon-to-be mother-in-law. He should be glad to see her and the crates the women were seated on. No doubt they held more much-needed provisions. Her being here would also save him and Grace the trip to Philadelphia with winter approaching.

But it was their wedding day and Prudence was... No, he should not think of his future mother-in-law that way.

Let him that is among you without sin, cast the first stone at her.

Mark cringed and bowed his head. *Forgive me Lord. I am far from without sin. If it be Thy will, help me find the right words to introduce Prudence to Thee.*

After he'd let the prayer settle, he looked up again. "Come, Naxa. They are friends, not foes." He led the horse from the thicket and down the hill while the wagons circled around to a more level entry into the valley. He arrived on foot about the same time that their drivers pulled the wagons to a stop.

Grace emerged from the forest with Anna, both holding baskets of whatever they'd found to add to dinner that evening. Anna took Grace's basket and motioned her to hurry on.

Grace ran to his side. "Mother is here. Can you believe it? 'Tis almost as if..." She searched his face.

"As if God brought her for our wedding?"

Her face lit like a candle in a mirrored holder. He almost took her into his arms, but Naxa bumped his shoulder, no doubt ready to unload the carcasses and join her fellow horses at the picket line.

"I must unload Naxa and picket her. Go and greet thy mother."

"Should I share our news?"

"If thee do not, someone else surely will."

"Of course." She looked down and then back up at him, a pretty flush across her cheeks. "Join us when you can."

"I shall." He watched her walk away, enjoying the view, until Naxa snorted, sending a shower of droplets across the side of his face. "Indeed. Time to get moving."

Nobody offered to help this time, the able-bodied among them all surrounding the wagons to unload and inspect the goods brought in by a sector of society to whom they normally would not give the time of day. And he was no better than the rest. Had he not proved that on the hilltop with his uncharitable thoughts? The women lived unsavory lives, of course, but they were not beyond redemption.

No one was.

Not an orphaned Indian boy, nor an illegitimate young woman, nor a woman of the street. They just needed someone to show them the truth, as Lucy had done for him. It was time he repaid her kindness by passing it on. The warmth that filled him, as if Lucy had sent down a heavenly hug, pressed tears against the backs of his eyes.

Blessed are the peacemakers: for they shall be called the children of God.

He wasn't meant to be a soldier. No matter that his bloodline went back through generations of warriors. No matter that he scouted for Nathanael, who he never could quite think of by a title. His calling, as Lucy would have worded it, was to minister to the practical needs of those around him. If he could help with their spiritual needs as well? That would be a privilege.

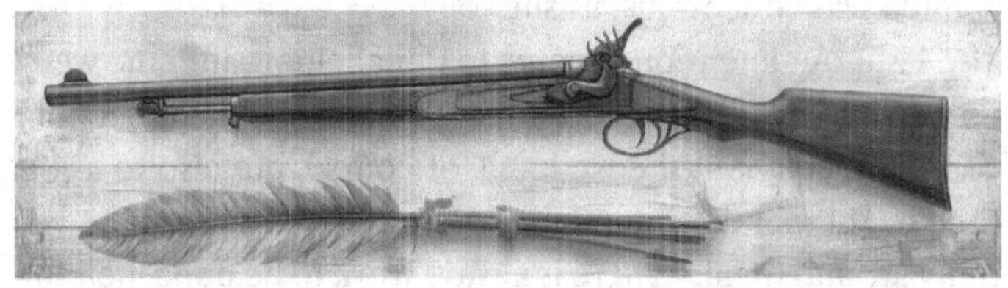

Chapter 34

"Prudence." Mark approached where Grace and her mother stood away from the hubbub of wagon unloading and crate sorting. "'Tis a pleasure to see thee again."

"Is it?" The woman tilted her head, peering at him. "I wonder, what with the news Grace has just shared. Had I known, I would have delayed a day or two."

"Nonsense, Mother." Grace took her mother's hand. "We are delighted that you will be here for the wedding."

"Both of you?" Prudence kept her eyes locked on Mark.

"Both of us, I assure thee."

Although she still looked skeptical, Prudence turned her attention to Grace. "Whatever will you wear?"

Grace smiled. "Mistress Geyer has given me a dress. 'Tis lovely."

He hadn't seen it, but it mattered not to Mark what she wore. Clothing and trappings were not important. All he wanted was Grace—just as she was.

"'Twas our intention to come to Philadelphia after the wedding to see thee." He ignored the woman's shocked reaction. "To tell thee about the wedding, of course, but also to ask if thee might join the camp here." He motioned toward the activity around them. "There is always work to be done, helping with the wounded, cooking, laundry, and such. Thee would be welcome."

At that, she lowered her brows. "Provided I changed my ways."

Grace put her arm around her mother. "You can, you know. Change your ways. Being here has changed me." She pressed a hand over her heart. "I have become a believer in the Lord, Mother. I cannot tell you how differently I feel. 'Tis..." Her eyes sought Mark in a silent plea for help.

"'Tis a wonderous thing, to be sure, and God's love and forgiveness are open to everyone."

"Everyone?" Prudence shot a glance at the other women in their colorful dresses, standing out among those of the camp, whose dresses were worn and stained, drab but serviceable.

"Indeed," Mark said. "All of them and thee as well."

"I cannot think I should be much help," Prudence said.

"You can learn," Grace said. "I did. And I believe the Lord will help me learn even more."

"You truly have become one of them?" Prudence's voice was barely a whisper. "A Christian?"

"I have, with my whole heart."

"I never envisioned that when I brought you here."

"I resented it at first, you know, being left here." Grace's voice was as quiet as her mother's. "But now, I see that 'twas the best thing you could have done. I am so different from the frightened girl you dropped off all those weeks ago."

"Nine weeks and five days." Prudence fumbled to grip her daughter's hand. "I have missed you each and every day." Her eyes shimmered.

"Then stay, Mother. Please."

"Where would I live? What would I do?"

"You vill live vith me and share my tent." Mistress Geyer appeared at Mark's side. "Excuse me for listening in, I vas vaiting to invite your mother to stay for the vedding, and I did not vish to interrupt."

"A tent?" Doubt filled Prudence's voice.

"Come and see." Mistress Geyer took the other woman by the arm and led her away. "Ve can always use another set of hands to share the vork." Her voice trailed off as they left Mark and Grace behind.

"Do thee think she will agree?" he asked.

Grace moved to his side, her arm brushing against his. "Can any of us say no to Mistress Geyer?"

He chuckled. "Not likely." Then he sobered and put his arm around her, pulling her to his side. "Even if she stays, it might take her a long time to come to know the Lord."

Grace gazed up at him. "Because she has lived so long without Him?"

"Because she has not trusted anyone in a long time, I think."

"She has not." Grace sighed. "Not ever that I can remember."

"With God, all things are possible. Hold on to that promise and pray. I shall do the same. Then we wait for the Lord to reveal Himself to her."

"As He did with me beside the river."

"Indeed." The Lord gave Mark no special word, nor did He bring any scripture to mind, but a peace settled over him all the same. When Grace snuggled closer, Mark's heart nearly hurt with its fullness.

The morning of the wedding had been thick with fog, but it had burned off, and by midday, the sun peeked through. Mark's Quaker outfit felt foreign against his skin after so many weeks of wearing his hunting clothes, and had refused to cooperate. He stood in front of Nash, who straightened the neckcloth Mark had fumbled with.

"Hold still, man." Nash squinted as he finished.

"I should have kept my Lenni Lenape necklace on."

"You are marrying the lass in front of a justice of the peace, not some witch doctor."

"Medicine man."

"Call it what you like."

"They do not perform marriages among the Lenni Lenape, anyway. The mother of the groom and the mother of the bride work it out."

"Women do the marrying?" Nash shook his head and stepped back to survey his handiwork. "Well, you will not frighten any small children, at least."

Which was hardly a confidence-boosting comment. "Have thee seen Grace?"

"The women will be fussing over her until the wedding, I am sure." He paused and looked Mark in the eye. "Is her mother truly staying with the camp?"

"At least for now." Prudence had stood beside them as the wagons and other women had left, but Mark was pretty sure she'd been on the brink of chasing them more than once.

Nash hiked an eyebrow. "Mistress Crenshaw cannot be pleased."

"I have assured her that Prudence will be under my supervision."

Nash chuckled. "So you are in charge of keeping her in line?"

"Something of that nature." Mark wasn't entirely comfortable with the arrangement, but it had unruffled Mistress Crenshaw's feathers enough to allow Prudence to stay. At least the Philadelphia women had brought bolts of cloth in some of the crates. Mistress Geyer had promised to help sew two new dresses for Prudence—as quickly as possible.

"You are a brave man, even if you will not fight."

"My work as a scout—" He was cut off when Nash's finger jabbed into his ribs.

"You are as much of a Patriot as I am, even if you never lift a gun." Nash grinned and then grew thoughtful. "I owe you, for what you said when my eyesight was gone. I feared it would never return. While you were gallivanting off to that valley you like so much, Grace wrote a letter to my mother for me, and I told her about our conversation."

Thank Thee, Lord, for using me to plant the seeds of faith.

"Now." Nash's voice boomed in the small tent with the lingering odor of freshly tanned hides. "Let us get you married."

Grace breathed in the scents of lavender and old leather that clung to the green dress. Mistress Geyer had slipped out of the tent, giving her and Mother a few moments together before they headed to the center of the camp, where the laundresses had stacked crates and covered them with greenery since it was past the season for flowers.

Mother, modestly attired in a dress borrowed from one of the laundresses of a similar size, looked her up and down. "You are beautiful, my dear."

"You think so?"

"I know so. Mark is a very lucky man." Mother took both her hands. "You are so much braver than I ever was. When your father asked me to marry him, I was afraid to leave the city and go with him. Afraid to give up my room and the little bit of security I felt there."

"Did you...?" Grace searched her mother's face. "Did you love him?"

"I did. But I was weak, not strong like you." Mother cupped Grace's cheek. "You are a far better person than I ever was, or ever could be."

Grace swallowed against the tears that gathered at the back of her throat. "If I am, 'tis because you raised me to be that way." Tears trickled down her cheeks, but she ignored them and the matching dampness on Mother's face. "I owe you everything."

"You owe me nothing." Mother dropped her hand and took a step back. "'Tis time to go."

"Mother." She waited for her mother to dab the tears from her face. "I am so happy you have agreed to stay."

"How could I not, when my daughter wants me near?"

"Will you miss Philadelphia?"

Mother nodded. "Some of it, but not all of it. Nothing there is as important as you. Now come on, before we are both in tears again."

Mother left the tent, and held the flap for Grace's exit. The laundresses stood in two lines, along with other women from the camp, making a path to where the crates had been set up. With Mother at her side, Grace walked between them, accepting their congratulations and well-wishes along the way. When she glanced forward again, Mark was standing at the end of the line, resplendent in his Quaker clothing.

How lucky—blessed—she was to be marrying him, the man who had rescued her from the panther, the cliff, and Dan Browne. A man of integrity and bravery who had seen past her lack of last name and lack of faith. Her hero. Her love. Her heart.

Mark's mouth went dry as Grace made her way toward him, speaking quietly to the women she passed, smiling and nodding and looking like the angel Nash had labeled her.

"Lucky man," Nash whispered from where he stood beside Mark, acting as his witness. "Glad I got my eyesight back in time to witness this."

Henry Colburn, *The Book of Common Prayer* in his uninjured hand, sent a glare that silenced Nash.

Grace finally stepped next to Mark, her mother going to her other side to serve as the other witness.

The ceremony wasn't as long as a Quaker wedding would have been, but that didn't bother Mark. The Lord knew his heart—and Grace's. They said their vows and were proclaimed man and wife to the cheers of those gathered around.

When the cheers subsided, Mistress Crenshaw called them all to the wedding feast of slow-roasted venison and turkey, boiled potatoes the women had brought, fresh bread, and hasty pudding with molasses. They'd managed to bake a pair of cakes, enough for everyone to have a slice. There was even a small barrel of cider to top off the meal.

"Well, Mistress Running Bear." Mark faced Grace as the crowd filtered toward the tables that had been set up for the feast. "Shall we join our guests at the feast?"

"In a moment." Those dove-gray eyes met his, and a shy smile curved her lips.

That was too much to resist. Mark leaned down and met her lips with his own, sealing them together as one.

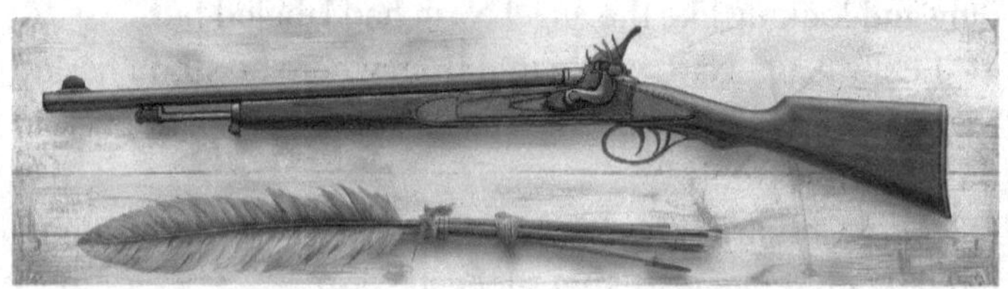

Epilogue

Birmingham, Pennsylvania, May 1784

Mark entered the house, the scent of newly milled boards still evident even with the windows open. Squeals of laughter were followed by the pounding of small feet down the staircase. Five-year-old Sammy appeared first, followed by almost three-year-old Lucy. Mark squatted and opened his arms. After wrapping one around each child, he stood.

"Where is thy mother?"

"In the kitchen cooking greens." Sammy wrinkled his nose.

"Greens will make thee grow big and strong."

"Like thee?" Lucy asked.

"Indeed. I had to eat a lot of greens to have muscles like this." He squeezed, setting both children to squealing again.

Grace appeared in the doorway, wiping her hands on her apron, exposing the rounded front of her gown. "Thee are a noisy bunch. I pray the next babe will be quieter."

Mark approached and dropped a kiss on the top of her head. "Where is Prudence?"

"Granny is in the garden," Lucy piped up. "She is planting beets with Granny Sarah."

Sammy wrinkled his nose at the mention of the vegetables.

"Go." He set the children down. "Fetch thy grannies in. I have news to share."

They raced for the back door.

Grace stepped into his embrace and lifted her face to his. After a lingering kiss, she drew back, eyes shining. "It must be good news."

"Indeed." He kissed her again, only stopping when the pounding of little feet grew louder.

"What is all the fuss over?" Prudence followed the children into the kitchen. "What news have thee today?"

It did his heart good to hear the Quaker *thee* in her speech, a new addition. After the war had ended, he'd brought the family back to Birmingham, and through the community here, finally, Prudence had come to accept the Light of Christ. Mark caught Grace's smile out of the corner of his eye and knew she shared his thoughts.

Hobbling in, with the help of a crutch Mark had fashioned for her, came Sarah. Wrapped in her traditional Lenni Lenape clothing, the old woman looked up at him and nodded. Her sister, Betsy, had died the winter before Mark moved the family back. He'd found Sarah alone in the bark hut, half-starved and stubborn as always. She hadn't wanted to move in with them until she'd seen the children. They had convinced her.

"My news is this." He spread his arms wide to encompass them all. "Thee are looking at the new *partner* of Charlie Brewer at the smithy."

"'Tis wonderful news!" Grace wrapped her arms around him again. "He could not have chosen a better partner." She grinned up at him. "I should know."

"Congratulations." Prudence looked down at the little ones. "This calls for a celebration. What do thee say, children?"

After the cheer, Sammy leaned forward and whispered loudly, "We cannot celebrate with *greens*, Granny."

"Indeed, we cannot. Let us see what we can find in the smokehouse, Lucy. Sammy, thee can fetch the sack of dried apples from the cellar." She left, the children scampering after her. Sarah sank onto a chair by the door, watching them go.

Grace leaned against Mark. "Well done, my husband."

"Did thee ever think we would have such a family?"

Those first years, they'd survived Valley Forge with its sickness and hunger. Following the army, living out of tents, the close calls and near misses where he'd been convinced the Lord had protected him. It had all come back to this. The meeting had voted to give him Lucy's lot, and the whole community had pitched in to help him build this house. Now Charlie, getting up in years and without a son who wished to take over the smithy, had made him a partner.

"A wise man—a true Patriot—once told me that with God, all things are possible." Grace smiled up at him.

Sarah nodded from her chair without looking at them.

Mark's heart filled near to bursting. "Look at what the Lord has done."

Author's Historical Notes

Several of my family members have worked on researching our family tree over the years and have come across people for whom they could find no last names. This led to more research and learning that, in Colonial America, while some illegitimate children were given their mother's last name, more common was for no last name to be recorded or used.

Distance was measured in rods during this period of Colonial American history. A rod equals sixteen and a half feet. If you have any farming background, that's just six inches longer than a hog or cattle panel, or a foot shorter than a regular cab Ford F-150 work truck. That's how I picture it.

The Lenni Lenape tribe is often called Delaware today. The tribe was once a mighty nation with territory covering what is now Delaware, New Jersey, Eastern Pennsylvania, and parts of New York, Connecticut, and Maryland. With the influx of European settlers, disease outbreaks, and wars between neighboring tribes—particularly the Susquehannock, they were pushed back into the Ohio Territory. After siding with the French during the French and Indian War, the Lenni

Lenape leaders who had converted to Christianity tried to stand neutral during the Revolution for American Independence. It was difficult, however, when most of the other tribes allied themselves with the British. In the end, the tribe split between siding with the British and siding with the American Patriots. Koquethagechton (Captain White Eyes) was an influence behind the Fort Pitt Treaty of 1778, in which he worked to secure lands in Ohio for the tribe as well as promises of their own state in the new nation and a seat in congress. In return, the Lenni Lenape supplied the Americans with food, horses, and other necessary items along with safe travel through their territory. They even allowed their young men to join the army as scouts and enlist as soldiers. But the newly minted United States defaulted on that agreement. The Fort Pitt Treaty was the first U.S. treaty with a native tribe to be signed... and broken.

Thomas Penn devised a way to strip more land from the Lenni Lenape with what was called the Walking Purchase. He claimed his father, William Penn, had signed a treaty fifty years prior with a Lenape chief. The tribe felt honor-bound to comply. But instead of walking off a distance of the land, Penn hired runners who increased the amount of land obtained by tenfold. The goodwill William Penn had established with the Lenape was fractured.

Major General Nathanael Greene was indeed a Quaker. However, he was barred from his Quaker meeting after he started drilling with the local militia in 1773. He was a large man with a stiff knee who battled asthma his whole life. An unlikely hero, he nevertheless saved Washington's army at Brandywine when he and his forces held the British at bay while the rest of the army retreated. After a stint as the quartermaster general, at which time he revolutionized the army's ability to get food and supplies to its troops, he was dispatched to the Southern states to face the British there. Outmanned and outgunned, his forces bloodied and bruised the British to the point where they withdrew from much of the countryside, earning Greene the nickname "Savior of the South." He is thought by many to be second only to George Washington as the best general of the Continental Army.

Mary Geyer was born in Sweden in 1735. She worked as a laundress with the 13th Pennsylvania and was at Valley Forge along with her husband, Peter, and their son, John. Peter and John were both injured at the Battle of Germantown, but neither seriously. Both fulfilled their enlistments. Mary died in Red Lion, Pennsylvania, in 1838—well beyond a ripe old age!

Joseph Townsend was a Quaker at the Birmingham Meeting. He was twenty-one when the Battle of Brandywine erupted around the village. He witnessed the battle unfold from the top of Osborne Hill and later wrote the most famous civilian account of the fighting. https://archive.org/details/someaccountofbri00town/page/n17/mode/2up

Private Peter Francisco was abandoned at the docks near Richmond, Virginia, at the estimated age of five years old. He was raised by Judge Anthony Winston (Patrick Henry's uncle). He was known to be over six feet tall, close to two hundred and sixty pounds, a veritable giant of a man in Colonial American times. He joined the 10th Virginia at the age of sixteen and was soon renowned for his exploits on the battlefield. He was recognized for his gallantry at the battles of Brandywine, Germantown, Fort Mifflin, Stony Point, Camden, and Guilford Courthouse. He suffered an array of wounds that would have sidelined lesser men. Legend has it that he once single-handedly carried a cannon off the battlefield to prevent its capture by the enemy. He finished his years as the appointed sergeant-at-arms of the Virginia legislature until his death in 1831.

The Battle of White Horse Tavern *(also called the Battle of the Clouds)* could have been a disastrous defeat for Washington's outnumbered forces. The rain, and the resulting wet gunpowder, made the battle impossible, and Washington's forces were able to escape to the northeast. But it wasn't a useless confrontation because it slowed Howe's forces and allowed the new Continental Congress to evacuate Philadelphia before the British arrived to take the city. It was not the only time weather helped determine the outcome of a battle—or lack of battle in this case—during the war. Washington himself would thank the Lord for His intervention at these times.

The Paoli Massacre was a solid defeat for the Continental Army. Brigadier General Anthony Wayne had been stationed there with roughly 1,500 men and ordered to harass the British and attempt to capture all or part of their provisions, which would follow in wagons after Howe's army. The Continental Army was always short of ammunition, powder, food, footwear, and clothing, so such a capture would have been a great asset. Instead, rumors reached Howe of Wayne's forces, and he sent out scouts. When their location had been confirmed, Howe dispatched Major General Charles Grey with roughly 1,200 men to engage the enemy. At ten o'clock that night, with bayonets fixed and guns not loaded, Grey's men charged the camp. Wayne's sentries had raised the alarm, and his forces were trying to escape, but some of them fired their muskets, highlighting their location in the dark. The British attacked with their bayonets, gruesomely slaughtering the men they encountered. After the battle, rumor was that the British cried "no quarter," meaning to kill and not take prisoners. However, the British took 71 prisoners that night, while only 53 men were killed, which does not fit with the cry of "no quarter." Still, that tale burned its way through the colonies and helped to flame the fires of rebellion.

Research proved that mares were used during the Revolutionary War as mounts for the armies. Geldings were preferred, as they didn't have the hormonal disruptions that a stallion or a mare would experience, but horses were not in such large supply that everyone could be picky about what they rode. I found an interesting collection of ads that had run in the newspapers in which officers tried to locate lost or stolen horses after a battle, firsthand accounts that confirmed some were mares.

While modern weddings happen just about anywhere, from a church to a beach, Colonial American weddings were almost always performed in homes of the bride's parents and would be performed either by their local pastor or justice of the peace.

While Washington was defeated at Germantown, the battle was something of a breakthrough for the Patriots. Howe was already in possession of Philadelphia, and in the British way of fighting and thinking, capturing the capital meant the war was essentially over. When Washington mounted an attack, even though he suffered defeat, he demonstrated to the French the determination and tenacity of the Continental Army, especially when that was followed by the surrender of Burgoyne's entire army that month at Saratoga. The French would go on to form an allegiance with the United States of America, sending reinforcements that would eventually determine the end of the war.

The Iroquois Confederacy consisted of different tribes, including the Oneida. Each tribe could be distinguished by their clothing, including the hats the men wore. The Oneida men wore a *kastoweh* with three eagle feathers, two that pointed upright, and one that lay to the side. The hats were made of three wood splints, usually ash, with one wrapping around the head, and the other two crossing across the top to create a dome. The splints could be wrapped in hide or cloth, or left open. The top of the hat was usually decorated with porcupine quills, small feathers, or other adornments. The Oneida split with the rest of the Iroquois Confederacy over the Revolutionary War, siding with the Americans. Without the many pounds of white corn brought to Valley Forge by the Oneida, Washington's army might not have survived the winter.

There were Quakers living in and around Valley Forge, about eighteen families in a small farming community, when Washington chose it for the army's wintering place. While some of the Quakers voluntarily helped to feed and clothe the army, others had provisions "commandeered" from their farms, including their horses. The British had been there before the Americans and had already taken much from the Quakers to feed and provision their army. The Quakers' activity was monitored by Washington's men and they were not allowed to travel to Philadelphia for fear they might be spies for the British. The suspicion and distrust added to the general tension of the winter.

Reviews are Golden

Reviews are the lifeblood of authors. Leaving a review on **Amazon**, **Goodreads**, and/or **BookBub** means that more readers will find our books! Reviews can be long or short—your honest opinion of the book. Shout-outs on any social media platforms also help!

About Pegg Thomas

Pegg Thomas lives in Michigan's Upper Peninsula with Michael, her husband of *mumble* years. She creates American stories with real history and fictional characters inspired by her ancestors who immigrated here in the early 1600s.

Pegg won the 2019 FHL Readers' Choice Award for novellas, was a double-finalist for the 2019 ACFW Carol Award for novellas, and a finalist for the 2019 ACFW Editor of the Year.

She was a finalist in the 2021 FHL Readers' Choice Award for novellas. Pegg won the 2022 Selah Award for historical romance and placed 2nd with her second entry. She was a finalist for the 2023 FHL Selah Award, placed 2nd in the 2024 Selah Award, won the 2024 Will Rogers Silver AND 2024 Bronze Medallion Awards, and was a 2026 finalist for the Selah Awards. Pegg spent 3 ½ years as the managing editor of Smitten Historical Romance.

PeggThomas.com
Facebook
Goodreads
BookBub
Amazon
Newsletter signup

www.ingramcontent.com/pod-product-compliance
Lightning Source LLC
LaVergne TN
LVHW040215110826
845146LV00005B/1298

* 9 7 9 8 9 9 2 9 0 7 9 6 4 *